MW00436227

Out of the Water

By Ann Marie Stewart

Hidden Shelf Publishing House
P.O. Box 4168, McCall, ID 83638
www.hiddenshelfpublishinghouse.com

Cover artwork: Megan Whitfield

Cover graphic design: Kristen Carrico

Editor: Rachel Wickstrom

Interior layout: Kerstin Stokes

Publisher's Cataloguing-in-Publication Data

Names: Stewart, Ann Marie, author.
Title: Out of the Water / by Ann Marie Stewart.
Description: McCall, ID: Hidden Shelf Publishing House, 2020.

Paperback: ISBN: 978-1-955893-90-9

Library of Congress Control Number: 2021911979

Printed in the United States of America

Siobhan = Sha-VAHN

Kildea = Kil-DAY

Giovanni = Ja-VAH-nee

Savelli = Sa-VEL-li

Saraid = Sah-RY

Aintín = AHN-chen

Saoirse = SEER-sha

Ántonia = An-to-NEE-ah

Marchand = MarSHAHND

Dedicated to Christine Alane Stewart

My firstborn daughter, a UVA graduate, and UVA Hospital RN whose gentle heart cares for patients young and old.

Chapter One
Siobhan

*The early mist had vanished and the fields lay
like a silver shield under the sun.
It was one of the days when the
glitter of winter shines through a pale haze of spring.*
—Edith Wharton, *Ethan Frome*

Deer Lodge, Montana
Saturday, March 14, 1931

Siobhan Mason stepped out into the cold March air and headed for the barn to gather the few eggs her hens still laid. Exhaling slowly, she watched her white breath hover in front of her. It was near the end of winter; spring was coming, she could feel it.

Nearing the chicken coop, she smelled the hay and chicken feather mustiness. Of her children, only Caleb liked the barn, because the three-year-old could shadow his daddy, following the big man in and out of the stalls.

Alone for now, Siobhan shushed the last hen and pulled out an egg to add to her basket, relieved. Six. They'd each have one.

The faithful cow sashayed toward her. Siobhan moved the stool into position to milk Maggie's swollen udder. She stroked the warm soft belly and reached for the teat. Maggie's back leg stretched and stomped, not in anger, just a testing, and then she let Siobhan's fingers pull forth streams of milk. Siobhan smiled at the sound of splashing in the tin bucket, and the image of her four children around the breakfast table, eating their eggs and licking at milk mustaches.

She liked having the morning hours to herself, when it was quiet and undemanding, just her and the animals. In the morning, the day held promise. But often by day's end, she felt defeated, beaten, and exhausted. Jack was the opposite. In the wee hours of the night, he rose and paced. He pored over bills, read the newspaper, and fretted about the weather. He couldn't simply lie in bed, no, he had to begin projects that would never be finished. That was farm life; a never-ending cycle of incompletion.

Turning Maggie out to the field, Siobhan spotted a mother ewe delivering a lamb. Her heartbeat quickened in excitement, as she tiptoed to the pasture. This was a rare privilege, as ewes delivered so quickly, arriving faster than any of the babies she had borne.

The ewe mother heaved, pawed the ground, and strained her neck upward. Then hooves and head emerged. The lamb dropped to the ground, and the mother licked away the sac. The sun illuminated the inside of the lamb's iridescent pink ears. Siobhan didn't move. There was likely another lamb. She would wait lest she cause the contractions to stop. When the afterbirth arrived, Siobhan resigned herself to a singleton, until she glanced across the wet and muddy yard and spotted what must have been the mama's first. A baby that had never been licked down and was probably dead, cold on the ground and unable to breathe through its slimy sac. This was the worst part of spring lambing. The harsh neglect and unformed breath. No life inhaled.

Siobhan sloshed through half-frozen muck to find the baby lamb and wiped away the membrane strangling its face with her apron. It wasn't breathing, so she stuck straw into its nose. "Take a breath, little wee one! Breathe!" She had seconds, not minutes.

With no response, she gently dislodged the lamb from the mud. The mother ewe paced nervously as Siobhan picked up the lamb by its back legs. Securing the lamb's legs with her apron so they wouldn't slip, she twirled the lamb as she would one of her children. At last, she heard a snort, and she slowed the rotations. When the lamb took its first breath, Siobhan gasped in synchrony then clutched the lamb close to her body and exhaled. What a morning to be alive.

Siobhan laid the lamb on the ground and began rubbing him, anything to get him to move, willing him to stand. Slowly, it got to its knobby knees, something she always considered a miracle. Unstable, wobbly, but nevertheless, standing. How strong and vigorous was a baby lamb!

She picked it up and took it to the mother, who sniffed it, then nudged it away with her nose.

"This is yours," she said softly. "Your baby." Siobhan lowered it near the mother's face, so she could smell it was of her womb, a reminder that she had only just delivered this little boy.

Molly's headbutt, full of such force, caused the lamb to lose its footing and fall to the ground.

"That's yer wee one!" Siobhan scolded. "And don't yer forget it!" With babies and lambies, she found herself reverting to her mother's voice, the Irish lilt and gentle singsong. "Oh, Molly May . . ." she tsked in a friendly but disciplinary tone.

She scooped up both lambs and held them under the nose of the mother, then inched backward as the ewe bleated and followed. The lambs mewed and Molly echoed in a low groan. Siobhan tried to soothe the creatures as she lured the mother into the barn, singing the same cradle song her mam had sung to her and she had sung to her four babies.

Sleep, sleep, grah mo chree
Here on your mamma's knee,
Angels are guarding
And they watch o'er thee

Siobhan's melody explored the grace notes, the slides and rolls as each pitch was first tenderly embraced by a series of surrounding pitches until each word found a home. Sung in the old style, her mother's voice carried across the sea, so deeply expressive and from the heart.

Once inside, Siobhan backed into a clean stall and set the lambs down. The mother followed her twins inside and Siobhan closed the pen. The female lamb nestled under the mother, first mouthing tufts of wool before the lamb found a teat and began sucking, her tail wagging happily. The other lamb copied, and the mother turned and sniffed, but then moved away, not allowing the boy lamb to feed. He kept trying, though Molly's back hoof denied him a teat. She would have nothing of him. With each hoof kick, Siobhan felt the sadness of that lonely lamb, remembering the times she herself had felt that same rejection.

Siobhan took off her apron and rubbed the female lamb and then transferred the residual wet scent onto the rejected lamb. The mother continued headbutting the lamb away. Finally, Siobhan put Molly's head in a stanchion and, while avoiding Molly's fidgeting kicks, grabbed a teat and squeezed, releasing a waxy plug and then a warm stream. She had but an hour, at the most two hours, or the lamb could die. This first milk, rich and golden, provided everything the baby needed. She picked up the smaller lamb—Siobhan was always drawn to the weakest—and tucked its head beneath his mama.

With the lamb cradled in her arm, she opened the lamb's mouth and connected it to the teat. Molly tried to smell the baby, and though unable to turn, her back legs were still restless and a danger. Siobhan sighed. This might take a while. Over and over the lamb lost the teat. At last, it latched, and she could feel the suction and let the lamb stand on his own.

His sister wobbled over, easily finding a teat again. The boy slipped off the teat and tried to recover it amid the straggly tufts of his mother's coat. The ewe had not been crotched, her underbelly a confusion of strands. When he reached the soft pink nipple, he nudged it with his nose and connected, suckling once again.

It didn't matter how many years they farmed; each new lamb was a miracle. The first lamb of the season signaled the start of life and each spring *she* felt reborn. Hadn't their farm also offered her a new beginning and a link to her homeland?

After five days at sea, the SS *Saint Paul* from Cobh, Ireland, neared Ellis Island. Her first memory of this new country—the woman holding the flame. "It was supposed to be a lighthouse," she overheard someone say. But Lady Liberty certainly didn't look anything like the Loop Head Lighthouse at the mouth of the Shannon. Weren't lighthouses supposed to warn people to stay away? Was the Lady trying to tell them something?

"How big is her hand, Aintín?" she had asked her Aunt Brigid. There was something ominous, almost frightening about the woman with the stone-faced greeting. A goddess with spikes coming out of her head. Eyes almost closed, looking down on them. No joy and yet no sorrow. Her only life was the flame that flickered hope.

Staring from Aintín to the statue, Siobhan had noted the similarity in profile. Both set and unsmiling—unlike her mother. How could Aintín even be related? People said her aintín used to laugh, and she had once been quite popular. Siobhan could imagine why. Aintín Brigid; an Irish beauty with her curly red hair, cool green eyes, and pouty lips. But Siobhan only knew her as cold, distant, and unforgiving. Never married, always bitter, Aintín had been such an infrequent guest in their home, Siobhan barely knew her. Siobhan had not looked forward to preceding her Mam and Da, Moira and Patrick Kildea, who, with insurmountable loss, had still not made it to America—and according to Aintín Brigid, never would.

In Siobhan's dreams, Mam and Dad came, and they lived in a home with a piano, a clock, and a fireplace. Aintín and Siobhan's Boston flat had none. The cityscape pulsed with congregations huddled inside buildings towering over narrow cobblestone roads, roads where she longed to find at least a weed growing in a patch of dirt.

When she fled that dreary city, however, it was not because they lacked material wealth or open space, but a lack of love that was killing her spirit.

Now in Deer Lodge, Montana, Siobhan had her piano, clock, and fireplace, and even better, she had family.

The two lambs stepped away from their mother and curled together in the corner of the pen, drawing warmth and comfort from one another.

"Now you be good, Molly!" she instructed the mama. "Your wee ones need you!"

The morning light sliced through the worn gray slats of the barn, and she wondered what the day on the other side of that door held for her. For them.

Jack has to be better today, she thought. *He just has to.* She squared her shoulders and leaned into the door with authority and purpose. She would make everything all right.

Chapter Two
Siobhan

As she slid open the barn door, the crisp morning air stung Siobhan's face. Life was everywhere. The Montana sky spun on and on, painted with streaks of billowing white, fringed with gray, hinting there could be rain later that day. The rooster weather vane twirled happily. The chickens flapped their wings in the barnyard. The sparrows flittered through the sky in what someone had told her was *murmuration*. Such a beautiful word. She hardly understood it but spoke it softly into the wind as she watched hundreds of birds fold in and out of one another. *Murmuration!*

The wind gusted, she shook her apron and let herself laugh, tossing her head back, before she brushed loose hay from her face. She wanted to believe the air was filled with promise. There was much to look forward to . . . including the new book waiting for her on the kitchen table, a novel called *Ethan Frome*. Antonio made sure her home library was well-stocked though they were separated by miles and years.

A light glowed from the kitchen. Jack was up. Perhaps she'd find the old Jack, the confident, loving man whom she'd married.

She shivered and rubbed her arms briskly. The promises of spring in the air could only work so many miracles. Their old cat Scattery slipped alongside her legs. Siobhan carried the wire basket up the back steps, feeling just the slightest bit queasy. She closed her eyes to draw a deep breath, smoothing her apron across her belly—the slight swelling only noticeable by her long fingers. Jack didn't know she was carrying their fifth. At this point, he worried enough about how to feed their four children and purchase the seed to help pay off the debts they owed; he might not want to know. Jack saw night, and Siobhan saw day.

Her husband brooded at the kitchen table, hunched over a cup of coffee. Silence. This depression was hard on everyone, everywhere, but Jack had been forced back into the mines. He lived in darkness, though Siobhan tried to be his light.

"Mitty Matty had a hen. She laid eggs for gentlemen," Siobhan chanted, setting the egg basket down, trying to cheer him up with her Irish rhyme and morning breakfast. "They're still laying. I'm surprised—since it's been so cold."

Jack nodded, cradling his coffee cup, still staring across the room. She wrapped her arms around his shoulders, jostling his cup and the black coffee within. She swept her apron across the table, capturing her spill, and laughed. Jack didn't seem to notice.

"Molly is in the stanchion. We'll need to make sure the two lambies are getting enough milk. I'll *make* that mother take to her wee ones!" Siobhan stroked Jack's rough face with the back of her hand, his dark stubble wildly handsome. She liked it when he grew a beard, though she wasn't certain if that was his intent or if he just hadn't taken time to shave that morning. Or the morning before.

She sat across from him, placed her hands over his, and drew his cup to her mouth. Sweet communion.

"Jack, we'll be all right."

He nodded slightly. He was a hollow shell of what she remembered. Theirs was an unsteady peace.

"I love you, Jack Mason."

He shifted in his seat; in his ghost of a smile, a tiny glimmer of the Jack of old surfaced. It wasn't that long ago when his laugh was enough to live on. Siobhan rose and sat upon his lap. She nestled her face against his soft blue plaid flannel shirt, a perfect match for his eyes. Their foreheads met, and she knew when she closed her eyes, he had closed his too.

These were not easy times, but she knew they would get better. Together they'd find a way. Nothing had been conventional about their love story. She knew 1931 would be a year they'd talk about in stories of perseverance, fortitude, and unity. She opened her eyes and placed her lips, soft and gentle, on his. Though his arms embraced her, she felt a hesitation in his kiss. Suddenly, he clutched her tightly, his rough cheeks scratching hers with a sharp pain she enjoyed. She ran her fingers through his hair.

"Breakfast?" she whispered into his ear. Jack wore no answer on his face, as if it were a difficult decision.

"I suppose so," he answered finally. "Yes."

She sliced the last of the bread. She could bake today! Yeast and warm water, flour and salt. Working the dough with the palms of her hands as she prayed away her problems. Then the warmth of the oven, and the smell that said home.

Siobhan cracked the eggs into the pan, sizzling in fat. Beautiful orange yolks she would not break. Strong and round like the sun. She had a few potatoes left over from yesterday's dinner, and a jar with peaches from last year's canning. She hoped the fruit would last until summer, but she would not worry about that now. This was more than some had. Soon they would start afresh. Fill up the cellar. She'd count each jar and stretch them to make it through the year. She'd line them up by colors, like books on a shelf, and go down to read them when the winds were wild, and they sat holding onto one another in their storm cellar. Their place of salvation.

"Siobhan," Jack whispered, coming to her from behind, his hands on her shoulders as she flipped the eggs in the cast iron skillet. "I'm sorry."

"Oh, Jack." She nestled her cheek against his hand. "We're going to make it. Spring will come."

His hands slipped over her arms and down her sides. She shivered at the possibility, but he stepped back. Could he sense it, too? Did Jack understand that fall would arrive with the birth of their fifth child? It had been so long since they had a baby in the house. She looked forward to the cries, the tears, the joy, and even the pain. Most of all, she looked forward to new life. Was it time to remind him that their love created beauty and hope?

Samuel and Paul bounded down the stairs, the boys a symbol of how their unusual family had come together and bonded: Paul was hers, Samuel was Jack's, now close brothers unrelated by blood, but loved by parents who thought of both as their own. She lovingly called them her "Irish twins," these boys from different fathers and mothers but born eight months apart.

Jack stepped back to let them pass. She saw him lift a smile, but his eyes were heavy and sad.

Their two youngest came down the stairs more slowly, eight-year-old Sarah holding little Caleb's hand with her one good one—she had been born with a short arm and three fingers, though she never let it slow her down. Caleb dragged a string like it was a toy. Siobhan marveled at how, together, her two youngest could make everything a game.

Guilt swept over her. She didn't spend as much time with Caleb as she should. She shook it off. She was doing her best under the circumstances, and if Sarah loved caring for him, what was the harm?

"Molly had twins!" Siobhan sang out as Sarah passed.

"What color, Mama?"

"That's a surprise for me to know and *you* to find out!"

The oldest boys had picked up two sticks from the kindling and were clashing at one another like fencers. She'd never taught them that. Why did it come so naturally? She wanted to stop it, but they'd just find other weapons and call it play.

"Not in the house, boys," she said and they both looked up. "Go find something else to do!"

"We're just *playing*, Mama!" they called out in unison. She sighed as they ran out the door. A mother could pray, but her boys would play.

Samuel and Paul were haunting reminders of her own brothers, lost in wars she didn't understand. The best she could hope for was an end to battles, before her boys chose to take up real weapons instead of playing with sticks.

Siobhan dipped the knife in the bacon fat, slapped it onto the pan, then added last night's potatoes. How ironic that Siobhan, here in America, still had lambs and potatoes. She'd come so far to find home.

Jack pushed his coffee aside and rose from the table, scraping the chair along the wood floor.

"What about breakfast?" Her eyes pleaded with him. "I fried eggs and potatoes."

"I'm not hungry." His expression sagged. "Give it to the children." She couldn't read his eyes so glazed and foggy. He seemed so unfamiliar.

As a teenager, Jack had fled West Virginia just as she had fled Boston, though he left in order to escape a life underground, where he'd been expected to follow his grandfather, father, and uncles into the mines. Settling in Deer Lodge, Jack took a job at the mill at Lower Race Track Creek, and soon dubbed the nickname "Lumber Jack." After he married Annabeth, they purchased a farm and eagerly anticipated having a baby. When Annabeth died in childbirth, the town had grieved for his loss.

Up until recently, he worked the farm by night and the mill by day. How he functioned with the uncovered blades and machinery whirring around him after but a few hours of sleep, she'd never understand. But he would do anything for his family. And that meant, with layoffs at the mill, even going back underground.

Jack began to believe that, like his father before him, he was fated to spend his days in that hated, stifling darkness. Even worse, the minimal pay didn't even cover their needs. As he stepped into the elevator and slowly descended into the shaft each morning, it seemed he returned home with more and more of that cold blackness seeping inside of him.

How many sleepless nights he left the warmth of their bed, she didn't know, but there had been enough early mornings when she heard him pacing the house or found him sitting at the desk in the front room going over the farm books. Worse yet were the nightmares. He would wake up gasping, his body tense.

"What is it, Jack? Tell me!" she had begged, resting her hand on his chest and feeling his heart race wildly. "Breathe!" He had turned away and sat on the edge of the bed, clutching the mattress with both hands, closing his eyes as if shutting out the pain. "Float." Hadn't he taught her that?

"What does it feel like?" she'd whispered in his ear.

In his weakened confusion, he had confessed. "Panic. Like something terrible is about to happen."

She put her arms around him and laid her head on his back as his

Out of the Water

body shook with each sob. She strengthened her grip as if she could squeeze out the tension.

What was happening to her Jack? This was all temporary, and yet it consumed him. She knew things were difficult, but they still had a roof, and food on the table, didn't they? And today presented another opportunity to work, plant, and grow.

Jack. Jack. Jack. Where have you been? I want you back. I need you, Jack Mason. I need the wildly courageous man who laughed with his mouth wide open to the world.

"I don't have your lunch made yet. I'm baking bread, so you'll want to come in from the fields."

He traced her face with his finger as if memorizing it, then turned to leave.

The screen door slapped shut.

For the next few minutes, the house was quiet. Empty. She cupped her hand in the flour, enjoying the silky weightlessness, then made a well in the middle where she added yeast, sugar, and salt. She poured warm water into the depression and let it sit and bubble. What was it about yeast that could turn a few ingredients into something so delicious? Later, she worked the liquid into the flour, closing her eyes as she kneaded the dough like clay. Pushing and pulling. Rolling and folding the soft elastic pillow.

The children dashed back in, and she served up the last of the old loaf and gave them each an egg and fried potatoes. When they were done with breakfast, she put away the dishes and swept the kitchen.

Outside her window, Samuel and Paul twirled the long rope for Sarah, who jumped like a ballerina. She wondered if Sarah's balance would be off, but she hopped from foot to foot and when she had to twirl the rope, she managed with one arm. This was a good game for Sarah. But not for Caleb.

"One, two, three; me mother caught a flea," the children called out together. Caleb, who sat outside the group of three, chimed in. He had always been a talker. Even at one, he had a strong vocabulary. But today he looked on sadly. She knew he wanted to join in, but jumping rope was beyond the ability of a three-year-old, even if he deemed himself able. She understood. Her own older brothers had played without her, and her older sister married when she was young. With such a gap between their ages, Siobhan had been left alone most of the time.

She put it in a teapot
And made a cup of tea.
The flea jumped out,
Me mother gave a shout
And in comes Daddy
With his shirt hanging out.

"Jump in now, Daddy! Jump in!" the children shouted. Jack stood on the outskirts of the party, watching with hooded eyes. *Jump in, Daddy,* she willed Jack, holding her breath that he might once again play with his children. "Me mother gave a shout!" she called as she opened the door.

The silly nursery rhyme was one that Siobhan had taught the children. Whenever she served tea, they lifted the teapot lid as if to find a flea. Once, she surprised them by trapping a fly inside. It flew out as if on command, much to the delight of all four kids and Siobhan, who wanted to make sure they learned the songs her mother taught her.

"Daddy, please jump in!" the children urged.

Jack shifted as if to leave. *Jack, Jack, Jack,* she willed. He turned and as Sarah hopped out of the game, the boys drew the rope higher, and their daddy jumped in. Just for a few skips. When they all cheered, she could tell how much it meant to them. And to Jack.

"Jack!" she called out in praise. Jack waved to her as the three oldest threw their arms around him. He ran his hands over each of their heads.

See! There would be more times like these. She was convinced of it. But then Jack's eyes shifted downward, and he slowly turned away, his shoelace dragging behind. She wanted to call out to him but did not know what to say. What would bring him back?

Sarah and Samuel took the rope and Paul began jumping. Siobhan stepped outside and sat next to Caleb who swung his little feet to the beat.

"Do you want Mama to twirl you? I'll swing you 'round and 'round!"

"No, ma'am."

She picked up a soft down feather.

"Feather me, Mama."

Siobhan ran the feather over his forehead, he giggled, but then pushed her hand away and looked back to his brothers and sister.

"You want to jump, don't you?" Caleb nodded in agreement. "Then why don't you practice without the rope? Here, take my hands." Siobhan took her boy's hands, and they began jumping up and down together. Rarely on the same beat, and often, one of them would lose balance. He smiled, even laughed. Though Caleb would trip and fall in the other game, jumping with a rope was what he truly wanted.

"Let Caleb try."

"Ah, Mama, he's too little."

"He'll get bigger. Let him try."

Sarah told him where to stand. Siobhan and Paul took the rope together. She coached Caleb when to jump in. Each time the rope slapped him; Caleb never winced.

"Let him start standing in the middle and we'll tell him when to jump. We'll twirl it around *him*," Sarah suggested.

Paul and Siobhan twirled it again, letting the snake stop on the ground so Caleb could step over it with one foot, then the other. When they picked up speed, his foot caught the rope and he fell to the ground. Still, he stood back up quickly and smiled at his brothers.

"See, Mama!" Samuel stomped his foot. "Let us play alone!"

Caleb looked to her, biting his lower lip. She had an idea.

"I'll get a shorter and thinner cord. Then you can practice by yourself for a while. You're still too little."

"I'll always be too little." His toddler voice cracked with sadness. She could see his hands dirtied and bloody from his tumbles. "Because they will always be bigger."

"No, you won't always be too little."

"How do you know?"

How *did* she know? The oldest, Samuel, was shorter than Paul. Samuel's mother had been a tiny woman, according to Jack, while Siobhan stood nearly five foot seven. She stacked Paul's father and Samuel's father next to each other in her mind, like books on a shelf, then smiled. With both, she'd had to reach up to touch their lips. Though similar heights, Samuel's father had a strong and rugged build. Her Jack. She smiled. Caleb would outgrow them all.

"Because of your papa. Look at him. He's so tall, and you are the most like him!" She didn't have to explain anything else. She hoped her three-year-old would not have any more questions about the very complicated Mason family tree.

"When you're ready, Mam will look for a rope for you. And one day we'll surprise the rest of them with how well you can jump!"

Sarah took Caleb's hand in her own, chanting another rhyme, naming each finger.

"Little Pea, Penny Roo, Rudy Whistle, Molly Wassle, and oold tom bum-bah-lo!" Caleb giggled. Had he heard the jingle before? Surely, Siobhan had played it with him once.

Perhaps Sarah had taught him when she'd taken Caleb under her wing. The wing that was not broken. Sarah could teach Caleb using the five-fingered hand on which Siobhan had taught her.

Siobhan returned to the house. Even without baking, the smell of yeast permeated the kitchen. She punched down the dough, knowing it would rise again twice its size, and sneaked a peek at her latest book.

After another chapter, she set the book aside and sought out something sweet to put on the bread. There was just enough honey left in the jar from their neighbors, and with the butter she and Paul had churned yesterday, they'd take a break and have a little party. The pan was hot, and she set it on a pad she had made from an old flour sack dress Sarah had worn out.

She could see Samuel, Paul, and Sarah. But no Caleb. No matter. He would be with his father. Outside, the laundry on the line rippled and flowed, bending, and succumbing to the wind. She had forgotten to take it down last night. It could dry and provide fun for her children as they ran in and out of the sheets in a game of hide-and-go-seek.

She rang the iron bell Jack had put near the kitchen door to signal time to come in from the fields and wash up, then headed back out to the barn, to check on Molly. She slid the exterior door open, revealing dust motes in a ray of familiar warmth. She lingered at the sight of the two lambs tucked in the corner together, Molly still in the stanchion.

The ewe would be set free when Siobhan felt more assured of the mother's care. Picking up the boy lamb, she felt its soft belly, slightly pudgy and reassuringly rounder.

"You could use some fresh straw in here and some hay to eat, ay, Mam?" Siobhan laid the lamb back with his sister and scratched Molly's furry forehead.

She then climbed the ladder to the haymow above. After hoisting herself onto the hard, wooden floor, she let her eyes adjust, before opening the haymow door slightly to let in a breeze and the midafternoon sun. The clouds, as if snowballs in the sky, slipped across the pale blue Montana expanse. She would come up here in the evening, when she knew the sun was setting, and watch the sky turn pink.

She'd bring Jack up here. Before dinner. She'd pack a little picnic like they did when their boys were babies. She'd spread their star quilt and the two would lie here and watch the sky change. And then quite possibly, Jack would caress her face and neck. She grew warm and tingled with the imagination. Well, she couldn't think of that right then. But, oh, how she loved that man.

She chose a bale and hefted it off the stack, tossing it over the edge of the mow to the floor. It landed with barely a sound, down below, the dust settling around it. As she raised her eyes from the floor to the beam over her head, she saw a boot.

Her brain shuddered. What was this? How odd that the brown rawhide shoelaces were not tied. Suspended in air, the denim pants, the blue plaid shirt. Didn't she know the softness of that flannel? Hadn't she only just felt it against the palm of her hands? And the unshaven face and open eyes.

"No! No! No!" Her head shook, punctuating each word. She clutched her belly, gasping in disbelief. Jack hung from a noose almost directly above her, his face discolored, his eyes unseeing.

"Jack! Jack! Jack!" She had to get to him. There might be life. Siobhan dumped a wooden box near the staircase and found a knife among the tools. She climbed the mountain of bales just like her husband must have done before her. When she got to the beam, she scooted her way across it. Had her husband walked along it? With the noose already fastened to his neck? She dared not look down. When Jack had fashioned a pulley for the boys to fly across the barn, she had tried it, unafraid of the heights. But now?

Now, directly above where the rope was tied to the beam, she reached for Jack.

"Jack!" she yelled. "Can you hear me? Jack?" She pulled at his body so that the rope had less draw on his life. And then she saw them. As his body turned, she saw the lifeless eyes. "No, no. No!" Her two fingers on his neck trembled as she felt for life. Then she reached for his elbow and held it up, vainly searching for a heartbeat. Life. There had to be life.

She sliced at the rope, gnawing each tine until it weakened. This she could do. She would saw the rope until the knife hit the raw wood below releasing the knot from the beam.

When there was but rope fragments holding her husband's body in the air, she tucked her head, covered her ears with her shoulders, made the final hack and groaned to cover the noise of his body hitting the ground below. Then she lay on the beam holding it like she had held Jack the night before when they had made love. They had made love, hadn't they? Hadn't she loved him enough?

She scooted slowly backward along the beam, retracing where she had just been, wishing Jack had done the same hours before. She lost her balance slightly and clung more tightly. But did it matter now what happened to her? Yes, it did. It mattered to the four children who were somewhere on the farm waiting for her to set another meal. For the loaves of bread to come out of the oven. Had Jack also considered what this would do to her, to all of them?

At that she shuddered and spun around to the door. Oh, that the children would stay out of the haymow. She wished there was a lock to prevent them from knowing what had happened.

She climbed off the beam and down the steps, standing in the middle of the barn floor like an actor alone on a stage with one ray of light spotlighting her face. She collapsed into a fetal position onto the hay bale she'd dropped, cradling her belly. She couldn't look at him.

What had he done? There was another child! Should she have told him? She would never know. She pounded the bale in anger. In horror.

In grief. "What did you do?" she yelled out to no one. "I can't do this alone!" And then all she wanted to do was to touch him again—but not in this way, his face so twisted.

"I love you, Jack Mason!" She wailed now, not in anger but in loss. How loudly had she cried out? Had the children heard? She sucked in and held her breath. How many seconds? Her head throbbed. She had to think. Her eyes searched the room wildly. She returned to the large wooden doors and closed them to within an inch, allowing just enough light for her to survey the barn.

He could not have hung himself. He was a good man. Everybody loved Jack Mason. He had four, no, almost five children. They needed to know their daddy never did this. They wouldn't want to know the truth. They *couldn't* know a truth that would forever change their lives.

It was an accident. Her husband had been in a terrible farm accident. He had been moving bales and he had slipped and fallen, and he had broken his neck. That was what had happened. Tragic, but believable. There were so many farm accidents. A farm accident was horrible, but the rest of the family could live with that. She wouldn't lie, she would say that he fell to the floor of the barn. She had witnessed it. That was the truth. *A* truth.

She was not going to think about *who* it was on the floor of the barn; she would just do what she needed to do. Kneeling beside the man's body, she took out the knife and slipped the flat side against his neck, slowly slicing the rope so tight against it. With very little space, it took twenty minutes for her to saw the noose. At last, the man was free. She considered the distorted body in front of her and could no longer deny it was her love.

"Oh, Jack," she whispered. "We could have made it, Jack!" She lay her head on his chest and sobbed as if he could return her embrace, by wrapping her in his arms. His flannel shirt felt soft and comforting. How long she lay there, she didn't know. Pretending they were together, that he was alive, that he would just get up and laugh. He would tousle her hair, pull her back down, and kiss her. Deeply. Warmly. Like the man who had accepted the pregnant girl off the train over ten years before.

Siobhan untangled herself from him and wound the rope in circles.

The rope would need to disappear. Never to be found. His obituary would read not that he had died suddenly, as some obituaries read when whispers suggested suicide. No, he died a farmer, a victim of circumstances. And in effect, that was exactly what he was. A victim. A victim of these times and of finances, and failed dreams.

This was what they would have to live with. She would protect them from what he had done. She alone. Picking up the coil of rope, turning toward the doors, she hesitated.

Tucked behind a ladder were two tiny hands, clutching the rungs. Two eyes gazed up at her. One silent witness.

Chapter Three
Geneviève

St. Denis, France
July 1918

Geneviève Louise Marchand, Red Cross Nurse, stepped off the *USS Cartago*, then headed to Base Hospital No. 41 in St. Denis, France, on July 26, 1918. Five days and almost six thousand miles behind her, the Statue of Liberty had seemed frozen in an ominous wave goodbye. "*La Liberté éclairant le monde.* Made in France," their NYC tour guide explained, unaware that Geneviève would be heading to France after being fit for her uniform and taking in the closing performance at the Bijou Theatre, ironically titled *Fancy Free*.

Though she was anything but fancy, she at once felt free and ready to make a difference. Base 41 was L'École de la Legion d'Honneur, a select all-girls school just outside of Paris originally set up by Napoleon.

Geneviève was one part of the Theater of Operations. Injured men from battalions on the frontlines were carried off by stretcher-bearers to the Battalion Aid Stations, then later to field hospitals specializing in gas injuries, surgical, or illness. These same hospitals could also mobilize into the trenches or no-man's-land. Base 41 was one of many last stops.

The French system of triage took on new meaning. Sort, classify, distribute. *Save. Maybe. No. Gas. Surgical. Sick.* The patient's hastily scribbled field card told Geneviève what stretcher-bearers or medical personnel closer to the front had diagnosed. Sometimes the acronym was of questionable help: ICT or *I can't tell.*

With little instruction or explanation, Geneviève Marchand was thrown into a ward dismally overwhelmed by patients in every level of agony, men who barely survived the shelling in the trenches or their charges into no-man's-land. One-third of the casualties were from mustard, phosgene, or chlorine gas—men who lacked a mask in the mandatory six seconds. She'd heard a soldier could urinate on a handkerchief and cover his face to protect from mustard gas. Or, at the first indication of chlorine, cover his face with a black veiling pad, ironically, made from women's funeral veils, and soaked in a chemical solution to neutralize the poison. But it only worked for a brief time.

She could hardly stand hearing the raspy breathing of gas victims, knowing the men would die an inevitable and painful death by suffocation.

Encourage the patient to vomit, keep the patient still, provide patient oxygen, clean patient's room of smoke and dust, initiate liquid diet, keep patient warm, facilitate oral hygiene, wash skin, irrigate then shade eyes.

She gave baths and cleaned gangrenous wounds. She dressed and redressed injuries. She nursed the blistering burns of gas victims, men who screamed with a relentless howling that continued through the night. She swatted at the flies which swarmed over infections. Sometimes she held the limb of a man while the doctor sawed, other times they attempted the Carrel-Dakin Method where she doused the wound with hypochlorite of soda to keep it wet, rigging the leg on a Bradford frame to keep it extended. The jar hanging above released fluid into the wound every two hours. Maybe the limb could be saved. Geneviève learned more than her textbooks could teach her about the debilitating effects of diarrhea, tuberculosis, chilblains, frozen feet, scarlet fever, pneumonia, dysentery, typhus, trench foot from wet boots, and trench fever from lice. Though each patient was new and intriguing, the ambulances and weary monotony of death had a horrible sameness.

She couldn't keep them all at arm's length, invisible and unnamed. She felt their pain and the inevitable grief. Each man claimed she reminded him of his sister, or girlfriend, or daughter, and that made them all brothers, or boyfriends, or fathers.

James Brown. An Australian stretcher-bearer was brought to her ward with *shell-shocked* on his field card. The man trembled with fear, unable to speak.

"There. There. Rest." But without warning, he jerked up, confused and ripping the cover from the bed. Like so many shell-shocked men before him, he couldn't obey simple instructions. She wrestled him back down with the aid of another nurse, then brought a warm tea and covered him with blankets.

Though he bore no external wounds, he screamed through the night. A fellow bearer came to check on him and explained his litter had become trapped in a shell hole targeted for days. At last, he returned to the trenches for rescues, but there were none.

She let out the breath she had held.

"The men were all holding hands, but they were all dead."

The terror the men must have felt. Geneviève instinctively touched the sleeping man's shoulder. She couldn't imagine climbing over the trench, running into the face of danger, risking her own life to search for another's, only to be a pallbearer at the funeral of war.

That night she tossed and turned, her back aching from a fourteen-hour day bent over making beds and changing dressings. She held the alien gas mask in her hand. Would this be the night she'd need it?

Soldiers came to her broken and bleeding from battlefields she couldn't pronounce. Meuse-Argonne, Chateau-Thierry, Saint-Mihiel, Saint Quentin Canal. When they survived and she sent them home, she felt the win. But what accomplishment was there when they headed back to another battle on foreign soil? Or when she couldn't heal them, and they died in her care?

As the days shortened, the workload increased, beginning with a few men complaining of body aches, muscle and joint pain, a headache, sore throat. Then fevers spiked to 104 with accompanying dizziness and weakness. Who could predict the hemorrhaging, vomiting, diarrhea, or constipation? Sufferers bled from their eyes, nose, even skin and ears as if from an invisible bullet. The sounds of rib-cracking, unproductive coughing and ragged breathing filled the ward, reminding her of pneumonia. Except it wasn't.

How could she explain it to her patients? Large tents were set up in the courtyard for the overflow and to keep the contagion down.

One soldier arrived with a leg so mutilated, it was held together only with cloth, necessitating immediate amputation. She wore a mask and tried to breathe lightly to avoid the vile stench. The odor wafted through her mask, she turned and vomited.

"My leg—" He lunged forward, his face cramped with pain. "Will I lose my leg?" His voice was raspy and etched itself on her skin in a way she knew she'd never forget. His field card noted shrapnel, but she knew it would soon read: DI, *dangerously ill,* which was code that he'd never be seen by a doctor.

The mahogany spots blushed on his cheekbones. He coughed up blood. Next came cyanosis, the bluing from lack of oxygen creeping over his face like a blanket of death. So blackish blue, some of her patients were mistakenly labeled *Negro.* So dark, some nurses called it a return of Black Death.

Did he really want the truth?

"You won't lose your leg." No, she wouldn't hold his leg while the doctor sawed. Only his hope. He would die by suffocation like too many others she couldn't save. She left him with a lavender sachet donated by someone somewhere who was trying to do something to help.

What had she expected when she left behind her former life working six-and-a-half-day work weeks at UVA Hospital, living in Varsity Hall like a lonely spinster nurse with too many other women barely existing on their eight-dollar stipends?

When Dr. Goodwin had begun recruiting alumni and students to staff a UVA Medical Base in France, she felt a draw. Then when Margaret Cowling, Superintendent of Nursing, personally asked her, she accepted the call. Was it for her country? Even she didn't know. But nursing was her calling and if America believed in this war, maybe she should, too. Perhaps saving lives would save her own.

Chapter Four
Erin

Spokane, Washington
July 1964

Erin May Ellis began compiling *Our Baby's Story* even before Claire's adoption and then completed the original storybook with photographs after her arrival. It was the first storybook Erin read to her and one of the first books the four-year-old Claire self-sounded out. Still, it couldn't answer all of Claire's concerns.

Her first questions were simple and childlike. "I grew in another mommy's tummy? I have two mommies? Where is the *other* mommy? How come I didn't grow in *your* tummy?" As Claire matured, so did the questions, their intensity, and frequency. Claire wanted to know, was there another daddy, too? What did the other mother look like? Was she nice? Did the other mother have any other kids that looked like Claire?

And then there was that sermon one Sunday at Priest Lake Community Church. The A-frame chapel overlooking the lake below was the perfect setting for the story of how Jochebed made a basket for her son Moses and sent him down the river where he was retrieved and adopted by Pharaoh's daughter. Claire was inquisitive on the ride home. "Why did they put him in a basket? Couldn't his mommy hide him? Who was the lady in the river? Couldn't the baby have drowned?"

Almost seventeen years later Claire's queries were a constant reminder that "Our Baby" was not Erin's biological child and that despite her best efforts, Claire felt rejected.

It probably didn't help that Claire looked nothing like her brother Evan or sister Elizabeth. Claire was a tall, wavy-haired redhead with porcelain skin; a few freckles dotting her nose. She was outgoing, but never as outrageous as her adoptive mom, the blonde, stick-straight haired, former cheerleader who stood five foot four in tennis shoes.

When Erin's two girls were toddlers in the grocery store, a clerk wondered aloud how two so close in age could be sisters. This happened frequently. "Are they both yours?"

"One's adopted," Erin explained and then the cashier apologized, just like they all did.

"You don't have to tell everybody!" Grandma jostled the cart out of the store. "People don't always have to know the whole truth."

Of course, once home, Claire then asked if it was bad to be adopted and if it was bad for people to know she was adopted. Was it supposed to be a secret?

As a UVA nursing student, Claire's OB rotation made the questions more personal. Prior to watching her first delivery, the sum of Claire's baby experience was the birth of her younger brother Evan, ten years before.

Over the phone lines, Claire narrated, making Erin feel she was in the delivery room.

"At first it was kind of boring, but then the contractions came faster and with more intensity. The nurse checked the patient's cervix and the doctor arrived." Erin knew she shouldn't be so impressed at Claire's use of terms; still her heart swelled at her daughter's knowledge.

"The head crowned. It was so amazing, Mom!"

Erin awaited the birth announcement.

Claire seemed to hold off for dramatic effect. "It was a *girl*."

Did that make Claire happy or sad? Erin couldn't tell. "But then the room went silent. The baby didn't cry." Erin sucked in a gasp.

"The mom got all worried and started asking why she didn't hear anything and if her baby was okay. I just ran APGAR over and over in my head. *Activity. Pulse. Grimace. Appearance. Respiration.* The little girl's hands and feet had a bluish tinge. The mom kept saying, 'Bring her to me. I want to see her!' The nurse kept rubbing the baby's back to stimulate its first breath. And rubbing and flicking the soles to illicit a response. Tactile stimulation.

"And then they said her SATS were eighty-seven percent, and her APGAR was four, and they called for an incubator for transport to the neonatal ICU."

Erin's grip on the phone had tightened.

"And then there was this little cry, and the baby wiggled."

Erin exhaled loudly. She hadn't realized she'd held her breath. "Was she okay?"

"Just some mucous in the back of her throat. She was low on oxygen. The nurses said she was six pounds, eleven ounces, and then the mom said that's what she weighed when *she* was born."

Erin felt the magnitude of that statement. That was something else she and Claire didn't have in common.

"And then they put the baby in her arms."

Erin waited for what she knew was coming.

"Mom, do you think she wanted to see me? Hold me?"

How was Erin supposed to answer that question?

"I want to find her, Mom."

Who was the "other mother?" Was it Claire's biological mom? Or was it her? Would finding her alter Claire's identity or allegiance? How would that affect Claire's brother and sister, Evan and Elizabeth, her husband Chase, and even Grandma who was already growing increasingly confused with life?

Now it was May 18, 1981, and Erin's firstborn was turning twenty-one.

"Five, four, three, two, one! It's 7:28! Happy birthday!" the Ellis family screamed in unison, following their tradition to celebrate birthdays at the exact time the celebrant was born. They all sang happy birthday to Claire. Evan, now ten years old, the loudest, and Elizabeth, the quietest. Erin smiled at her husband, Chase, who sat at the end of the table next to his mother.

As the song hit a crescendo, Elizabeth said, "Not so loud or the puppy will pee!" lowering her palms in caution.

"What?" Claire shouted over the family choir.

"Ginger pees at loud noises." Elizabeth nudged Claire, adding a parenthesis of explanation.

Claire rolled her eyes, then blew out the candles on the pile of pancakes, sending a smoky haze into the room.

"Remember when Mount St. Helens blew up on your birthday?" Evan reminded, grabbing four pancakes with his bare hands.

"What?" Grandma asked.

"Mount St. Helens!" Evan yelled rudely.

"You don't have to shout, Evan!" Claire scolded.

"Helena?" Grandma turned quickly. "Helena?—I think I've been there."

"*Mount* St. Helens, Mom," Chase corrected, placing a pancake on her plate and spreading it with butter. "That was some birthday gift."

"Harry Truman died there," Grandma said, and lowered her head respectfully.

"Harry Truman died a long time before that, Mom," Chase corrected.

"Actually"—Elizabeth pointed her fork at her dad—"there was this eighty-two-year-old guy named Harry Truman who died up there. He wouldn't leave his house."

They looked to Grandma, who smiled.

"Maybe GinnaBee relates to Harry," Claire said softly.

GinnaBee. Firstborn Claire stubbornly attempted the name Geneviève long before *Grandma.* The name had stuck. And yes, GinnaBee probably did relate. The passing of her husband, the Honorable Judge William Charles Ellis, meant GinnaBee's move from their longtime home of over forty years had exacerbated her already deteriorating memory. After her stroke, nothing had been the same. At eighty-seven, she'd flooded the bathroom, wandered away, and called 911 for no particular reason. Never a dull moment at the Ellis home since GinnaBee moved in.

"Evan, are you feeding that puppy pancakes?" his father asked. Evan's guilty hand hung down with the forbidden morsel. "If you feed her from the table, she'll always beg. No more of that, Evan."

"With the girls in college, I don't think getting another dog was a good idea," Erin pointed out.

"It's good for a boy to have a dog," Chase countered.

"Then the boy should care for the dog."

Ginger whined as if in agreement.

"Maisie never begged," Elizabeth reminded.

"Let's not talk about Maisie!" Claire pleaded.

Claire's request was fair. It was her birthday after all, and losing Grandpa and Maisie all in the same year had been hard.

"Okay, I've got something else to talk about, anyway." Claire bit her lip and hesitated. "I don't want to be dramatic or anything, but . . ."

"Since when are you not dramatic?"

"Thanks, Evan."

"You bet."

Erin could feel it coming. But why now? In the middle of her birthday when they were all together?

"And I don't want anybody to feel hurt." Claire studied her family as they passed around the syrup.

"Great start. Now you have us worried. Did something happen to the car?" teased Elizabeth.

"I'm not trying to be funny, Biz." Claire's voice was so low and sober, Erin put her fork down and smoothed the napkin across her lap. The breakfast rush slowed.

"Since I'm twenty-one . . . I'm thinking about looking for my . . . mom." It sounded more like a suggestion, a trial balloon.

"Look no farther." Evan gestured toward Erin.

"*Birth* mother. I have another family."

"Yeah? So, we're not enough?"

"Oh, you're *more* than enough!" Claire laughed. "You know it's not *that*. Wouldn't you want to know *your* birth parents?"

"Depends on who they are." Evan wrinkled his nose. "And only if they're better than the ones I got," he added before Elizabeth hit him.

"Be serious. Wouldn't you want to know what they were like?"

"I can't imagine why you *wouldn't* want to find out. It's your choice. And we support you." Erin eyed her husband. "Don't we, Chase?"

Erin regretted blindsiding him. This had always been a tender subject. She shouldn't have spoken for him even though he was always so silent. It was a familiar joke in their family that Dad had a mere three thousand words per day and used up twenty-nine hundred at the office.

Chase's mouth was as firm as the frown on his forehead. The only one eating now was GinnaBee, who had poured out most of the pitcher of syrup.

"At least you don't have to worry about getting what GinnaBee has." Evan smarted off. "I hope it's not contagious."

"You mean *hereditary*," Elizabeth corrected.

"That too," Evan nodded then stabbed his pancake with a war cry. "HyyyyyYAH!"

Chase remained stoic. Was he worried about getting Alzheimer's?

"I'm not sure it's a good idea."

"Why not, Dad?"

"Not everybody wants to be found. If you didn't want to be found, would you appreciate her dropping into your life?" Chase didn't even call her *the other mother*. It was just *her*. "You never know what you'll find. It might hurt. Is it worth the risk? Especially when you have a family right here."

"That's what *I* said," Evan concurred.

The twenty-one candles still towered on her birthday pancake, filled with twenty-one blueberries.

"Dad, I *know* I have a family. But what about my medical history? That's important. And where did my ancestors come from? There are people out there who are related to me. I could learn things about them."

"Like why they gave you up? Do you really want to know *that*?" Evan asked.

"I'm curious," Claire admitted. "Like Mom said. It's part of my life."

"Just think about it first." Chase set his fork down. Where did this negativity come from? Was there something she didn't know? Why couldn't they all just get along?

"So, you're against it?"

"Like your mom said, it's your choice. But I don't think you should."

Her husband was not without expertise in the matter. The Moses Project, a nonprofit Chase had formed, helped aid the homeless, refugees, widows, and orphans.

"You have a family. We love you and that should be enough. Why open Pandora's box?" Chase pushed back from the table, snatched up his plate, and strode into the kitchen without finishing his breakfast or waiting for Claire to open her presents.

"It's not like I don't think you're enough." Claire called out after him. "It's me," she murmured. "I wasn't."

"You know adoption is being *chosen*—" Elizabeth quoted from Claire's baby book and rolled her eyes.

"And some babies are a *surprise*—" Evan added, elbowing Biz.

"And some are an *accident*—" Elizabeth glared at her brother.

"Hey, you're all special. You're all gifts."

Elizabeth smirked. "That's what parents are *supposed* to say."

"I wouldn't take a million dollars for any one of you," Evan began, imitating his dad's familiar saying before they all chimed in on the punchline: "But I wouldn't pay a plugged nickel for another!"

Evan stuffed the last bite of pancake down with a slurp of milk. "I gotta go."

"You're not going to that video arcade!" Erin said, a nonnegotiable statement.

"No. Robert has a new RC Piper Arrow. His dad's taking us to the football field to fly it."

"Be home in an hour. Remember you have a certain chore to finish."

Evan frowned, then paused at the door. "Hey Claire, good luck with finding someone who's more like *you*. I hope they still like you if they are." He quickly slammed the door behind him, getting in the last word.

"No! Ginger!" Erin jumped to her feet and ran to the puppy who was piddling on the floor. "No slamming doors!"

The three Ellis women looked at one another, then down at the puppy, and laughed.

"You know, Evan doesn't mean that," Elizabeth said, heading to the kitchen. "Look, whatever you do, just be careful. You might get hurt."

"How could the truth hurt?" Claire asked innocently enough.

After Elizabeth cleared the table, Erin and Claire finished up the dishes. Erin dipped each plate in the soapy water, then rinsed, while Claire dried. They were the only two in the family who liked doing the dishes. Erin knew the shared time was what Claire looked forward to most; she teased that Biz and Evan had no idea what they were missing.

"Are you okay with this?" Claire asked, seemingly unable to give *this* a name.

Erin looked out to their patch of grass and fenced backyard that she assumed had kept her children safe all these years.

"I've been okay with this since you first asked questions." Erin held a plate in the soapy water. "I'll never know that longing, but from all those books I've read, it's pretty strong."

"It's like . . ." Claire twisted the towel in her hands. "It's like I'm missing something. A piece of me." Her eyes wrinkled into an apology. "But I don't want you to feel . . . sad."

"Maybe I'd feel worse if you thought your adoptive family was so crazy weird you didn't want to take a chance on knowing another one."

"Hmm, I never thought of that!"

"Or if you couldn't stand us, so you had to find your other family."

"I don't want you to think you're not enough."

"I don't." Erin scooped up a few bubbles and blew them at her daughter. "And sometimes I get curious about her, too."

"Really?"

"Of course."

"Like why she'd give me up?"

"Maybe that. But more because I know who you are, and I wonder if she acts like you. *Looks* like you." Erin stopped and turned, tracing one soapy finger under Claire's chin, "Or whether some of the things you do are just because I am your mom."

"You *are* my mom. You will always be my mom, no matter what happens." Claire reached into the soapy water and pulled out the stopper.

"There's one more thing you should know."

Claire dried her hands.

"There was something I didn't put in the baby book because I wasn't quite sure about it, and I needed to find out more. But it might be helpful." Erin took a deep breath. "And I had to wait for the right time."

Claire raised her eyebrows.

"The attorney's office where we signed the papers was Cramer, Davis, and Morgan. It's a small law firm. The lawyers were in their thirties. I'd be willing to bet they're still practicing."

"Well, that's a start." Claire grabbed a pen and paper off the counter.

"There's more." Erin sat down at the kitchen table and Claire pulled out a chair across from her. "When we were signing the papers, I was looking at one of the documents on the lawyer's desk across from me." Erin could almost reenact the scene. "I tried to read the certificate upside down. I saw a name and I think it was hers. Your mother's name." Claire's eyes widened. "I only saw her *first* name. It caught my eye. I was curious. But then he moved his arm and I never saw anything else."

"Only a *first* name? How would that help?"

"Because that name is *Aria.*"

"Aria?" Claire asked, as if she hadn't heard the name before. "So, this name I've always made fun of—it's real?"

"Aria gave you to me, so I gave her something back. In the only way that I could. *Aria.* Your first name is hers. *Aria.*"

Aria. The name Claire had always said was too weird. In first grade, Aria suddenly announced she wanted to go by her middle name *Claire,* discarding Aria as if she were a kindergarten friend she'd outgrown on the playground.

"But you never told me."

"Yet," Erin explained, "I would have; and I did, at the right time."

"All those times I complained about not having a normal name?"

"Well, you solved *that* problem, *Claire.*"

"You didn't see her last name?"

"No. I'm sorry, honey."

"And that's the whole truth? There's really nothing else?" Claire raised her eyebrows in expectation.

"Nothing that I know of, honey." Erin shook her head, wondering if the truth was worth the unburying of secrets.

Claire tapped the table nervously.

"They warn you that sometimes parents don't want to see their child. That you should have counseling to help prepare you."

"I can't imagine *that* happening!" Erin shook her head. "That would hurt." The last of the water made a sucking sound as it swirled down the drain. Erin hoped she'd dispelled her daughter's fears.

Later that morning, Elizabeth and Claire lay side by side in their shared bedroom, both reading books like an old married couple. Above their heads, their bulletin board looked like a high school time capsule. Elizabeth's track ribbons, a photo of Claire as Nellie in *South Pacific,* or "South Pathetic" as Evan called it. And there he was playing Matchbox cars on the shag carpet under their bed.

"*There* you are! Evan, you were supposed to finish weeding the front walkway!"

"That's child labor."

"Yes, it is. Reparative and retributive punishment, too. Next time think twice before throwing snap-its all over your bedroom wall." After putting herself through college as a legal secretary, Erin Ellis could parry with the best of them. Even Evan. *Especially* Evan.

"How was I supposed to know it would do *that?*"

Erin swatted his behind, then stepped aside so he could march down the stairs. She never knew if girls or boys were easier. It was a tough call with a kid like Evan. She sighed as she sat at the foot of their bed.

"So," Claire began. "After we drop you off at the U, Mom and I have a meeting at RAFT. About finding my birth parents."

"You're kidding? *RAFT?* That's what it's called?"

"It's an acronym. Reuniting Adoptive Families Together."

"Wow. So, you're really doing this," Elizabeth said. "What happens first?" She sat up on one elbow. Air Supply playing in the background.

"At the meeting, they make you talk about the emotional stuff. In front of everybody."

"Emotional stuff?"

"Like how I'd handle it if my mom or dad didn't want to meet me. Or if I were disappointed."

"Or if *they* were disappointed."

Claire whacked Elizabeth on the head with a pillow. "Biz, you never had to wonder what Mom was like." Erin smiled and shrugged.

"And *you* never had to wonder how a biological brother could be *so* different." Elizabeth tilted her head. "Emphasis on *different!*"

"Sometimes I wonder if I've ever bumped into my mom or dad. Would I recognize them? Or what if I have siblings?"

"You *do* have siblings." Elizabeth corrected, then softened, "One pretty great little sister!"

"Sometimes I wonder if they're good at the same things I am or if they like the same foods or television shows or whether they have the same laugh or sense of humor."

"Yeah, but Evan and I aren't always like Mom and Dad, but sometimes you are. I mean, Mom's outgoing and so is Evan. But I'm kind of an introvert. Dad is good at the math and sciences and I'm not, but you are. And even though you don't look like Mom, you look a little like Dad."

"I don't think I'm anything like Dad," Claire argued, silencing the debate on nature vs. nurture.

Erin's eyes watered and, in the blur, she could see the resemblance between Chase and Claire.

"I'm sorry, Mom," Claire said suddenly, reaching toward Erin. "But sometimes I wonder if I might be more like the *other* dad. And then maybe I could talk to *him.*"

Erin longed for the day Claire and Chase would forge a better relationship but recognized her husband was sometimes emotionally shut down. Closed off.

"HyyyyyYAH!" Erin heard from outside and opened the window to yell.

"Evan, that's *not* what I asked! Get back to work!" She shook her head, her hands on her hips.

"I'm going to call the . . . the Department!" Evan matched her stance, his hands on his hips, as he struggled for words. "The Department of Social . . . of . . . Social Security on you!" Evan yelled upward. The girls collapsed laughing but Erin had to bite her lip before she yelled back, "You do that. I'll get the phone book."

⌒

That evening, Evan took out his electric racetrack with Nite-Glo and set it up on the floor in the family room. Sitting in the dark, his back against the couch, with his small feet sticking out of his Luke Skywalker pajamas, Erin was reminded how little he really was and how he was probably still looking for a superhero.

Evan raced two cars at the same time, one controller in each hand. The two cars sped up hills and around circles and over a few jumps he had created. He pressed all the way down on each controller, and both cars flew off as they simultaneously rounded a tight bend.

"And the cars are in a roll," he narrated as if an Indy reporter.

"Hey." Claire settled in on the couch.

"Hey," Evan echoed back, focused on putting the cars back on track.

"Can I play?"

Evan glanced up, wide-eyed and open-mouthed.

"Or better yet," she suggested, "I could be your . . . your setter-upper."

"Pit crew," he corrected.

"Pit crew," she agreed. "I'll just put the cars back on the track."

For the next twenty minutes, Evan made all the sound effects, narrating the races, while Claire crawled around the tracks, tightening them, and setting each car back in its lane when it flew off. For a mom, sitting invisible in the kitchen, it was a sweet moment in time.

"There's a new movie coming out." Claire set a car back in the groove.

"A Star Wars one?" Evan asked, swiftly stopping the cars, and rising onto his knees.

"No, it's called *Raiders of the Lost Ark.*"

"Oh," he sat back down, "Like Noah's Ark?"

"No, but it's an adventure, and it has Harrison Ford in it. The guy who plays Han Solo."

Evan frowned. She was surprised he didn't look interested.

"No. He should only be Han Solo. I don't want him to be anybody else."

Erin smiled. Evan was such a Star Wars loyalist.

"Well, then, we don't have to see that one." Claire paused. "I did see *The Empire Strikes Back* is returning to the Fox. Maybe we could see it tomorrow?

"Awesome!" Evan's face lit up. "Then maybe stop at Ferguson's for a chocolate milkshake?"

"And you can eat it straight out of the mixing cup!"

Evan turned serious again. "Don't go away, Claire. I still want you for my sister."

"You'll always be my little brother, Evan." Claire gave him a quick squeeze. "Nothing is going to change that."

Chapter Five
Anna

Darrington, Washington
September 7, 1965

Anna Hanson surveyed her music classroom. It was the first day of school. Along one wall she'd posted the stepping-stones of solfège symbols. Julie Andrews had recently made sight reading fun with *The Sound of Music's* "Do Re Mi." Now Anna would turn it into a game.

The third through fifth grade classes had been surprisingly successful with Name That Tune and Name That Note. At lunchtime, she didn't feel up to her modest sandwich and apple. She knew what was next. It should have been the easiest.

Her lesson plan was a simple game of each child singing "Yoo-Hoo" on "So-Mi" so that she could learn all their names. Then they were going to play Lucy Locket.

"I would like to be taught by you." Kindergarten teacher Mrs. Hewitt smiled as she studied Anna's decorations. "I've heard you sing. You sound even better than Julie Andrews."

Anna frowned. She didn't realize her voice could be heard through closed doors. She would sing more softly.

"You'll like kindergarten," Mrs. Hewitt encouraged.

Possibly. But she hadn't forgotten that the girl would be in kindergarten now, the same age and size as her new charges. The girl in her imagination could even be in her classroom. Anna had assumed it would all get easier with time, but it was only getting worse. This was no way to live. Always wondering. Always longing. Always looking. She stood too quickly, and the room went dark.

"Miss Hanson? Are you all right?"

Anna grabbed the music stand, but it tottered. She staggered, leaning back on the chalkboard, and closing her eyes.

Mrs. Hewitt grabbed a chair and sat her down.

"I get dizzy when I stand up too fast."

"I'm going to get you a glass of water." Mrs. Hewitt took the mug off Anna's desk and left for the drinking fountain.

All those mothers who brought their kindergartners to school with tears in their eyes. She wasn't that mother. She'd lost that chance and didn't deserve another.

No congratulations, no birth announcement. No baptism.

She couldn't even remember signing the papers. Nobody talked about it afterward. Something hidden, never happened.

But oh, how secrecy bred shame. Would anybody anywhere still like her if they knew what happened? She alone bore a complicated and continuous grief.

Mrs. Hewitt returned with the water.

"You'll be fine, honey."

She wished she could believe it.

Chapter Six
Siobhan

Here at our sea-washed, sunset gates shall stand
A mighty woman with a torch, whose flame
Is the imprisoned lightning, and her name
Mother of Exiles.
—Emma Lazarus, *The New Colossus*

Boston, Massachusetts
April 1919

Seventeen-year-old Moira Siobhan Kildea had now lived in Boston with her Aintín Brigid for a year. Though different from Kilrush, Ireland, the big city in Massachusetts had not lived up to its promise of prosperity and power, only poverty and prejudice. In the year 1918, Boston won something called the World Series, though played by Americans with red socks and somebody named Babe. They had experienced a plague, a deadly molasses flood, and now witnessed war from both sides of the ocean.

Not a day went by that Siobhan didn't hope her da and mam had saved enough to join her, so the three could be a family again and she'd be relieved of her cold and callous chaperone. Siobhan could only hope the coins in the money jar hidden behind the flour would one day bring her parents to America.

Siobhan often strayed from their apartment in Charlestown. The bridge over the Charles River beckoned her to new adventure in the North End, an escape from everything that reminded her of home in Ireland and everything that was not home in Charlestown.

The people on the other side of the river, the North End, celebrated family, food, and faith. Their language was a beloved concert. She loved how the Italians bounced the ends of their words and rolled their r's, and ended sentences with "no?" The second to the last syllable was always accented. Spag*het*ti. Ravi*o*li. Ling*u*ine. Cal*zo*ne. The lyrical sound was almost as delicious as the taste. She compared her Irish voice with its strong *r* and dropped *g* at the end of words. Sometimes she sat on the curb and watched them speak a language of hands and gestures.

A strong aroma permeated the air, deliciously alive with garlic, oregano, basil, and thyme. She had stumbled upon a new world and imagined, for a moment, that someone was cooking for her and that she would step inside and sit down to dinner. A dinner with a big family. Lots of brothers. "Siobhana!" they'd call out.

As the youngest, and separated by fifteen years from her closest sibling, she had never known what it was like to have a relationship with sisters or brothers. Her two older brothers had been killed—one in a war off Irish soil, and one in the never-ending war within. Her older sister was just that, older and with a family of her own. She could have been her only sister's *daughter* instead of the baby of the family. In Boston, she searched for something. She sometimes explored narrow alleys linked by fire escapes running up the sides of brick buildings and tried to pronounce the names of the various shops. Prince Macaroni, Romana Florist, Giordanis Store, Notario Publico, Zattoli Samoset Chocolates, Banca Italiana, Dolci and Confetti.

Siobhan peered into the windows of restaurants, feeling much like the outsider she was. It was Saint Leonards of Port Maurice Parish at 320 Hanover Street and Prince Street where she felt most at peace. She loved the sanctuary garden with its statues, especially the one with the man and the children.

She tiptoed onto the checkerboard tile floor inside and studied the detailed ceiling with the angels floating above her, the figures frozen in stained glass windows, and the beautiful people surrounding her in the apse. The chandeliers drooped above.

She liked St. Anthony, a monk who welcomed children, and St. Joseph holding a child. But her favorite was the strange St. Lucy with her red hair, displaying eyeballs on a gold platter. Lucy meant light. Lucy avoided darkness and sin.

There was no St. Brigid in this church built by Italian immigrants. Brigid was the saint who had prayed for a blind nun's sight. But at the miracle, Dara the nun realized that sight blurred her ability to see God and asked Brigid to return her to the beauty of darkness. Could darkness be beautiful? The rows and rows of candles in red glass jars shined brighter in darkness.

For her, light was knowledge. She remembered when she first understood that letters formed words, and words formed stories. Irish literature was nostalgic and romantic, full of legends and fables. In Kilrush, stories were told, but when you could hold them in your hands and read them, you had new power. Books took you far from your village, or held you close with foreign emotions. Books taught what the government disallowed. Her Irish hedge schools had given her a window on learning that had continued into the Catholic school in Charlestown.

The day she found the bookstore on the other side of the river was the day another door opened in her soul. The bell on the door jingled as she closed it softly.

Rows and rows of books lined the walls, with titles on every end unit. It was a labyrinth she followed to the back of the store. Perhaps the quietest and darkest place in the bookstore might speak the loudest.

Thomas Hardy. *Tess of the d'Urbervilles.* She opened to the middle and began reading, silently at first and then in a hushed whisper so that she owned the words and their sounds, repeating captivating phrases.

"*A strong woman who recklessly throws away her strength, she is worse than a weak woman who has never had any strength to throw away.*" She reread it, hoping to commit the verse to memory.

"*'Tis because we be on a blighted star, and not a sound one, isn't it Tess?*" a foreign voice finished.

How long had he been standing there? He was unobtrusive in height, yet confident in presence. She blushed.

"You startled me." She clapped the book shut and coughed at the sudden dust.

"You read very well." He sounded like he thought himself a teacher.

"For an *Irish* girl?" Siobhan suggested. His lilt had given him away. She already knew how Italians felt about her people. Too many times, she had been given a look, a derogatory comment, or an unwelcome stare.

"You read very well," he repeated, cocking his head, and smiling. "Antonio." His name confirmed her suspicion. He reached out his hand, but she offered neither hand nor name.

Antonio. It had to be his smile, wide and honest, with the bright twinkle in his eyes. Everything about him laughed. Was it at her?

"I know a place where all the books are free."

"And you think I don't have the money to buy this?"

"I think you would like to own every book in the store, no?"

She slid the book back to its home and ran her finger over the spines on the shelf, stroking them as if flirting with the stories they told. "I think a place like that is in your imagination."

"There is a library down the street. Not far from here. You can check out any book they have," he tempted. "And for me, it feels like home."

"To live in a library!" she scoffed and then caught herself.

"Don't laugh! There's a fountain and statues. It's quite beautiful. My brother Giovanni goes there just to study the pieces."

Everything within her longed to see this place. To escape with this boy—this almost man—to a place that felt like a home.

"I could show you, no?"

"I have to go now. My aintín is waiting."

Her aintín. Aintín Brigid would frown at the idea of Siobhan even entertaining a discussion with a boy. Then again, Brigid wasn't here.

"I see." He checked the door beyond. "It was nice meeting you . . . ?" His sentence ended in a question mark, waiting for a name.

"And how many other girls do you invite to the library, Mr. Antonio?"

"None." He frowned. "I have no time for anything but books. My studies will take me to the university and beyond. No girl can do that. No girl will *stop* that."

"My name is Siobhan."

"Tomorrow same time, Siobhan. Meet me here."

Siobhan ran through the narrow alleys, then followed the road along the water. She hit the bridge and stopped; gripping the railing and closing her eyes, she inhaled deeply as if to smell the salt from the ocean beyond. As if she could share the same air, the same breath as her parents. She walked more slowly on the metal strips, peering through the slats to the water below.

To live in a library near the water would be lovely. Much better than the house she'd never call home. Her feet slowed as she touched the ground of Charlestown and dragged as she came to a narrow block filled with clapboard tenements and boarding houses. She squinted up at one of the many bay windows on the long street, eyeing their third-floor rooms, then made her way up the stairs.

"You're late," Aintín scolded, as she took off her apron and spread it on the back of the chair. "Me feet are knackered an' me noggin 'urts." Aintín Brigid could be quite beautiful if she were not so miserable and didn't make everyone else feel miserable, too. Had she always been like this?

"I'm sorry," Siobhan apologized guiltily. Siobhan was supposed to keep their flat clean and make the evening meal. She sat near Brigid and rubbed her feet. "I picked up a loaf of bread. Just like you asked."

Aintín worked long hours as a housekeeper for an established family in Boston and then took the streetcar home. Oddly in America a *brigid* was a maid or cook in an upper-class home. Brigid abhorred her job and kept speaking of taking secretarial courses. Siobhan once asked if Brigid would have to change her name; Brigid had neither laughed nor denied the possibility.

Though related by blood, there seemed no connection between the two except their looks. When so many were dying of influenza, they had both survived. "It's our Irish blood," Aintín Brigid declared. And yet Siobhan had seen the priest with a wagonload calling out for her fellow Irishman to bring their dead.

Once Siobhan had run home quickly and felt flushed and dizzy. Did she imagine it, or just wish it had happened, or could it be that through the night her Aintín had sat near her, stroking her forehead?

"You'd best start de supper, lassy." Brigid pulled her feet away.

"You're right. I'll get to it." No more talk. The discussion was over.

The next evening, Siobhan purposely veered off her course and found Antonio on the street corner where she had met him the night before. She had thirty minutes before Aintín needed her. Thirty minutes to see every book in the world.

Could there be a place more magnificent than Boston Public Library in Copley Square? It towered proudly with a sloping red tile roof and copper tainted green verdigris. Inscriptions and names of people. Who were they?

"The great masters," Antonio explained. "That's Minerva, the goddess of wisdom." Antonio led her beneath the triple arches. Siobhan couldn't even whisper, the vestibule with its marble floor, statues, and the vaulted domed ceiling took her breath away. Domes, columns, archways. She was a princess in a great castle.

Heavy bronze doors left her wondering if anyone was imprisoned in her castle. Not a bad place to be locked inside. The main staircase urged her on. She counted each step of the ivory-gray marble mottled with fossil shells until she arrived at the two great lions at the turn and then ran up the remaining stairs.

"It's modeled after an Italian villa." Antonio's arm swept over the interior as if he owned it.

"And the books!" She gasped at a room with endless rows. He was right. Inside those books she could travel far.

"But wait, there's more." He guided her up the stone steps, her hand skimming the marble banister until they arrived at the top floor filled with paintings. What kind of museum was this? Each painting told a story she wanted to read. She knew the scenes had to be religious and so she stopped and studied each one and then closed her eyes to imprint the memory on her eyelids. She had never seen such grandiose beauty.

"Tomorrow." He spoke with urgency, his eyes so eager and true. "It's open on Saturday. Tomorrow we meet here, no?"

Did she even need to answer?

Every Saturday morning thereafter, they met at the library and read together. Antonio showed her fiction, nonfiction, and the Dewey Decimal System. Each book they shared was followed by intense discussion. They read Hugo, Dickens, Austen, and Melville, traveling to France, and England, and many places she'd never heard of. They lived in poverty and riches. They collected phrases like precious stones on the beach. She noted quotes in her little book so she could hold them close to her heart. Together they went far and stayed close.

Antonio found gems from the past but continued to look for those recently published. She liked that he selected so many female authors because she imagined herself writing a book one day. When they read *O Pioneers!*, she fell in love with Cather's prose. Lyrical but not overdone. Antonio chose it for its themes of perseverance, family, community, and fate. He loved to tell her about themes and motifs and most recently, allusions.

She could decipher certain themes in Hans Christian Anderson and *The Swiss Family Robinson* and even Henry Wadsworth Longfellow. But that Emil and Marie's tragic romance echoed Pyramus and Thisbe from *Metamorphoses*? How did Antonio know those details?

"I hated that sense of dread and that sad finish. Next time I'm reading the ending first."

"That dread is what keeps us reading. That tension. That *foreshadowing*." Antonio's arm spread before him, as if granting access to royalty.

"But if I know the worst that can happen, I can go back and sort through all the middle things and see the hints," Siobhan exclaimed, defending her stance.

Antonio gritted his teeth, smoothing a lock of dark brown hair from his forehead.

"I still wish it could have ended better. She didn't need to kill them both." Siobhan began rewriting a new ending in her mind.

Antonio joked that she preferred Pollyanna; Siobhan argued against reading a book that began, *"This is the saddest story I have ever heard."* *The Good Soldier* was anything but a good book.

Antonio shook his head and smiled. "Siobhan, everything can't have a happy ending." Her look must have convinced him otherwise.

"All right. Next book, I'll give you fair warning." Antonio laughed then nudged her. "Go ahead and read the book in whatever order you choose."

One day his older brother met them at the bakery. She'd heard of Giovanni, the one who had gone to war and only just returned. Antonio bought one zeppole, which they shared under Giovanni's watchful eye. The sky turned dark, and Siobhan knew she'd have to make a run for it to beat the rain.

"Gio did that," Antonio whispered, nodding to the brewing tempest. "He has that stormy way about him, no?"

She peered back at Antonio's older brother. So quiet, aloof. Almost haunted. She took one last bite of the sweet dough and licked her finger as Antonio opened the door to thunder and lightning. The rain began draining off the awnings and onto passersby. Her dress stuck to her skin and her hair fell loose on her face. She glanced back to see Giovanni's gaze through the rain-peppered window, then ran for home.

After that, Giovanni accompanied the two to the library. Giovanni was as reserved as Antonio was outgoing. Words spilled from Antonio while Giovanni brooded. Antonio could be seen from the outside in, but Giovanni was a book unread, a mystery untold.

Whether Giovanni had been instructed to chaperone or came by choice, he now became a regular on their library days. Antonio seemed less friendly when Giovanni was there. Was it because Giovanni didn't seem to share a love of books? Or did the brothers have a relationship more complex than she understood?

Giovanni's eyes wandered out the window or down the stacks, and then sometimes on Siobhan. She felt it and kept her eyes in her book, reading the same sentence over and over, though the words made no sense. Her cheeks grew warm under his scrutiny. What was this feeling?

"Let's go, Antonio," she said, her breath hurried. "We've been here long enough."

Siobhan stood as Giovanni pulled the chair out and placed his long-fingered, olive-skinned hand on the small of her back.

And from that place where he touched her, something exquisite.

An excruciating shock ran up her spine and reached her heart. She was sure it exploded. How could it be that there was nothing to like about this silent man but everything to love?

He was needy, he was confident. He was attentive, he was aloof. He was troubled, he was understanding. He felt familiar. Exciting and frightening all at once. *"He's more myself than I am. Whatever our souls are made of, his and mine are the same."* She and Antonio had only just begun *Wuthering Heights* and she'd committed Catherine's quote to memory. She tried not to, but she couldn't help picturing Heathcliff as Giovanni. Was she Catherine?

Chapter Seven
Geneviève

Western Front (France)
September 1918

"There's a need for at least three more nurses at a frontline Casualty Clearing Station. I don't know for how long." The doctor frowned. "And you realize CCS is a more dangerous assignment." Geneviève listened, surmising that without volunteers, the awkward invitation would turn into a difficult draft. She didn't need any inducement.

Geneviève raised her hand. Two others followed. From what she had seen with the sacrifice of the soldiers, she could offer solace to the wounded, and, selfishly—learn more about medicine.

Now in the proximity of the trenches, the sound of explosions and gunfire rang louder, and the activity was faster and more focused. Everything felt imminent. There was little time to think, only to make quick decisions.

Change dressings. Administer fluids. Move the soldier to a field or base hospital with specialized care. But she had learned some treatment was as simple as applying balm on cracked lips, running a comb through a weak soldier's hair, or offering water. Some men refused to be undressed by the nurses, their embarrassment and horror over lice-riddled uniforms too great. Others tried to kill the lice by holding their uniform seams over a candle. And still, the battle with influenza raged on.

Her shifts had no beginning or end; each day blended into night and another day. From bending over stretchers, her back felt permanently crimped. From walking miles up and down the five city blocks of beds, her feet were sore and tired.

For the third straight day, the rain pummeled their mobile tent city as if competing with the peppering gunfire nearby. Stretcher-bearers, wet and muddy to their thighs, came and went to the swampy environs. What should have been a short run took hours for each litter. And unlike at the base hospital, her patients' wounds were fresh.

The bandaging work of the previous men was sometimes skilled, but sometimes so contaminated, she cringed at the potential for tetanus and infection. Geneviève always dreaded removing the clothes to see what she'd find. Missing limb? Hemorrhage?

One man had holes in his skull, his face embedded with shrapnel, cloth, and mud. Where could she begin? Another, faceless with burns from gas. After sixteen hours of work, when the last litters had returned, she noted one of the new patient's field card read: *basket case.* She thought herself strong, but nothing prepared her for a soldier needing a carrying basket because he was missing limbs. She couldn't cry. Not yet.

One stretcher-bearer remained through the night; he, too, had to have been tired. Why didn't he get rest?

"Ma'am, do you know anything about Private Harold Petrelli?" *Petrelli.* The basket case.

"I'm sorry, I wasn't the nurse on his case."

The man's face fell, so she added quickly, "They're still working on him. I know he's alive."

He closed his eyes and blew out relief, then loosened his belt, nearly hidden by encrusted debris. Mud and blood stained his familiar five-buttoned uniform. He held his Brodie helmet, and his neck belt hung over his shoulder as if he couldn't bear to be off duty.

The drubbing rain slowed. Quite possibly tomorrow she would see the sun.

"I don't believe we've been introduced. You're new here?"

"Geneviève Marchand."

"William Ellis." He rummaged in his pocket and retrieved a cigarette, fumbling with the match. She took it from his hands and then drew back.

"What happened?" She turned his hands face up to study his blisters and calluses. The scars and cracks ran in patterns across palms threaded with slivers of wood.

She fumbled in her kit for tweezers as he sat down on the bench near a table with a small light.

"They don't provide you with gloves?" She sat next to him and took his hand.

William's smile was slow but endearing.

"They do."

"Ever thought of wearing them?"

"We lose our grip."

"But your hands? How?"

"The poles. They get wet, they dry, they splinter, they're shot, they rot."

The map of his palms was a battlefield of infection, blisters, and roads of wood fragments. Like everything out here, it would take hours to clean it up, and tomorrow it would repeat itself. Though she poked and massaged, William never winced.

"Sometimes we wrap our hands in wire, but it cuts." He sliced one palm with the finger of his other hand, then lifted them both up, as if offering a gift. "You'll always know a stretcher-bearer by his hands." Then almost jokingly added, "Or his neck and shoulders."

Geneviève had seen the backs of other stretcher-bearers. The deep burns from the strap and collar around the neck. Now she felt small in the shadow of his broad shoulders, holding his raw and rough large hand. She turned away, surprised at her sudden desire.

"I like the night." The man rubbed mud off his helmet with his free hand. "Less confusion and distraction. One goal." His voice crawled to a whisper. "We call out, very softly, hoping the enemy doesn't hear, and then listen for wounded amid the cries of the downed horses."

Geneviève trembled. She was tired, weary, and cold, but for some unknown reason, this man not only needed a response to his call from the wounded soldiers in no-man's-land, but perhaps from her, too.

"A little sound, a little light. But not enough to attract enemy fire. Just enough to see . . ." His voice trailed off. She filled in the blank with what she heard about the labyrinth of upturned trees, duckboard pathways rotting under the weight of mud and dead soldiers, and decomposed corpses caught in the chaos of twisted barbed wire.

"And sometimes there's a faint smell of thyme."

Time. For a moment she questioned how to smell time until she realized he was talking about the herb. *Time* would have been more appropriate in the battlefield of life and death.

"Even when I go to bed, I still hear the other stretcher-bearers call and I pray for a soft answer. Not gunfire."

She considered the position of her's and William's hands; to an onlooker it might have appeared as if they were praying.

"So, how did you get here, Miss Geneviève Marchand?"

She liked his directness and answered with an unfamiliar ease. "I wanted a little change. And this certainly did it." She barely smiled. "And you?"

"I grew up on a wheat farm. I wanted a *lot* of change." He cocked his head and smiled. Was he teasing her?

"I was drafted. But when I had a choice, I realized I'd rather *find* life than take it." He stopped short. "Do you know how hard it is to look away from a soldier you don't think can be saved? One guy even waved me on. He knew he'd only be deadweight."

"This place is filled with the wounded you've saved." She squeezed his hand. "The men must appreciate you."

"Only in no-man's-land." He shook his head. "Before that, in the trenches, we're the ones they don't want to see. The cleanup crew." His words were not sarcastic, just factual.

"The men climb out of the trenches with guns, and we call out 'Bearers up!' and follow them, listening, watching, always running toward danger to retrieve them."

So *this* was the first line of triage.

"Tell me about your field medicine, Dr. Ellis."

He removed the panier from his shoulder, set it down on his lap, and displayed *The Stretcher-Bearer War Manual,* splint limbs, dress wounds, blue morphine pills, maps made of oil skin cloth. "And these are my scissors," he shrugged. "I've never lost mine. Most people lose their scissors in the mud."

She noted the respirator and Dickie Bird gas hood, which he omitted.

"We had ten weeks of training in tetanus inoculations, tourniquets, ligatures, shock, foot care, frostbite, and lice. The rest was training on the field. Mainly we try to control hemorrhage, apply dressings, splints, and protect from gas. Most of it's trial and error." He shook his head, as if embarrassed. "Sometimes the best I can do is morphine."

"The crayon mark on the forehead." She remembered that meant not to give the patient any additional painkiller. "Do you write the field medical card?"

"Sometimes." He looked at her and smiled. She wondered if she'd ever received one of his patients. Such a strange connection.

"Should I try sending you a message sometime?" he asked, as if reading her mind.

Send me a message. Yes, send me a message.

"It rained today. We all put up our hands to feel the rain." He pulled away and raised both arms. "It must have looked like we were praying. And maybe we were. But it felt so good." He lowered his hands and she poked at another wound.

How long had it been since someone had held *her* hand? Once, just once, she longed for a tender hug, or soft caress. Was he her patient or her friend?

"On the other hand"—he shifted his hands—"it's hard to move in slow motion. The mud up to our knees. Shell fire everywhere. Can't get stuck or we'll be a frozen target."

She looked up to see why he had stopped.

"And we can't rock the patient. Steady. Steady." He was as still as she imagined he would be holding a wounded shoulder. "The jostling can send your patient into shock."

She worked a splinter with her thumb.

He cocked his head to the side.

"You remind me of my sister . . ."

"Or cousin, or daughter, or mother. Or girlfriend." She shrugged. "I hear it all."

"No." He shook his head. "You don't remind me of my mother."

He hadn't responded about the other choices. She'd seen no ring on his hand but that meant nothing.

The rain started up again. Would he have to go out tomorrow? Would he ever have a chance to dry off?

"Take off your boots."

"I'll check later."

"No. Take off your boots. Now," she repeated with more force. She had learned much about massage and treating her patients with trench foot.

William struggled to release his boots as she prepared for the worst. Men standing in water for days, for weeks on end, their socks growing into their feet. Blackened toes, any remaining red skin stretched taut across the foot. Trench foot. Gangrene. The eventual amputation.

"I haven't been dancing lately." His words were an apology. Though William's feet were as ugly as his hands, they were not infected. She sighed with surprised relief. "Now that you have my boots, what are you going to do to me?"

"Stay there."

She returned with supplies to wash, dry, and bandage his feet, then knelt to hold his battered foot in her hands. She couldn't bear to look up, certain he would see her tears. What would it feel like if someone washed her feet and rubbed them after she stood for sixteen hours dressing wounds or standing at the operating table? She was giving him what she knew she needed. She felt his hand on her head.

"I can't. I . . . I thank you. But I must go."

He clumsily attempted to shove his feet back into soggy boots, tucking the filthy socks under his belt.

"You're not heading back out tonight?"

"No, but I have to redraw the maps."

What did that mean? Her face betrayed her question.

"The battlefield and trenches change. The hazard areas. We draw maps and report back."

She rubbed the salve across his blistered palms, massaging with her thumbs. So gently. And then, before she realized what she'd done, she blessed his hand with a kiss.

Chapter Eight
Erin

Spokane, Washington
May 19, 1981

E rin couldn't help but feel a nervous excitement as they drove over the mountains and dropped into Seattle and then the offices of RAFT. Everything could change with the other mother—for good or for bad. Was Claire opening a can of worms or Pandora's box like Chase suggested?

Erin noted the logo used all four letters, but the vertical line of the T was a pier, and the cross bar was an extended rope tethered to a raft. So appropriate for Washington State with its lakes and waterways.

"RAFT is a nonprofit dedicated to reuniting families," Kelly Peake began, sitting in an office surprisingly clinical. The smell of stale coffee permeated the room. Files and papers littered her desk. "We don't just serve adoptees. Sometimes birth families and adoptive parents come in. Everything is done through a third party. It's safer that way."

"Safer?" Claire asked.

"Protects both you and your parents."

"I don't understand."

"Although your records are sealed, recent changes in procedure allow adoptees to petition the court. We can obtain the legal access to sealed records. Judges don't refuse to sign a court order to open a sealed file."

The records were sealed because the mother or father didn't want to be found. Erin hoped that wasn't the case for Claire.

"We assign the case to a Confidential Intermediary. The CI will search for your birth mother and then contact her. But a signed consent form must be obtained before any information is exchanged." Ms. Peake paused, seemingly weighing her next words.

"And in the event of death, we submit a court order, and the death certificate is released to the closest blood relative."

Death? Claire would be heartbroken. What if her mother had died in childbirth? The guilt. Sorrow. Disappointment. Lack of resolution. Claire's hands were positioned on the vinyl-covered metal chairs as if she prepared to spring away.

"We also have support groups in case you want to talk with people who feel like you do. Adoptees, birth parents, adoptive parents, family and friends."

"No, thank you. I don't live in the area." Claire tapped the desk with her fingers.

"You need to know, more than ninety percent of the people contacted want to meet their child." Ms. Peake's statistic sounded positive, and yet her voice was cautious. "But there are some birth parents who do not." Ms. Peake stopped. "Do you have a support system or a counselor that you're seeing?"

"My family is incredibly supportive. My mom came with me to Seattle. My sister gets it."

"I understand, but it's helpful to have a counselor, somebody who can talk you through this."

"Well, it's not like I'm going to jump off a bridge or something."

The woman frowned, and Erin turned to Claire and shook her head.

"Sorry, I didn't mean to make light of it. It's just that I've lived this long without my biological parents. If it doesn't work out, I'll be okay."

Mrs. Peake looked to Erin who could only think, *I know. I know.*

"If the birth mother does not want to meet . . ." Ms. Peake stopped and held Claire's gaze. "We cannot give you any of the information."

Erin couldn't picture that happening. Who wouldn't be curious to meet her own child? Especially if her child wanted to meet her.

"We have to caution you about the possibility. Many feel they've been rejected again. That they've come so far only to be turned back."

Erin was overwhelmed by the information. She could only imagine what Claire was feeling. Was it possible that the truth might never be known—that documents might not exist or people who knew her story would be unreliable or deceased?

"I won't stop just because I'm afraid." Claire took out her checkbook. "Who do I make this out to?"

∽

Claire began her summer job, not coincidentally as a nurse tech at Sacred Heart Medical Center where her grandmother had worked some fifty years before. Erin eagerly anticipated Claire's three months at home before she returned to UVA.

As the days wore on, more and more of Claire's sacred nursing skills were needed in their own home as GinnaBee became increasingly unreliable.

"Grandma sometimes wanders off and we have to drive around the block to find her. All the neighbors know to look out for her," Erin explained when Claire returned from her shift.

"Once the police even brang her back!" Evan raised his hand as if testifying, then resumed eating the cold pizza he had rescued from the fridge.

"Brought," Claire corrected.

"Brought what?" Evan picked off an olive and discreetly dropped it to the puppy below.

"We could get some bells on the doors, so we'd know when she goes out."

"And then there's the oatmeal," Erin added. "Grandma left it on the stove. Who knows what all was in that pot, but it scorched badly and caused a lot of smoke damage. Luckily, she didn't burn down the house."

"That was cool! The smoke alarm went off and lots of fire engines came!" Evan started to jump on the couch.

"It's not a trampoline, Evan. Finish your pizza."

It was so hard to talk to Claire about it. They hated the word *Alzheimer's,* but Claire also loathed *dementia.* As if her grandmother could be demented.

Claire understood the elderly because William and GinnaBee had put the *grand* in grandparenting. Claire would choose Geriatrics as her specialty.

She could still see William and GinnaBee down on their knees, eye level with four-year-old Claire, spinning her around the hardwood floor, jazz standards playing in the background. Grandpa learning to braid her long red hair, Grandma taking her to dinner at Clinkerdaggers Restaurant at the Falls, Claire curled in the crook of her grandpa's arm, tracing the lines of his hands, which told a story he would never explain.

"I don't know what will happen when you go back to UVA. I don't think we can keep this up."

"Somewhere inside, she's the same WWI nurse. The wife, the mother . . ." Claire stopped. "The grandmother." She continued. "If we move her," Claire's brow furrowed. "Will she just keep drifting farther away from us?"

Erin couldn't answer that. She only knew she felt sandwiched between addressing Claire's questions about her grandma and about Claire's mother, never suspecting how Claire's search would unravel all their lives.

Chapter Nine
Anna

Arlington, Washington
May 8, 1981

Spring in Bloom featured all Trafton Elementary grades in concert, but Anna was most interested in a certain first grader.

Her daughter walked across the front of the stage dressed as a butterfly. Unscripted, the little girl hugged each child. The caterpillar, the sunflower, the bumblebee. Then Emma spoke her lines, briefly, though not clearly.

"Spring makes everything grow flowers." Emma's mouth was too close to the microphone and her breath hissed throughout the auditorium after *flowers*. "Oh." Emma backed off in surprise and then resumed as Anna's husband mouthed along, having practiced every night since Emma was given the part by her first-grade teacher, Mrs. Lundquist.

"Spring makes everything new. We can all change and grow, too." And then she took a deep bow. Not because it was planned but because that was what Emma always did. Like any proud mother, Anna grabbed her husband's hand without looking at him and drew a shaky involuntary gasp.

Emma's eyes searched the audience, those beautiful almond eyes that turned down not unhappily, but as if in a relaxed, sweet, melancholy smile. She squinted against the light and tented her eyes with her chubby little hands. Then she stepped downstage to see everybody. When she waved, they all waved back. The spring concert resumed with the audience standing to sing the rhyme Mrs.Lundquist had written for the program. "We can change, we can grow, be a butterfly, you know . . ." Anna joined in with conviction.

"You should go back to singing," Ben whispered, encouraging her yet again. Anna laughed, Mrs.Lundquist's butterfly jingle hardly an audition for the Met. Though she had once dreamed of performing in opera houses around the world, the Mozart arias Montserrat taught her during college. Tonight however, while watching her daughter take the stage, she experienced a new satisfaction. She only wished their other two were here so she knew they were safe.

"I think I should go call the babysitter."

"They're *fine*."

They probably were. But what if? That nagging fear.

She glanced down the program to see how much was left.

TRAFTON ELEMENTARY UPCOMING DATES

She shuddered. *May 10th, Mother's Day. May 18, 1981, Parent Child Conferences.* The irony. Her stomach squeezed and her heart raced. She sat down and caught her breath, then bent over, lowering her head to her knees, certain she would be sick.

"What is it, Anna?" Her husband sat down and put his arm around her back. "A dizzy spell?"

She couldn't move. Her face felt hot. She tried to take a deep breath.

"Anna? Are you all right? Honey? Are you worried about the kids?"

No, she was not all right.

Would there ever be a May 18th she wouldn't think about *her*? Impossible. Besides, it wasn't just May 18th that brought her to mind. It was Thanksgiving and Christmas and the first day of school, as well as the last. It was the visit to the OB/GYN, when they asked her about how many children she'd given birth to.

Anna had no picture beyond that birth day. That baby was frozen in time. Anna could only imagine the significant moments. The first food in the high chair. First steps. First day of kindergarten. Braces. Her first dance. High school graduation.

She would never forget or stop asking questions. Did she have red hair? Did she look like her? Did she like to sing? She would never stop worrying. Did the girl feel wanted? Did she wonder about *her*? Did the girl have any brothers and sisters?

She'd be twenty-one in days. Was she in college? Did she have a boyfriend? Where did she live? So many questions that would never be answered.

She'd once spotted a little redheaded girl at the ice-skating rink that could have been hers. Anna's heart beat faster and she found herself approaching the little girl. But what would she say?

She just had to check. See if the girl was happy. She wore white tights, a little blue skirt and Nordic sweater. So young to be taking lessons. Then someone came between them. A woman with red hair, carrying the little girl's backpack. Anna turned away quickly, ashamed of coveting another mother's child.

"Anna, talk to me. What's wrong?" Ben's hand on her shoulder felt weighty. "You mustn't worry so much."

The years of holding back were tormenting her. But the longer the lie, or the hidden truth, the greater the tension. How, after this much time, could she tell him? What would he do? Theirs was a strong marriage built on love and trust. But would he accept this?

The piano accompaniment grew louder to cover the fifth graders filing onstage for the grand finale. Anna rose unsteadily and Ben took her elbow. She needed to get home.

Chapter Ten
Siobhan

Why didn't you tell me there was danger?
Why didn't you warn me?
Ladies know what to guard against,
because they read novels that tell them of these tricks;
but I never had the chance of discovering in that way;
and you did not help me!
—Thomas Hardy, *Tess of d'Ubervilles*

Boston, Massachusetts
June 1919

S iobhan loved Saturday mornings best of all, running about the
city with the Savelli brothers. She preferred the narrow maze of
winding streets along former colonial cow paths and breathing
the air above ground, to the subway below. With the bustle of horse-
drawn wagons, delivery trucks, and farm fresh produce, life was a
beautifully repeated rhythm. And Saturday market was her favorite
stop. What a contrast to the quiet hours that would follow when
Antonio and Giovanni met her at the library!

Giovanni taught her that Quincy Market was Greek Revival. She
wasn't sure exactly what that meant but she loved the coolness of the
granite, the columns, and arched windows. It wasn't the Irish coast,
but she found beauty where she could. Faneuil Hall with its copper
weather vane, a grasshopper! She loved to stare at buildings and
discovered the connecting Zs made by black grated platforms and

diagonal staircases casting shadows against the brick. She thought Giovanni would have liked it, too.

Giovanni knew so much about art and especially the works in the Boston Library where he seemed to feel most at home.

His words were few and saved mostly for art, so she listened intently though she didn't always remember all he taught her about the Puvis de Chavannes Gallery and the nine muses of Greek mythology or the Abbey Room with the Quest of the Holy Grail and a ceiling modeled after the Doge's Palace in Venice.

Antonio brought words to life, Giovanni made pictures and sculptures come alive. Even the painting of a weary Homer was more intriguing when Giovanni pointed out that the spear and the oar next to the blind poet represented his great epic poems, *The Iliad* and *The Odyssey.*

But it was the courtyard she loved best, a peaceful retreat with its arcaded promenade. Here she felt safe. Enclosed. Untouched by war or disease.

"It's *exactly* like the arcade of the Cancelleria Palace in Rome." Giovanni sat on a bench, leaning over, and resting his arms on his legs, loosely clasping his hands together.

"Have you been there?" Though not touching, she could feel his warmth.

"Not yet." Had he smiled? Perhaps slightly. "We're from Sicily."

"Do you remember much about it?"

"I was eight."

Siobhan considered that. She had lived fifteen years in Ireland. "You went back to Europe. Where were you in France?"

Giovanni stared out at the water and the fountain. She shouldn't have brought it up. Giovanni's fingers trembled, his thick black eyebrows knit together. He was clearly disturbed by her question.

"Meuse Argonne." Giovanni cleared his throat and shook his head, removing it from his memory. He turned his palms upward and studied them as if he didn't recognize his own hands.

Why did she want to take his hands in hers? As if she could bring him comfort when he saw something she could never understand.

Footsteps approached behind them.

"There you are!" Antonio said, joining the two.

"I'm learning about great Italian masters!" Siobhan stood and smiled at Antonio.

"Giovanni is attracted to great beauty." Antonio looked toward his brother and back to Siobhan. "Works of art." Antonio tapped his brother on the shoulder. "Papa will need us at the shop. We'd better go."

In early June, Antonio took her to the North End Park, where they sat on the beach and watched swimmers dive from the floating dock. The Boston Naval Yard, Charlestown Shipyard, and Bunker Hill Monument stood off in the distance, the Old North Church and Copp's Hill stood tall behind them.

"Sometimes I think I can still smell the molasses." Antonio waved his hand toward the water.

Siobhan shook her head. Months after the accident, the wreckage remained. Boston Harbor stained brown, and the molasses aroma now made sickly sweet by summer heat.

Who would have thought a river could be made of molasses? It might have been funny if it had not killed twenty-one innocent people and injured another 150. The molasses tank exploded on Commercial Street, unleashing a powerful thirty-foot wave of hot quicksand-like molasses. The thirty-five-mile-per-hour sticky surge buckled railroad tracks and knocked buildings off foundations, drowning victims and leaving two million gallons of molasses in its wake. On that cold January day, the molasses hardened as did the hopes of many North Enders, still reeling from the terror of influenza, which had claimed more victims than the war.

No danger at Devens. Fear kills more than disease; the newspapers had claimed. Fear did make them all hide out in their homes, but they were being lied to; this was no ordinary flu and there was no way to fight it. The Red Cross issued masks, but people died of influenza within twenty-four hours. Too many horse-drawn carts collecting corpses on cobblestone streets. Corpses without coffins, stacked like firewood, then rolled into mass graves. One US doctor claimed it appeared worse than any battlefield in France.

With school and church canceled, Brigid and Siobhan had been imprisoned in their small apartment far too long. "Cover up each cough and sneeze. If you don't, you'll spread the disease." And yet she had never been sick. Not even when she crossed the Atlantic. "It's the Irish in ye," Aintín had declared, keeping her behind closed doors, letting her go out only with a mask.

"I had a little bird, its name was Enza. I opened the window, and in-flu-enza." Nobody wanted to see anybody and yet they needed each other. They couldn't go to church, but she could pray. On her own.

And then in those wee morning hours when she gazed out the window or stepped onto the streets, she'd discover how many had died during the night. Most people were her age or older. Orphans were left starving in the streets.

But now wasn't the weather warming? Wasn't there a crowd on the beach? Street vendors, families in the laundry, changing area, and children's tent. Summer loomed and she wanted to think happier thoughts. She needed a new season.

"We survived," she stated the obvious.

"My mother put garlic around my neck. That's what we do."

"Brigid pinned camphor balls to my clothing." She plugged her nose and they both laughed.

Antonio cupped sand and let it trickle like sand in an hourglass.

"The beaches at Kilkee, they are beautiful." A year away from Ireland seemed as many years as the miles on the boat from Cobh. She wished her parents wrote more often but the correspondence had slowed, as hesitant as their penmanship.

"Where are you from?"

"Kilrush."

"Kilrush, like Kildea? I like the sound of that."

She had never thought that her own accent made music. Brigid's words were not pretty. But now that Antonio praised her with the gentle imitation of the hush of her town, a lump formed in her throat.

"Say more names."

"Shannon," she said. "The Cliffs of Moher. Dromoland Castle. Carrigaholt." The dialect made her homesick. "What do you like about the sound of my language?"

"Wa' do ye lahk abou' de soun' o' me language?" Antonio was a poor imitation.

"You're making fun of me."

"Nahhh, ahhm nah makin' fahhn o' ye. 'Tis because ye talk so fas' I kin 'ahrrrrrrrrdlee understan' ye! An' it all sahns lahk a quessshion."

This had to be what having a brother was like. She enjoyed it.

"What about your Italy? Tell me about *that*."

"I don't remember much. I was three when we left Sicily." Antonio shrugged. "Giovanni and Luca were older." He stopped and looked out to the water beyond as if he could find them there. "What about you. Any sisters or brothers?"

"One sister." Siobhan stopped. The rest was past tense. "My brothers . . . they . . . they are gone." She was surprised at how disconnected she felt. As if she couldn't feel sad because their graves were miles away. Couldn't they just be far away in Ireland, alive and well?

"Giovanni was not the oldest." Antonio scooped another handful of sand and let it sift through his fingers. "In our family, we would have no slackers. You know what I mean?"

Siobhan nodded yes. No one wanted to be unpatriotic.

"Two brothers went to Italy and only one came back." He smoothed the surface of the sand, as if wiping away something he needed to forget. Boston was encouraged to "Pack Up Your Troubles," go "Over There," or "Keep the Home Fires Burning." What had the war taken from all of them?

"Gio came back, but he's not the same. Maybe it's better . . ."

"No, it is not," she said defiantly.

"Giovanni likes to work with his hands. He wanted to go to study with an Italian sculptor, Ernest Pellegrini, who's from Verona. Now he trains young sculptors in Copley Square. I don't know if Papa ever knew that. If Luca would have come back, he and Papa would have run the family business. But now Papa needs Giovanni and me." Antonio sighed. "That's why I have my books. I find no beauty in scissors, and razors, and brooms."

Siobhan shivered despite, or perhaps because of, the heat.

"Papa wants to disprove the labels on my people, and Mama just wants her boys to live and work with Papa. *Via vecchia*—the old way. Obligation and authority. It feels like such a weight."

What did Mam and Da want for her? Why had they sent her to America?

"What do you want to do, Siobhan?"

What a thought! She was only a girl! Why would she have a plan? But then again, she couldn't read books all her life. What *did* she want to do?

Giovanni had a plan even if it was not to be. Antonio wanted something. Did Aintín have a dream?

Siobhan only wanted to see Da and Mam again. Life would begin again when they joined her in Boston. Maybe when she was seventeen. They would figure things out then.

"You? What about you?" She threw his question back, hoping he wouldn't pursue what she couldn't answer.

He let the lingering silence suffice.

"I want to go to college. Boston College. I've already spoken with a professor there."

She gasped. His dreams were large.

"I want to study and write and teach about what I learn." Antonio stood up and walked the boardwalk. "Good morning, I'm Professor Savelli and today we'll be discussing . . ." And then he stopped. Siobhan tossed back her head and laughed.

"You are too funny. But what are you *really* going to do?"

Antonio's face fell, but he didn't take his eyes off her.

"That is what I'm going to do. And you nor anybody else will stop me."

Antonio was calm but serious.

"I . . . didn't mean . . ."

"You did." He stepped off the boardwalk and sat beside her.

She put her hand on his. "I believe you now."

She needed a plan as well. Wasn't that what the books taught her? Thomas Hardy? *Things willed.*

"The beauty or ugliness of a character lay not only in its achievements,

but in its aims and impulses; its true history lay, not among things done, but among things willed."

"And one day after that, I will marry." Antonio continued. "I'll be a papa who'll teach my own children to read." He looked out beyond her as if that dream meant going away.

"You *will*, Antonio. You will!" Then she laughed gaily. "All five of those little Savellis!" Her heart beat faster at the thought, yet it made her sad. He was not going to stay. He would go away to school and become something great. She knew that. But what about her? What would be *her* true history?

Chapter Eleven
Geneviève

Base Hospital 41
St. Denis, France
September–October 1918

By mid-September, at least a third of Geneviève's patients were dying of something more deadly than a bullet. In October, when Geneviève returned to Base 41, after her time at CCS, there had been little improvement.

"In the trenches there's a chance of surviving a bullet or gas. But not this." Fellow nurse and friend Celeste sat on Geneviève's bed, collapsing backward onto her pillow. A desperate look invaded her red-rimmed eyes, the corners of her mouth sagged. The rising body count in her ward had brought her to tears. "Some say it should be called the *German* Influenza and that it was all part of their attack."

"Mom wrote that back home the schools, colleges, theaters, movies, all closed. Church is outside. Funny thing, officials confiscate moonshine and turn it over to drug stores for flu prescriptions."

"And that's supposed to help?" Celeste sat up quickly.

Geneviève shrugged. "The base in Fort Devens went from three cases at the end of August, to thousands ten days later. I heard eleven hundred in one day."

"If the epidemic continues its mathematical rate of acceleration, civilization could easily disappear from the face of the earth within a few weeks," Celeste read from a news flier. "That's from our Surgeon General." Celeste put the paper aside.

"Well, that's encouraging." Geneviève sighed.

Celeste scratched her head and frowned.

"I feel like I have cooties."

"You forgot that in your list of trench hazards." Head lice was rampant, as well as the diseases it carried, but Geneviève had to make a joke. "You've pulled your hair so tight, you'll give yourself a headache."

Celeste unbraided her hair and scratched her head. "And how's your soldier?"

"He's not *my* soldier. It was nothing. Really."

"Well, you *kissed* him!" Celeste ran a brush through her silky brown hair.

"On the hand!" Genevieve clarified. "Besides, that was a mistake. I don't know what came over me." She met a man and nursed his wounds as she would have wanted someone to care for her.

"I'm just so tired, Ginna. I need it to be over. I've never worked this hard in my life."

"It's for your country!" Geneviève pointed upward.

"Where we have no voting rights!" Celeste had a point.

Geneviève removed her nurse's cap and scratched her scalp. How did she look after a day like this? Her girlfriends teased her about her big brown eyes, pert little nose, and lips that smiled without trying. But would those lips smile again?

After a troubled sleep, Geneviève donned her nurse's uniform, shoes, and hat, and trudged to her ward—dressing, redressing, consoling, combing hair, smoothing balm on chapped lips, and offering water. Doing everything with a sense of tired sameness.

"Do you know what I had to do to get into this place?"

Geneviève whipped her head around at the familiar voice.

"Mr. Ellis?"

"They didn't know what to do with me, so I told them to send me to Base 41, that I had friends in high places."

Geneviève read his field ticket. Unwrapping his leg, she tried not to shudder. He had shrapnel embedded deep, causing an angry infection. Purple marks painted his leg. She placed her hand on his forehead, which was warm to the touch. With the risk of clostridial bacteria from farm dirt unearthed during shelling in the field, his leg would need extensive treatment.

"When was the last time you urinated?"

"Now is that any way to greet someone you haven't seen for weeks?"

"I'm your nurse. What happened?"

"Well, it's kind of private, ma'am."

His pulse was 125. Her immediate concern was blood poisoning. "I'm not talking about going to the bathroom," she snapped, wheeling the medical cart between the two of them. "And you can be a private and not be private."

"That's what I missed about you." He stretched his hand across the metal tray. "I'm neither."

At that point, the doctor came in and took a look at the field ticket, then William's leg, and wheeled him away. The shrapnel had to be removed, and the wound thoroughly cleaned and irrigated, or septicemia was imminent.

Though she had fifteen other patients to attend to that night, she stood in the door of the ward and surveyed the sleepless men, and the ones resting under medication, with her eye on William Ellis. *Mr.* William Ellis. *Stretcher-bearer* William Ellis. She would keep this formal. She navigated the floor, offering a sip of water, fluffing a pillow, or consoling the men crying out in the night, stopping at William who was among those in an uneasy sleep. Startled by her presence, he tried to rise on one elbow.

"I need to go back," he grabbed her arm. Tears streamed down his face.

"No. You need help. You're not well. Go back to sleep." Was he delirious?

"It's like quicksand. I couldn't move. I had to step on them. Bodies. So I didn't sink." His arms trembled. Was it fever or memories? She stroked his forehead with a wet washcloth. "We lost one of ours." He closed his eyes against the tears. "I picked up our carry." His breathing grew agitated, and she checked his pulse.

"Settle, William. Calm."

"Shell burst. I dropped him." William grabbed her hand as if pleading an urgent case. "In that mud. I had to dig him out and then dive for shelter." He fell back on his pillow. "Three days. It was three days before the firing stopped."

Geneviève nodded, understanding why his infection had been so bad.

"We couldn't move or talk, or they'd find us. He tried to scream. What could I do?" Will's eyes pleaded with her.

"Who treated you?"

"Aid post, battalion aid. Then a field hospital."

"You're here now. We'll get you on the mend."

"About my leg," he winced as she touched above his incision. "Before I return . . ."

"Before you *return?*" Her voice sounded scolding.

"Now you really do remind me of my mother."

She gritted her teeth. The streaking on his leg, the days in mud. How could he even consider returning to the field?

"*To sleep, perchance to dream . . .*" he murmured sleepily. Was it better to be lucid or under? She offered him a glass of water and another quarter gram of morphine.

"*O sleep. O gentle sleep. Nature's soft nurse,*" Geneviève whispered back.

"Well, if it isn't my angel of the battlefield," William declared the next morning.

"I'm no Clara Barton."

"Close enough, Ginna."

She wasn't sure what to make of his teasing endearment, though the idea of being that kind of nurse was inspiring.

"You probably remember nothing of last night." She took his pulse as William eyed her curiously. "Oh, you *do* talk," she added, noting his quickened heartbeat.

"So, now that I'm pinned here, what stories do *you* have?" He sounded wary.

"You only get my attention when I'm working on you." she scolded. "I need to stay professional."

"Would that include a kiss on the hand?"

She blushed. They both needed to forget that.

"I wouldn't want to risk any possibility of influenza."

"If you prick us, do we not bleed? If you tickle us, do we not laugh? If you poison us, do we not die?"

"Just because your name is William doesn't make you Shakespeare." She studied his leg. *"Merchant of Venice."*

A slow smile took over his face, and then he laughed. How strange. She'd always been practical and to the point; she'd never been humorous. She removed the dressing and checked the color, then cleaned the wound.

"How many in your family?" William prodded.

He closed his eyes and clenched his teeth against her swabbing his gash and answered, "Only child." She'd keep him distracted for his sake.

"Sisters." He held up two fingers.

"Let me guess, you're the oldest and boss them around and torment them unmercifully." Geneviève teased, a frown developing at the thought of his pain.

He laughed through his pain but nodded in agreement.

"And where are you from?" William winced.

"Richmond, Virginia," she answered.

"Spokane, Washington." He inhaled deeply and held his breath as she doused the wound. "I come from a long line of farmers. It stops here." He pointed at himself. With his potential for future immobility, that was probably a good thing. "What about you?"

"My father is a state senator."

"A state Senator?" William perked up. "And he likes his career?"

"Yes, and yes, and too much." Geneviève sighed.

"Then why your frown?"

"He's gone too much of the time and politics can be very stressful."

Will cocked his head and rubbed his chin as if considering her words.

"Favorite place?" William inquired, changing the subject.

"Blue Ridge Mountains. Skyline Drive." She stopped for a moment. It was fall. Home. The mountains a quilt of red, orange, and yellow. Peaceful and quiet.

"Priest Lake, Idaho," he followed. "And so many other beautiful lakes."

Idaho. What a strange name for a state and a place that seemed so very far from France.

"Pend d'Oreille and Coeur d' Alene," William added.

"*French* lakes in Idaho?" Geneviève shook her head as she redressed his wound. The color still wasn't good, but the surgery had helped. She hoped this time they'd found all the shrapnel.

They both quieted as she placed the stethoscope on his chest and listened for any signs of fluid in the lungs.

"Did you know the stethoscope was invented in France?" she said at last, trying to fill the silence.

"I thought all aspects of the heart were invented here."

She blushed and tried to remember the rest of her story. "Not far from here, actually. Paris."

Will smiled knowingly and she quickly explained.

"The doctor wasn't comfortable, listening to the heart that is, with his ear on a woman's chest." Her face felt hot. Why had she stopped to explain this story to a stranger?

"What about me?" William relaxed, seemingly relieved only to be touched by her stethoscope. "What do you know about my heart?"

She couldn't answer as she attempted to listen, and process whatever was going on in her heart as well as his. What could she say?

"I think you have a good heart, William Ellis."

Each night when Geneviève returned to her bed, she recalled his answers and remembered the way he looked at her with those sincere hazel eyes. And then she'd remember the look of his legs. The muscular thighs. His back and shoulders scarred with stripes from the leather strap attached to the stretcher. She knew him while he slept and while he was awake. She knew him far better than he would ever know her. When she traced her finger down the scars, applying ointment, she memorized his body.

Each day, she checked him first. Pulse. Normal, though her own heartbeat quickened when her fingers touched his broad forearm. Lungs. Heart. Blood pressure. His wound had nearly healed. It wouldn't be long, and she would not need to clean the infection.

"I'm improving. Might be another week and I'll return to the field."

She stopped midmotion. She had worked on his body, loved on his body, only to send him back? Not to America but to no-man's-land? A hundred-foot barbed wire hell. Or the trenches filled with excrement, rats, and rotting bodies? What was it all for?

"*I have seen a medicine that's able to breathe life into a stone.*" William seemed oblivious to her furor.

She closed her eyes tightly and resumed the cleansing. Breathing life into stone? Hardly.

"But first I'm to help with some of the mapping. Teach some of the younger fellows."

Geneviève finished rewrapping the wound.

"You're unusually quiet," he said at last.

She moved to her next patient.

"Geneviève. Come back."

She turned around, expressionless.

"Three questions." His game began again. Pulling her in with questions and answers. Making her know him better than she had a right to.

"No," she smarted. "I have three for you." Her voice was surprisingly cold as she spit out her interrogation. "Do you think you'll survive this time? When do you think it will end? What good has come of it?"

Will never blinked. "I'll outlive the war and I think that means I'll be home for Christmas. This was supposed to end all wars, but war is in our hearts and there will be more. Perhaps leaders can make changes to prevent another world war."

Home for Christmas? She could only dream.

"Geneviève, when I go . . . you need to know that everything . . ."

"No, I don't have to hear all of this. Really. I'm a nurse and you're my patient. And you're not a very good one at that."

"There's someone back home, Geneviève." He blurted it out as if it would make it easier for him, but certainly not for her. "We're engaged. Her name is Audrey."

Audrey? Did he have to say his *someone's* name? Would a name help Geneviève accept that the fiancée was real? Couldn't he just have returned to the front without telling her? Did she need the truth? God forbid he died without her ever knowing. Would that have been so bad? Or that he returned to his home and she to hers, their friendship a treasured memory. But this was an honesty borne of guilt that she now shared. She had kissed his hand. She had imagined more about this man than their relationship permitted.

She should be happy for him. He might make it home, and when he did, Audrey would be there waiting.

"And you needed to tell me this because . . . ?"

"Because of us. Who we were together."

"Because of *us*?" She scoffed, shaking her head in disbelief. "There is a *we*?" The past tense *who we were* had not escaped her.

"I was worried that . . ." He tried to sit up and she pushed him back down.

"That I might think there was something more?" She tried not to sound bitter. To toss off the mere suggestion. "You're the one using *us* and *we*." She was fueled only by anger.

"Thank you for caring for me. Any assumptions I made . . . I ask your apologies with sincere gratitude."

"No need. You're here to recover and I'm here to work."

Tourniquets. Applied too loosely, the patient bleeds out and dies, applied too tightly, cut off circulation and the patient loses a limb. That was her heart. Opened, and her love flowed out until she lost everything. Closed, and something died.

She was in surgery and conveniently missed their goodbye. Silly, she thought, how one soldier could make such an impression. That he could change how she felt about the war. That now she would have someone to worry about each day he went into battle armed with a stretcher and ruined hands.

Never mind. This war could not be over too soon for her. And going home for Christmas would be her salvation.

Chapter Twelve
Erin

Spokane, Washington
June 10, 1981

"I guess I'm one of a kind." Claire plopped down near the flowerbed where Erin had spent the morning weeding. This year promised a beautiful garden without the inundation of volcanic ash. "My other mother didn't want to RAFT anywhere with me." Claire looked both wounded and angry. "Of all the birth mothers who gave up their babies, mine was the one in ten who didn't want to be found."

RAFT had finally called three weeks after their trip to Seattle. Who knew this year would have volcanic activity of a different type? Erin hadn't prepared for this. Where was the instruction manual for adoptive parents? What could she say?

"I'm sorry, Claire." She only knew what not to say. Now was not the time to tell her Claire had been forewarned but had clung to the statistics of reconnection. And yet, it was difficult for Erin to fathom that the other mother didn't want to meet the daughter Erin had raised.

"There are probably other ways of finding her." Claire knelt next to Erin and tugged at an ugly weed.

Erin winced. If her birth mother gave her up once, and then twenty-one years later denied the opportunity to connect, knowing her daughter would face that second rejection, it might not be a smart idea for Claire to pursue a third. But how to convey there was no *Reuniting Together*? No RAFT pulled to the dock?

"You know, if you would have waited a little longer, you wouldn't have needed to adopt me." Claire yanked the weed and let the dirt fly. "You would have had your own girl and then your own boy."

"If I had waited a little longer, I wouldn't have had *any* children."

"What do you mean?"

"I don't know if I ever would have gotten prgnant with your sister, if we hadn't started the adoption process for you. We were married for ten years without a baby. When we started the adoption process and I knew I'd get to be a mom, I was *so* happy. I don't think I could have been more excited than if I were actually carrying you." Erin took off her gloves and lifted her baseball cap to wipe her brow.

"For months, I planned and read, staring at every baby and mom, knowing that would be *me*." Erin touched Claire's face in remembrance. "And then a funny thing happened." Erin slapped both hands on her lap in amusement. "Five months into the proceedings, I realized that everything irregular and emotional about me wasn't *all* about adoption."

"You could have stopped the adoption when you knew about Elizabeth."

"I suppose I could have." Erin nodded in agreement. "But just because I wasn't carrying you didn't mean you weren't in my heart." Erin rested her hand on her chest. "Why, it was like expecting twins."

"And when I went in to sign the final papers that warm spring day, I wore a big heavy coat. Afraid that if they had chosen us because we were childless, they might turn me down or think I couldn't handle two babies." She sighed. "I didn't even tell Dad."

"Mom, that doesn't sound like you! To hide the truth."

"No. It doesn't." she answered matter-of-factly.

"So, you think Dad would've said no to the adoption?"

Erin drew a line with the trowel and then focused on a weed. She shrugged, poking deeper until the weed was out. "Dad was cautious about adoption. Telling him was a risk I couldn't take."

"Why was he so afraid of adoption?"

"I'm not sure." Erin frowned. "He was always evasive when I brought it up. Maybe it was just the unknown. Your hidden backstory." She smiled and pinched Claire's chin. "But you turned out pretty good."

"But he wanted me, right?"

"Oh yes. The Christmas before you came, Dad gave me two thirty-three records from *Penny Serenade*."

"That sappy movie about adoption?"

"Remember the songs?" Erin tapped her on the nose and attempted the tune of "I'm Tickled Pink with a Blue-Eyed Baby."

"Except I have green eyes." Erin stopped and switched to the other song, singing, "You Were Meant for Me."

"You were meant for me." Erin paused her singing, smiling in remembrance. "That year I gave dad a record player. It was sort of one of those *Gift of the Magi* moments."

"So, how was it different when you had Elizabeth?"

"I dreaded going to the hospital and leaving you. Thank God for Geneviève! She was always a capable nurse and could handle anything. Your grandma should have had more kids."

Claire nodded.

"And then there was Grandpa. I think he loved you more because you were adopted. You were his first grandchild. And you can't argue—his favorite."

She let that sink in. Let her daughter remember how beloved she was and is.

"Now, when your brother came along ten years later, my goodness, that was something." They both laughed at the shock of that surprise. "Claire, I'm not adopted so I don't know what it feels like. And you've never been in my shoes. But as your adoptive mom, what I love about you is that everything is a little bit of a surprise." Erin packed the trowel and gloves in her wicker basket. "Your looks, your talents, your tastes. You were a gift I got to unwrap." Erin smiled broadly and laughed.

"But then when you did something that *I* might have done, or liked something *I* liked, or said something like *I* said it, it felt like a compliment. It felt like nurture dominated nature and that maybe imitation was flattery." She cocked her head and studied Claire. "Selfish, I know. But I think every parent looks for some way their kids are like them."

"And Dad?" Claire brushed the dirt from her clothes. "Did he really want me?"

"Of course he did! Dad insisted on naming you. When I said you had to be Aria, he announced, 'Aria Claire.' He gave you your middle name."

"Where'd he come up with it?"

"I'm not sure. Maybe he wanted the first letter from his own name. Maybe it was the first C name he could think of. Or maybe he named you after someone he cared about.

"All I know is he loved not only your *name*—but *you*. And our lives would not be complete without you. We *wanted* you."

"But *she* didn't," Claire said, facing her disappointment.

"Well, you don't know that. You don't know the circumstances."

"Mom, we both know she turned me away. Not once but *twice*." Claire's face puckered and she bit her lip.

Erin always bit her lip to keep from crying, too. Sometimes it worked. But not today.

"I wonder . . . if abortion had been legal . . ." Claire's eyes teared up even more, giving them a deeper shade of green.

Erin rubbed her forehead as if debating what to say. "Your mom made the right choice." She took Claire's hands in hers. "She had you."

"But what I'm trying to say is I think she would have done something differently if she had a choice."

"She may *have* had a choice."

"An illegal one."

"Don't put people on a pedestal they can fall off of."

"I didn't put her on a pedestal."

"I'm not talking about *her*." Erin paused. "Look, her choice gave us you. I'm thankful for her."

"I know, it's all in the book." Claire took a deep breath and sighed.

"I keep telling you that story, so you know you're chosen."

"You and Dad chose me," Claire quoted, and then softening, added, "I'm thankful for that." Her voice wavered. "But I still need to find her."

Erin knew Claire needed to hear the story of why she hadn't been chosen by Aria, but she also recognized Claire was swimming in the deep end.

"I'm not sure that's a good idea."

"I can do it myself."

Erin pounded the ground with the trowel, knowing Claire's curiosity would take her somewhere regrettable until she found the answers. There was little that Erin could do to dissuade her firstborn from her search; but she could join her. From the first question to that final answer, Erin could be there to catch her if she fell, or if she started to drown.

Chapter Thirteen
Anna

Arlington, Washington
June 8, 1981

Anna picked up the phone, holding Mei Mei in her left arm as Aaron clung to her leg, twirling the long coiled line in his fingers.

"Hello." The voice on the other end was unfamiliar. "To whom am I speaking?"

How odd that the caller didn't know. Ben had taught them all never to say their names when a stranger called.

"Who is this?" she asked.

"We're looking for Aria Hanson. Or Aria McMahon."

"Yes. This is Mrs. McMahon." They knew her first name. Her real name.

"Mrs. McMahon, I'm an intermediary with RAFT. Reuniting Adoptive Families Together."

Aaron stretched the cord and yanked it back. Anna grabbed the stool nearby and sat down. Mei Mei clutched at dangling earrings and Anna extracted her little fingers. *Adoption. Adoption. What kind of call was this? Who wanted to know? Whose adoption?*

"I think we should consider adopting," Ben had said one night so many years ago as Anna lay cradled in his arms. She turned to him in surprise and smiled when he added, "Not as a fallback, but as our first choice."

But he didn't know it had already been her first choice. Somebody had adopted her daughter. The child she'd never spoken of after giving her up.

"I want our child . . ." Ben had stopped and corrected himself. "Our *children* to know they were chosen." She'd nodded in agreement. Oh, but did her own daughter feel chosen?

"Would you think about something?" Ben had hesitated. Why was he so cautious? "There's a long line for perfect babies, but there are so many children who will *never* be chosen. What if we adopted a child who was perfect, just not in the world's eyes?" Anna would remember this moment because she couldn't believe she had married a man such as Ben.

"Mrs. McMahon? Mrs. McMahon?"

How long had she stood there? She was afraid to answer. Her eyes blurred. Who was this about? Would someone come and retrieve her children? Their Emmaus Joy, a beautiful blonde-haired girl with Down Syndrome. Ben couldn't be prouder of naming her *Emma & Us.* And that's exactly what they were, until Emma became a big sister to Aaron James, a biracial boy who hadn't fit into either of his parent's world, but he fit theirs.

Their youngest was a Chinese baby with cleft palate, their Little Jade, Xiao Ying. *Shee ow Ying.* Anna loved how the Chinese language incorporated pitch into meaning, almost musically. But when Emma was told that the crying new baby was her xiao *mei mei,* or little sister, Emma's response not only quieted, but renamed their baby *Shhhhhh Mei Mei. Shhhhhhhh.* It sounded like a lullaby.

They had a beautiful family. When people thought it was "so nice" what they had done for their kids, it troubled Anna. These kids weren't a charity project, they had saved her.

"What do you want?" Her voice sounded scratchy as if she had a terrible sore throat when everything about her felt sore.

"It's about a baby born in 1960."

That baby. Who knew it would all unravel with a phone call? *That* baby would be twenty-one. Anna bowed her head and closed her eyes. It was happening. After all these years of silence. It was happening.

"Mommy, are you okay?" Aaron patted her arm, his chubby brown hand warm against her skin.

"I assume you know why I am calling?"

"Yes." Her voice was a whisper. Her stomach twisted like Aaron coiling the telephone line.

"Your child is an adult now and is requesting contact."

She couldn't speak. Those files were supposed to remain closed.

"Your child . . ."

"My *daughter*."

"Your daughter. We don't always know if parents know the gender of their child."

She knew. She knew.

"You have the option to decline or to meet with her. We do not share any information with her. No names or addresses. This was a closed adoption."

Closed. Closed. Closed. How could she respond? Closed but no closure. And what about Ben?

"I know this may be a surprise. It may even be difficult."

They couldn't know. "How did you find me?"

"There are a number of steps. Birth date. Obituaries. No one else has been contacted. Your daughter signed a release of liability, we have copies of her driver's license. We know that this is the baby you gave up for adoption."

She wanted to hang up and she wanted to ask questions all at once.

"Would you like to connect with your daughter?"

Yes of course I want to connect with my daughter, I've wanted that all my life. I want to know what she looks like, and what she does, and tell her how much I love her. I want to know that she's healthy and happy and ask all the questions I've always needed answered.

"No. And please don't call again."

Chapter Fourteen
Siobhan

If an offense come out of the truth,
better is it that the offense come
than that the truth be concealed.
—Thomas Hardy, *Tess of d'Ubervilles*

Boston, Massachusetts
Saturday, June 14, 1919

"I don't want you seein' dohs boys anymore." Aintín said when Siobhan returned from another Saturday excursion. Aintín lay on the couch with her feet up.

"They're my friends." Siobhan placed the two books on a chair and set the bread of appeasement on the table. If only Aintín would just be thankful for the fresh loaves from the bakery.

"Make lads wi' some nice Irish boys."

Siobhan stifled a smile. Aintín liked the Italian bread but not the Italian boys. She had once told Siobhan she'd rather see her married to a German Jew. "Aintín, you're so old-fashioned."

""You know they don't like us. We're not like dem, they're not like us. It's not right"

"Aintín! This is America."

"Exactly. I came 'ere for dis?" Aintín kneaded her shoulder and then rolled them as if she had a crick in her neck.

"What do you know of these things? You've never even been married." Siobhan turned her back and headed to the stove.

"An' now I may never."

"And that is somehow my fault?" Siobhan whipped back. Brigid had to stop accusing her and blaming her for everything that was wrong.

But strangely, Aintín didn't respond. Instead, she pursed her lips and held her words.

"What is it, Aintín Brigid?"

"You would never understan'."

"I could, if you gave me a chance." She reached out and put her hand on Brigid's. Aintín pulled her hand away as if Siobhan's touch burned. "We could be family, but you push me away with your cruel words."

"And why Mam and Da sent me with you, I will never understand." Siobhan ached with the longing for her parents. "I didn't want to leave."

"Neither did I!" Brigid slammed her hand on the table.

"But you *chose* to leave Ireland." Siobhan folded her arms across her chest and eyed Brigid.

"I went cause I 'ad no future." Brigid sat up on the sofa. "*You* 'ad no future in Irelan'."

"We weren't so awfully poor," Siobhan defended, circling the davenport. "But look at us now! A tenement on the third floor!"

"You see everythin' clouded. You don' see that the best went to you. We were al' poorer cause of you." Aintín scowled. "When you're out of school, you can take care of *me*."

Siobhan shuddered. She had no intention of living with her cantankerous aunt for the rest of her life.

"It will be different when Mam and Da come."

Brigid sniffed as if scoffing that idea.

"That can't be long now." Siobhan's voice sounded like a pathetic question. The letters from Ireland never seemed to mention them coming.

Brigid drummed her fingers on the table. Siobhan hated it when she did that.

The next day was Sunday, June 15. After mass at Our Lady of Siena, they walked back to their row house. Siobhan could hardly wait for the upcoming Bunker Hill Parade, just over the bridge from Boston in their Irish enclave.

Last year on that day, she had sat on their roof to watch the carnival atmosphere of confetti, firecrackers, and a long parade. One of the first happy memories she had of their Charlestown, just over the bridge from Boston. How ironic for the Irish to celebrate a British victory. No matter. This year the festivities included sporting events in football, hurling, and baseball. And the bands would play "The Rose of Tralee," "You Can't Deny You're Irish," and "When Irish Eyes are Smiling."

"What would Mam and Da think about the parade? Just imagine!" Siobhan longed for her mam to greet them at their third-floor tenement and spend the day as a family. Just like Mama Rosa and the Savellis.

"I won' be goin'. *Me* work don' stop for a party."

At that Siobhan smiled; she was free.

"We'll be a family again when they come." Siobhan took the stairs slowly, considering how much better things would be then.

Brigid didn't even acknowledge her with a glance.

"Oh, I wish they'd come *now!*" Siobhan stomped on the last step to their attic apartment.

"I don' know dat they will. Ever." Brigid eyed Siobhan as if relishing her reaction, then opened the door.

"Oh, don't be mean, Aintín. They'll come!" Siobhan flounced onto the sofa.

"You're so childish." Brigid sat in the big chair. "Start de soup. I'll be restin' me feet."

Siobhan poured the split peas that had soaked overnight into the pot on the stove. She chopped an onion, added water, and a piece of dried pork. Then she checked the jar hidden in the cupboard behind the tea. The money wasn't growing; it seemed to be shrinking.

"This is for Mam and Da!" Accusation laced her voice.

"And for me secretarial classes." Brigid defended.

"No! Not until Mam and Da come!"

Brigid only raised her eyebrows and turned away as if she had her own secret.

"We have to save our money for *them!* How dare you steal it!"

"I'll no be workin' like a dog fer the rest of me life!" Brigid hated that here her name was a derogatory slur for an Irish woman who worked for other families cooking, cleaning, babysitting. A *Brigid.* "Do you know what de master of de house said yesterday? He said dat I was no smarter than a gray-haired negro!" Brigid could be so ugly, so prejudiced, just like so many who hated others. Irish, Italians. Jews. When would it feel like home? Oh, she just needed her Mam and Da!

"They're my parents! They *said* they'd come, so they will!" Siobhan hit the counter with the wooden ladle. "Why would you say that they wouldn't come? What have I ever done to you to make you hate me so?"

"You're so selfish, Siobhan. Moira and Paddy spoiled you."

"How would you know? You weren't even there. They love me. You're miserable, but don't blame me for your unhappiness."

"I shouldn't blame you?" She laughed. "I shouldn't blame you?"

"No," she responded feebly. "I don't imagine there's a reason."

"There are too many reasons." Aintín's voice was a whisper. "So many, you couldn't understan'."

"Maybe not. But you are my *aintín.* We could have been sisters. But you're cold. Like a stranger—or worse." Her eyes narrowed at her Aintín. "A stranger would have at least been indifferent. A stranger might have been kind.

"Why don't you send me back? Or you go back and let my mother and father come!" Siobhan poked and prodded, but Aintín kept staring out the window as if not even listening, so Siobhan left the soup.

"I just want them here. Don't steal their way back." Siobhan pointed at Aintín.

"Yer Mam and Da wouldn't care."

"How dare you say that! Why would you say that?" Siobhan stomped her foot. Why wouldn't she listen to her?

"Oh, Siobhan, stop your whinin'."

Siobhan knew she sounded like a child. Her aunt rose from the chair as if leaving.

"Just stay away from dohs boys." Aintín turned to the loaf of bread as if she wanted to end the discussion and hacked off a thick chunk.

"What does it matter if I have friends? I have no family here." Siobhan sensed something unfinished and poked at the tail of the discussion.

"A fella can lead to other things." Aintín wielded the knife, pointing the tip at her.

"I don't *have* a boyfriend!" Siobhan pleaded.

"Maybe not yet. But dohs Italian boys will want somethin' more." Aintín set the knife down and braced herself against the table, Siobhan directly across from her.

"Aintín, you don't know anything about them."

"I know more than ye do, lassy!" Aintín sliced another slab of bread and the knife thudded loudly.

"You know nothing of love and kindness and men. You will always be a lonely, hard-hearted spinster."

Those words became spittle in the air and Siobhan couldn't believe they'd escaped from her secret thoughts. Since she'd begun, she might as well continue spewing the feelings pent up for months in their tiny apartment.

Aintín spoke not a word but raised her head to look Siobhan directly in the eyes, her lips curled upward.

"I know what comes of dees things with boys who are not men. An' I'm not gonna see it 'appen again." She pointed her finger at Siobhan who now cowered, thankful the knife had been set aside. Aintín drew her sleeve across her reddened face, her eyes small and mean above her arm. Something boiled within her which would burn everything in its path. "I know more than you tink. You're not ready to raise a child, and I'm not gonna raise a grandchild!"

Aintín stopped hastily, her stiff arms now slack at her sides. Brigid's fire had died out, now Siobhan felt an unexplained chill, a cold horror seeping through her body.

"No . . . that would never happen," Siobhan said slowly. "You are not my mother." She needed to speak that. To make sure it was truth.

The longer Aintín remained silent, the more Siobhan dreaded what Aintín would say. Was what Siobhan imagined as awful as the truth? Siobhan shifted her weight from one foot to the other.

"What an odd thing to say. How could you misspeak so?"

"You. You spoiled, whiny chil'." Brigid's voice was cold and calm. "You need to learn a few lessons."

Siobhan shook her head slowly. Whatever was coming was something she didn't want to hear.

Siobhan scooted a chair, a wall, between Brigid and her, the sound shrieking along the floor. She sat on the sofa. The day should have been warm, but she was shaking. She tucked her hands beneath her, barely able to breathe.

"We 'ad to start over." Brigid measured her words.

Did she mean to say it in past tense?

Siobhan heard the soup bubble, hiss. Spit. Its aroma was changing.

"I 'ad to start over. An' dat meant you, too. Yer reputation. *Our* reputation."

Siobhan's face wrinkled, she glared beyond to where she'd tacked her prayer cards. One of the crucifix, one of Mary and Joseph, and the other of the Sacred Heart of Jesus. She wasn't sure if she'd posted them as a reminder to pray, or to antagonize her Aintín.

Though calm on the outside, Siobhan's heart beat so quickly she could barely catch her breath. Could the question mark be more hideous than the answer? An awful sensation consumed her from the inside out. The air in the room had gone stale. Siobhan wanted to run to the window and gasp.

"I can't . . . I can't hear . . ."

"Oh, now, you've started somethin', Siobhan, though you'll be sorry I'm a finishin' it."

"I don't want you to be my mother!" Siobhan pushed away the potential truth. "You shouldn't be *anyone's* mother."

"Believe me, I didn't want to be *anyone's* ma, least of all yers. But that's what 'appened."

"Why did you have to tell me? I didn't need to know the whole truth."

"Ha! You don' even know de 'alf of it." Brigid's voice was so calm it scared Siobhan.

"And my . . . father?"

"There was someone in Ennis."

Siobhan put the new facts of who she was in one pile and discarded everything she wanted to be. The memory of almost sixteen years in Ireland with Mam and Da now tainted by Brigid's revelation.

"I loved him," Brigid said in the softest voice Siobhan had ever heard from her. ""Maybe 'e loved me, but not after I told 'im I was in de family way." Brigid picked up speed and volume as if this story had been reignited from within, pent up inside too long, now a raging fire threatening to burn everything Siobhan had known as truth. "His name was—"

"No!" Siobhan interrupted. If Brigid didn't say it, then the man, her father, wouldn't have a name, so he wasn't real. *Da. Paddy.* Patrick was the only Dad she wanted to know.

But Brigid spewed the truth like a volcano, killing everything in its path. "Denis."

And there it was. Her father's name was Denis. And over Siobhan's tears, Brigid continued. "He said, 'Maybe if it's a *fella*.'" Her father didn't want a daughter and her mother didn't want a baby. "I went to the workhouse."

The prayer cards. *Mary, Mother of God.* What could she pray to make her stop? Siobhan knew about the workhouses for those with no job or money. And she'd heard rumors about unmarried women who had gotten themselves in the family way.

"Ya know who else was there?" Brigid asked as if reading her mind. "There's women who are too juicy, or whose family thinks they've disgraced dem, or maybe they've been taken advantage of, or maybe they jist felled in love." Her voice dropped off in a sigh.

"We needed a pretend name. Mine was Theresa O'Sullivan. We couldn't talk to each other. Our clothes were taken an' exchanged for ganky uniforms. I hated dat petticoat of linsey-woolsey an' striped jerkin dat as much said I was a prisoner. Like I 'ad committed a crime. Prison would 'av been better. Less rules an' better grub."

"A wee spot of meal to one gallon of water, wi' onions, pepper, salt, an' root vegetables thrown into de witch's cauldron. I know cause sometimes I cooked dat rank stew. Sometimes we 'ad rancid butter an' stale bread."

By the smell of the soup on the stove, she knew the soup would need stirring, but she wasn't getting up. Instead, she eyed the loaf on the counter, then her eyes wandered up to Brigid who also studied the bread.

"Yes. I 'unger for fresh bread."

Siobhan never lowered her glance. It was a stare down.

""Six weeks after you 'ad yer sprog . . ." Brigid stopped and glared at Siobhan. "Your baby," she corrected herself. "You could leave. but only if you could pay. I worked de laundry to pay off me debt. Don' you ever wonder why I don't want to be a *brigid*?" She said her name with disgust, disdain.

If her heart didn't hurt so badly, she might have felt sorry for Aintín, but she didn't know what to feel.

"So many sick an' lonely babies. So, after you were born, I wrote to Patrick—not to Moira—I wrote to Patrick cause he wus different from most men."

Siobhan closed her eyes remembering Da and how he read to her by the fire when all he probably wanted to do was sleep after a long day of work. But Da wanted her to learn, even if she was a girl. He was different. Her heart ripped at the memory of sitting at his knee.

"Moira practically raised me; seein's our folks were so old. So why would Moira want to raise de wane?" *De wane*. Siobhan thought. That was me. *The child*. Couldn't she even call her *my child*? "Patrick must 'ave talked to 'er. They figured out what to do."

"Me own Da was near dead from drinkin' an' me Maa from worryin' over him. I might of stayed if Da 'adn't of club me so badly. I 'ad to get out of dare." Brigid stopped. Siobhan would not look up at her lest the tears spill down her cheeks. Her tears might be a sign of weakness and a reason for Brigid to further despise her.

"I told 'im, you'd be the 'shakins' of de bag.'"

Siobhan choked at Brigid's crude term, horrified that Brigid could suggest Siobhan be thought of as the last dregs of Mam's womb.

"But Paddy tol' a tale in town about one last lambie in de flock. Moira stayed away from people an' her heaviness hid de lie."

Siobhan knew the rest of the story, and it was a good life with Mam and Da, but now she would never see them again.

"Who named me?" Suddenly that seemed important. She wanted that significant gift to be from her parents.

""Me."

Siobhan sighed. Brigid went on, not comprehending Siobhan's

disappointment.

"I wanted to name you *Siobhan*, but de priest wouldn't christen you except with de name of a saint. As if I would name you after a saint!" Brigid looked at Siobhan as if she might spit on her. "They all tart themselves so holy but for de love of God, they 'ad no kindness in dem."

""So I named you *Moira* Siobhan. I gave you me sister's name. An' maybe she was a bit of a saint to 'av to raise another man's child." Siobhan waited for more. There would be more. "An' do you know Moira means *bitter*?"

Of course it did. But was her Mam bitter? Surely not. Her Mam had loved her. It was Brigid who had not. It was Brigid who had ruined everything.

"You could have come by yourself."

"Patrick an' Moira are auld. Jist like me own maa an' da. An' no dowry to spake of. They were afraid there'd be no one to take care of you. No one." Brigid seemed to take delight in her argument. "And they were afraid you'd "An' they were afraid you'd be like me, wi' parents too old to watch out for you." out like me with parents too old to watch out for you."

"I could have stayed with Da and Mam. They were good to me."

"But den rumors started." Brigid leaned in, her eyes widening. "Lassy, yer must see yer look jist like me?"

Yes, Siobhan was a younger, softer version of Brigid, but she didn't want to be.

"We 'ad no choice but to come 'ere by ourselves, Siobhan. You know Paddy and Moira are too old."

"The port in Cobh County? Cork?" Siobhan asked, the reality of her departure washing over her. "That was my last goodbye?" She thought of her parents hugging her. She thought they were going to be reunited. This was just the first boat ride for a fifteen-year-old adventurer. She hadn't cried!

Da! Her Da who loved her more than anyone! Da who taught her to read. She'd barely said goodbye. What was he thinking when she skipped down the ramp? Did he know how much she loved him? That she treasured cleaning the barns with him and reading by firelight?

Her face stung with hot tears.

She would have touched her mother's face; she would have told her how much she loved her. If only . . . she would have asked her mam to sing another lullaby in her low alto voice. Something Brigid had never done. Never done for her own daughter. *Daughter.* The word now horrified her.

"Did you ever feel anything for me?"

She waited for the answer. How could a mother not respond?

"I never saw you til yer were five. It was when I came for me mother's wake." Siobhan had a vague dark memory of a guest who was coarse and sharp with a beauty that scared her. When she laughed with Siobhan's older brothers, it was a hard chortle. Even then Siobhan didn't like Brigid. Had Brigid ever liked *her?*

"You looked so like me I could 'ardly stan' bein' in de seem room. Everybody 'ad to know. I came back two or tree times, an' each time you looked more like me." Brigid wrapped the bread back in its paper.

"That's when Moira said de rumors were too strong an' she an' Paddy were gettin' too old. If me an' you stayed, you'd be labeled a langer, an' me a 'oor." Bastard. Whore. Siobhan cringed at Brigid's language. There was no way to make it sound pretty. But, the words were true. Except she hadn't asked for those names.

"You never wanted to see me before that?"

"There was a moment I tried." Siobhan turned keenly, the unfamiliar softness in Brigid's voice returned. "De nuns turned their backs on me as they took you away." Brigid's eyes looked unfocused. Siobhan couldn't fathom anyone could do that to a new mother. "I asked, 'Can I look at 'er?' But they didn't answer. They jist formed a wall between us." Brigid's fists were clenched on her lap. "I 'ated dohs women. I don't know what made dem choose to be nuns, but it wasn't for de love of God."

An odor of burnt peas warned Siobhan she'd ruined their lunch. Brigid would be angry. Couldn't she smell it? But why did Siobhan always have to take the blame?

"Maybe it's not my fault. Maybe it's yours."

"How dare ye!" Brigid rose. Her sudden slap stung Siobhan's face. But despite the pain, Siobhan felt better. She had seen the slap coming because Brigid had done it once before when Siobhan tried to teach her something Da had once shown her. Brigid had whirled around and surprised her with a slap across the face. "Do you tink I'm dense?"

Siobhan hadn't thought Aintín Brigid stupid until she had raised the question and her hand.

Though she had always known Aintín would strike her again, she was unprepared for Brigid to turn her hand and slap the other cheek with her backhand. Brigid looked shocked, perhaps at her fury. But no apology.

"I might've married 'im! Instead, I make a livin' cleanin' other peoples 'ouses." Her voice was cold and unfeeling. She knew how to hurt. "You'll always be a *noose*."

"I didn't want to know! You said it just to hurt me!" Siobhan had no idea what to do or how to strike back. She only knew she had to get out of there and headed for the door.

Turning around, she stared at the woman she could not call Mother. What could she say? What last words would linger? Like mother, like daughter, her voice sounded just as cold and unfeeling. "I could never love you." Siobhan slammed the door behind her.

Chapter Fifteen
Erin

Seattle, Washington
July 1981

Cramer, Davis, and Morgan still practiced on the second floor in a small firm that smelled oddly like the dentist's office next door, combined with the smoke from nervous clients dipping their cigarettes in ash tray side tables. Everything seemed the same as it had twenty-one years before, though Mr. Morgan no longer handled adoptions. Roe v. Wade 1973 had pretty much extinguished those opportunities.

Soon after arriving, they were ushered into Mr. Morgan's office where they each sat on a vinyl chair across from his formidable desk.

"Twenty-one years ago, my adoptive parents . . ." Claire suddenly motioned to Erin. "This is my mom, Erin Ellis." Claire drew a quick breath. "They were here signing papers. Now I'm here for information about my *biological* parents."

The attorney nodded as if he understood but not in a way that said he'd help.

"You may be familiar with open adoptions, but years ago, that wasn't how they were done. The records for your adoption are closed. As the attorney for your birth parents, there is no information I can share. Those files are protected."

"And so, for someone who might need to find her mother, there's no way?"

"There are a lot of reasons why parents choose closed adoption.

Some people do use RAFT—to help locate their birth parents. It's still no guarantee though, because your mother or father might not want a reunion. Are you prepared for that?"

Erin cringed. No, Claire hadn't prepared for that.

"Doesn't it bother you that the information is somewhere in those file cabinets, and you can't help me?"

"It would bother me more to do something illegal and betray someone's secrecy."

Erin stared at the display of family photos behind Mr. Morgan, two sons, one daughter. The girl looked familiar.

"I'll let myself out." Claire pushed the chair back.

"I'm sorry I can't help you." Mr. Morgan followed Claire, nodding to his secretary, "No charge today."

Erin caught the eye of the teenager slipping manila files in the cabinet, recognizing her as the girl in the photo. This was likely her summer job. What would it take for her to open one file? Was she vulnerable? Maybe. Was it worth it? Probably not.

As the door closed behind them, Claire turned, her lips pursed, her eyes focused.

"I have another idea and I'm not leaving here until I've tried it."

Chapter Sixteen
Siobhan

There are only two or three human stories,
and they go on repeating themselves as
fiercely as if they had never happened before;
like the larks in this country, that have been singing
the same five notes over for thousands of years.
—Willa Cather, O Pioneers!

Boston, Massachusetts
Sunday, June 15, 1919

S iobhan stumbled down three flights of stairs, blinded by her tears and infuriated by her Aintín's words. Where would she go? Her feet took her all the way to the bridge without stopping, where she leaned against the railing, heaving in deep breaths. The pilings below blurred. She could faintly smell the salty sea air and closed her eyes to drink it in. She had once heard that the ocean was made of tears. She understood that now. When she opened her eyes, she glanced around to see if anyone was watching. Bunker Hill on one side, the draw of that white steeple on the other. She stood between two worlds not knowing where to go or who to be. She couldn't return to Ireland. They had sent her away. They had parted with her for a reason. To undo that would be cruel. And conceivably they really didn't want her. Or had never wanted her. Mam and Da were never coming for her.

Staying with Brigid was impossible. She couldn't even call her *Aintín* any longer.

The water shimmered. It wasn't that far down. But was it far enough? Did it matter? She had never learned to swim. She considered which direction she could plunge but knew she lacked the courage or the foolishness to do something that reckless. Would it matter to anyone if she did? Brigid would never tell Paddy and Moira. Moira would assume she ran away.

No, if she was going to run away, she'd run away with purpose. But where to? Siobhan walked the metal bridge until she set foot on ground. She was certain she could smell the molasses, the oregano, the basil, home. She'd find Antonio. Antonio would listen. She could tell her friend. That's what he was. Her *best* friend. Brigid had made it sound like so much more. Like it was dirty or wrong.

Her eyes were a blur and she stumbled on the uneven bricks, barely able to see the shops she passed. She didn't have to look at the signs, she knew the zigzagging mazelike path that enclosed her. *Illegitimate. Unwanted. Bastard.* Why couldn't it remain a secret? What had Mam and Da's generosity cost them in Ireland? What had they lost in shipping Brigid and her to America?

She couldn't go back, but where was the way forward? She had nowhere else to go. She had no one.

Siobhan ran toward the bookstore. No Antonio. But of course, it was Sunday and closed. If she had to go near the barber shop everybody would see her. What difference did it make now? "Antonio?" she cried out, blinded by tears. "Antonio!" She panted and her heart raced as fast as her feet, which sloppily carried her down the road. And there it was at last—the barber shop, with him standing uncharacteristically tall on the doorstep, the closed sign hanging behind him. She kept running and just shy of the step, fell forward and into his arms. In her anger, she pounded her fists on his chest which seemed strangely broader in her weakness. "No! No! No!"

She expected his arms around her in comfort. But Antonio was silent and took her wrists in his hands and hushed her. His grip was strangely firm. Antonio seemed so angry. Except it wasn't Antonio. In her shock, she quieted. Those eyes so brown. Not a smile. No words.

He pulled her into the alley and there, in privacy, he wrapped his arms around her and held her tightly. She was hidden. Her back pressed against the brick wall, protected by the bulk of his body, she felt small and contained. How long had it been since someone held her? Loved her? She felt as though she would faint. Was it just a dream? It didn't matter because he would keep her from drowning.

The metal staircase upward was a direction she had never considered. The fire escape. *Escape.* Such a perfect word of ascent. They climbed it together and when they reached the top, he took her hand. She had never seen the North End from such heights. The smell of oregano from the rooftop garden of the Savelli's building permeated the air. The sound of cheerful chatter in the music of their language drifted up from the streets below. The boats droned by in the Charles River, which would take her away across an ocean and home.

Here she was invisible. This was another world, protected from the hurt below. Giovanni picked a sprig of rosemary, crushed a needle in his fingers, then touched her nose. She deeply inhaled the earthy, woodsy scent. She had never cared much about flowers, but now this perennial herb with its needlelike leaves and colorful flowers connected her to him.

"Rosmarino." He spoke the word as if it were the name of his lover. "Rosmarino." It sounded so beautiful; she would have taken the name for herself.

Giovanni guided her toward a private space formed by laundry blowing in the warm summer wind. As one sheet curled upward, a sail on a ship, it exposed a cot hidden behind a half wall. She could imagine this was where he spent much of his time. Siobhan had witnessed the chaos of their household with seven younger brothers and sisters. Giovanni would seek solace.

She took a long breath to steady herself. She could almost smell the ocean beyond the thyme, oregano, and *rosmarino* growing in Rosa's rooftop garden.

"*Ros*—dew. *Marinus*—Sea. Dew of the sea." He touched the branch to her cheek and slid it under her chin. Everything within her shivered.

What could she say? Was it enough to sit beside him under the intensity of his stare? He slowly lifted the hair off her neck, and she trembled at the touch of his fingers. She turned her face toward him until he cupped her cheek in his hand. Tenderly, he toyed with her curls and her scalp tingled.

Giovanni spoke a different language with his fingers. His hands told her what she needed to know. She was cherished.

"You are sad, no? Put this under your pillow to chase away the bad dreams." How could he know about bad dreams? Today had begun on the other side of the water, in a church of her people, praying to a God who seemed so far away. But she had crossed the water. Taken a bridge to where? And now she was here in a congregation of two.

The next morning, Giovanni was gone, and she slipped down the same staircase she had ascended the night before. But this time she was different, felt different. Knew something and knew someone. Now what?

She passed St. Leonard's where morning mass was over. Oh, but she needed mass. What had she done? Everything Brigid had warned her about. She sat down in the pew, profoundly changed. She stared at the cathedral ceiling. How many times had she prayed to those statues along the walls? Brigid was right, she should not share the name of a saint. *"Our impulses are too strong for our judgement sometimes,"* she whispered the words of Hardy.

"Mary, Mother of God, I have sinned." Did the statue hear her? Or was there another presence in this building that did? Maybe she needed to go back to Charlestown and find Our Lady of Siena Church. Would the lady there know what Siobhan had done?

When she was certain Brigid had left for work, Siobhan did return to Charlestown and changed her clothing. Had Brigid missed her? Doubtful.

A warm wind blew into the open window, and she looked out on the life that had significantly changed since yesterday.

She thought back on *rosmarino*. The way he had crushed the needles of the sprig. The way he had tickled her body with the treelike herb. Then the softer herb, *"timo,"* he said and finally *"origano,"* and then the feel of his soft lips on hers. His body against her. She had never known the way between a man and a woman. The exquisite pain. His cry. Was he in pain, too? His release and how she had stared up into the sky, the stars blurred with her tears. The cot was so narrow that they faced each other, his breath warm against her. Lazily he opened his eyes. Still no words. He touched her lips with his finger. Even now she shuddered in remembrance.

Later that day, she met Antonio as she wandered through the streets. Could he tell that everything was different? That nothing would ever be the same? That she no longer knew to whom or where she belonged?

"Siobhan!" he called out, running to her. "Siobhan!" Antonio panted in excitement. "Dinner with us tonight. Can you come?"

Her heart expanded. Everything within her wanted to be with Gio. Antonio looked so happy. Siobhan winced.

At dinner that night Mama Rosa dished a soup from the pot, thick with beans and vegetables and sprinkled with rosemary. *Rosmarino.* She couldn't eat.

Rosa and Roberto spoke Italian from opposite ends of the table. For all she knew, their conversation could be about her. Like many Sicilians, Rosa knew little English. Antonio said he thought she still hoped to go back. *Birds of passage.* That was what they were called.

Giovanni sat across from her in silence, never meeting her gaze. Perhaps he regretted what happened. "What's wrong with you tonight? You're so quiet." Antonio touched her shoulder. She felt only the remorse of guilty pleasure for what she had done. She couldn't go back to the way it was.

She couldn't tell him she had no place to go, that she had no home, and that the previous night she'd slept with his brother over Antonio's head on their very rooftop. That in a garden from another world, they had done something that was a surprise to them both. Adam and Eve trying to remake their lives.

After Rosa's cannoli, Siobhan and Antonio sat quietly on a bench in front of the barber shop.

"Antonio!" Rosa came out the front door and nodded for him to come back inside. She said something in Italian and Siobhan heard "Padre" and what sounded like a command, then her own name. "Siobhanna. Night. Your zia."

The door closed behind her friend and his mother, and she stood on the sidewalk considering where to go. She dragged her feet toward the church, where she hoped to sleep in the garden. So peaceful, surrounded by St. Anthony and the children. A Catholic church built by Italian immigrants providing an Irish girl a quiet respite.

The next morning, she returned to the apartment where she left no mark of her presence. Everything was closed in Charlestown for the holiday. The idea of a parade and confetti and celebration now seemed like a childish chaos she couldn't endure.

Taking only what Brigid would not miss, she headed out to the North End and to the library where she pored over newspapers for jobs and housing. But that night she lingered by the barber shop, until Giovanni took her elbow and returned her to Eden.

The next morning, once again Siobhan slipped down the fire escape. But when her feet touched the ground, she saw Mama Rosa leaving the barber shop. Siobhan stood still and when she thought it safe, headed down the sidewalk in the other direction.

"Siobhanna." The voice was not a command, but neither was it warm.

"Yes, Mrs. Savelli." Siobhan felt the stolen herbs in her pocket, crushed so she could smell them whenever she wanted to remember that place. And Giovanni. Even now she knew that the aroma carried her guilty secret. *Rosmarino.* She fingered them, unwilling to withdraw her hand with its lingering fragrance.

"My boys, good boys. You live over river, no? We live here." Each hand represented one side of the river. "No more." Her hands separated, cutting the two places apart.

Siobhan shivered. How much did she know?

"You capisce, no?"

But if she wasn't welcome at the Savelli's, then where?

To Rosa's horror, Siobhan's answer was to do just the opposite and walk across to the barber shop. What would Rosa do? Standing in the open door, she waited for Giovanni to notice her. Rosa remained on the sidewalk.

"I have nowhere to go, Giovanni."

Gio glimpsed behind Siobhan's shoulder to his mother on the sidewalk. Siobhan could see his father behind him.

"Do you want me?" Her voice sounded pathetic and small.

"What are you talking about? You need to go back to your zia."

"I cannot go back there. She doesn't want me." She'd never told him about Brigid. Theirs was a language of few words, only touch.

Gio was silent.

"We could be together." She spoke low enough that neither parent could hear her words.

"Not here." Gio's voice was a hissed whisper of a snake, looking back and forth between his Mama and Papa.

"Then let's leave. Go somewhere we can be husband and wife. You can study sculptures and I will . . ."

"You will read books."

She couldn't tell if he was teasing or taunting.

"Giovanni." She reached up to his face. He caught her hand and lowered it, squeezing it too tightly. Controlling her movement. Hiding her gesture from his mother.

He sighed and, in that moment, she saw how he lacked her courage and that his love did not match hers. Giovanni's reason for staying was greater than his feelings for her. She had nothing in Boston, he had his family and a vague vision of a future that didn't include her.

She thought of the sprig, crushed between his fingers. She was that herb, and she longed to be broken by him again. But he had also told her that rosemary was for remembering. That people put it in the casket of a loved one so as not to be forgotten, and that brides and grooms carried it in their wedding as a symbol of love and commitment. Was this the death of their short love or a sign of commitment for their future?

"I will go away then. Alone."

She said it partly to shock him and partly to make it real to herself. Or to force him to claim her. And if he didn't—there was nothing left here.

"I will go far away." Not back to Ireland but farther west. To one of the many places she had read about in those newspapers. She would find something to grab onto. She would have a dream, like Antonio.

"Siobhan, now you're being silly."

"Silly? You think me *silly?*" She laughed and then swatted him petulantly on his arm. "You think I'm just a child. You're so much older and wiser but you don't know what you want." She thought of her hypocrisy. Until the night on the rooftop, she was still waiting for her life to happen. "And even if you did, you lack words to say it." Her words spat to the sidewalk below. How could she feel so much hatred in her love? "Could you even say it now? If it were the last time you would ever see me? Could you say, *I love you?*"

"*Rosmarino.*" Giovanni used the word as if it was his only language.

"I will not beg, Giovanni. I will not. I will just leave. Relieved I found out you are not a man who lives from his heart."

"Oh, Siobhan . . ."

She shouldn't have kept hoping. And yet, as she turned to leave, she still wondered if he would run to her. She walked slowly. Her feet quiet on the bricks. He didn't stop her.

And yet when she was five paces away, she thought she did hear him. It was quiet but even over her soft footfall, she might have heard him say, "I love you, Siobhan." Or was it her imagination? Wishful thinking.

She didn't turn back because she knew that she could not. She knew that his words changed nothing.

Chapter Seventeen
Geneviève

Richmond, Virginia
Winter 1918

The Armistice of Compiègne was signed on November 11, 1918, at 5:45 a.m. and enacted at 11:00 a.m. Still, more than eight hundred and sixty servicemen would die that day.

And on that day, three thousand patients remained at Base 41. This had become a bleak house, but home nonetheless. Here, Geneviève knew what it was to be needed and wanted. She had a purpose and a focus. Every bit of the frivolity of social life in Richmond or Charlottesville seemed a thing of the past.

At the beginning of December, she and forty-two other UVA medical staff were shipped back to the States. She returned to her room in Varsity Hall where nothing felt the same and she longed for someone who could understand her. *The war is over, Geneviève Marchand! The war is over!*

But it wasn't. Her mind was filled with the faces, the stories, and the scarred hands.

On a dark December afternoon, after her second day back at the hospital, she walked the UVA grounds, tired, cold, and worn out.

She wasn't ready to return to nursing. Was there something else she could do? When a doctor described an autopsy with words like lungs—*swollen and blue, tissue diseased, gelatinous, surfaces wet and foamy, alveoli filled with fluid, hemorrhagic tracheobronchitis,* she was intrigued, and considered that in research there was hope. In research there was help.

A light dusting of snow covered the UVA Grounds and Geneviève felt the cold reach to her bones. Students retrieved wood from stockpiles outside their rooms to fuel the fireplaces in their courtyard dorms. She shivered as a wind swept from Cabell Hall, past the pavilions and colonnades, all the way down the grassy lawn.

Snow could be so beautiful, but now it struck her as monochromatic and gray. As the sun went down, the world turned as blue as she felt and the idea of returning home for the holidays made her shudder. Especially to a stately Richmond Colonial, a mansion compared to the field hospital tents, evacuation hospitals, and Base 41.

Upon arrival in Richmond, she felt like a stranger at her homecoming, lost in an unfamiliar world. The house seemed different because *she* was different. The holly and ivy, the Christmas tree in the foyer; a stark contrast to Base 41. She felt tired and weary. In a lifetime of nursing, she'd never again see so many people die. Had she failed?

She was haunted by what she'd seen and what she couldn't do. Every day, too many men had died on her shift. She had heard their delirious cries caused by debilitating injuries. Even now she couldn't silence their agonizing pleas.

One night she cried out in her sleep, only to hear her father's slippered feet on the stairs, a sliver of light illuminating a path when he opened the door.

"Ginny?" his voice a whisper. She closed her eyes against the pain and felt her tears dampen her cheeks. He waited. She feigned sleep. "If you want to talk . . ." He knew her too well.

"I can't, Daddy." Her voice was a snag on material, a catch that could pull into a cry and unravel everything.

"When you're ready." The door closed slowly, leaving her wondering when that would be, and even if she could explain her feelings, would anyone understand?

Theirs was a quiet holiday season. Her mother and father didn't invite anyone for Christmas Eve or Christmas Day. Geneviève had defined her expectations and so their greenery covered door was closed for entertaining. That was why two days after Christmas, her mother's announcement both surprised and annoyed her.

"There's someone come calling." The breeze from her mother whisking the door open contorted the fire, as if the flames were as angry as she at Mother's disturbance. Her mother waited expectantly in the open doorway.

"Really, Mother, not now."

"Geneviève Louise Marchand, pick yourself up and receive your guest." Her mother turned on her heels and slammed the door, further fanning the flames.

Geneviève unwrapped her robe, picked up yesterday's dress hanging over her chair, then buttoned it, as well as her shoes, grumbling even as she did so. She caught herself in her full-length mirror and frowned. She was one button off, but she didn't care. She ran her fingers through her disheveled chestnut curls and smoothed the wrinkled dress, then gave up. Much to her mother's dismay, she no longer cared about her appearance. Her mother would say she was unpresentable. It was a good thing her mother had never seen her tending to patients near the front.

Halfway down the winding staircase she saw her parents below, waving her toward the parlor with great anticipation. Her mother inspected her up and down, frowned, and then put on a smile she knew was only for her benefit. Geneviève Louise Marchand hadn't passed inspection. She crossed by them, then entered the parlor.

"Hello, Ginna."

Her eyes blurred at the sight of a man known only to her on a battlefield in a faraway land, half a world away, a place that still felt more like home than Richmond, Virginia.

She was in the middle of her parlor, but where was he? No-man's-land.

She turned back over her shoulder to see her parents, confused, then at her look, turn quickly away.

"It's a beautiful night." William's extended arm invited her to the door. He walked slowly, favoring his good leg. He should have healed more quickly.

William steadied himself against the door as she selected a cape to wrap around herself and then inhaled the cold December air. She motioned for him to sit on the porch swing, but she remained standing. What was her place?

"You must be surprised."

"I'm thankful you're alive."

"It's strange to see you here. In Virginia. When I only knew you in the middle of . . ." The swing creaked slightly.

She nodded, biting back the tears, closing her eyes against the scenes that threatened to reappear like a movie in her mind. The tears were warm against the chill of the air.

"Nothing feels the same, does it?"

What was he trying to say? That whatever friendship they'd shared in France was not the same?

"We shared so many things. Faced the same enemies." He paused. "Became friends."

She knew what they shared. They had shared fear and grief. The sorrow for all the boys who would never be men and for the men who would never see their children grow up. The recognition of family and friends in every wounded soldier, and every wounded soldier becoming family and friends.

Something was coming and she feared it would be hard. She held her breath against the thought of one more disappointment. One more death. Tighten the tourniquet.

"Audrey and I cannot be together. Too much has changed."

She could not exhale. Her heart pounded and then, slowly, involuntarily, she shuddered.

"I brought you two gifts. Your choice." William took a rectangular package from an inner coat pocket.

She slowly opened the present. "Scissors?"

"I never lost mine on the field. That wasn't the only thing I didn't lose."

Below the scissors was a shiny new stethoscope.

"The choice is yours, Geneviève. Keep the scissors and I leave." He snipped with his fingers. "Or . . ." He closed his eyes and took a long, deep breath. "I was never honest about my heart. You can check it now, Nurse Geneviève."

This couldn't be happening. Her rib cage tightened. Breathe. An uncomfortable silence stretched between them.

"*Who could refrain, that had a heart to love, and in that heart, courage to make love known?*" His voice was steady. Firm. Confident. Now she'd let him quote Shakespeare anytime he wanted.

She looked beyond the front yard. When had it started to snow? White silk covered their grass, snowflakes trickled through the light of the streetlamps. As a child, she sat in her upstairs window seat for hours, studying that view, celebrating the first magical winter snow. But she was no longer a child.

"I'm applying for Law School at UVA. I'm hoping that you'll be patient with this patient. That we will have time to get to know each other."

"I'd like to keep the stethoscope."

William patted his hand on the porch swing, and she sat down. Closer than she could have imagined. She allowed herself to embrace the tingle and breathlessness. William took her hand and moved even closer, so his frame shielded her from the wind. He had become her definition of handsome: chiseled face, a smile worth waiting for, and those hazel eyes.

When he leaned toward her, she instinctively tucked her head on his shoulder, her cheek imprinting on the rough herringbone pattern of his coat. He smelled like wet wool and an earthy cologne. She almost laughed in her tears.

His hands were open. She took them in hers. Those poor hands, so cracked and scarred. She smoothed her palm over his and then lifted it. She ran the calluses over her face, enjoying the rough texture and knowing what it meant. Knowing that, like a bearer, he would never give up on her.

"Your face is so soft." Will placed both hands on her face and lifted her head, kissing her as gently as the soft snow falling around them.

Chapter Eighteen
Siobhan

I have not broken your heart—you have broken it;
and in breaking it, you have broken mine.
—Emily Brontë, *Wuthering Heights*

Boston, Massachusetts
July 7, 1919

"Write to me," Antonio said as they waited at North Station on Causeway Street. Siobhan sat on the leather-upholstered oak benches, the chandeliers lighting the columns. "I will miss you more than you can know."

But she did know. Because she would miss him that much and more.

"And I, you, Antonio."

"And you'll write when you get there, no? To this Washington on another ocean?"

Siobhan was thankful for the newspapers and the advertisements for finding a destination, for a place to stay with Antonio's friend in Washington, and then for the money jar in Brigid's apartment, which she emptied.

Washington was on another coast and another ocean. If she couldn't have what she wanted in Boston, then she needed to be as far away as possible where she could still breathe in the salt air.

"I suppose I'll write," Siobhan teased, knowing that the kinship she felt with Antonio would continue.

"Maybe one day you'll come back."

"To what?" Siobhan laughed but her voice held derision. "To Giovanni married to a Sicilian girl making him ziti? To see you reading books to your five children? I don't think so."

Antonio frowned. "And your Aintín? She will be all right?"

"Ha! You're too kind. Brigid has no need for anyone. She can take care of herself."

There were no goodbyes with Brigid. She'd send Da and Mam a letter, but not her. She relished knowing Brigid would be ignorant except what Mam and Da told her. And maybe if she didn't use all the money in the jar, she could still see if she could bring them to America.

"If I were to say, 'Come with me, Siobhan.' Would you?"

Her heart skipped at the thought. What would that mean? Would she one day have the kind of love for Antonio that she had for Giovanni? Or would he always remind her of the one whose love was not enough? And would Antonio ever go to college if they ran away together?

"You see?" he said. "You know what you want to do, and I need not ask." Antonio smiled sadly, but Siobhan saw the relief at having an excuse.

"I love you, Antonio." She took his hands in hers and placed them to her face as if he were her brother. "I will never forget you."

"No, you will not," he said, pulling his hands out of hers and rubbing his shoulder to his cheek to wipe away a tear. He took from his wide pocket a book wrapped in brown paper. The only marking was AMS. "This is for you. There is a special address inside. You must write. Then I'll know where you are, and I'll send you another book."

Antonio knew the way to her heart.

His fingers held fast to the package. It was as though the book demanded a commitment.

She traced her finger along his initials. AMS.

"What's your middle name?"

"Don't you want to know what's inside?"

"That's what I mean, Antonio M. Savelli. What's in the middle? What does 'M' stand for?"

"Maybe one day I'll tell you. Maybe after many more books!"

"That sounds like Rumpelstiltskin!" She tugged on the book.

"Every time you write, I'll send another."

She had her hands on the treasure, while he held fast. His eyes twinkled; he had her trapped. This was an agreement, she would write, he would send books. She had but three in her satchel. *The Bible, Jane Eyre, Wuthering Heights.* Whatever was beneath the brown paper would be her fourth.

"*I am no bird; and no net ensnares me: I am a free human being with an independent will.*" Siobhan quoted *Jane Eyre.* How she had loved that story and even more their discussion after reading it. She teased with another's truth.

"*I need not sell my soul to buy bliss. I have an inward treasure born with me,*" Antonio countered.

"Thees ees ah gooda story, no?" Siobhan asked in her best imitation Italian accent, ignoring his quotation to negotiate.

"Uh laaahng wan. Pairfec' fohr yer jairney an' for yerrrr." Antonio's Irish slipped away with his smile. And then he quoted in his own beautiful accent, "*Her coming was my hope each day, her parting was my pain.*"

Siobhan's eyes stung and she blinked back the sudden feeling that she, too, might cry. Why couldn't Giovanni have felt the same? And now it was too late with Antonio. She had tainted their friendship.

"I'll always know the right words for you, Siobhan."

"But they will always be someone else's?" The quotes, the sayings. What belonged to him?

"You'll probably finish it before you leave the station." Antonio left her question unanswered and reached into his other pocket to retrieve a second package also wrapped in brown paper and tied with twine. Her curiosity temporarily exceeded her loneliness and fear.

"A *fifth!*" She jumped up and down. "I'm going to number all of them! I'll have my own library!" And impulsively she threw her arms around Antonio as the whistle blew.

Chapter Nineteen
Erin

Seattle, Washington
July 1981

Erin dropped both suitcases on the floor of their Seattle motel while Claire took out a brand-new phone book for July 1981 through July 1982, zeroing in on Seattle Public Schools. "I have half of a name and the possibility Seattle was her home." Claire pointed to the list of high schools. "Aria is an unusual name. There can't be more than one."

But it didn't matter if Claire's biological mother's name was *Jennifer;* Erin knew Claire would visit every high school in the Seattle area, scanning every yearbook within a certain time frame until her mother was located. And if she exhausted Seattle without success, she would draw concentric circles around the city until they included the high school her mother attended. She'd visit every high school in Washington state if she had to. Her mother might not want to meet Claire, but Claire was determined to meet her.

Claire counted eleven public high schools listed in Seattle: Ballard, Cleveland, Franklin, Garfield, Nathan Hale, Ingraham, Rainier Beach, Roosevelt, Chief Sealth, West Seattle, and South Lake.

Claire calculated aloud that she would search ten yearbooks per school. The odds were that someone giving up a baby was between the ages of fifteen and twenty-four. She just had to look at the four classes from 1954, six years before she was born, through 1960.

That yearbook face would unknowingly smile back. What would that moment be like for Claire? When she saw Aria's name, would there also be a face that resembled hers? That face couldn't turn away. That face would lead her to the reason she had been rejected.

They began with Franklin and Garfield. When they came up empty-handed at Franklin, Erin wasn't surprised, she knew it couldn't be that easy.

Garfield was next. Garfield was a spectacular three-story brick building with huge windows. A sweeping staircase fanned upward leading to three arched doorways. Had Aria climbed these forty-plus stairs each day? Once inside, they looked for the library.

Claire opened the 1956–1957 yearbook, and Erin took out 1957–1958, and they began. Garfield High School Bulldogs wore purple and white and were highly successful at sports and music.

At first Erin scanned faces, curious how all the senior pictures looked alike: bouffant hair, pearl necklaces, and V-neck dresses. The photos were all ten years older than Erin. Soon she concentrated only on names, focusing on the female ones. The same 1940-era female names popped up: Mary, Linda, Barbara, Patricia, Carol, Sandra, and Nancy. Maybe having an unusual name wasn't such a bad thing.

When she hit the last yearbook for Garfield, she said a quick prayer that it would hold the answer—that Aria was a Bulldog, and their search was over.

There were a few A names which made her pause—*Angela, Amanda, Arnold. Arnold* made her stop and check the young man's face just to be sure. She laughed when she saw the peach fuzz mustache providing necessary comic relief.

But no Aria at Garfield. Claire was right. If in fact she found an Aria, it would be the only Aria in the Seattle area.

No matter, they still had time for one more school that day and chose Roosevelt High School near the University of Washington. The Roosevelt librarian was especially helpful, and he seemed curious about her search. "We keep ours in the library but remember that some schools store theirs in the main office. And it might be simpler to go to the local newspaper. They keep headshots in the event of accident or for obituaries." Claire shook her head. Erin knew she preferred the possibility that she studied in the same place her mother had once studied.

The green and gold Roosevelt Roughriders' yearbook was oddly titled: *Strenuous Life*. Erin examined the faces of girl after girl as Claire traced her finger down pages for someone who could have been her mother, who by now was possibly someone else's mother. The library would be closing soon. They had one more yearbook that Erin flipped through as quickly as possible, not wanting to miss anything, but also not wanting to waste time necessitating a return.

Suddenly, Erin spotted *Arie van der Riet*. That was the closest she got to Aria that day. She dropped the cover and closed the chapter on Roosevelt.

Eight more schools. The next day, instead of feeling renewed hope, each new yearbook that failed to turn up an Aria meant fear. How many high schools were there in the entire state of Washington, and what if they had to circle out of state? Just how far could Claire's search take her? How far was she willing to go physically and emotionally?

Chief Sealth and West Seattle didn't have a full set and that made Claire feel anxious, but she made a note of it and decided not to assume the missing yearbooks were the only link to her mother. Rainier Beach and South Lake followed. It was Friday when they hit the final three schools: Ballard, Ingraham and Nathan Hale. Erin could sense Claire hadn't prepared for the empty feeling when the northernmost school yielded nothing.

"What exactly are you looking for?" The librarian hadn't been particularly inquisitive before, but perhaps now that Claire was sitting in a daze and near tears, the librarian took more interest.

"I'm looking for someone. Everything is kind of a guess, but I think she went to high school in Seattle between 1956 and 1960. I've gone to eleven high schools this week and searched through so many yearbooks."

"This is a first for me." The librarian smiled, adjusting her glasses. "A hunt for someone!" She clapped her hands. "My name is Adele by the way." She extended her hand. "This sounds so fascinating."

Adele was the most sympathetic figure they'd encountered.

"All *eleven*. That must have taken some time. You might not know this, but since then some schools have closed. At least three. Their information is in archives at District Admin. There you'll find school newspapers, yearbooks, everything."

Three more chances.

"Broadway, Queen Anne, Lincoln." Adele wrote them on a piece of paper and handed the lifeline to Claire, who hugged her.

"It only takes one book. I hope you find what you're looking for."

It wasn't *what*, it was *who*.

"It's a sad thing when a school closes. A little bit of lost history." Lost history? Adele couldn't know.

Chapter Twenty
Siobhan

That it would always be summer and autumn,
and you always courting me,
and always thinking as much of me
as you have done through the past summertime!
—Thomas Hardy, *Tess of d'Urbervilles*

Train from Boston heading west
July 7–10, 1919

Siobhan resisted opening Antonio's book until the train pulled out of the station, and then even longer as they left Boston and she saw the city from a new perspective. This was an aboveground subway bullet shooting her across the nation. Her heartbeat quickened. What had she done, leaving everything she knew?

She clutched the book to her chest and sat back in her seat. The country fanned out beside her and she fell asleep holding her treasure. When she awoke, she had just enough light to see the package.

Should she open it now or just savor contemplating its contents? As soon as she knew the title, one of the joys of the present was gone and she'd have less to look forward to. But if she opened the package, she could just hold the book for a while and wonder what was inside. Should she limit herself to a few pages a day, unlike Antonio's prediction? Or should she begin immediately and read the book over and over, cover to cover?

She could even mark in this one; it was hers alone, not one of the many they read together in the library. Or was it? Maybe he was sharing a book that was special for them both? *Oh, Antonio—why did you know my heart better than your brother?*

At last, she peeled back the folded paper, knowing each precious crease was from Antonio's loving hands.

Siobhan was afraid to read too fast but unable to take it slowly. She was hungry for the plot, the setting, the characters, and the theme. All those fancy words she and Antonio had whispered about in the stacks of the Boston Public Library.

My Ántonia, by Willa Cather.

She studied the cover and felt the spine. Firm, sturdy. She opened the first page to see Antonio's handwriting.

For Siobhan, my friend across miles and words.

AMS

All the sunlight hours the next day were spent studying the landscape enfolding around her and reading her new book. Antonio wrote in the margins, responding to thoughts on the page. He asked her questions. He underlined passages. Reading the book and his notes by herself was almost better than reading it with Antonio. She knew his every thought and he cared about hers.

She liked that an orphan named Jim was riding the train like she was. But she became stressed when Mr. Shimerda killed himself. She resisted the urge to skip around.

Books were not as fixed to her as they were to others. If she disliked the story, she would lay in bed and imagine how different it could be. She fashioned other endings or skipped to the last page so she could relieve the pressure building within her. If she knew the resolution, she could go back and read, prepared for whatever unfolded ahead. She knew that devastating things happened between pages, and she knew that some characters survived and were stronger because of it.

As the train moved across the Midwest, her journey paralleled Jim's vision of *"never-ending miles of ripe wheat, by country towns."* Antonio sometimes underlined sections so beautiful, she blushed at the thought of his eyes sharing those pages; his fingers touching them. The words made her heart ache with the loneliness of his absence.

"I have a feeling that if you go away, you will not come back. Something

will happen to one of us, or to both. People have to snatch at happiness when they can, in this world. It is always easier to lose than to find. What I have is yours, if you care enough about me to take it."

The underlined passage was so personal. Why had he waited to share it until she was on a train leaving him behind?

Imaginably for the very reason he knew he had a different future ahead of him. No matter, she was moving away, in another direction, in so many ways.

Reading had proven oddly dizzying. The unfamiliar motion of the train, not seeing forward, and being trapped inside had left her feeling ill. She stepped to the back and unsuccessfully tried to keep the rollicking feeling inside her. Was this influenza? Not now! Not while she was on a train with no one to care for her! The passengers would be alarmed. She stood on the back of the train and finally convulsed what little she had eaten that day. The taste in her month repulsed her. Beads of sweat now dripped down her brow and suddenly she heaved over and over with nothing to show for her rhythmic spasms. Her hands gripped the railing as her body shivered and shook. So, this was how she would die. On a train bound for Washington.

When at last there was nothing in her and she was too weak to stand, she returned to her seat, folded her arms across her chest and doubled over. When the wave passed, she took out her book. She could only hope reading would take her mind off her nausea, but keeping her eyes down in a book only made the words swim in front of her. How she longed to read Antonio's second gift. *Pride and Prejudice* by Jane Austen. Another female author!

I declare after all there is no enjoyment like reading!
How much sooner one tires of anything than of a book!
—When I have a house of my own, I shall be miserable
if I have not an excellent library.

After three days, they entered Montana, which she learned was very wide. It could take days and she still had two states to go after that. When would this sickness go away? So many had died gruesome deaths, and yet she had experienced none of the other symptoms. She awaited blood from her ears, eyes, mouth, nose, but nothing. She checked for splotches. None. Was it as her Aintín said, something about the Irish?

The realization that little food remained was no hardship. A woman across the aisle continued to study her, then handed her a package wrapped in waxed paper and folded at the top. Uneeda Biscuit.

"This will make you feel better."

Siobhan opened it and nibbled on the cracker.

"Where are you headed?"

"Washington. I have a job as a cook in a logging company."

"Does your husband work there?"

"I'm not married."

"I see." But did she? Her former generosity now seemed tainted by criticism.

"You think you can work like that?"

"I'll be better by then." Siobhan blushed. Did the woman suspect she was contagious?

"Maybe. Maybe not. But you'll be in no position to be cooking for loggers."

"What do you mean?"

"Your condition."

"My condition?" Siobhan was embarrassed. The woman must know about the influenza. Would the woman make her get off the train?

"Surely you know."

Siobhan eyed the woman quizzically.

"You're with child."

Siobhan almost laughed. "I'm . . . I'm not . . ." she began, but then she had to consider the possibility. She knew so little. Giovanni was gentle. Giovanni said he was careful. But what did that mean? Her mother had never told her anything and certainly not Aintín. All she ever said was to stay away from those Italian boys. Was she really such an ignorant girl?

It was unthinkable that she could be traveling away from the only man she ever loved, carrying his child. Alone.

The compartment seemed to spin, and her head felt light. What was happening?

She had to get off the train. She couldn't keep moving farther away from Ireland and Boston. She needed time to figure out what to do.

She could always go to Seattle later. But she couldn't go any farther now. Words spun. *"I wish I were a girl again, half savage and hardy, and free . . . Why am I so changed?"*

Heathcliff. Catherine. Would it make a difference if Giovanni knew? Would he come for her? She remembered his last words, "I love you." But she also remembered they were to her back, in the safety of her walking away, and perhaps only in her imagination. Antonio? How would he feel knowing she was carrying his brother's child? What did it matter now? She didn't have the money to return home, and she certainly couldn't go back to Brigid. No, Boston was an impossibility. That would be worse than death. The next stop was Deer Lodge, Montana. Siobhan was getting off.

Chapter Twenty-One
Geneviève

Charlottesville, Virginia
January 1919

Villiam Ellis became her main patient. Both Field Hospital and Base Hospital had never successfully removed the shrapnel from William's leg, resulting in persistent, recurring infections. Another surgery at UVA Hospital removed what they hoped to be the remaining pieces. Now the wound was cleaned, and William's walking orders were to have the leg massaged, the bandages changed regularly, and additional therapy for full range of motion. Geneviève's attention to all aspects helped speed up William's recovery.

One doctor advised dancing for full range of motion on the leg. William hesitated, but Geneviève delighted in that prescription. And despite William's reluctance, it was doctor's orders, after all.

"I've been sentenced to dancing!"

"And you may not appeal."

"I'll tell you what appeals to me, Nurse Geneviève." He pulled her toward him and wrapped his arms around her. "I finish in May and take the bar exam at the end of July. Let's set the date."

"And if you *don't* pass the bar?" she teased.

"Oh, ye of little faith!" William laughed. "This defendant, pro se, pleads the question: Are our nuptials contingent upon my success?"

"Nolo contendere." She pounded her hand on his shoulder. Indeed, it was no contest. "You already sound just like a lawyer!"

"I won't just pass the bar. I'll raise it for all!"

"Well, let's see how you do on the dance floor first."

William groaned and twirled her until she landed in his arms.

On their first outing, William hid discomfort with humor.

"Don't you find it disturbing that all the dances have animal names?"

It was true: grizzly bear, turkey trot, bunny hug, camel walk. But dancing the foxtrot and listening to ragtime made Geneviève feel happy.

No matter the song, William tried to sing it, never even close to the pitch. But with his lips close to her ear, whispering "Look for the Silver Lining" and other songs full of hope, it didn't matter.

The instructor Bernard's voice was deep and husky. "Listen to the beat of the melody. Now try swaying to the left, then to the right. Or for the women, the right, to the left. Excellent! Now you can see you're mirroring each other!"

William started to laugh which gave Geneviève the giggles.

"Keep listening to the beat. Now we're going to try walking counterclockwise in a circle. Don't stomp, this is not the Virginia Reel."

"Step lightly. Use the balls of your feet. Not such big steps, we're not in a hurry. Now add the swaying motion. Always sway toward the foot that is moving. Your sway will cue your partner about the direction of your feet."

Apparently, it didn't work that way for William and Geneviève.

"Ouch."

"I'm sorry, Ginna."

"Now lead away from your partner, then step with the other foot, sway with that foot. Turn clockwise. Oh, Mr. Ellis, don't run into anything."

"When do we get to tango?" William suggested, too loudly in her ear.

"You're a little way from the tango, Mr. Ellis."

"War injury." Will pointed down at his foot and Bernard nodded sympathetically.

Later that night, they celebrated over floats.

"I don't really think about the pain when I'm with you."

"But I do," she said, rubbing her feet.

"Here, let me check." He bent down to the floor on his good leg. "Don't do that!" she cautioned, still worried about undue pressure on his leg. "Be careful, Shakespeare!" His one pair of suit pants would be so dusty when he stood.

"Geneviève, you always care for me." He reached in his pocket and extracted a box. "I want to care for you, too. In sickness and in health. Will you marry me, Geneviève Marchand?"

And then he started humming. So dreadfully and out of tune, she had no idea the song until at last he sang the words "Let me Call You Sweetheart" and all she could do was laugh.

Chapter Twenty-Two
Siobhan

If she be all tenderness, she will die.
If she survives, the tenderness will either be crushed out of her,
or—and the outward semblance is the same—crushed so deeply
into her heart that it can never show itself more.
—Nathaniel Hawthorne, *The Scarlet Letter*

Deer Lodge, Montana
July 10, 1919

Siobhan stepped off the train at Deer Lodge and headed toward the lights of town. She walked past Hotel Deer Lodge and then found Main Street, a place far different from the boroughs and warrens of Boston. Looking to her right, she saw a terribly imposing structure. With each turret lit and a guard standing sentry, it appeared to be a castle. What was it and where was she?

Siobhan smoothed her disheveled hair and lugged her small suitcase along the sidewalk, wondering where she should go and how far her money would take her before she needed to start working, and if she could find a job in her *condition*.

"Kate's Place's back thatta way." A man leaned against the building, his voice thick and his breath reeking of alcohol. "Katie Sullivan'll take care of ya." Siobhan squinted. The way he gawked at her made her uncomfortable. But maybe she should head in that direction? What was Kate's Place?

A woman came from behind and took her elbow.

"Is that what you want?" Her voice was husky but warm, as if she could've been a jazz singer. "It's a bordello."

Bordello. That word from a book she began but never had time to finish. *Oliver Twist.* A boy born in a workhouse and a woman—Nancy, who worked for men. *Bordello.* A place where women were paid to do what she had done with Giovanni for free.

"Whorehouse." The woman guessed her ignorance. "Look, just don't talk to someone like that." She studied Siobhan up and down. "You're new here. Do you have a name? A place?"

"I . . . just got off the train." Siobhan's head felt light. A bordello? This wasn't what she wanted. Not for her or the baby. "Miss Kildea. I need a job. A place."

The woman smiled. "You're a long way from home."

She was. But what was home now? How could she answer.

"Sometimes this hotel hires in the dining room or kitchen. It's a busy place." A *Brigid.* Like mother, like daughter. "You look like you need to sit down. Here, let's go in the lobby."

Housing. Job. Baby. Her head was swimming and she barely got in the door before she doubled over, holding her hands over her face. The woman pushed her down a hall and into a bathroom near the rear. Siobhan raced to the ceramic bowl on the dresser top and once again was sick.

The woman turned away politely, then from the pitcher poured water onto a linen and wiped Siobhan's face. "It could be this way for nine months, or it might only last for three."

If Siobhan were reading a novel, would this be the most climactic part? Would this be where she skipped to the final pages to find out how it all resolved? Could there be a happy ending for the main character?

"My name is Millie. Maybe I can help."

Millie's hair was thick and shiny. She seemed older than Siobhan and yet not. Millie had thrown a shawl over her dress—a dress Siobhan would not see in any Boston church. Everything about the dress seemed as if it were meant to come off, with little beneath.

"You? You work at Kate's Place?"

"Don't judge a book by its cover." Millie leaned against the marble wall. The entire room felt nearly elegant enough to be in the Boston Library. Millie put her arm around Siobhan and guided her back into the main lobby of the hotel, then left, returning with a glass of water.

"I don't think you're here to work for Kate." She sighed and looked around the lobby like she needed to leave, as if there were something important out there in the night. "But I can't leave you like this. I don't know what you're doing here. So, you need to talk. Now."

Siobhan had never met someone quite so direct, but she also didn't think there was another person who could help her. Millie had already figured out why she had gotten off, so she told her story.

"You don't have a lot of options." Millie was so honest. Painfully honest. Millie tapped her leg as if perplexed. "Wait here. There's someone you need to meet."

The Hotel Deer Lodge was stately and handsome, perhaps one of the grandest hotels she'd ever seen, with its oak woodwork, marble slab windowsills, and ornate vent covers. Siobhan studied the twenty-foot ceiling of the lobby. The hotel had a rugged elegance, sturdy, protective, a manliness about it that said it could take care of her.

Could she afford this hotel? If not, where was she sleeping for the night? Then what about the next night and the night after that? How soon could she get a job? She collapsed on the velvet sofa. Another wave of nausea rose within her, and she tensed her body until it passed. How long could she work if she were this sick? When was the last time she'd eaten anything?

Siobhan curled her body inward and set her head on the armrest. When was the last time she'd had a night of uninterrupted sleep? There had been too many changes too fast. Her life felt out of control, and she felt so alone.

"Hello, ma'am." A voice. A pleasant but unfamiliar voice, gentle, almost soothing. "Millie sent me." He stood over her. Did she know him? "Are you Miss Kildea?"

Who was he? Where was Millie? Why was he here?

He took off his hat and fanned her face, then sat on the couch facing her. He was a blurred figure. She blinked quickly to adjust her eyes as she sat up, straightened her clothing, and smoothed her hair.

"I'm sorry to wake you. Are you Miss Kildea?"

"My name is Siobhan Kildea." Of that she was certain. Everything else was muddled.

He tilted his head as if something surprised him.

"*Shah-vahn.*" He spoke her name like someone who had never been confused by the spelling. "Siobhan Kildea." He smiled.

Her eyes now focused, she estimated he was five to ten years her senior. Brown hair, slightly wet and combed as if he had just cleaned up. Crisp shirt and pants. Nothing fancy. He held his hat in his hands. His eyes studied her. Blue. So very blue.

Kate's Place. No. No. She couldn't do this. How could Millie even think . . . ?

"I'm sorry. I . . . I cannot."

He shook his head. His eyes full of concern. "I understand. I wasn't sure I could either."

There was something sad about him. As if life had done him harm. She would have to explain.

"I just got here. I was supposed to go to Seattle. To cook." Siobhan was waking up, but from what? Why had she left Boston? Was she crazy? "Millie . . ." And then she found herself crying.

"I'm sorry." The man pulled out a handkerchief. "Here." But instead of handing it to her, he began to dry her eyes as if she were a child. "Sorry. Don't have a lot of practice at this. My son is just a baby."

"You have a son? Where is he?"

"With Millie."

Siobhan frowned. He left his son with her?

She wanted to ask: *why would you do that? Why Millie? Where was the boy's mother? Or was Millie the boy's mother?* She was so tired, and nothing made sense anymore, she still couldn't believe that she, herself, was going to have a baby.

"My wife just died." His voice caught as if he needed to clear his throat. "In childbirth." He wiped his forehead with his arm like a farmer in the field.

Siobhan cringed for so many reasons. At her rash judgment of a man who had just experienced such loss, the sudden fear she had for herself, the panic of who would take care of her own child, and the idea that he would consort with Millie so soon after his loss.

"I have a small farm and I have a job at the mill." He wrung his hat between his hands. "That provides for us. But now, I don't know how I'll be able to work and take care of him."

"Does he have a name?" Somehow it seemed strange he spoke of the boy as a stranger.

"We never really decided. It was always going to be Anna if it was a girl. My wife's name was Annabeth."

"I'm so sorry."

He nodded, then cocked his head. "I was thinking of Samuel." He stared off into the distance as if trying the name on for size.

"It's a very good name." Siobhan's voice came out so weak she wondered if he heard.

"And my name is Jack." He extended his hand. "Jack Mason." Then he repeated her name softly, "Siobhan," sounding it out so slowly as if savoring the syllables.

"And *Samuel*. Yes, I think Samuel Jacob. Thank you for helping name him."

She didn't think she deserved any credit. She had just listened. Just like he was doing for her.

He helped her move to her sofa, leaving space between them.

"I wonder where Millie has gone?" Siobhan searched around for the only person she knew, to relieve her of their imposed date.

"I like the sound of your voice," he said, breaking the silence.

"I'm sorry I can't be who Millie wants me to be." Siobhan tapped her fingers on her knees nervously.

"No, it's asking a lot. I understand."

"Did she say she'd be returning?"

"I don't know. I'm not sure." Jack looked about the lobby. "I suppose you'll want to be on your way." Jack seemed to share her discomfort with the situation.

"I don't know. I'm not sure," she repeated, then rolled her eyes in apology. She hadn't meant to imitate him or make fun of his answer.

How much had Millie told Jack about her condition? Would Seattle be any better than Deer Lodge? Was there a way to stay here? At least for a while until she figured out what to do next? She didn't dislike the place, then again, she'd only seen it by dark.

"Sometimes ranchers or bankers need a nanny for their kids. You could stay." He paused. "That is, if you wanted."

Did she want to? Ranchers and bankers? She didn't know any ranchers or bankers.

"Or maybe you still want to go to Washington?" His last sentence sounded like a disappointed statement, not a question. But it needed answering both for him and for herself.

"My neighbor and his wife have two children. They have a little bedroom in their home. I could ask Naomi if you could rent it? If you really want to cook, there might be an opening at the hotel?"

A room? That was all she heard. She felt like Mary to his protective Joseph. She could have been kinder to him. He must have his own needs.

"It was too much. I knew it. To take on a child that's not your own." Jack's voice was so soothing. "Marry someone you don't know. Hoping you might fall in love over time?" He shook his head as if in disbelief and smiled to himself.

Jack's words took all the air out of the room. Siobhan felt dizzy, lightheaded. Confused. Was that the arrangement?

"That's what you're asking?"

"Well, yes. Millie had thought . . ." His voice drifted off and he focused directly on her. His eyes were so blue. "My child needs a mother. I wish I had time to find someone who would want to be my wife." He wasn't embarrassed, just honest, frank. She liked that. "But he's not well, and I don't know anything about babies." He was back to twisting his hat. "I love my son. *Samuel.*" He tried out the name, so unfamiliar and nodded.

"Did Millie speak to you? Did she tell you about me?" Siobhan wrung her hands like he did his hat.

Jack took a deep breath and took his time figuring out what to say. "She said we both might have to love someone else's child. And she said with that, we might learn to love each other."

Siobhan gasped. That was a shock. So much from a woman for whom, only an hour before, she felt such disdain. Did Millie know more about Jack than Siobhan could give her credit for? Was Millie looking out for them both? Why would she care at all?

Was this ridiculous arrangement a reasonable solution? Whatever was wrong with Jack's son, maybe she could help. Samuel needed a mother and the child she carried needed a father. A home.

Giovanni? She didn't think he would come. She could go back, but there was no room for a pregnant Irish girl in the Savelli family. Brigid? Never. She could write Antonio, but that would take time and what if he didn't come? Or worse, what if he *did*?

Would she destroy Antonio's dreams when she had already turned her back on him? She would owe Antonio a lifetime of missed opportunities. She owed Jack nothing. He owed her nothing. She would start out on equal footing. He didn't love her, and she didn't love him, but there was enough to like.

"Millie could be right." SSiobhan tilted her head and almost smiled past the stabbing pain in her heart. Jack's eyes were warm. Was it just his grief or relief that a decision was made? Whichever, he nodded to her, and inside she felt the beginnings of hope.

Chapter Twenty-Three
Erin

Seattle, Washington
July 1981

If Aria couldn't be found in a high school library, Erin had her doubts she'd be found in the basement of the Seattle School District Administration Building.

"You can at least rule out Broadway High." The woman guarding the tomb of cardboard boxes waved her arm dismissively. "It was shut down before that time. The other two only recently closed. Just this June."

Would Aria be in one of those two boxes? She could hope, couldn't she? Where to begin? The process always took so much time.

"Queen Anne or Lincoln, Mom?" Claire asked.

"Well, Lincoln is your favorite President and Grandpa drove a Lincoln, so . . ."

"Lincoln it is!"

Lincoln was a three-year school, which, after seventy-four years, had closed in June. What were the odds? They perused the shelves until arriving at Totem yearbooks from which they pulled 1956 through 1960. Erin scanned '56–'57, while Claire worked on '57–'58. Erin calculated that if Aria were a sophomore in '57, then Aria would have given birth at about age nineteen.

The Lincoln Totem was in crimson and black with Homer M. Davis as principal. Erin scanned the fine print down the edge of each page for three grade levels. Instead of feeling like they were narrowing their search, it felt like something was floating away. That somehow the process got harder. She didn't have many more Lincoln yearbooks to search. Then Queen Anne. Erin was already anticipating throwing her net wider, to Shoreline or Northshore or Lake Washington.

Claire gasped with a shivery breath.

"Mom!" Her daughter pointed a shaky finger at a page.

Aria K. Hanson. Hanson. She had a last name. *Hanson.* And a middle initial. Erin didn't want to look at the picture. What if Aria looked nothing like her and they didn't know what to do? Without matching the side list with the number of faces, Erin scanned the page to see if she could recognize her.

It wasn't difficult. Aria gazed at her with a quiet confidence, eyes warm and dark. Erin thought it would be easy to talk to somebody like that. Or at least, it should have been, if Aria wanted to meet Claire.

Claire then laid out the next two years on the table. Her mother's junior and senior years. One year her smile was big, bright, happy. Almost as if she couldn't contain her joy. Her eyes sparkled, and she looked like someone who made everyone laugh. As in so many pictures, her hair was parted down the middle and hung below her shoulders; thick hair, like Claire's. If only the book were in color, so they could find out if Aria's hair was reddish brown like Claire's. Each time they opened a new yearbook, Erin hoped Aria was there and had not moved away or worse yet—quit.

By looking at the back section with alphabetized names and pages, they discovered Claire's mother's involvement in choir, tennis, the Totem school newspaper, and the Lincolnian talent show. In addition, Aria was in the Honor Society and French Club.

In Aria's senior year, she was listed on fifteen pages. "Where are they going next?" was the section where the seniors listed their colleges. There was a full page spread on how Aria had won an audition that let her perform with the Seattle Opera. Aria was going to New York School of Music and Drama.

But it was the last listing that made Claire smile. Aria had played Julie Jordan in Carousel. And more importantly, her mother had graduated.

After copying every page her mother was listed on, the librarian pointed out there were school newspapers as well.

The Totem was published three times a year. Aria Hanson was found in every newspaper during her junior and senior years. She had sung at church events, Memorial Day celebrations, Lincoln Day, and even a ribbon cutting. Then there was a half page write-up about Lincoln seniors destined for greatness. There she was, with a description of her full scholarship.

From the payphone at the library, Erin made phone calls to the Conservatory, trying to reach someone before the offices closed. Here the trail ran cold for forwarding addresses. Aria Hanson had never graduated. Maybe that's when Claire had interrupted her life.

The two then headed to the King County Courthouse where they learned that in 1971, eleven years after giving birth to Claire, Aria Hanson had become Aria McMahon. There was a Benjamin McMahon listed in Arlington, Washington. Finding the address and phone number was easy with a name.

Back at their motel, they argued about what to do next.

"We need to wait, Claire."

"I know. I know." Claire dropped back on the bed and exhaled loudly. "Dad doesn't think I should do it."

"That's true. Aria didn't want contact." Erin thought of all the things Chase and she had talked about late into the night. *She doesn't want to be found. What if there are reasons for secrecy? What is this doing to her? And the worst question: what if her own family doesn't know?*

Erin was touched at the tender concern Chase had about the birth mother's feelings. Sometimes, though, he seemed to care more about the birth mother than Claire. He claimed it was all *related*. Ironic choice of words.

"I think if she sees me, that will make a difference. She just has to *see* me," Claire pleaded.

Erin closed her eyes and said a silent prayer. She didn't know if she was more afraid for Aria, or for her daughter, or for herself.

"I just wonder what she sounds like. Then again, calling might not be a good idea. She might just hang up."

"And what if someone else answers?"

As if on cue, the phone rang, putting their discussion on hold.

There was a message for Erin to call Chase at her earliest convenience. She didn't know what to expect. Elizabeth? Evan? What was wrong?

"Honey, I need you to come home." Chase's voice was calm but urgent.

"We've just found her, Chase. We're going to Arlington." Erin blurted.

"It's Mom. Geneviève's in the hospital." Chase sighed.

"What happened to her?" questioned Erin, her voice full of concern. Claire lifted her palms and gave Erin a questioning look.

"She walked there. I think she thought she was going to work or something. I don't know. I never know anymore." Chase's voice sounded exhausted and sad.

"Is she all right?" Now Claire came close to try to hear both sides of the conversation.

"Just shook up. I have her back at home now. But I need to activate the opening in Summer Meadows."

Did Claire hear that? She wasn't going to like this.

Chase continued as if needing to justify his decision.

"She fell. She was laying by the side of the road and somebody found her. Here I am running an organization to help widows in their distress, and I can't even protect my own mother." His voice held the weight of guilt. "I can't do it all, Erin."

"I can be there tonight. I'll get a late flight. We'll figure this out together."

When Erin got off the phone, she updated Claire on GinnaBee's accident and cautioned her that they couldn't keep GinnaBee safe anymore. There was another room available; it was time to activate the reservation. She needed a place with full-time care and rehabilitation. For once, Claire seemed to understand.

"What tests did they do? Activity. Pulse. Grimace. Appearance. Respiration. What do they do for someone like GinnaBee?"

"I don't know, Claire. I'll find out and then we'll sort out your information. I'll help Chase move GinnaBee into the new place and get her situated and then I'll fly back. Then we'll go see Aria together."

She couldn't say it. She just couldn't call her *your mom*. Not yet. Maybe never.

Claire stared ahead, seemingly processing everything.

"Did you know that it was really someone's name? Dr. Virginia Apgar. She saved so many lives. She was a really good doctor. Like GinnaBee was such a good nurse."

"Oh, Claire. Just hold tight. Go to the Seattle Center. Woodland Park Zoo. Go on a ferry. Take a ride up the Space Needle. I'll be back in a few days and we can do this together. Just promise me you'll wait, Claire. Promise me you'll wait."

Chapter Twenty-Four
Siobhan

The miracle happened;
one of those quiet moments that clutch the heart,
and take more courage than the noisy, excited passages in life.
—Willa Cather, *My Ántonia*

Deer Lodge, Montana
July 10, 1919

After the world's shortest engagement, there was little romance in Jack and Siobhan's wedding ceremony that followed. Especially since she was a pregnant Irish Catholic girl at a Presbyterian church in the middle of nowhere.

It was nothing Siobhan had ever imagined from her days in Ireland. But she did have one Irish lace handkerchief made by her mother. Though other Irish brides needed a special handkerchief to dry their tears, she doubted she'd cry. Millie had picked a few roses and Siobhan wrapped the flowers in the piece of woven cloth. Someday she would repurpose the lace into a christening bonnet for Samuel. She had asked Jack for a horseshoe and a rope, and he had supplied both without question. She laid the horseshoe on the front pew for good luck. Before the vows, she had instructed the minister to tie Jack's and her wrists together. The minister only agreed to the handfasting ritual after she explained that it was a part of two becoming one. He then included that verse in his message.

She wore the only other dress in her satchel, an appropriate dark green one that highlighted her red hair. In Ireland, blue was the color of innocence and purity, not that anyone in Deer Lodge knew about her or would care about that tradition.

The minister asked a few questions. Questions that seemed so permanent. *Do you promise to love?* What was love? She felt nothing for this man. Was it a lie? Or just a decision? *Honor and cherish?* Would he do this for her? In the little she had observed, she could only hope. *Till death do us part.* Now till death, her life was tied to his. There would be no more Giovanni. No Antonio. Her life was his. Her child was his—or so she hoped. Was this a good thing? Her heart raced. She glanced at Millie, who smiled and nodded.

"I do," she heard herself say. He slid the ring of his first wife on to her pinkie.

They had made a trade. *I will love your son if you will love my child.* Whether they loved one another would come with time. Though a marriage of convenience, two children forced a commitment that would not be broken.

You're not ready to be a mother, you're not ready to be a mother rang in her head. Brigid's prophecy. Ready or not, soon she'd be the mother of two.

"By joining hands, you are consenting to be bound together as husband and wife. You are promising to honor, love, and support each other for the rest of your lives. By the authority vested in me by the laws of the state of Montana, I now pronounce you husband and wife." It was a good thing the ceremony was short because sickness came quickly as Siobhan ran for the door.

Millie, now her oldest friend in town, embraced her. Jack picked her up in the carriage instead of his car. She held Samuel in her arms as they neared the little bungalow lit by moonlight.

Jack made no apologies. In fact, he seemed to sit taller and thus, in her mind, so did his little house. He nodded to the barn, and the fields beyond, as if he had been longing to get out of town and back to his first love. But how could she, Siobhan, be the heart of a home that had only just lost the wife? What rights did she have to assume Annabeth's hearth, her child, and Jack's warmth?

The moon was almost full. Just a smidge shaved off. A porch swing swung slightly in the breeze and Siobhan smiled though she knew not why. Jack jumped off the carriage and came to her side, taking one hand as she held the baby in the crook of her arm. It wasn't natural yet. Not the way she should hold a child, or carry a child, or even to be touched by a stranger who was now her husband. He glanced up and smiled, too, and she wondered what he had to smile about. Were they smiling because it was all so strange?

Not long ago, his wife had died, leaving him with a colicky baby. Now he had married a stranger who was pregnant with another man's child. She was quite sure life had dealt him harder blows than hers.

He released her until they got to the front porch, where he took her elbow and guided her up the stairs. He stood a head above her, and with his broad shoulders and stance, Jack seemed like a giant. He was so serious, but beneath those deep blue eyes was laughter. One day she could make him laugh.

Jack opened the door and then stopped and looked at her expectantly. "Sometimes we carry the bride across the threshold."

"No." She shook her head, moving forward before him as they both sighed with what she assumed was relief.

With the room lit, she took it in. The main floor had four rooms anchored by a staircase. Compared to her Bostonian apartment, this was spacious.

Somebody had once kept this house neat and orderly, but no longer. Blankets strewn on the couch. Stacks of papers, a floor that needed sweeping, laundry in a woven basket, and the smell of the diapers. Her stomach churned. Jack had not known that he'd bring a bride across the threshold this evening.

She was drawn to a dark corner; there stood an upright piano. She ran her fingers over the top, leaving tracks in the dust.

"Do you play?" Jack opened the lid, and his fingers ran scales, both hands working in parallel motion.

To have music meant there was life in the room. She could try to poke out a melody.

"No. Not really." She sat down on the needlepoint piano bench. The ivory keys were chipped and broken, but that made the piano more beautiful. Like a face with wrinkles, having laughed and cried a lifetime of songs.

Still holding Samuel in one arm, she played a few notes, enough to hear that the piano was grotesquely out of tune, which made her love it even more. The off-kilter sound had character, infused with an extra vibration or twang that could only come from being hauled from somewhere else and having endured seasons of both warmth and cold.

"This was my wife's. She could play." How many people had crowded around this piano and sung a carol? There was no way Siobhan could make those kinds of sounds on the piano—orchestrated, composed, purposeful. Siobhan's would be playful, inventive, creative. She would never be as good as Annabeth.

"A piano makes a house a home, I think." Siobhan rose, then lowered the baby into the cradle. The cradle that Annabeth had never placed her child within. Jack pointed out the sitting room. "This is where we eat. The sun comes up here in the morning." The four small rooms were sparsely decorated. Plain but simple and Siobhan liked that. He led her to the kitchen; he showed her the bottles and milk for the baby, then the bedroom off the sitting room with a double bed and a wedding ring quilt, no doubt made for Jack and Annabeth. On the dresser was a picture of their wedding.

What should she say? What was next? She'd never slept on a bed with a man. He didn't look at her.

"This will be your room. No stairs. That will be good." Then he pointed upward. "There are two rooms upstairs, one on each side. One day the baby and his . . ." Jack stopped. "And the other baby will have rooms."

Jack took the photograph off the dresser and headed upstairs alone.

Later that evening, when the baby was fed and sleeping, she crawled out of bed. Her bare feet tiptoed across the wooden floor of the sitting room. Her white nightshirt glowed in the dark. Heavy on her shoulder was her single red braid laying across her breast. She found pen and paper and an envelope in the beautiful rolltop desk that had been Annabeth's. She moved aside the stamp of AM, placed it in the bottom drawer, and began her first letter as Mrs. Mason, though for now, she would just sign it as Siobhan.

Dear Antonio . . .

Chapter Twenty-Five
Siobhan

I don't think I was homesick. If we never arrived anywhere,
it did not matter.
Between that earth and that sky I felt erased, blotted out.
I did not say my prayers that night: here, I felt, what would be would be.
—Willa Cather, *My Ántonia*

Deer Lodge, Montana
July 11, 1919

Siobhan awakened to the sun rising in her window, a beautiful pink glow. Where was she? It was such a strange bed and unfamiliar bedroom. Was it just a dream? Or a nightmare? Or had she made one of the most impulsive decisions of her short life?

Then she remembered a terribly fitful night of crying and pacing hardwood floors and then the crying continuing up the stairs like a lingering fragrance until a door was shut. She yawned in confusion.

Siobhan drew the comforter about her shoulders and moved to the window, taking in the extended farmlands and the mountains beyond. Inspired by the wide-open space, she slipped out of bed and ran to the kitchen for a better view. Never had she seen that much blue sky and endless mountains, and it was right in her own backyard. How different this was from her Charlestown fire escape. This was new and alive, and an untamed beauty.

Siobhan had slept in much longer than he had, and the smell of bacon and coffee remained, setting off her stomach. She ran outside and lost whatever she had last eaten. When had she last eaten?

Sheep bleated a greeting, chickens ran free in the yard, and Jack's laundry hung on the line. Men's long johns. She had to blush. The man whose body fit in that underwear was her husband. She was married. She ran her hand along the rough-hewn zigzag of the jackleg fence and was greeted by a zealous pig.

And then the smells and her tiredness overcame her and once again she felt the telltale signs of the life within her. After relieving herself, she walked the vegetable garden, studying what Annabeth must have planted earlier this spring. Everything seemed parched. When was the last time it had been watered?

Then she heard a baby cry and remembered, it was hers! She rushed back into his house, *their* house, and found the child. His diaper was soiled through. Holding him with one arm, she searched the house for a clean cloth, hoping that in his short life, they had not already exhausted the supply.

When taking off the heavy, soiled diaper, Samuel sprayed wildly until she grabbed a dish cloth and covered him. "Oh my!" She giggled, tickling his tummy. Then she wrapped his bottom and legs and gave him his bottle as a reward. "I'm sorry, Samuel. I have to admit I'm not too good at this whole thing yet."

She smoothed her hand over his head. To be truthful, there was nothing cute about him. His face was shriveled, and his limbs were scrawny sticks. Was it normal that a baby's arms and legs should be so long? And his fingers? They looked as if a child's! But his head was that of a little old man. She hadn't really seen a baby so bald before. But then, as the youngest child, and infrequent visitor to her sister's family, she hadn't really seen many babies. Jack didn't know she was the youngest and had no experience with babies. To think he was entrusting his only child to her care.

Samuel had a sweetness she'd never smelled before. His skin was so soft, almost as if dusted with flour. She soon figured out she had to hold his head carefully. Samuel liked it best when he was nestled between her chin and shoulder. If she sandwiched him and pressed her cheek down, he settled in. But when he fell asleep and she tried to put him down, he fussed. At last, she gave up and left him in the cradle to cry. What would Annabeth have done?

I am so sorry, Annabeth. She ran her fingers along the piano keys to drown out his cries. She created tunes from memories in her heart and Samuel's sobs softened. Perhaps he was familiar with this piano, grown in Annabeth's womb next to these very keys. Except Annabeth probably played much better.

Siobhan put on her dress to explore the front yard. The front walk lined with flowers was a work of art now drooping in the heat. The blossoms clung to life in the dry dusty soil, but their master gardener was gone.

Now Siobhan wanted to know all their names, but she could hardly count the varieties. The garden was a faded rainbow of colors in ordered stripes. Siobhan thought she would have preferred throwing seeds and having a garden of disarray. But Annabeth must have loved order. She would have been sad to see her flowers dying. Oh, what was she like? Was she happy here? Did she ever get to hold her baby? There was so much Siobhan didn't know.

Turning back toward Jack and Annabeth's house, a little white bungalow with blue shutters, she wondered what her Mam and Da would think. This was nothing like the mud huts in Ireland. The clachan, clustered homes of one-room cottages with dirt floors and a hearth with a fire where people told stories, recited poems, and sang. Where potatoes roasted over fires of peat bogs and spongy soil. Or even the cabin-like house she'd grown up in while living in Kilrush. Certainly not like the walk-up tenement in Boston. Here the ocean was grasslands rolling and waving in the wind. Cattle with long horns. Tall purple flowers whose name she wanted to learn. Mountains that framed the valley and a river that appeared to cascade on forever.

Back inside Jack's house, the grandfather clock kept time moving forward even when she wasn't sure what she should do all day. Siobhan went to her room and rummaged through her suitcase to find her treasures. Over the hearth, next to the stuffed bunny, obviously an unused baby gift for Samuel, she placed six books. The beginning of her library. She would write more letters and the library would grow.

After washing every diaper she could find, Siobhan took off her apron and cradled Samuel in it, securely fastening him about her neck.

Still barefoot, the straw and hay crisp beneath her feet felt unusual but pleasant as she explored the barn.

She could call this place home. It had a fresh and earthy warmth. It was just as Johanna Spyri's *Heidi*, one of her favorite books, had described and everything she'd longed for. Tentatively, she climbed the ladder to the haymow where she opened the upper barn doors and let in the summer breeze.

She cradled the baby so his head nestled beneath her chin. Here she felt safe and Samuel, too, had quieted.

"Samuel," she would say and touch his nose. "Samuel." One disrupted bale displayed a rustic softness. She spread a horse blanket over it and pretended just for a moment that she really was Heidi in Grandfather's loft, where she prepared a bed beneath the circular window that looked out over the mountains. She thought perhaps she had never felt so at peace.

All night she slept soundly on her bed of hay, dreaming of nothing but of shining mountains with red roses all over them. . . . Heidi was awakened early the next morning by a loud whistle; the sun was shining through the round window and falling in golden rays on her bed . . .

"Siobhan! Siobhan! Siobhan!"

She heard a voice. But whose? Where was she? A barn? Where was the baby?

It was a man. She was up high, but not on a rooftop. It was not Giovanni.

"Siobhan!" The barn door slid open and then began to close until she heard a tiny mewing beside her. Like a lamb, but different.

"Siobhan!" Who was yelling at her? His voice sounded angry. Her head spun. "What are you doing up there!"

"I . . . I was looking at the view." Her head spun.

"Where's the baby? Where's my son?" He stood at the bottom of the ladder. "Where's Samuel?"

She wondered, too.

Samuel whimpered softly as if to answer.

"You took him up there?"

She fastened the sling and secured Samuel within, then descended the ladder. Jack put his arms around her hips to steady her, then took the baby from her which made Samuel break into screams.

"Why did you do that? What were you thinking?" He clutched his son. "Don't ever do that again!"

"I can't go in the barn?"

"No. I mean yes. I thought . . . I just thought. I was so scared."

"You thought *what*?"

"No. Never mind."

"You thought *what*?" Her voice was steady. There was something wrong.

"I thought you left. You took him. Your suitcase." Jack yelled over Samuel's sobs.

"It's under the bed. I haven't unpacked."

"There's nothing for dinner."

"I fell asleep."

"You can't do that."

"Fall asleep? Or not make dinner?"

He gasped and let out a shuddering breath.

What had she done? Did she really marry him? Who was he but some terribly broken man with a hot temper?

"You thought I ran away." Who did she sound like? Cold and mean.

"What else could I think?"

Her mind reeled. So that was what he thought of her. That she could pick up his son and leave. That she was not strong enough to last a day in Montana.

"You ran away from Boston."

"Did I?" Her voice sounded so sharp.

"Well, I don't know . . ."

The baby's sobs continued, she reached for him, and Jack finally let him go. She nestled Samuel's head beneath her chin. She might not be a good mother—yet, but she knew he was hungry. She had kept him too long without milk. This poor motherless little boy with only a child for a stepmother. No, she'd never be a child again. That part of her was gone.

"You left and I don't know why." He studied the way the baby curled his head against Siobhan's neck and the way she tucked him in.

Was he asking her? Or was he just afraid she'd leave again? If he didn't know the reason she left Boston, would he worry that it would happen again? Did he deserve an answer?

"Because there was no one to love me. No one." Her voice was cold and hurt and broken. Why not tell him? There was nothing to lose. Start off with honesty. "And it seems it is the same in Montana."

As she passed him, he reached for her arm, but she shrugged him off.

"Samuel is hungry." She slid the door closed between them.

The child's suckling silenced his sobs and when she heard his father enter the house, she put the baby in the cradle and the bottle by his bed, then slammed the bedroom door. She put her fist in her mouth so that Jack would not hear her own involuntary sobs, drawing blood biting down so hard, but preferring that pain to the one ripping through her heart. Her head pounded holding back her grief. She couldn't have left Samuel! That funny-looking bald child who looked more like an old man than a baby. Could no one understand her?

She did not come out for dinner. Let him make his own. And though she heard Samuel cry, she was reassured by Jack's pacing. He hadn't even removed his boots. Nothing was going to get her to leave her room.

The next morning, she heard the knock. Should she answer? She had slept in her underclothes from the day before and still smelled of hay.

"Siobhan!" His voice was firm.

She answered through the door, separated by inches. She was Brigid. She was everything Brigid ever said about her. She was a bad mother and she had married a man she didn't even know. Maybe he was a man just like her father. Who was her father? How did her father imprint her life?

"He wants you." She considered that idea. There was something in it that sounded beautiful. "He needs you."

Her palm rested on the door. Steadied her. Was his on the other side? She said nothing.

"I . . . want you . . . to come out." It wasn't a command. There was something gentle in his voice. Firm, but it said he wanted her, too. The door wasn't locked. He could come in at any time. It was his home, after all, and she was his wife.

She thought it strange he didn't try the door. Was there any part of him that wanted to come in? To see her again? How were they to be married if he didn't? Then again, she hadn't exactly invited him into her life.

She slowly turned the handle and opened the door, and with it perhaps a piece of her heart. Jack had signs of exhaustion written on his face, his eyes were swollen. There was a measure of relief to his expression when he saw her. He studied her as if seeing her for the first time. Then again, they had only just met, barely any daylight hours had passed between them. Annabeth had only been in the grave for a little over a week and here Siobhan was, standing in front of the widower in barely a nightgown. What had she gotten herself into?

He reached his hand to her hair and shyly pulled a long piece of straw as if part of a magic act.

"You said you left because no one loved you. You thought it was the same here." His gaze was intense, but she didn't look away. Never had she seen such blue eyes. Giovanni's were so dark she couldn't tell their color. Antonio's? As warm and brown as the earth around this farm.

He took her suddenly in his arms and embraced her. Not gently, but abruptly. She almost fought except that she needed to be held and she thought perhaps he did, too. She tucked her head against his neck just where she had cradled Samuel against her. She wasn't sure what any of it meant except that she drew on his strength and she would let him feel her warmth.

Chapter Twenty-Six
Geneviève

Richmond, Virginia
August 2–December 1921

Dorothy Louise Marchand chose St. Paul's Episcopal, situated directly across from the Virginia State Capitol, for William and Geneviève's wedding. Geneviève barely recognized herself in the beaded flapper wedding dress; a hobbled straight skirt, lace neckline, dropped waist with fluid draping bodice, and floral cloche hat and veil. The dress was beautiful, but straight out of *Vogue*. Geneviève would have preferred wearing a serviceable suit, as had so many war time brides. A white blouse beneath a collared coat, a floor-length skirt, and a simple hat. But that was not the dream of Dorothy Marchand who, for the two years William finished law school, perfected her daughter's wedding.

After the reception at her grandparent's estate with three hundred guests spread across their lawns and gardens, William and Geneviève would leave for the Wild West to follow her husband's dream to return home. But if William Charles Ellis had his way in politics, they'd be back in Washington, D.C. soon.

Their honeymoon was the cross-country train ride to Spokane, Washington, where William resolved to practice law. He would one day run for office, and she would heal the sick, both motivated by what they'd witnessed on the battlefield.

They purchased a small home on the South Side, where they foxtrotted on the hardwood floors, sashaying to their favorite music.

As long as William didn't sing, she could focus on her feet.

With renewed purpose, Geneviève donned her nurse's uniform at Sacred Heart Hospital and assisted in the delivery of babies. This was a fulfilling vocation and, compared to the frontline, a vacation. With each day, she helped bring life into the world, not to return her patients to the battlefield.

At first, the thought of having her own baby was almost frightening. She had no siblings, but William did. Her work was important and fulfilling. What did she know about raising a child? Besides, she enjoyed the intimacy of two and felt unsure about how that would change with a baby.

But each day in the hospital, watching a man become a father and a woman become a mother, her heart was filled with wonder. What would William and she be like as more than husband and wife? With each child delivered, she anticipated the day her definition of family would grow.

Chapter Twenty-Seven
Siobhan

I have to remind myself to breathe—
almost to remind my heart to beat!
—Emily Brontë, *Wuthering Heights*

Deer Lodge, Montana
July 26, 1919

Jack rather proudly educated Siobhan about his town, named for Warm Springs Mound; the outlying ranches with tall native grasses and willows spread out to the mountains beyond. The Shoshone had called it *"it-soo-ke-en-carne"* or *Deer's Lodge*.

The second oldest town in Montana had the first college (now closed) and the first prison. She could explore Main Street from beginning to end in five minutes unless she went into the shops or stopped for a soda at the drugstore. Much of Main Street was consumed by the castle-like structure of the Montana State Prison.

If she started at the prison, she passed the Orpheum Theatre, the M & M Building with the Rialto Theater, the fraternity club, Larrabee Bank, Keystone Drug, and the Kleinschmidt Building. Hotel Deer Lodge was across from the Bonner Building, which boasted one of the largest glass storefronts in America. Then she'd stroll by the Coleman Lansing Building, Trask Hardware, the post office, city hall, and arrive at the other end of town.

The railroad with the Chicago, Milwaukee, St. Paul, and Pacific ran right through the town, making it a hub of interest for ranchers, miners, and lumber workers. The climate was extreme, with hot summers and bitter cold winters. The soil was dry, rocky, and sandy, but with irrigation could grow the hay needed to support the cattle in harsh winters. This high desert was perfect for ranching.

Though it didn't have an ocean, the Clark Fork River, which ran alongside the town, split the valley in half. Jack had warned her not to go in the water because it was polluted from the smelter upriver. He must have sensed her disappointment because he suggested that Saturday they ride up to Rock Creek Lake.

Siobhan rode with Jack on the horse. She held onto his waist, his baby securely nestled in her apron and tucked between them, and her own baby within. She felt oddly that they were a family of sorts.

Rock Creek Lake was sapphire blue surrounded first by evergreens and then the mountains beyond. She settled on the shoreline and laid Samuel on her apron. He was sleeping soundly, probably due to the gentle rocking on horseback. She imagined one day he might be a cowboy. She set their lunch under a tree and scanned the water.

Jack pulled off his shirt and pants and then dove into the lake. A part of her was jealous of the freedom he had to plunge into the refreshing lake water.

"Do you want to swim?"

"I can't. I don't know how."

"Then you're in luck!" Jack walked back toward the beach. "I taught every one of my nine brothers and sisters." Siobhan hesitated. She considered Samuel.

"He's sleeping." Jack extended his arm. "C'mon, Siobhan. It'll feel good after the long ride."

Siobhan turned away to slip out of her dress to her bloomers and camisole below and then giggled at her modesty. She stood in front of this man, practially a stranger, in her underwear. And yet, he was her husband. She was in a stranger new place. How had she ended up here?

They focused on one another as if daring the other to retreat. She walked straightaway down the hill, wading into the water where Jack stood.

She gasped. The lake was icy but terribly refreshing, awakening every nerve in her body. She tingled. First her feet, knees, and then she slowed as the water reached her hips.

"In the winter, the lake can have sixteen feet of ice."

"I believe it! It's still frozen!" She clenched her teeth and shivered as the water reached her waist. Then she didn't know if she shivered from the cold, or the fear, or because Jack was standing so nearby, but she had to stop. Her breasts stung with the chill. Was this good for the baby?

"All the way to me, Siobhan."

Every part of her wanted to scream "I'm afraid," but he hadn't stopped looking at her and she couldn't admit her fear. Not yet. She was the girl who boarded a train from Boston and ended up married a few days later. She was the girl raising one man's child while carrying another's. She took another step and the chilly water swallowed her up to her shoulders. A searing cold, stabbing pain. Her heart raced. She wanted him to come to her. How could she risk her footing? She could lose her step and plunge beneath the water, which was not yet her friend.

"Siobhan, take the last three steps. It's not over your head. Come to me."

"Jack . . ."

"It's all right, Siobhan, take each step slowly. I'm here."

One. Two. Three. She was so close to him, to everything about him. His rough afternoon beard, his blue eyes, his muscles sculpted by hard labor.

"Do you trust me?"

"Yes . . ." she answered too quickly and with a shiver.

"Put your face in the water."

Siobhan couldn't imagine how that had anything to do with swimming, but she lowered her head until her cheeks felt the biting chill, then pulled her face out and shook the water off.

"Now blow bubbles into the water." His smile teased.

Siobhan giggled. Was he serious? "It's so cold!" Still, she lowered her lips and made bubbles in the water.

"Put your whole face in the water and blow bubbles. Then I want you to turn your head, take a breath, and turn back and blow more bubbles."

Siobhan smiled. He had to be tricking her. This wasn't swimming. This was child's play.

She lowered her face again and blew out the air, then turned slightly and took a breath, which she released into the water. After the third time, she gasped and inhaled a gulp of water. Suddenly she stood upright, choking.

"Jack!"

He took her hands to steady her, and she coughed and snorted until she was breathing again. The water burned her nose.

"What does this have to do with swimming?" she accused. "You're toying with me!"

"Siobhan, do you trust me?"

This time she wouldn't answer because she did, but she didn't need him to know that yet.

Siobhan's teeth chattered and her body shook in the frigid water. She crossed her arms in front of her to warm herself, realizing by touch what he must already see.

More than anything she wanted to run to the beach and lay in the sunshine until she was dry. To sleep beside the baby and dream of ocean waves and the wind in her hair. Samuel seemed so peaceful sleeping on her apron. She could be there instead. Why didn't he wake up so she would have that excuse?

"Look this way, Siobhan. Step closer now."

She inched forward, narrowing her eyes. Why was he pushing her when this was all so new? What was she mad at? Was she mad at him, or the water, or her fear?

"The next step is floating." He sounded like a teacher. "You will spread your arms, lean back, take a deep breath, expand your chest and let your feet rise to the surface. You're going to just let go."

Siobhan laughed. That was never going to work. But he was serious. He waited for her to obey. She didn't have to do this. And yet the idea that the water could hold her was so unbelievable, tantalizing, alluring.

Siobhan slowly spread her arms, closed her eyes to the bright sun

show you how to stroke."

Her arms moved beneath his, alternating windmills in the water. Her breaths shortened into gasps, and she wasn't sure whether it was the cold or that his arms were so strong.

"Now when your right arm goes back, take a breath to the side, and when it goes forward, blow into the water." She had never been this close to anyone except Giovanni. She tried to concentrate on her movements, but with his muscular arms surrounding her thin wet layer of underclothes, she started to laugh, and he joined in.

His laughter. Was this the first time she had heard it? It was the most beautiful sound, so hearty and melodious. Was it good that he could feel joy so soon after loss? When she turned to him, she could see he was smiling. Was he teasing? She scooped the water and splashed his face but in so doing stumbled and went underwater.

She tried to stand but her clothes were heavy on her body and she lost her balance only to be caught by him. He steadied her body, her clothing clinging so that every curve was revealed. Now the baby awakened, just when she wanted to stay.

"Samuel." He nodded to the beach, taking her hand to guide her unsteady footsteps. "You're a good student." His voice was soft and gentle.

"Your tenth?"

"I was the oldest." He spread a blanket near the baby. "Then six girls and three younger brothers. I practically raised them."

"Where are they?" Siobhan gave Samuel the bottle.

"Back east. West Virginia." By now Samuel was wailing but she couldn't pull him to her chest because she was so cold and wet.

Jack draped a towel over her shoulders and Siobhan wrapped the baby in it, snuggling Samuel's head in her arm.

"But you left them?" Her own running was her choice, and she left no one behind.

Her look must have worried him because it took him a long time to answer. She tickled Samuel's cheek. He was gaining weight.

"Have you ever felt trapped?" She felt Jack's eyes on her.

Siobhan turned away from the baby and studied her husband. He talked so differently. Not like Giovanni, who said very little. Or like

Antonio, who connected through the words of others. No, Jack asked her questions to try to marry their experiences. "Like you couldn't breathe?"

Siobhan remembered the moment Brigid told her the truth, and then the moment Giovanni could not or would not, and then falling into the water just now. She nodded.

"It was a coal mining town. I was going to spend the rest of my life underground. One day I went down and knew I could never do it again. There are places where no light can reach. Total darkness." He held his hands out. "You can't even see your fingers." He curled both hands into fists, grimacing as if the memory was painful.

"So, you . . . ?"

"I just left."

"But your family?"

"I don't know. One less mouth to feed." He closed his eyes and lowered his head at the memory.

She couldn't speak. *He left his family.* He ran away.

"I loved them." His eyes were sad, and his voice was an apology. He traced a line across Samuel's head with his finger and she remembered *rosmarino*.

"And now? Do you wonder about them?"

"I send them letters. I tell them I'm all right. That I have a little farm."

"Are *they* all right? What do they say?" She rose on one elbow. Would she ever send a letter like that to Ireland?

"I've never put a return address on the envelope."

"Why not?"

"That connection was too strong. The responsibility." He shook his head. "There was another baby every year. Twins one year. My parents weren't much older than me. I had to leave."

She knew that feeling. Completely different but familiar. A life of your own. To feel like you were underground instead of breathing. She had seen the blackness of the Charles River and wondered whether she could be swallowed into its depths.

But today was different. Today she had learned to float and potentially one day she would learn to swim.

"You have family, too." He picked up his son and laid him on his chest. "You left somebody." Now they were laying side by side, the sandy beach was their bed.

"I didn't want to leave home. I thought my parents were coming, too."

"What was home?"

Siobhan found herself smiling. No one had ever asked about her homeland. Antonio liked the sound of names and accents and words and stories, but Jack, Jack wanted to know about *home*.

"Kilrush. County Clare. That's where I come from. Everything is water. The River Shannon. The Atlantic Ocean. Cliffs and coastline."

"It must be very beautiful."

"There is a place on the mouth of the Shannon." She put her arms up and parallel. "Two rugged cliffs are nearly touching. They call it Lover's Leap." She turned and smiled. "I guess it takes faith to make that jump."

"I guess so!" He smiled back, and she hoped he understood her metaphor. "And on Scattery Island there's the ruins of an old monastery. Older than anything you see here. Da says *scattery* means treasure." She smiled remembering her father and hoping he was still alive and wondering if she would ever see him again.

"Loop Head is the farthest west point of County Clare. It's a sliver of land separating the Atlantic Ocean and the Shannon Estuary. When you stand on the tip, you can see the Connemara Mountains, Blasket, and Aran Islands." She extended her arm as if pointing out the islands on the placid lake.

"What do you remember best?"

Had anyone ever asked her that question? Had anyone ever cared about her Ireland? Had she ever talked this much?

"Once, my father took me out with him fishing and I saw needle-nosed dolphins."

Jack shook his head which made her frown.

"I'm sorry. It's not that I don't believe you. It's just that this place"—Jack stretched his arms out—"must seem so different." She filled in what had to be on his mind. Can this be home?

Siobhan looked out across the lake, water contained by land, imprisoned like the inmates. But not this sky. It rolled on forever above the land like the waves of the ocean. She didn't hate this place called Montana. It had its own wildness.

He took her hand and entwined their fingers. "We're family. You're his mother now."

She felt the heat rush to her face. "You took a chance. Marrying me. Making me the mother of your child!"

"We both took a chance. Lover's Leap. Now we have to trust."

Float, she thought. *He understands me.*

"Just look at you." He sat up and pointed at her. "You left Boston, got on a train, got off a train in an unfamiliar town, married a perfect stranger—emphasis on perfect—and became a mother. You are quite a woman, Siobhan."

Why, it was true! When he put it that way, she sat taller and laughed in agreement. Maybe she was as wild as the wind, and this west, so foreign and new.

"I like it here. Though it is different, so far from the sea."

"That's something you miss." He spoke so softly, she leaned in to hear and to answer.

"There's a white lighthouse on Loop Head at the mouth of the Shannon to warn sailors of the jagged cliffs." She felt a flash of homesickness. In her mind, she could hear the deafening cries of the seabirds mixing with the waves crashing against the stark stone face of the shoreline; she could still see the white light flashing four times every twenty seconds. The scent of the sea. Would she ever smell it again?

Then she was silent. There was little left to say. Her home was ruggedly savage, but so was life in Montana. There was beauty at home and there was beauty here.

She was seventeen years old and maybe she was wild, but sometimes she was scared, and she didn't know how to navigate this new life. How much older was he? Could he understand?

Maybe not. The wind picked up and tossed her hair about. Then he fixed his gaze on her. His eyes were sapphire blue like the lake, as if she could dive deep into them as she would one day dive into the water. He would teach her. She would grow stronger, she would trust, she would float, and one day she would swim.

Tenderly he pulled a curl from her face and tucked it behind her ear.

"Siobhan, I'll be your lighthouse."

They arrived home just after sunset. As they cleared the gate to their farm, Siobhan gasped at the awesome spectacle. A golden hue hugged the mountains, lighting the sky with shades of beautiful pink. The intensity of the colors encompassed her in a warm calm, a sigh, the end of a day.

"Alpenglow." Jack answered her unspoken question. "It's the sun below the horizon. It happens when—"

"No." She raised her palm and her fingers almost touched his lips. "Don't explain it. I just want it to be magic."

They fed Samuel, but after his long sleep lulled by the ride home, there was no putting him to bed. Jack rocked him and cooed, forming the various vowels in the alphabet as if Samuel was ready to imitate. Siobhan made them both sandwiches and they kicked up their feet on the coffee table and sat there, two married strangers, comfortable without words.

"This is a bad year for most farmers. I have to be honest." Jack patted his son's back.

"But not for you?" She tried not to look at Jack. She could tell by his voice that something was hard to say.

"I've just gotten started, only just bought the farm. I didn't plant a crop. But with the drought, many farms have gone under. It's always a risk, this life."

What should she say? What she knew of farming was from Ireland where it was difficult, too. What did Jack want from her? An acceptance of shared hardship in this joint venture?

"It's not going to be easy."

She nodded and took his hand in hers. She wanted to say that this life was already a shared risk.

Samuel cranked up his colicky cries. Siobhan went to the mantel, removed the stuffed rabbit, and tickled the baby's nose with the bunny's ears.

"No. Don't. Please." Jack took the bunny from her and replaced it on the shelf.

"I thought it was a toy." Now Samuel screamed louder.

"It was a gift. From Annabeth's father. I just thought I would save it for him." Jack sounded apologetic. "For later."

Siobhan carried Samuel to the keyboard. Was this a bad idea too? Holding him in one arm, Siobhan's right hand fumbled at melodies from her past, begging the music to come out of the piano. Annabeth's piano. Annabeth's house. Annabeth's baby. Annabeth's rabbit. Annabeth's husband.

The louder she played the disconnected melodies, the less Samuel cried. Her embarrassing tunes somehow lulled Samuel to sleep and Jack laid him in the cradle.

When Jack joined her at the piano, she was afraid to stop playing lest Samuel awaken. Jack reached his arms around her and placed his hands on the keys to take over the melody. She felt his body behind hers as he leaned forward playing something that sounded all at once unfamiliar and exquisite. Siobhan froze in place.

"How did you do that?"

"My grandmother played. Back in Tennessee. I would listen to her for hours. It's all by ear."

"I play by heart." Siobhan turned around and smiled at him over her shoulder, his breath in her ear, his heartbeat against her back. He placed his hands over hers, shaping them over the keys, their fingers spooning not unlike her earlier swimming lesson.

Jack gently spread her fingers to reach every other key. Thumb, third, then fifth finger. His hands were so much larger than hers. Strong, rough. He lowered her hand and she heard notes that sounded particularly pleasant together. "That's a chord." They played three white keys at a time. "It's like a family." Yes, like a family, but on Annabeth's piano.

"Annabeth was the youngest of four girls. Her father was German." Jack's words seemed to answer her question. "He represented the train company that hammered the last stake at Deer Lodge.

"We met when she and her father came out one summer, but Annabeth never left." Her fingers rested on the keys, unmoving. "He bought us an automobile for a wedding present. That was the last time

I saw him, until the funeral. He came and left. I don't think he'll ever be back."

She waited until she was certain there were no more words.

"I'm sorry."

"I didn't have a name for his grandson." Jack let out a deep sigh as if this story was difficult. She had no idea what to say or if there was more to the story.

"I'm tired. I'm going to turn in."

To Siobhan's delight and surprise, three weeks later a brown paper package arrived at the post office. Jack handed it to her when he came back from town, never questioning the return address or the initials AMS. What was Antonio's middle name? She loved the mystery and intimacy of middle names. Especially since she went by her middle name, strangely, the one Brigid had given her. That brought back a familiar sadness. Had she truly repeated her mother's story? No. She had made a different choice, hopefully the right one, and hers would have a different ending.

What about Giovanni Carlo Savelli? She knew his middle name. What was he doing now? Did he miss her? He didn't know she was married. Did he regret letting her go? Her heart skipped. Had she been a hasty, fearful fool who jumped into a marriage of convenience? Were there other solutions to her problem? What would have happened if she had run into Antonio's arms that fateful night? Did that one night dictate the course of the rest of her life? Of their lives? Of all four of their lives—or the six of them, if she included the Savelli brothers?

A month ago, she had shared her post office box with Antonio. Would Giovanni suddenly arrive? Or Antonio? What would she do if they did? Go back to Boston? Leave baby Samuel?

She had grown to love the little boy, the joy of responsibility, and the possibility she could help him. Though he screamed through the night, she had moved his cradle into her room for company when she felt lonely. She liked to watch the rise and fall of his tiny chest.

She ran her fingers along the package, knowing it had come from Antonio and Giovanni's home. It could have been Giovanni's manila paper and ink. She undid the tape without tearing the wrapping; the paper could be reused. She flipped through the pages, checking for a hidden message. No letter fell out because the note was inside the margins, filled with thoughts and questions and paragraphs underlined, special to Antonio. *The Odyssey* by Homer. The significance of the reminder of art from the Boston Library did not go unnoticed. She even wondered if Giovanni had suggested the book.

"We do have a library in town." Jack smiled. "If you run out of books." Jack was watching her. Was this a book he had read?

She could only imagine what a library in Deer Lodge would look like. Hadn't she been to the best one in the world?

"Conrad and Augusta Kohrs lost their son William in 1902. He was studying Electrical Engineering at Columbia and died of an appendectomy. They had the library built in his honor."

She couldn't imagine losing a son at any age. Not Samuel. Not Giovanni's baby.

The next day, Jack dropped her off at the front of the William K. Kohrs Free Memorial Library, which, like so much of the architecture in Deer Lodge, was remarkable and displayed a grandeur she hadn't expected.

Siobhan climbed the nineteen steps up to the four sandstone columns. She could almost hear Giovanni narrate its Classical Revival and Beaux Arts tradition. Siobhan opened the door and gaped at the central dome of colored glass in the ceiling.

"Hello, my name is Lilian McCalm." The woman's accent had a slight Scottish lilt, as if she'd listened long to someone with that singsong sound.

"I see you're reading *The Odyssey*." Lilian pointed at the book Siobhan clutched to her chest. "You might be interested in our stained glass window."

Lilian directed her to a window, where Siobhan studied a familiar face. The artist titled the work *A Reading from Homer*. She'd seen this likeness in the Boston Library and now laughed at the idea that a much younger Homer had followed her across the country. Was this a connection? Some sort of sign?

Siobhan's fingers wandered through the shelves, studying the titles on the backs of the various books, and she finally settled on a chair near the stained-glass window and sat down with Homer.

There is nothing more admirable than when two people who see eye to eye keep house as man and wife, confounding their enemies and delighting their friends.

Who knew Homer's *Odyssey* could be so funny? Antonio still had a sense of humor, or perhaps he had married? Lilian raised a surprised eyebrow upon finding her giggling. Her smile was friendly. "You might be interested in our Women's Club. We're a part of the American Women's League. We meet about literature, art, music, culture."

A club? A place to discuss literature like she and Antonio had? Her heart quickened. She could make friends.

"Thank you for the invitation."

"800 Missouri. It's the bungalow."

That night, when it started to hail on their tin roof, Jack laughed at her shock.

"It's August and it's hailing." Siobhan palms were extended, and she shrugged as if in disbelief.

"That's Deer Lodge, Montana. Right now, I'm just thankful it's some form of precipitation."

"But it's damaging the flowers. It could punch a hole in something!"

"Sometimes it does. This year, we have nothing to lose. But in the future, an event like this could be a tragedy." His eyes begged for a response. Forgiveness, consolation. Was he asking her if she would leave?

She took his hand. If he was slow in making physical contact, she would signal that his touch was welcomed. Touch was another way to communicate.

He traced her cheek with the back of his hand and smiled at her. She felt shivery and hot at the same time.

"I made a friend," she said. He was looking at her so intently. Maybe she should have said two friends. Though this man was not her lover, he was becoming her friend.

"There's a Women's League."

"Ah, yes," Jack smiled and nodded knowingly. "Does this mean you can tell me what goes on behind those stucco walls?"

"I don't think it's some sort of secret society." Siobhan frowned in confusion.

"No. They do champion a woman's right to vote. You might be my little suffragette."

"You do tease." She nudged his shoulder playfully.

"No. You should vote." Jack became serious as if he didn't understand she was joking.

"I actually hadn't thought much about it. American women have far more freedom than what I saw in Ireland. But if I could talk about art, and music, and literature . . ."

"I want you to have what you need, Siobhan. *Who* you need." He took her in his arms and hugged her. "And I hope I can be just that."

She did, too.

Chapter Twenty-Eight
Geneviève

Spokane, Washington
Christmas 1924

On their third Christmas together, Geneviève decorated their little house with cross-stitched memorabilia, knitted stockings, and crystal ornaments from her past, which her mother had finally sent to deck their halls. Theirs was such a cheerful home. It really was. She could be thankful for so much.

Geneviève had December 23rd off and used it to bake gingerbread men with two neighborhood children. The house smelled like cinnamon, ginger, and pine. The newly chopped tree stood in the window, announcing their home was ready for Saint Nick's arrival.

When William arrived home from work, he was in an unusually mischievous mood. She shoved a cookie into his mouth, and he closed his eyes, as if savoring it to the fullest.

"GinnaBread!" He took another bite. "The taxi will be here shortly so you're going to need to get dressed." He took another bite and continued with his mouth full. "This is for you."

The box was perfectly wrapped with a matching bow.

"*You* didn't wrap this." She cocked her head quizzically.

"Open it. Open it!" Will was like a child at Christmas.

Lifting the lid, Geneviève gasped as she lifted a beautiful emerald green sequined ball gown from the box.

"Do you think it will fit?"

"Perfectly. I tried it on." He laughed teasingly. "Yes, of course!" He was definitive. "I know your figure and your shape, and you will look stunning." Will ran his hands down the side of her body, tracing her hourglass figure. She shivered. He did know her body.

As she slipped off her dress, she felt his eyes study her, but she did not turn away. Then she picked up the box and went into the next room where she stepped into the fitted floor-length gown.

"You tease! You tempt!" he called out.

No. There was a mirror in the room, and she didn't want to disappoint if his dress didn't fit.

The bodice was sheer mesh with a leaf sequin design and capped sleeves. The dress hugged her body all the way past her hips where it flared out in flowing material. She could imagine how she'd twirl on the dance floor.

He was right. The dress fit perfectly. She wished it didn't. If she had given him a child by now, this dress might not fit so well. This was elegance, but she'd be overdressed for most of Spokane. She returned, just a little bit pleased with the sensation she might cause.

"Oh, honey, you look beautiful!"

"It looks so Christmassy. But I don't think I can wear it at the hospital," she teased.

"I think it's a flapper dress. But I won't tell if you won't."

She smiled up at him. He was irresistible. Irrepressible. Nothing ever daunted him.

"Where to, Jeeves?"

William slyly removed her luggage from beneath their bed and in his best French accent, mimicked what he thought the Louis Vuitton ad might sound like. "Show me your luggage and I will tell you who you are."

"Oh dear. I don't think the luggage matches my dress."

"It's all packed." William beamed. "Trust me. We don't need to wear much." He winked.

"William!" Why she blushed, she did not know.

The taxi arrived and he held her hand the entire ride to wherever they were going. She sat back, wondering what dreamy event he had planned this time.

She was so lucky. He was everything she had wanted in a husband.

Was *she* all he wanted in a wife?

Though they were *we,* and *us,* she thought a family was more than two. Their first miscarriage had been sad. Perhaps painting the little bedroom had been a mistake. They had invested into the future when the present of a child was not there.

If the first loss was sad, the second was devastating. What was happening to her? What was she doing to the child within? After that loss, she was no longer the nurse; William held and consoled her. How spoiled she was with a man like William. Wouldn't he make a wonderful father?

William continued at the law firm, and unlike their family, the practice and his client base grew. At the hospital, she asked to be transferred from Labor and Delivery to Post-Op care. She liked talking to the patients when they came out of surgery, and it stung less than watching new mothers experience something she feared would never happen.

The taxi drive wasn't long, but as she neared Post and First, she realized exactly where they were going.

Taking up one entire city block, thirteen floors tall, stood the Davenport Hotel, the newly constructed architectural wonder of Spokane, of which she'd heard so much about. Fifteen thousand pieces of silver, Irish linen, the first hotel with air-conditioning, ice water in the rooms, a pipe organ, ten-thousand-dollar chandeliers. Perhaps if she had the chance, she would order a Crab Louis, named after Louis Davenport himself. That would be pure decadence and extravagance.

A line of Model T's, electrics, and taxis pulled up to the hotel. They stepped out of the car, and into the lobby.

The lobby was a place so sophisticated and graceful, she felt an imposter. It was truly a wonderland of old-world beauty, culture, and history, with architectural nods to France, England, Spain, and imperial Russia. She listened to the foreign accents and words she couldn't understand, but which felt oddly recognizable from her time on the front.

While William checked in, she studied the symbols of various animals, then left the fountain and stepped over to the fireplace, so elegant with gold leaf. Fine art covered the walls and the music of songbirds filled her ears.

That night, they danced at the ball in the Marie Antoinette Room.

"The floor is suspended on cables, so we'll stay light on our feet."

"I think it might take more than that," Geneviève teased, but had to admit, the two had improved, swirling about on the inlaid quartersawn oak dance floor.

A balcony surrounded the floor, making every dancer center stage in this swirl of society. They danced every dance they'd been taught. They were a team. He led and she followed.

When they left the ball, they returned to the lobby and sat by the fire to relax.

"I don't remember when I've had so much fun." Geneviève liked the feeling of her hand in his.

"Merry Christmas, darling."

That night, they fell into bed and a deep sleep. He was right; he'd packed lightly.

The next day, William and Geneviève toured the hotel and its concert hall, shops, and various nooks and artwork. Even the Hall of Doges, with its crystal chandeliers, balconies, and ornate ceiling. Now she felt they were in Italy. The ballroom itself was built with steel girders all the way to the basement to minimize the sound of dancing feet. She learned about the four hundred and fifty telephones and the twenty-four synchronized clocks. And Louis Davenport introduced himself and shook Geneviève's hand.

For a town like Spokane, with its roots in mining, timber, railroads, and agriculture, to have a hotel like the Davenport was astounding. Many had commented this rivaled Chicago or New York.

The next morning, room service brought eggs Benedict. Lying in bed together, William cracked open *A Christmas Carol*, as they had every Christmas since they were married. It was always a reminder to be thankful. To treasure the past, the present, and the future. But last Christmas and then this one, it was hard to treasure future, when she wasn't sure what it would bring.

Geneviève stumbled as she read about the crutch in the empty corner. And then again at the words from the Ghost of Christmas Past: *"For it is good to be children sometimes, and never better than at*

Christmas, when its mighty Founder was a child Himself."

"Christmas needs a child. I see the baby in the manger and I long for our baby in the cradle."

"Geneviève, it's only been two years. We have time. We're young. We have each other."

"I just hope to read this to our own children one day." Did she really need to explain? He kissed away her tear. She didn't want to mar Christmas, but she also felt the emptiness of a childless household.

"We're a family. We *will* be parents. I'm convinced of that. And even if not . . ." And here he paused, and she hated that he had made a concession, that he had admitted the other possibility. He wiped the tears from her cheeks and kissed her forehead. "You are my life."

Chapter Twenty-Nine
Siobhan

*And here I have lamely related to you the uneventful chronicle of
two foolish children in a flat who most unwisely sacrificed for each other
the greatest treasures of their house.
But in a last word to the wise of these days let it be said
that of all who give gifts these two were the wisest.*
—O. Henry, *The Gift of the Magi*

Deer Lodge, Montana
Christmas 1919

That first Christmas, Jack and Siobhan had so little and felt so rich. Jack had chopped a Christmas tree at Emery Mine, which they had decorated with ornaments from a box in the attic, memorabilia from Annabeth's past, and he had shot a turkey for Christmas Eve dinner. Siobhan had made two gifts for Jack. It would be a real Christmas.

"Skinny malink, melodeon legs, big banana feet." Siobhan tickled Samuel's toes and then kissed them one by one.

"What does that mean?" Jack carried in a load of wood for their first Christmas Eve together. She could feel his breath, warm and sweet against her neck, the clean and woodsy scent of evergreen pitch on his clothes.

"I don't know," she said. "A jingle my mother used to say. I can't remember the rest of it." She couldn't tell him that he took her breath away, as well as the rest of the words to the nursery rhyme.

"So, it's Irish?"

"I think so."

Then he left and returned with something large and wrapped in newspaper.

"I'm supposed to wait?" she asked incredulous.

"Not if you don't want to."

She eagerly ripped it open to find a beautiful, handcrafted bookshelf. Six shelves and almost as wide as she could stretch her arms. She ran her hand along the wood. So smooth it felt like butter except it didn't melt under her touch. Perhaps only her heart. She imagined him sanding, then staining each plank, running his firm hands over each board to ensure its smoothness. All for her. A shelf to put books from another man.

"It's for your library." His smile was shy. This was so like Jack. To do things quietly, never ask an opinion but to surprise her with exactly what she needed. "You have all those books. And maybe more to come!" He laughed heartily. Jack—never asking questions, so accepting of the mysterious books from a person he unknowingly invited into their home.

He could have been jealous. If he was concerned, he didn't say. The return address was AMS. What would she say if he asked who the books were from? Was "a friend from Boston" good enough? It wasn't a falsehood, but if you hid the full truth, did that count as a lie?

There were other secrets in their lives. Giovanni—the man who didn't know he had an unborn child. Annabeth—the ghost, a shadow who lived on through the scrawny baby who cried more than he laughed. And what about the baby to come? Would that child look too much like another man's child?

"And this is for you." She reached under the tree and brought out two packages. She sat near him, hardly able to contain her excitement. Perhaps it truly was better to give than receive.

He untied the string, tore open the paper, and studied the small gift inside. A photograph of the three of them had been taken at a church social. Siobhan had found an empty frame in the attic.

"It's us." Jack smiled, tracing their faces on the glass. A chord not easily broken.

"Open the other one, too!" She almost squealed. Christmas had never been like this with Brigid.

He peeled off the paper carefully, seeing the backside. "'To Jack, who makes our house a home.' Very nice handwriting, Siobhan." She was never certain if Jack was teasing.

"Oh, Jack! Turn it over!" She waited, her hands clasped together, certain he'd love it.

"You made this." His voice was low and quiet, almost a question.

"It's our house!"

Siobhan clapped her hands together in delight that he liked her original needlepoint bungalow with *Mason Family, established 1919.* She'd created the design and worked for hours poking threads through the cloth until she fashioned a decoration that said their house was a home. *Their* home.

He fingered the detail she had put into the picture. Touching the weathervane, Annabeth's flowers, the porch, the barn in the background, and the cottonwoods. The tiny petti point MSM in the corner. Her signature.

"This is more than the picture. It reminds me that you've made us a family." He reached out and squeezed her hand. "I love it. Should we hang it above the fireplace?"

He stroked her cheek, at last reaching around her expanding frame to draw her close. But then he suddenly withdrew, startled.

"I feel it!" The baby had moved within Siobhan and she laughed. "She's a little kicker!" Siobhan had just begun enjoying the pregnancy now that the sickness had left her.

"You think it's a girl?"

She had to think it was a girl. A girl would not remind her of Giovanni. How could she explain why a girl would make it so much simpler?

Jack located an existing nail and hung her needlepoint on the wall above the fireplace. On the mantel with the bunny and the new family photograph, and the books that she would soon transfer to her bookshelf. Their gifts to one another made her feel complete.

"If a chord is three notes, what do you call four?" she asked, stroking where the baby was kicking.

"A chord can have two notes that are the same but separated by an octave. They are like bookends protecting the other two notes. That's us."

Siobhan took the most recent book off the shelf and opened it. Antonio had sent a short story of a newlywed couple named Jim and Della. Their gifts to one another of a comb and watch fob chain were borne of sacrifice and, though less successful than Siobhan and Jack's first Christmas gifts, shared the same generous spirit. *Comic irony,* Antonio had written between the lines. Before the embers went out, Siobhan finished reading the book with Jack sitting at her feet, his head against her knee.

Antonio's book was touching, and it made her wonder what was happening in Boston. She imagined that Giovanni married a fine Italian girl with hair down to her waist. Mama Rosa and the Catholic Church would be proud. Giovanni would never be a sculptor but most likely worked the family business cutting hair. Antonio was probably following his dream. Would he marry, too? It now mattered little to her.

After Jack climbed the stairs to bed, Siobhan knew she had a letter to write. A letter that would extinguish all chances of a reunion with either brother, knowing with confidence that whatever would happen was the best for all of them.

Dear Antonio:

It is winter and there is so much to look forward to! You know that I love spring and with this new season will come a child. We enjoyed The Gift of the Magi *and* A Christmas Carol. *What beautiful Christmas presents! I shall indeed make merry all the year long! These books are so expensive, but I want you to know that I read and reread them all. Sometimes I read them to my husband, Jack, before he falls asleep. He works so hard at the mill and on our farm. I notice you have a university address! Keep studying, my fine friend.*

Siobhan

Chapter Thirty
Geneviève

Spokane, Washington
March 1925

With each pregnancy, something beyond hope grew within her. She considered names, treasured the secret knowledge personal only to her body, and anticipated a birthdate not so very far in the future. With each miscarriage, Geneviève felt stripped. Smaller. They had been whole as Mr. and Mrs. Ellis, why was there now such a hole within her that would never be filled? So many babies had slipped through her womb that only she knew the count, because she was their mother.

William knew about three. But after that she bore the losses alone. He would have felt each period of sorrow and grief, but he had not experienced the life within. Did he really need to know that whatever tiny baby began in her womb, never made it into their family alive? To bear the thought that his wife was failing and that she might not deserve to be a mother. That he might never be a father? He was a protector who couldn't protect the baby or her, and so William busied himself with clients, settlements, and court dates. She couldn't heal her body. She returned to nursing where she might be able to help someone else.

When he tried to reason, she couldn't listen. "We could adopt," he suggested, wanting to fix her problem. But for her, taking another mother's baby should never be second choice, a substitution, a replacement. Besides, why would another mother give up a baby when each baby that Geneviève's body gave up, wounded her beyond grief? What was wrong with the baby? What was wrong with the mother? And what if she couldn't love another mother's baby? No, she couldn't risk learning the answers to those questions.

Chapter Thirty-One
Siobhan

*So I shall just imagine myself for a fortnight or so
at one side of the fireplace of a country cottage,
with a sympathetic soul opposite me.
And I shall go on talking, in a low voice
while the sea sounds in the distance
and overhead the great black flood of wind
polishes the bright stars.*
—Ford Madox Ford, *The Good Soldier*

Deer Lodge, Montana
January 8, 1919

At seven months, Siobhan was barely showing, but she had developed a round enough and thickened belly that she couldn't fasten any of her clothing and they could no longer be let out. Annabeth's clothes were nowhere to be found and she couldn't ask Jack what he'd done with them. Not yet.

Jack had never seen her body, so he hadn't detected how she'd grown. Would he ever want to see her? At first, she thought it was in respect to Annabeth. Then later, she attributed it to her discomfort and sickness. Then again, Jack did work hard and there was so little time, but as the months continued, she had to accept that it could be disinterest.

Would Jack ever see her as physically beautiful? Would he love her? She needed to be loved. Had she made the right choice? Should she just have returned to Boston? Would Giovanni have accepted his child?

Why did she bother second-guessing herself when the decision was made? Jack was her husband, and whether he loved her now or ever would, they had a family.

She thought of her parents often. By now Da and Mam knew she lived in Montana and was married and expecting a baby. Oh, how she missed them both. Though she had come to an understanding that she would never see them again, that didn't take away her longing for a mam who could help her during this time.

Millie. Millie would know something about clothing. Millie would know how to have dresses made without suspicion. And Millie would listen. With her shawl securely wrapped around her, Siobhan made her way to the only person who might help. There was still a chance that this child could be seen as Jack's instead of the bastard that some might call it.

Millie's apartment was up three flights of stairs in an alley off Main Street. Siobhan knew the saloon wouldn't be open for another hour, so Millie should have been home.

After a pot of tea and a piece of leftover pie from the saloon, they sat on her couch.

"You're still not noticeably big. With a higher waistband we might hide your stomach."

"Everything is getting tight." Siobhan shifted uncomfortably.

"Have you felt him yet?" Millie traced the curve of Siobhan's belly with the palm of her hand.

Siobhan smiled and blushed. "Oh yes, she's a busy girl."

"Like his father?"

"No." Siobhan answered immediately. And yet, Millie posed an ambiguous question. Millie didn't know Giovanni. Jack would be the only father her daughter would ever know. Jack was the opposite of the slow-moving, lethargic Giovanni.

"I mean . . . I don't know." Siobhan wrung her hands.

"Jack is a very busy man." Millie seemed to know her husband.

"Yes, but . . ."

"Siobhan, Jack is this little fellow's father. All answers are about Jack. Everything forward, stop looking back."

Siobhan nodded as if obeying Mam. Millie was so practical.

"This little *fellow*?" Siobhan prompted for more information.

"Gotta call him something!"

"What about Annabeth's clothes? Maybe I could wear them?"

"Hah!" Millie laughed. "No. That will never work. Annabeth was a whisper of a woman. You're the wind."

"I see."

"Do you?" Millie sat down on a well-worn sofa. "Now, Siobhan, I'm telling you things I would never share, except that Annabeth's gone."

"I feel like the shadows linger."

"I don't know why, Siobhan." Millie's voice held correction. "I'm sorry to speak ill of a woman in the grave, but the shadow was small. In so many ways, you will never fit into her clothes."

"But . . ."

Millie took Siobhan's hands in hers. "You're young, you don't feel well, everything is strange, and you're married to a man you hardly know. But you have fire and spit, Siobhan." Millie made her stand in front of the full-length mirror. "Look at yourself!"

Siobhan tried to see what Millie saw. Chestnut red hair framing a heart-shaped face. Jewel green eyes against porcelain skin.

"But then why . . ." Siobhan faltered.

"Why what?" Millie's question had no lift. It was a statement. It was as if Millie already knew what Siobhan was asking but would make her say it herself.

"We don't know each other. We haven't known each other yet."

"You haven't made love?" Millie spoke so easily. "Well, there is more to love than making love. Ask the women in the Burnt District at Dumas. Pleasant Alley. Nothing pleasant there. Though they make love, there's little love in what they do. It's just a service and for most of them, the love doesn't ever grow."

Siobhan turned away. This talk was coarse and made her ill at ease. Millie had left Butte. Siobhan wasn't completely sure of all that Millie did. Though Millie had a past, she hoped it wasn't Millie's present or future.

"What do you want from me, Siobhan?" Millie turned Siobhan around. Siobhan reddened, suddenly aware that her words and actions depicted someone who thought themselves better than the wiser woman before her.

"A friend." She raised her chin and stared intently into Millie's eyes. Millie met her gaze without changing expression and then burst into laughter so loud, Siobhan looked around to see if anyone could hear.

"I'll get you the clothing, Siobhan." Millie took out a measuring tape. "I know someone. And with her dressmaking skills, she'll make you a few dresses." Siobhan felt dismissed by Millie's lack of response about friendship.

As Millie took measurements, Siobhan turned away, uncomfortable. "Tell me what you did last night."

Siobhan felt confused. Though her face questioned Millie's inquiry, she answered.

"I made dinner and was reading—"

"What did you *two* do last night," Millie interrupted, talking through the pins between her teeth.

Siobhan took a deep breath and tried to remember. "I read by the fire and then I fell asleep. He took the book from my lap and helped me to my bed, but then I said I just wanted to sit for a while. And so he stayed. He sat near my feet. He told me about coal mining and his mother, and his brothers, and sisters, and his father, and his father's anger, and how he wanted out of West Virginia and, in the glow, I thought how lovely his hair looked and I touched it. And then he held my hand."

"And what did you two do *yesterday*?"

Siobhan laughed. "Our new sow gave birth! He taught me what to do. I wasn't at all good at helping. I slipped in the icy pen, and I was mud-covered and chilled, and I laughed. But he looked concerned and picked me up. I said I was fine, but he seemed so worried and held my hand as we walked back to the house."

"Siobhan Mason." Millie's disciplinary tone made Siobhan wince. She knew she was about to be reprimanded. Then Millie sported a hint of a smile. "I think perhaps I might be a matchmaker." Millie stared knowingly at Siobhan, as if testing for a reaction which Siobhan didn't want to acknowledge.

Siobhan warmed. Her arms tingled, and she felt breathless. It was true. There was something she felt for Jack Mason. But did she want him because she missed the act of love or because she was in love? He was like no man she'd ever met. But she was young and hadn't met many.

"Siobhan, I don't think Jack will lie with you until after this baby is born. That's my guess. But girl, think about this. Though you can't see it, you're the most beautiful woman in town. Take those words from an honest friend."

Friend. Millie had used the word.

"He's just like you. He may be oblivious to your feelings. He may have no idea you're in love."

In love? *In love?* Was she in love?

"I'm not saying much more, but you need to know that the spark that came before you is pale warmth to the heat of your flame."

Siobhan could feel the flare in her face. The inappropriateness of the talk. The thought that she was more than just a girl but a woman with desire and a woman to be desired.

"There are other ways to know and be known. It sounds like you and Jack are getting to know each other in a way that's best."

Ironically, Millie's message sounded more like a sermon.

"Don't try to guess whether the man loves you. Just love him. He'll warm to everything you are." Millie helped Siobhan back into her dress, fastening the button tightly about her waist.

"I think I see passion in your future." Millie smiled without laughing and Siobhan desperately wanted to throw her arms around her. And then Millie did something that surprised her—Millie did just that.

Chapter Thirty-Two
Siobhan

And it was a most remarkable, a most moving glance,
as if for a moment a lighthouse had looked at me.
—Ford Madox Ford, *The Good Soldier*

Deer Lodge, Montana
March 10, 1920

"Skinny malink and malinky skinny . . ." Jack attempted the little Irish song and Siobhan laughed softly to herself as she spied on the two in the kitchen, Jack unaware she was awake. Jack stroked the baby's face and took Sam's little hands in his much larger ones and raised them to his face to feel the child's caress.

Jack loved that boy. So much so that he was willing to marry a woman he didn't love. Each night when Jack came home from the mill, tired and drained, he headed out to do his farm chores. He'd sometimes help with the dishes, tell Samuel stories, always ending saying "I love you" to baby Samuel. That sounded strange to Siobhan's ears, as her Irish family had never been as forthcoming with those three little words.

Last night after they'd put the baby to bed and Jack had gone upstairs, she'd felt twinges. As she did so often, she went upstairs to Jack's bedroom and removed his boots and covered him with his quilt. He worked so tirelessly. She would never awaken him.

The twinges continued throughout the night. She'd had them before and by what their neighbor Naomi had said, they might not be true contractions. She wouldn't want to tell Jack yet. *Especially* if they were real. Even if it meant she was alone when the baby arrived.

If Jack could make the sacrifice of marriage for his son, could he love *her* baby, too? Could he take on whatever questions would come his way about the woman he married right after Annabeth's death? And the baby that came too soon?

That morning, she grabbed the bedpost and clung to it through each contraction, then laid back down on the bed and rested. After Jack left for work, Siobhan cleaned the house, washed diapers, and folded laundry. Just in case. Then she counted the hours until he arrived home. All day, she measured contractions and time and frequency. She had wanted Jack to arrive when it was too late to go to the hospital. If the baby was premature, no one could question them about its parentage. Then afterward, Siobhan planned on staying away from town for a few months and hiding the baby from scrutiny.

When her water broke, she cleaned up the mess and began pacing the living room. When Samuel cried, he distracted her from the pain. What if Jack didn't come home in time? Was she being foolish in waiting? What if she were alone when she gave birth? What about Samuel?

At last, the back door opened, and Jack entered the kitchen with a gust of wind and snow. She wanted to run over and grab him when the next contraction began, but she still wasn't sure how much time there was before the baby would be born. Jack would not want her to deliver here alone; he'd make her go to the hospital. Especially after Annabeth.

Siobhan scrambled eggs and placed a slab of ham on his plate before doubling over at the stove, holding back a silent scream. After dinner, the contractions came quickly and forcefully, and she gripped Jack's strong arm.

"It's time then, let's go to the hospital, Siobhan."

"It's too late."

"When did this begin?"

She gritted her teeth, a clenched scream erupting from her throat. The stabbing pain subsided but she did not let go of Jack.

"I think I should get someone."

"No! You can't leave me! I'm scared."

"You could be in labor all night. I can go and come back in an hour."

"No! It's coming now. You can't go."

"Then I have time to get Naomi! I could go there and be back in a half hour."

"I want you!"

She gripped his muscular arms and shrieked against the pain.

"I have to get someone."

"No! She's coming now. *Early.*" Siobhan clenched her jaw.

Jack frowned and then took her hands in his. "Our baby doesn't need to come early. He's my son no matter what anyone says. I'd rather have a doctor here and you two safe."

Oh, she had been selfish. He had lost someone before, losing her now would be too much, and with not one, but two children. She groaned at the thought and the ensuing pain.

"Siobhan!" he said in fear. "I have to get someone!"

"No! I don't want to be alone. You can't go. Not now! You can't go!" She screamed against the next wave of pain and dug her fingernails into his skin because it somehow made her feel better not to bring pain but to share it.

"Then we'll do this together." *Together.* She relaxed at the word and the waning contraction and the memory of all the times he had said we and us and *our* and *second baby.*

There were small cuts on his arms where she had drawn blood and inflicted pain.

Though she had relaxed, he clenched his fists. "I wasn't there when Annabeth delivered. There was a doctor. And still . . ."

And still Annabeth hadn't lived. She shook her head. The only person she wanted here was Jack. Or maybe Giovanni. Oh, Giovanni. Why would she want him now?

"It's God. He's punishing me. I was bad. Just like my mother." She tossed her head back and forth, her hair strewn about her face. She felt like a wild animal caught in a trap, unable to avoid being ripped apart.

"I can't do this!" A low grunting scream came from deep within and she flailed her arms.

"You're strong. You're so strong, Siobhan!" He took both hands.

"God is gracious." His voice was soft and gentle in her ear. "Your name means *God is gracious.*"

"What?" She had never heard that. Brigid would never have chosen that name if she had known. Why had Brigid given her that name when bitter Moira was so much more appropriate?

"I like to think about names. What are we going to name him?" Jack stroked the hair from her face.

Jack always called *him* a boy while she called *her* a girl. It reassured Siobhan that Jack thought of the baby as a him, as if maybe Jack could accept another man's son.

A name? She liked names, too, but she had been unable to think of anything. She had an idea.

"If it's a boy you name him. A girl, I name her." She couldn't name Giovanni's son, but she could name his daughter. She'd give her a fine Irish name that would remind her of home, a name that would keep this girl close to her always. That would erase all things Italian.

Her next contraction brought another long, low, guttural scream. She had never heard something like this before. She was an animal and he was seeing her at her worst. How could he ever love her after this?

She clung to him as she arched her back in pain. He clutched her fists in his hands lest she claw him any more.

"Float, Siobhan. Float." He said nothing else until the ocean wave curled and folded and left her panting and counting the seconds until the pain resumed.

"I like a good Bible name. Here. Look."

She pushed the Bible away. "No. Not now. I can't."

"We could name him Matthew, Mark, Luke, John, Peter, David."

"How about Moses?" she asked. She had a moment between spasms. She could be funny in this short reprieve. "Oh, Jack, I'm just teasing." And then he laughed, a deep, happy laugh. How she longed to stroke his masculine forearms and to hold his hands for strength. She wanted to be wanted.

"Hezekiah?" he continued.

"Methuselah," she added, before the next wave of contractions.

This was a closeness she'd never felt with him. Would it be the beginning of something, or the end? *A daughter. Please a daughter.* He could—no, *she* could better accept the daughter of another man's child.

Oh! The exquisite pain. This was her penalty for stealing Annabeth's child and the love the child had for his birth mother. If anything happened, would Siobhan's child ever know about her? She coughed and sat up suddenly. "If anything happens . . ."

"Shhh, Siobhan . . . I am here." His shushing blurred into her name, and then she bore down against the pain and knew that this was the moment. Jack touched her where she felt the pain. Touched her where he had never touched her before.

"I see the head, so much hair. Lots of black hair."

All Siobhan could see was the dark, brooding face of Giovanni with his back to the wall, a shock of black hair over his forehead.

"You can love the baby?" She gasped. She had to know. The pain was a burning, ripping pain and she was certain she would die. And then what? Did he understand what she was asking? There was a rush and Jack had something in his hands and the burning pain lessened and she lay back in relief. Every bit of her was expended on that bed. She felt so exposed, so naked, but Jack had delivered her firstborn.

She lay back unsure of what should happen next. She heard the cry and Jack was doing something with her baby.

"The baby?" Jack didn't respond. "*The baby,* Jack. Answer me!"

Jack wrapped the baby in blankets sewn for his firstborn. His eyes were wet as he placed the baby in the crook of her arm. "Here's our son."

She'd never seen a baby so new, and she couldn't remember one so handsome. He was dark, with ink black hair, and his tiny frame made Samuel seem large. But he didn't look like Jack.

"His name is Paul." Jack said, stroking her head. "Paul Jonathon Mason." He chucked the baby under the chin. "We have two sons, Mama."

She sighed at the thought. She was tired and having two baby boys eight months apart seemed almost incomprehensible and certainly impossible. He bent low and kissed the tiny olive-complexioned baby with a full head of jet-black hair.

"That's my boy." Jack's light brown hair swept over his forehead, and she longed to brush it off his face and look into his eyes, and then into his heart.

"I'm so proud of you, Siobhan." That made her cry though she wasn't sure why. The pains continued and Jack explained them away as afterbirth.

Jack ran a hot wet linen over her forehead, and she closed her eyes as he continued wiping her neck, stopping at the top of her nightgown. Then she felt the warmth on her legs as he stroked downward to her feet where he stopped to massage them. Then he dipped the washcloth in the bowl and returned to her legs and upward to where she had just given birth. He was gentle and caring. With her eyes closed, the tender act was natural. Then he sat beside her, stroking her hair and studying the newborn.

"He needs you," Jack said, touching Paul's lips as they pursed. "You need to feed him now." Her breasts ached with an unfamiliar heaviness and her heart pounded as Jack set Paul in the crook of her arm and turned to leave.

"I . . . I . . ." She didn't know what to say or do. "I don't know how . . . I've never seen . . ."

"Should I get someone? Naomi?"

"She . . . Annabeth?" Siobhan named the invisible presence. "She fed Samuel?"

"No." Jack's face softened as if in remembrance.

Siobhan sat up and gently slipped the nightdress off her shoulder, exposing herself to the baby. Jack stood gazing at her. She turned the baby to her full breast and tickled his lips, enticing him with a nipple that felt strangely foreign to her. At last, Jack stepped forward, tenderly coaxing the tiny child's head while cupping her breast to meet the baby's lips. He tickled her nipple into the baby's mouth. When Paul latched, she lay back, discovering a new and tingling sensation, and understanding a rush of exquisite relief. Still, something felt incomplete.

"Bring Samuel."

"You're tired. He can meet his brother tomorrow."

"No, Jack, I have an idea."

In so many ways, she felt full, warm, and that her breasts had only begun to offer life and sustenance. When Jack put their older son in the crook of her other arm, Samuel looked at the unfamiliar nipple, but Siobhan squirted milk into his mouth until he hungrily drew what he had missed for months, and a tingling sensation rushed through her breast. This son was not of her blood but of her breast.

At last, she leaned back with one baby cradled in each arm and her night dress still open and she smiled and even laughed, which made Jack join her. She thought this might be what she could call a family.

Dear Antonio,

Jack and I are now parents. We hope 1920 will not have the drought conditions of the past years. The farm is busy. I love the sheep and am getting used to the chickens and the pigs, though the rooster is not my favorite. Your postmark is from Boston College! Imagine that! I am happy for you.

- Your friend, Siobhan

Chapter Thirty-Three
Geneviève

Deer Lodge, Montana
October 1926

After five years practicing law in Spokane, Geneviève wasn't surprised when William had been flattered into serving on an investigative team for Montana's maximum security prison. Especially when the job could lead to a position as prosecuting attorney.

But she couldn't help but feel leaving his Spokane practice was an admission his career would take precedent over family. Her body had failed them. She couldn't heal her womb or the emptiness she felt. Deer Lodge promised something new for William. But what would it offer *her*?

"Starting over can be good. Saying goodbye to say hello!" William claimed, poring over the paperwork covering their Spokane dining table. Maybe this would be good. A fresh start.

"Hey honey, two for the road!" Then enthusiastically William read from a railway pamphlet, of all things she'd missed, describing Deer Lodge as *lovely year-round, with rich soil and conditions favorable for all classifications of farming, and finally, abundantly restorative*. The advertisement sounded too good to be true.

Previously known as LaBarge City, Spanish Fork, and Cottonwood, Deer Lodge City rested in a valley five to ten miles wide. Grizzly bear, deer, elk, and buffalo ran free on the sixty miles of streams, farms, and foothills framed by the mountains.

And yet in this beautiful setting, there was a prison modeled after Alcatraz, originally built in 1871 when Montana was but a territory. On paper, they read the prison was a medieval fortress with round, crenellated towers surrounded by twenty-foot-high Romanesque walls, which the prisoners themselves had built.

They were told that portions of the prison were state of the art, even boasting of the first prison stage in America. But there were problems, and in 1921, longtime Prison Warden Conley had been fired from his position.

Montana State Prison was only a photo and words, Deer Lodge a description in a Railway Pamphlet. But when they first arrived, Geneviève made Will drive up and down Main Street four times in disbelief.

"I had no idea it was this large. Or that it was such a . . . a castle."

"There are over six hundred prisoners in there."

"Well, I guess Montana *is* a big state." She smiled at him, still shaking her head in disbelief.

Finally, they turned their eyes to the storefronts on the opposite side of the road and the reassuring feeling of Americana. Keystone Drugstore, Coleman Jewelry, Deer Lodge Bakery, Toyland. If they put their backs to the prison castle set against a painted backdrop of valley and mountains and focused on the town beyond, they could almost forget about crime and punishment.

"Let's go find our house!"

"No, let's save the best for last." Geneviève squeezed Will's hand encouragingly.

They traveled past the train station and roundhouse, then to the outer edges of town where they saw ranches, sawmills, railroads, and even mines. They drove the streets named after various towns or states in America, seeing everything from cottages to mansions to log cabins to decorative Victorians surrounded by weeping birch.

At last, they located their house on Milwaukee Avenue, a stunningly beautiful Victorian, more elegant than Geneviève could have imagined. A large quaking aspen awaited her in the front yard, its white bark a striking contrast to its gold leaves.

The house was such a home. Wood floors with inlaid patterns, and banisters, and framing. The two ran through the rooms and up the stairs to the bay windows, turrets, angled walls, and cubby corner rooms where children could play. It would have fit a large family. She bit her lip at the thought.

"Plenty of room to dance!" William whisked her around the parlor and swirled her in front of the bay window. Her shoes clicked along the wood, a steady percussion. He dipped her backward and then kissed her. "That's so everyone knows how much I love you." He twirled her into his arms. She knew he was still working on selling her on Deer Lodge.

"You have your work cut out for you buying furniture." She could buy the furnishings, but this house would still be missing something. Her definition of home meant family. "In the meantime, Mrs. Ellis, we could stay here . . ." William took her by the waist. "Or I could take you to the Rialto for a show followed by a stay at the Hotel Deer Lodge. We never really had a honeymoon." His voice echoed in the empty room. "*Honeymoon. Honeymoon. Honeymoon*," he repeated in jest.

As the sun lowered, the sky turned brilliant swaths of colors. Not a rainbow but a soothing band of illumination that reminded her that life was still rich.

"How? What is it? What makes it?"

"Alpenglow." Her husband gave it a name and then continued with a satisfyingly scientific description.

She moved to the front porch. He took his hand in hers and they sat in silence on the steps. If she ignored the prison, the beauty of this valley and their little town was growing on her.

"Let's go out on the town, Mr. Ellis. A second honeymoon."

She kept her expectations low. Deer Lodge's Rialto was no Seattle Fifth Avenue Theatre, where William had recently chosen to celebrate their fifth wedding anniversary and its grand opening. Where dance bands entertained the crowds on every intersection of the seven blocks of closed streets and thousands sang along with the words projected on a giant screen. "The Magic Sign of a Wonderful Time" over the marquee, spotlights, klieg lights, and flares.

And yet, this Main Street theater with its Beaux Arts architecture and red Spanish tile roof, contrasting a creamy brick exterior, was quite impressive.

"What are we seeing?"

"Harold Lloyd and Jobyna Ralston. They've got real chemistry."
William squeezed her hand and winked. "Just like us."

That twinkle in her husband's eye always made her catch her breath.
How could she respond?

"It's a gag film. We'll laugh." And that's exactly what he did. Laugh.
As if everything about this new beginning meant a happy ending.

"So what's it about?"

"A millionaire by the name of J. Harold Manners." William
pronounced his name as if announcing a royal subject. "He falls in
love with a girl named Hope." His eyes focused on her, so gentle, so
loving. "For heaven's sake, that's me. A guy with everything he could
ask for smitten by the girl of his dreams."

Genevieve smiled when she read the marquee: *For Heaven's Sake.*
What a title!

William opened the door to the marble flooring and wainscoting,
the arches, and painted murals. But the opulence of the theater itself
with its old French-style side panels with roses and velvet stage curtain
was a complete surprise. She collapsed into a burgundy velvet seat as
someone began playing ragtime on the Cremona Theater organ.

Tilting her head back, she studied the huge chandelier surrounded
by seven smaller ones. Will took her hand and squeezed it so
reassuringly. She loved him more than she could ever explain. Were
they whole as a family of two? *Alpenglow.*

What a curious place. So wild it invited exploration. A newly
discovered love sonnet they could read together. Maybe it was about
hope.

Chapter Thirty-Four
Siobhan

Love of man for woman—love of woman for man.
That's the nature, the meaning, the best of life itself.
—Zane Grey, *Riders of the Purple Sage*

Deer Lodge, Montana
Spring 1920

Siobhan had hoped that the boys might miraculously look similar, but Samuel was a wiry boy with sandy-colored hair like his mother and a face shaped like his father's, with deep blue eyes and a wide smile. Paul was a hefty little bambino who looked nothing like Siobhan or Jack. And though Samuel thrived at her breast, younger Paul began to outgrow him.

Siobhan had been nearly invisible in Deer Lodge for the two months prior to Paul's birth and hadn't ventured into Deer Lodge after, knowing the day she brought baby Paul to town would raise eyebrows. As the months went by, she hoped it would draw less attention to Paul's birth date.

This meant endless days at home with two babies and a longing for adult company. When Jack came home from the mill, then finished his farm chores, she found herself drawn to his warmth, the smell of the hay and everything honest and earthy about him. And especially the relief he spelled with the boys.

One evening when the babies were crying, too tired to fall asleep, Jack and she paced them around the front room. Siobhan finally collapsed on the sofa and began laughing.

"It's not that funny." Jack bobbed Samuel up and down.

"I know. But at least it's man-to-man defense." The two had enjoyed watching the high school basketball team last November and she was rather proud she could reference that in her description. "It's better than when I'm all alone."

Jack dropped down beside her. "Are you lonely, Siobhan?" Samuel's cries suddenly quieted as if he wanted to hear the answer or else appreciated the proximity to his mother.

"Sometimes," she admitted. "When you're at the mill. I'm lonely for friends."

He stopped bobbing Samuel, who now reached for Siobhan.

"Not that you're *not* a friend," Siobhan corrected. Samuel's little fingers petted her cheek. "I mean, you are my friend." She couldn't quite explain herself.

Jack's eyes saddened and he sighed.

"But perhaps if I knew more people in town. Had friends that were like sisters."

"So, you consider me a . . . a b*rother*?" He leaned in for the answer. His blue eyes so soft and yet intense. Samuel's look mirrored his father's.

"Oh, no!" She shook her head and felt a rush of warmth. Samuel yawned and rubbed his fist in his face, signaling sleep.

Jack lay Samuel in the crib. As if on cue to compete with his older brother, Paul's eyes closed, and Jack took him from Siobhan's arms and laid him beside his brother. Jack returned and sat on the couch next to Siobhan.

"You need to get out. The weather is warming. Go back into town."

"Yes, but Paul is such a big boy. Almost the size of Samuel!"

"I don't care what people think. You need to make friends."

Maybe Jack and she were just friends. She had no idea what he was like with Annabeth. Maybe they were soulmates and Jack could never love Siobhan like that. Did he wonder whether she still had feelings for Paul's father? Could they both leave the past behind and go forward? Was it her responsibility to let him know that she was ready?

She closed her eyes and tipped her head back. How lovely to feel her neck conform to the back of the davenport, her hair draped loose and wild.

"You're beautiful, Siobhan."

She opened her eyes to see his face close to hers.

"Never would I have imagined I could marry a woman with such strength and fire."

Millie's words echoed in her memory. Siobhan was strong indeed. She reached out and stroked his cheek. She loved the feeling of unshaven stubble on the back of her hand. She traced his lips until he brought his hand up to hers and held it.

Her heart pounded wildly, and she wondered if he knew it or whether his beat with the same intensity. Resting her palm on his chest, she knew. Then he placed his hand to her heart and nodded. His hand dropped slightly, almost accidentally, as if testing, and then he cupped her breast and gasped. His eyes were closed. She trembled and he drew away. *Oh, stay!* But he took her face in his hands instead. They were rough, calloused; he was gentle and strong. His fingers then slowly tickled through her hair. Maybe he was lonely. Maybe he was longing for something any woman could give him, but to her what he was doing seemed like something more. His hands dropped to her shoulders where he touched her skin so lightly, she shivered.

He scooped her up and carried her for what she hoped was the answer to her longing. To what she anticipated would now be *their* bed.

Very slowly, she untied her bodice so that his fingers could then caress her arms. A single feather lay on the pillow and he picked it up and traced it across her forehead and down to her neck. Soon his lips found hers and she knew that there was a way they fit together. An exquisite lock and key; his lips were soft, gentle, and kind, and full of intent that one day, Paul and Samuel might have a brother or sister.

The next morning, she awakened to a man in her bed. Their bed. This was something she had never experienced, and she smiled at the thought. The rooster crowed and yet the babies slept, a gift to them both.

Where Jack and she had previously been shy and cautious, she now could not get enough of touching him and knowing every place on his body. She ran her fingers through his hair and down to the hair on his chest and felt the muscles of his arms and every other curvature, and oh how he laughed.

"Do I pass inspection?"

She rolled atop him, her hair tickling his face. "More than you could know."

Chapter Thirty-Five
Siobhan

*The ghostly winter silence had given way
to the great spring murmur of awakening life.*
—Jack London, *The Call of the Wild*

Deer Lodge, Montana
Summer 1920

Another book arrived and she threw her arms around Jack in excitement, then ran her hands down from his shoulders to forearms, as sturdy as planks run through the millworks.

"What are the boys up to?" He winked at her gentle caress.

She didn't answer. "I have something for you." She took a small package from the dresser.

Jack opened the package tenderly, pulling the string. Inside was a framed photo of the four of them, taken a month prior, an update of her Christmas present. "And now I have one more gift." She smiled as she led him toward their bedroom. The new book could wait.

Her room was now *their* room. They collapsed on the two down pillows and then Jack undid her bodice as he had unwrapped the picture of their family. He picked up a stray feather off the comforter and tickled her from head to toe. She would never grow tired of his touch.

"There's a concert at the W. A. Clark Theater. I don't remember the name of the group, but they're here from Minnesota. I think we should go."

Siobhan shook her head, not at the tickle but at his suggestion. She hadn't wanted to make an appearance in Deer Lodge. Not yet. It was too soon. The longer she waited and the longer before townspeople saw her boys, the greater the chance Paul would pass for Jack's son.

"Siobhan, you can't hide out here at the house forever. And besides, I don't care what people think." He ran his eyes up and down her body. "We could leave the babies here. Naomi and Walter would take care of them. They're just down the road. You trust them. Then we'll just be two in a crowd of hundreds. It'll be good for you."

"The idea of being in a prison. I don't like it. Especially after Sheriff Warburton's murder."

"That wasn't in the prison. We'll be in the theater in the yard. Only the women prisoners will be with us. All three of them. It's the first prison theater in the US." His voice bragged with authority.

She dangled one of her red curls across his chest.

"You have me captive." His voice cracked with what she hoped was longing.

Prison. Wouldn't Brigid think that fitting? What a contrast that Jack wanted into a place so many people wanted out of.

"They even have a thirty-piece uniformed prison band. People come from out of town to hear the concerts."

Siobhan considered the offer. Jack was serious. He wanted to take her on a memorable date in the prison the townspeople called the House of Forget.

"We missed the opening, but it's time we got out, Siobhan!"

Her friend Lilian had already told her about the theater. Invisible from outside the walls, it hardly seemed real to Siobhan with its classical portico and balcony. Lilian's husband James had sketched it in pencil and Conley had it constructed using prison labor and the dollars from W. A. Clark. The theater seated six hundred in the main section and four hundred in the gallery. On April 2, "My Sunshine Lady" had entertained all the male prisoners.

Finally, she accepted Jack's date. The calendar said spring, but it had snowed the day before and the ground was cold beneath her feet. What she loved about Montana was that the sky was bright blue and clear. If she could climb the mountain range, she'd see that the sky went on forever.

As they entered the prison gates, her boundaries were defined. Siobhan inhaled deeply and blew out, watching her breath. Somewhere beneath the cold, she could smell spring. She wondered if the prisoners could sense it too.

They crossed the yard and saw the white brick façade of simulated stone and the large pilasters and columns that announced the theater entrance. Neither Jack nor she said a word as the stepped into the theater. The stage and orchestra pit were huge, and the ceilings reached at least eighty feet high. Hanging at the back of the stage below the proscenium arch was a painted curtain that Lilian said was done by one of the inmates, depicting DaVinci's *The Last Supper*.

"That isn't some sort of gallows humor, is it?" Jack turned to her with a wink.

The Renaissance-style theater with its Corinthian columns, paneled walls and ceiling, and an octagonal stained-glass light was one of the grandest rooms in Deer Lodge, an irony not lost on Siobhan.

The prison band began, and Siobhan was back in Boston with the parades. She clapped her hands together in delight. Jack leaned over and kissed her. He was right. Though she loved being home with him, she needed this happy ragtime music.

As Jack drove home, Siobhan sang in his ear, "Kiss Me, My Honey, Kiss Me" and Jack answered with "Dreams, Just Dreams," another song from the night. They were both drowsy and relaxed.

"By day, I can almost see our home from here. Now all I see are the stars."

Siobhan's heart swelled and then she exhaled with a deep and satisfying sigh, then remembered the theater. "I hope the prisoners can see them, too."

Jack tensed. His hands gripped the wheel. "I don't ever want to know that kind of darkness again."

Siobhan knew she had plunged him into the memory of the mines, and she needed to get him out.

"What do you want to do, Jack? What's your dream?" The same question had been asked of her on North Beach in Boston.

"I want to farm. Have enough land that I don't need to go to the mill. I want to love you more than I do today, which sounds impossible. I want our children to go to school so they never live in darkness."

Jack had fears and he had dreams. Did she? Or could it be that her dreams were to follow his?

They picked up the boys from the neighbors and enjoyed the baked bread and beef stew Siobhan had cooked the night before. The house smelled warm and satisfying. Jack sat at the piano and mimicked the songs they had heard, and Siobhan thought that perhaps her reality was better than any dream.

In August, Siobhan enjoyed her first Deer Lodge Farmers Picnic and Fair with a basket lunch in a shady nook listening to the band, dancing at Milwaukee Hall, watching baseball, bulldogging, calf roping, bareback and wild horse races. Why, even President Roosevelt made an appearance proclaiming, "Those who look backward are inclined to say, 'Those were the good old days.'" She believed she'd vote for him in the next election.

The Rock Creek Labor Day event was especially exciting when the range stallion broke loose. Then fall arrived with hayrides, followed by sleigh rides, and ice skating on College Hill. When spring came, the hollyhocks burst into bloom followed by the purple clematis, and they planned and planted for the next year. Their married life became an ebb and flow of hard farmwork and making the most out of a simple thing like a feather.

She rarely thought of Antonio except when the books arrived. Most of what he wrote was purely academic, revolving around characters, setting, theme, plot, and discussions of terms. Though Antonio's initial love of literature was self-taught, she could tell that his comments were now tempered by his education.

She read everything between the lines, hungrily devouring not only the typed font, but the handwritten notes in the margin. Each book connected her to Boston or places she'd never been to in Europe.

Her letters to him were a one-page analysis of the book. She would have felt guilty offering more—as if she had betrayed Jack with an emotional affair on paper. She owed Jack more than that.

Jack enjoyed a few of Antonio's books more than she. When Antonio sent Zane Grey's *Riders of the Purple Sage* about a woman saved by a gunslinging avenger, she wondered if the book wasn't more for Jack's benefit than hers. The cover could have been the two of them riding together on the back of a horse to Rock Creek Lake. After flipping through the pages without finding any notes, she gave it to Jack for the first read. And then when *The Call of the Wild* arrived, a survival tale set during the Klondike Gold Rush, Siobhan gave him that one too; after all, it did have his name on the cover. Jack loved it.

Siobhan measured time by the books on Jack's bookshelf. In the first year of marriage, she had ten. Each year thereafter, it multiplied. Sometimes she wrote less often, and the shelf grew more slowly. Other times she raced to the post office with words on a newly scribbled letter; then from across the country, his words tucked inside a book quickly answered.

That past December, Antonio sent a bottle of scotch for Jack, *North and South* for her, *The Five Little Peppers and How They Grew*, and peppermint sticks for the children. When she tried to explain who had sent them such a lavish present, she had slipped and called him Uncle Auntie. Her children laughed and thereafter dubbed him Uncle Auntie. If it troubled Jack, he never let on.

Now as the years put time and distance between Boston and Deer Lodge, Antonio and Siobhan had known each other in correspondence longer than in person. And sometimes it surprised her that though they'd never meet again, Antonio was true to his promise.

Chapter Thirty-Six
Geneviève

Deer Lodge, Montana
Spring 1927

Geneviève found work at Doctor Briggs's office in the hospital. He was a good man, a competent doctor who also worked part-time at the prison. With so many male prisoners, he was often making calls and so she served the patients who came to the office. It was simpler and quieter than hospital work in Spokane and she found purpose in using her skills.

"I need you to accompany me to the prison," he asked her one morning. "The *women's* prison."

Though there were hundreds of male prisoners, she knew there were less than ten in the women's prison. One of the rare occasions he needed special assistance.

She had avoided the end of Main Street and the monstrosity that consumed her husband's work by day and his thoughts by night. The red brick façade was, in so many ways, a castle of crime and a curious blight on an otherwise perfect horizon.

"There's a female prisoner that needs medical attention." Doctor Briggs packed his bag. "I don't go into that section without another person. A *woman*."

The prison, on the outside, stood quiet and stoic. Geneviève had to admit she had once been curious about the inside, but not after William's stories about the horrors of the place seeped into their home. William despised what he saw and nightly worked out the cage of his thoughts, for which she had no key.

"It's overcrowded, understaffed and overworked. There's no individual plumbing in the original section. There are three showerheads for six hundred men. Ventilation is so bad it reeks of human waste and sweat. And in the winter the wood stoves and oil lamps make breathing difficult. And the roof could go like that." William snapped his fingers and made a *fsst* sound to demonstrate its flammability.

Doc Briggs and she left the hospital and headed toward Main.

"When he was warden, Frank Conley built an empire while his prisoners built a cage for their confinement. Now he's the longest serving mayor in American history." Doc Briggs was a professional and private man who rarely said anything about prison or politics. His conversation surprised her.

"I don't understand how he's still the mayor when he was fired from being warden." She could picture the extremely large man at six and a half feet and about three hundred pounds. Her husband claimed he had more hair under his nose than on his head.

"Didn't you see the town give him a standing ovation at the Fair? They love him. They see roads and bridges, and buildings built by prisoners, so they don't care that those same prisoners aren't being educated or treated well. Or that Conley used them for his own personal interests."

"What did the prisoners think about him?"

"Back in 1908 there was a revolt. One guard was killed, and Conley was stabbed and cut fifty times. His throat was slit, requiring a hundred and three stitches.

"It was an eighth of an inch from his jugular." Doctor Briggs touched his throat. "Conley hung the men responsible in the yard for all to see and yelled, 'Vengeance is mine!'"

"That's awful!"

"Not surprising from a man who claimed half the prisoners are physically diseased or mentally insane." Doctor Briggs let that hang.

At Tower Seven, Doctor Briggs knocked on the door. "I guess we're all guilty of giving thanks for the twenty-four-foot wall that separates us."

They were let into the first vestibule where a key was lowered down. This key let them into the next section where the key was exchanged for another key lowered to them. Geneviève watched in fascination. Then they were released into the yard, where the prisoners sat in the warm sunshine.

After another gate, they were finally in the women's yard, a narrow strip of land surrounding a small building, with outer walls so tall, the prisoners would never see the sky. It made Geneviève claustrophobic.

Once inside, the matron ushered them into a special room where their patient, a gaunt woman with a flushed face, awaited medical attention. Geneviève first assumed she had a fever.

"I cough. Real bad." The doctor checked her lungs. Geneviève took her pulse. "Just so tired." The woman wheezed. "Can't get my breath and my chest hurts. It hurts real bad, Doc."

"How are you sleeping?"

"Just hot and then I sweat and then it feels cold."

"Describe your cough."

"Dry. Sometimes a little blood."

They both knew what was wrong and what was her new sentence. She had to be removed from the contained environment as soon as possible before the others were condemned with TB.

Geneviève knew the infection was from the inside out, and so was whatever evil was festering in the walls of the Montana State Penitentiary. She wanted out as quickly as possible.

Chapter Thirty-Seven
Siobhan

Deer Lodge, Montana
April 1923–1928

It was three more years before Siobhan was expecting again. This time, her pregnancy was complicated by two toddlers running around the farm. The two brothers were close but often fought like Jacob and Esau, vying for her attention.

Samuel didn't look like Jack and was significantly smaller. Siobhan could never determine if he was unhealthy or had inherited his mother's genes. He was fair-haired but melancholy, quiet, and withdrawn. Samuel was clingy and, as he grew, so dependent on Siobhan, townsfolk no doubt forgot that he was another mother's child.

Paul would one day be tall, dark, and swarthy. She tried not to see Giovanni in Paul, but God had not gifted her with a son that bore any resemblance to herself. His olive-colored skin never burnt in the sun like his blond older brother's. His cheerful disposition was that of Antonio. Paul would always be a reminder of the brothers Giovanni and Antonio and the painful way they were all connected.

Oddly, with this pregnancy she had no sickness. Jack talked names for the new arrival. He would name a son and it would be a Biblical name and she would name a daughter. Siobhan practiced Irish names: Shannon, Brianna, Caitlin, Catriona, Deirdre, Fiona, Maire, Saoirse. Her daughter's name would be unique, and because its spelling would challenge her friends, it would give her daughter a reminder that she came from another place.

The birth was so long and difficult, and with so much loss of blood that Jack had gone for Doctor Briggs. When all was quiet and she still awaited the baby's cry, she feared trouble. Her first thought, her secret longing had been *please let it be a daughter.* But when there was no rejoicing, she feared something was wrong with her child. *Please not with my child! Please let it be me. Please let it be me. Pleaseletitbeme...*

"It's a girl." Jack's voice was flat.

What was wrong? Something was wrong. "Let me see her, Jack."

"Your daughter has a minor problem." Dr. Briggs continued examining the baby, his back to her.

"No. There is no problem," Jack interrupted. "She's beautiful." The doctor whispered to Jack as he wiped the baby with a wet washcloth. Jack wrapped the baby in a blanket and placed their daughter in her arms.

Siobhan gasped. "She *is* beautiful." In relief she cried and collapsed backward. It was over now. She had a daughter! The baby rested in the crook of her arm. Siobhan touched her button nose and ran her fingers over the wisps of curly blonde hair. "She has blue eyes, Jack. Just like you." Then Siobhan unwrapped the blanket.

"Not yet, Siobhan, I need to finish with some things on you first," Dr. Briggs cautioned. "You should wait."

But Siobhan couldn't. She wanted to see her baby's fingers and toes and the place where they had once been connected—the beginning of something she knew would go on long after her daughter left home and long after Siobhan died, because that was how it should be with mothers and daughters. Even though that had not happened to her with her own mothers.

When Siobhan counted her baby's fingers, she found there were not ten. One arm was shorter and had only three fingers. Her baby's hand was a misshapen piece that looked like her garden trowel.

"Oh," she whispered in a long exhale. Jack bent down near Siobhan's face and took the little three-fingered hand so unlike any others and blessed it with a kiss.

"She's perfect." His face was wet with tears, but they didn't seem to be tears of sadness. He was hopeful and he displayed such happiness, so she would be happy, too. Her daughter would be stronger because of this.

"She's a princess." Jack traced the crown of her head.

"Saraid," Siobhan answered as if trying it on for size. "*Sah-RY.*"

"That sounds beautiful." Jack smiled at them both.

"That's *Sarah* in Irish. It means *princess*. You just named her, Jack." They gave her a Biblical name that was as beautiful as she was. Her Saraid.

As Sarah grew, Siobhan caught the eyes that lingered on Sarah's strawberry blonde curls hanging in ringlets down her shoulders. Sarah had Siobhan's porcelain skin with peaches and cream cheeks. Her blue eyes sparkled with a smile and lit up in a fight with her older brothers. This only made others laugh and tease. She had a spirited radiance about her. Alpenglow.

She was daddy's little girl and the boys never minded because she was theirs as well. Samuel had been disinterested by the cherished gift of the stuffed bunny from his grandfather. Paul had never so much as gazed at the toy on the mantel. But Sarah asked about it, so Siobhan was not surprised when Jack took it off the mantel.

"His name is Wilfred. He's in the funnies: Pip, Squeak, and Wilfred. They're all orphaned. Pip is the dog, Squeak is the mother, and Wilfred is the little boy bunny." Jack handed the rabbit to his daughter. "It's yours now, princess."

The irony of the orphaned bunny did not escape Siobhan. Samuel's grandfather could not have known Samuel would also lose a parent, or that his first toy would be a precious hand-me-down to a younger sister. Though Wilfred did not retain his mantel condition, Sarah's gentle care kept him safe. Being a little mother came naturally to their daughter and good practice for her future.

Chapter Thirty-Eight
Geneviève

Deer Lodge, Montana
March 7, 1928

William was now a prosecuting attorney. He didn't love his new position any more than he had loved investigating the prison. In fact, now that he knew what was happening to the men he put inside, he sometimes vacillated about his career direction. Geneviève hoped that might prompt a move away from the prison town.

Geneviève focused on her career, the steady stream of patients, and at thirty-three, almost accepted her status. Most all her friends, like Lilian McCalm with two sons, were *haves*. But Geneviève was childless. She was a *have-not*. One of the rare women in town without the title of Mother. And yet, even in her work, every child reminded her of the ghost children that had come in and out of her life, never to stay. Every pregnant mother reminded her that her body would never let those children stay.

It happened again on March 7, 1928.

"It's my wife!" The man rushed into the waiting room. "I think this one's coming faster." Geneviève didn't recognize the anxious husband, but Doc Briggs did.

"Siobhan's not due for another month, Jack."

"She's downstairs. Should I bring her up? You know what happened last time."

Geneviève didn't know and couldn't decipher what happened last time, probably before she came to Deer Lodge, but whatever it was must have been bad. The husband was stricken with worry.

"Bring her up and if we need to, we'll move her to delivery." Doc Briggs nodded and Geneviève immediately prepped the table. When Jack brought Siobhan up, it was obvious his wife wasn't going to the delivery room. That baby was coming now and if it was a month early, there could be problems.

"Siobhan, I'll be in the other room." Jack squeezed her hand, bent over, and kissed her forehead. "I love you, honey."

"No, stay, Jack. You've always been there." Siobhan clung to Jack. Geneviève thought she'd never heard a voice so lovely. Irish?

Jack looked to the doctor who smiled. Doc Briggs had delivered his own four babies. Why would he deny Jack?

Geneviève had never seen such a fast delivery.

"This little fellow had a quick exodus!" Doc Briggs announced and laughed. "And considering he's a month early, he's a big fellow."

"It's a boy?" Siobhan's voice was thick with emotion.

The baby let out a healthy cry. Geneviève snipped the umbilical cord as Siobhan gazed at her son. Then Geneviève took the baby aside and cleaned him off, Jack standing over her shoulder as if monitoring her work.

"He's all right?" Siobhan asked. Why were they so concerned? What had happened before?

"Everything is fine, Siobhan." Jack's rich baritone sounded reassuring.

This baby was more than fine. He was near perfection. Geneviève cleaned his eyes, wiped his tiny arms and legs slower than necessary. She wanted this moment. She doubted he was premature for when she put him on the scale, he weighed seven pounds, three ounces. Then she wrapped him in a blanket and held him close, his face soft against hers and his aroma so sweet. This one was special. Unique.

"Caleb Andrew." Jack's voice was a suggestion. Geneviève handed the baby to him. "What do you think about that, Siobhan?" He snuggled the baby into the crook of her arm. "Caleb Andrew Mason." The three were so beautiful together.

Would Geneviève's children have been so perfect? Surely William would have been that attentive. He would have loved a son. All she ever wanted was for even one of her children to survive. *O God, where were her babies now?*

Chapter Thirty-Nine
Siobhan

*Our souls are like those orphans whose unwedded mothers
die in bearing them:
the secret of our paternity lies in their grave, and we must
there to learn it.*
—Herman Melville, *Moby Dick*

Deer Lodge, Montana
March 7, 1928

Siobhan could not honestly say she loved one son more than the others. All were children of a man she'd loved. But Caleb, who looked nothing like his brothers, was the perfect combination of Siobhan and Jack, and this made him different. Special. Unique.

It had been five years since Sarah was born. Perhaps that was why Jack and she so celebrated the arrival of their fourth child, a son, the easiest and quickest delivery to date.

His older brothers thought little of the new baby, but Sarah adored him.

"I have something for you, baby." The little girl kissed and then squeezed Wilfred, placing the bunny on the table near Caleb's cradle. Sarah didn't need Wilfred any longer since she had a real baby to play with. "Mr. Bunny will give you lots of hugs when you get bigger." Siobhan was quite sure Jack teared up at his daughter's generosity. So much so, he asked Siobhan to make Sarah a Raggedy Ann doll. After all, that was how they afforded toys: spools for homemade tinker toys and Jack's Lincoln log creations.

From the start, Caleb was Sarah's little charge. She was his little mother and filled Siobhan's absence when Siobhan worked the farm. Wasn't that what a farm family did? Even in Boston, parents sent their children to the factories, or left them behind when parents went to work. You had to do what you needed to do to keep your family alive.

With the Great War in the not-so-distant past, anti-German sentiment was still strong and seemingly gaining in strength.

"They called me a Kraut!" Samuel ran up to Siobhan as she waited outside Keystone Drug. Siobhan considered how the wars could influence their family. Would the truth come out on the playground?

The wind whipped down Main, unleashing snow from the awnings. Siobhan shivered and hugged Samuel close. They hadn't kept Samuel's parentage a secret, they had never lied, they had just never explained the truth. The fact that Annabeth died shortly after his delivery still did not make Siobhan his biological mother, but it did in all other ways.

She had overheard the boys taunting but had not intervened. Nobody wanted to be German these days, not even a little boy who never knew his real mother, or been told who she was, or that she was of German birth.

"What did you say when they teased you?" Siobhan treaded carefully.

"I said just because you have red hair doesn't make you a Kraut and that your name was Siobhan *Kildea* and that you came from Ireland!"

"Well then! There you have it!" Siobhan brushed it aside. *Make this go away. Make this go away.*

The door jangled as one customer left, and Siobhan moved down the sidewalk to let him by.

"But George asked me if that was really my mother's name. That I should check the birth certificate. That you are a Kraut!"

Siobhan peered up and down the street. Nobody had heard. Somebody in this town remembered Annabeth. What could she say?

She had no response.

"*Are* you a Kraut?" Samuel pronounced Kraut with disgust. Sauerkraut was now Liberty Cabbage. Did he even understand what any of it meant?

"No, of course not." Siobhan laughed. "And I don't like using that word. Can we just say *German*?" She thought of Annabeth. What would Annabeth tell her son?

"Is your real name Siobhan Kildea?"

"Why of course! You know that, Samuel." Her voice sounded scolding. Could she steer him off this topic? "Well actually, it's *Moira* Siobhan Kildea Mason."

Samuel frowned as if trying to make sense of the latest information. "That's a lot of names. And my real name is Samuel Mason?"

"Samuel *Jacob* Mason. Your middle name is after your father. He wanted that! II remember when we named you." She took his hand, and they began walking. "Did you want to stop at Keystone and have some penny candy?" The fact that she was not there nine months before should not be the hidden key that unlocked the story.

She took his hand, and they began walking. "Did you want to stop at Keystone and have some penny candy?"

That evening she joined Jack in the barn where the children would not hear what she knew would come to an argument. It always did. He pitched hay in the stalls while she watered the animals.

"Jack, we have to tell them."

"We will. When they're ready."

"That's not what this is about. It's about when *you're* ready."

"Maybe." He stabbed the loose hay and threw it into the newly cleaned stall. It cascaded like snow to the barn floor and Siobhan sneezed. "Why do they need to know?" Jack began on the next stall. "Annabeth is gone. Samuel can't know her. And Paul's . . ." He eyed Siobhan. "Do we know where he is?" It was the closest he had ever asked about Paul's father. Did she owe that to him? They shared everything. Everything except Giovanni. What was she afraid of? Or was it really Giovanni she was afraid of?

She shook her head. No, she didn't really know anything about him at the time, she could only speak of the past.

"Do you want to know about him?" There it was. Her question and possibly his.

Jack stopped and sat down on the hay bale, laid his pitchfork aside, and wiped his forehead. She knew that whatever his answer, it would be the last words on this topic. He would say something that ended all discussion. That was Jack. He tilted his head thoughtfully and smiled. She drew in the smell of fresh hay. She loved this barn and she loved her man.

"When a child is born, we look for what's like us, both the good and the bad. Sometimes I see things I have taught, and I'm so proud. Then there are surprises and I think, maybe this is the best part of being a father . . . to see something new and fresh and unexpected." He smiled and paused as if seeing a memory in the distance. "When I watch Paul, I see you. I do not see the man who . . . who is his relation. I don't know that man. I can't picture him, and he has added nothing to this child except the blood that flows in his veins. Everything else is what I've taught him. And so, while there is a curiosity, I don't want to know this man or his name. I want to continue to be surprised and I want to continue to see how I have nurtured Paul to manhood."

So, this was how he viewed it. He didn't want the full truth, so she didn't have to tell it. She didn't have to reveal that up until three months into their marriage, Giovanni had been the love of her life. That her love for Jack had grown in a way that far exceeded anything she and Giovanni could have ever known.

"Now, what do you think?" He took her hands in his. "Do these boys need to know about people who no longer have any influence on their lives?" Siobhan shook her head slowly, but it didn't take away the nagging feeling that they did have an influence and that one day her boys would find out.

Chapter Forty
Siobhan

He was ready to give up, he felt.
He did not know how it had come about,
but he was quite willing to go deep under his fields and rest,
where the plow could not find him. He was tired of making mistakes.
He was content to leave the tangle to other hands.
—Willa Cather, *O Pioneers!*

Deer Lodge, Montana
January 1931

The crash of a stock market in a big city two thousand miles away, at first, seemed unrelated to anything in rural Montana—particularly the stories of people jumping from tall buildings to their death. That couldn't happen in Deer Lodge, where residents pulled together as a community.

But when banks failed and the endless drought continued, Siobhan began to understand the trickle-down effect of the depression. Two years before, wheat went for ninety-three cents a bushel and now it was thirty-six.

Jack shielded her from the worst, taking on the full burden. She read their finances like she read a stressful book; she just knew they would find money for seeds, and the story would finish well.

Each day teased Deer Lodge with cheerful sunshine while the wind blew the dust everywhere. She wanted to stand in rain and hold her hands to the sky and let the showers wash over her. It would look like revival in Deer Lodge. They would all be washed clean. In the meantime, she told stories, sang songs, and made sure they were all fed, looking to spring to change everything.

On Caleb's birthday, Jack gave him a coin from his father, and to Paul, his beloved pocket watch. They had little extra for niceties like birthday presents. When Jack seemed distant, she'd suggest they get out to a concert or the theater. But Jack never wanted to leave the farm. He resisted even a soda at the Deer Lodge Bakery or the free passes to the Orpheum.

"I'm not taking handouts."

"You work so hard, Jack. You can't keep on like that."

But he did keep on just like that—only harder.

When Jack lost his job at the mill, he was "lucky" to have another option: Anderson Mine, where he donned a carbide headlamp and descended in the cage to utter darkness where he mined for phosphate underground. Work was hard to come by. When Montana Power Company advertised job openings in out-of-state papers, Montanans cried, "Montana Work for Montana People." She wished Jack had been hired there instead of the mine.

Jack said very little to Siobhan about the mining job. He showered at the Dry and came home clean, leaving behind his clothes and all talk of life underground. But she knew that there was a sacrifice in returning belowground, and that he'd ridden the train from West Virginia to escape it so many years before.

He doubled down at home. In the back field, he labored on a project, most likely digging holes for additional trees to shelter the farm animals. Or maybe it was for seeds that would be planted if they had enough money to buy them, when she knew he hadn't paid off last year's loan, and would those seeds ever grow if it didn't rain? By now, Siobhan knew all about blackleg, coyotes, hog cholera, and potato wart. There were so many ways to kill an animal, or a crop, or a man's spirit.

Siobhan knew these things without Jack's warnings. He tended to himself these days, and it was a rare moment for him to bring up the troubles of his heart. How she longed to share the burden of what was on his mind but could only share in the physical toil of farm life. If only he would talk.

She enjoyed working parallel shoveling stalls or the teamwork necessary in hauling the feed and distributing it to the animals. They'd sometimes call out to one another, focused on pitching hay or carrying buckets, and the physicality of the labor. Usually, they'd share small talk or chatter about the children, and on rare occasions deeper communication.

"I know you're thinking about those predictions. But they're only that. Just predictions. We don't know that's how it will turn out with the weather and all."

"They say it'll be like 1919."

"We made it through that year," Siobhan answered, hiding her surprise at his response by lifting another load of straw.

"It was hard, but I didn't have a crop to lose." Jack turned his back and dug deeper into the muck of the stall.

"Was it so terrible?" she asked. "That was the year you met me. In the lobby of Hotel Deer Lodge." Now she stopped her work and joined him for what she hoped would be a reminder of better days.

Jack didn't smile. She nuzzled his face with hers. What a year that must have been for Jack. He had lost Annabeth, became a father to a baby boy, and experienced a severe drought. Then Siobhan arrived, oblivious to the depth of his despair. Had she brought him something good?

"Are you glad you met me?" She took both hands in his.

"Are you glad you met *me*?" He echoed her question.

"Oh, Jack!" She wrapped his arms around her then hugged him tightly. "I only wish I had met you sooner." What else could she say? She had never loved anyone as much as him. She only hoped she'd been more than a distraction during that horrible year and this one as well.

What could she do now to help? This year would be more difficult with four children and one on the way. If *her* dream had been to help him with *his* dream, then they couldn't lose the farm.

They stood embracing one another, holding onto their memories as well as fears. What was he thinking? Antonio had sent another Cather book. *Prairie Spring.* Like the title, what they felt was merely a season. Now the words lay heavy on her heart.

The growing wheat, the growing weeds,
The toiling horses, the tired men;
The long empty roads,
Sullen fires of sunset, fading,
The eternal, unresponsive sky

"Talk to me, Jack!" she pleaded, whispering into his ear. "Other people are going through the same thing. Or talk to someone." But the slight crack had closed, he seemed tired, unresponsive, at last pulling away and shaking his head.

"I can't do this, Siobhan."

At the time, she hadn't understood what that meant.

Chapter Forty-One
Erin

Seattle, Washington
July 25, 1981

With GinnaBee settled at Summer Meadows, Erin was preparing to fly back to Seattle when the phone rang.

"Mom? Mom?"

"Claire, you don't sound good. Are you all right?"

Erin heard only hiccupping sobs.

"Were you in an accident?"

Claire's speech was garbled and unintelligible, but Erin did hear a no.

"I can't understand you, honey. Slow down." Still more crying. "Breathe. Claire. Breathe. What happened? Are you hurt?"

"No." She choked. "No."

Erin let out her breath in relief. Claire's sobs continued until she confessed.

"She didn't want to see me."

It took so long before Erin responded. What could she say? Erin had to admit she was mad. She had asked Claire to wait. But Claire was headstrong and now faced the third rejection. And alone. *I told you so* wouldn't help. Apparently, Claire needed to learn by experience. Take the field trip.

"I'm so sorry, honey. So sorry." What had she done? "Did you call her?"

"No. I drove up to her house."

Erin shook her head and rolled her eyes, thankful Claire couldn't see her reaction.

"Where are you now?"

"I . . . I . . . I don't know where, just outside of Seattle."

"Come home."

"I can't, Mom. Dad would say, 'I told you so. Don't stir the pot.'"

Well, it was true. Claire hadn't just opened the proverbial can of worms, she'd gone fishing.

"You are *my* daughter. I raised you. I love you." Erin's emphasis sounded selfish, but she didn't care. "Do you know how hard this is for me?" She was both angry and desperate. "I want you to come home whenever you want to!" Her voice sounded tight. "I want to be enough!"

"I'm sorry, Mom. But . . . Dad . . ."

"Then how about the cabin?" Erin's voice calmed. "You haven't been to the lake this summer."

Erin knew the thought of having a sleepover and falling asleep in the big bed would lure Claire to the lake. The quiet. Time to think.

"I know it's too much driving for today. Not safe after all you've been through," she added. "But if you wait and head out . . ."

"I'll meet you there by six. Six *tonight*." Claire hung up before Erin had a chance to say no. So impulsive. Headstrong. Where did she get that from?

Chapter Forty-Two
Siobhan

The return to reality
was as painful as the return to consciousness
after taking an anesthetic.
—Edith Wharton, *Ethan Frome*

Deer Lodge, Montana
Spring 1931

Siobhan buried Jack out in the field near a tree under which they had once made love. The hole had already been dug on a day when the earth wasn't frozen, but his hopes were.

If anyone questioned why not Hillcrest, the cemetery less than a mile from their home where the graves of other Deer Lodge residents were marked with headstones, she would claim it was because she wanted him nearby. If the coroner argued, she'd let him dig Jack up by himself with the children standing by.

The funeral was simple. No wake. No black ribbon tied on the front door. She didn't cover the mirrors. No midnight rosary. Nothing like she remembered from Ireland.

When her grandmother had died, the body had remained in her Mamó's living room for days. People came to sit by the body. They sang, they drank from Belleek china teacups, never mugs. Not for a wake. They danced, talked of the weather, the farm, others who had died recently, and they talked about her grandmother as five-year-old Siobhan sat at the foot of the bed and Brigid stared at her from the other room.

Jack deserved a better send-off. But in Montana they had no wee wan or small port. No "Sorry for your trouble." She didn't shave Jack's face or change his clothes. She couldn't even afford a headstone, so she found a large rock and wrote *Jack Mason. My Lighthouse.* No one would understand and the rain would wash it away anyway, much the same way she felt a part of herself carried away.

What would she ever do without him?

She could remember the boats off the coast of Kilrush and then Boston. They moved with a longing purpose to head home, or to leave port for new adventure. She had neither purpose nor adventure, and her bed was cold.

Waves of grief threatened to drown her. *Float. Float.* Except he wasn't there. Jack had taught her to swim. But was it enough? She'd bolt awake in the middle of the night, gasping for breath. A sucking chest wound, perhaps a heart attack. She was powerless to stop the stabbing pain. All she could do was tread water, keeping her mouth above the churning waves. Sometimes she found footing but only until, yet again, an undertow of grief pulled her beneath the swells, leaving her desperate for breath.

She didn't think anyone could miss Jack more than she, but to watch her own grief in the eyes of her children was worse than facing it alone.

Samuel's and Paul's sadnesses manifested in anger. They were sometimes aggressive, sometimes mean. "What's wrong with Caleb?" They didn't seem to ask out of concern but as if he were at fault for everything that had happened. Samuel and Paul demanded her attention when she had nothing to give. More than once, embarrassed friends commented that the boys were playing too roughly with their children. The teacher told Siobhan she was having trouble with them in school.

Nobody knew the truth of Jack's death except Caleb. Why was he in the barn that day? How much had he seen? What did Caleb think about the woman who crawled across a beam and let his daddy fall to the ground? How did he feel when she was screaming? When she was crying? She shivered at the thought.

How could she ever begin to ask him? She had so many questions and only Caleb held the unspoken answers. Now her formerly chatty little three-year-old once filled with songs and stories was mute. Her penance was watching Caleb's emptiness.

What was the last word Caleb had uttered? She couldn't remember. Was it for his daddy? When she had peeled his fingers from the ladder, she had held him close. She had told him "Daddy's gone." She had said, "I'm sorry." But nothing brought his daddy back—and nothing brought back Caleb's words.

"What's wrong with Caleb?" Sarah would whisper. "Why doesn't he talk to me anymore?" What could Siobhan say? Her little girl not only missed her father, but also the dialogue with her best friend.

"Cat got your tongue, boy?" townsfolk asked when they went to town.

"He'll get over it," others predicted.

They didn't know the half of it.

Chapter Forty-Three
Siobhan

She could no longer borrow from the future
to ease her present grief.
—Nathaniel Hawthorne, *The Scarlet Letter*

Deer Lodge, Montana
Summer 1931

March had drifted to April to May to June with little rain. Then a July heatwave nearly drove her to distraction. Each day came and went without precipitation, and the blistery dry heat persisted. The week of July 21–27 was the hottest on record, water levels were low, and the valley was a dust bowl as farmers abandoned their crops, declaring them a complete failure.

When Edwin Merchant from Larabee Brothers Bank arrived, he tipped his hat and apologized. They stood on the land Jack had tilled, looking toward the house Jack and Siobhan had brought their babies home to. Her hands were on hips, her apron hiding her growing stomach, and she had listened politely as Mr. Merchant explained the debt and that the land was no longer theirs and that he was sorry and that she wasn't alone because these were troubled times and people all over were losing their homes.

She appeared strong but inside she withered. The baby kicked. *She's got more fight than me.* Then she considered the fields, and the barn, and house again, and thought what it would mean if it weren't hers.

"That's fine."

Mr. Merchant turned back to her in surprise.

"I don't want any of it. We need to start over." She gave him a steely stare and then turned away.

"Yes, I can imagine it would be like a noose around your neck."

She whipped around so quickly, her neck stung. He didn't know. He *couldn't* know. No. He had only sympathized that the farm was a relentless, day-to-day operation dependent on weather and whim. They could have hail or snow in the summer and the narrowest margin of spring and fall bookending the longest of winters.

This was Jack's love, and her first home, but it was nothing without him. She did not need any of it.

Two days later, Siobhan and the kids moved into a one-bedroom apartment directly over Coleman Jewelry, across the street and down from the Montana State Penitentiary.

The kids shared a room and she slept on the couch in the front room, which faced the prison. The kids were surprised she'd brought the crib. Paul jokingly claimed it so he'd have a bed of his own.

Once again, she was in the unenviable position of being without a husband and with a child on the way. But this time, she had four other children, no income, and nobody awaiting her at Hotel Deer Lodge.

But she still had the same post office box. When she wrote Antonio, would he see words and white space and know that something terrible had happened?

Dear Antonio,

I look forward to hearing how you are doing. I read to my children regularly. We enjoy The Wonderful Wizard of Oz. *Summer in Montana is so extremely hot. We've had no rain for months. They say it could be worse than 1919.*

Siobhan

She couldn't tell him their food supply was low, that she was a widow, that her baby couldn't speak, that she was having another baby, and that it would not rain.

And she couldn't let on her sorrow to the children. They were too young to understand and didn't need to share her burdens. She would still do for them what she could.

On Saturday mornings, she made pancakes, their favorite. She still had a few jars of canned applesauce they could use for topping. Even now, in the apartment, Siobhan mixed the last egg, the last bit of flour, and stretched it into a watery mixture. She melted a tablespoon of lard into the pan and made six small pancakes, and then wondered how she could still miscount. No matter, Paul would eat two. Sarah would eat a half of one and then say she was full and give the rest to Caleb. Because Paul would eat two, Samuel would be jealous and so Siobhan would share half of hers to even things out. Siobhan would have offered all of hers except for the baby nobody knew about.

After that, she wasn't sure what they were eating. She needed a job. But how would she find one? How could she be away from the children?

The aroma was sweet, warm, and inviting. The sunlight on her daughter's hair made a halo around her face. Sarah flipped the pancakes one-handed, just as she had taught her while Caleb watched from the table, his face cradled in his hands.

"Caleb, will you get the applesauce from the box in your room?" As she did so often, Sarah began singing a little rhyme.

As I went up an apple tree
All the apples fell on me.
Bake a pudding, bake a pie
Did you ever tell a lie?

Siobhan grabbed Sarah's hand. Over and over her mind replayed the line. *Did you ever tell a lie? Did you ever tell a lie? Did you ever tell a lie?* Was it a lie if you didn't tell the truth?

"Mama, that hurts!"

"I'm so sorry, Sarah." But what was it she was really sorry for?

"Pancakes for breakfast!" Siobhan called out.

Paul ran in first. Siobhan hadn't realized how dark his eyes sunk in their sockets. How he no longer looked like robust Antonio.

"That's not very many," Samuel pointed out.

"Pretend each bite is one huge pancake and let the sweetness sit on your tongue for as long as you can."

"Too late," Sarah said, pointing out that Paul had already devoured one and was eyeing the last cake.

"He doesn't get two." Samuel's fork was up.

"We can all share." The script was playing out just as she imagined. "Mama, I think *you* need mine." Sarah's suggestion surprised her. "No, Sarah." She raised her palm. "I mean, thank you, honey, but you've got to eat."

She stared at Caleb. Had she told him she loved him that terrible day? Had he said, "I love you, too, Mommy?" Would she have remembered that? She wanted to hear him talk and sing in his innocent and childish voice.

Caleb pressed his hands together as he did before each meal. What prayer was in his head? He used to clasp her hands in his, his smaller hands bookends to hers. But not today. Sarah moved her fork around with her one good hand. The other wrapped around Caleb to keep him from falling from the bench they shared. Siobhan kissed the tops of each head.

"What a celebration we're having today!"

Caleb motioned to Sarah, who had worked out their communication. His hands and fingers made small dancing movements like sign language. Caleb looked to Sarah as his voice and she answered his every thought, even when Siobhan could not.

"Caleb wants to know if there is any more milk." How frustrating that Sarah would ask that question when she had just seen them use up the last bit in the batter.

"You need to let Caleb find his own words. Don't talk for him."

Caleb gripped his sister's hand, his eyes staring straight ahead as if he could not understand anyone else.

"You can hear me. I *know* you can hear me." Siobhan's voice grew louder. "Caleb, look at me!" She bent down to his eye level.

"Mama, stop it. You're scaring him! He's just a little boy!" Then she slid him off the bench. "Caleb, come with me."

"Don't you leave this house, Sarah Kildea Mason."

Her daughter stopped but didn't turn around. "You don't know what you're saying right now, Mama. You're sad." Sarah took her little brother out the door and away from her.

Siobhan felt jealous and helpless, and her daughter was right, she was sad. And this time, Siobhan had no plan for what to do next.

Chapter Forty-Four
Geneviève

Deer Lodge, Montana
July 1931

Geneviève was surprised when two children came into the office unaccompanied. They made a curious pair. The strawberry blond girl was like a little mother with one arm around the boy's shoulder and spoke to him in a hushed whisper. The other sleeve hung limply. It was a boy's shirt that was certainly a hand-me-down. The child silently clutched his bunny. They sat together; their feet, not reaching the floor, hung still, so unlike the other children in the waiting room who carelessly swung theirs back and forth.

The afternoon had heated to over a hundred degrees and still no rain. Everything was dry and dusty, and the patients she saw, especially the farmers, looked weary. The depression had done damage, but the drought conditions had been equally as cruel, forcing many from their farms. Crime increased and so did the number of prisoners William was putting in prison.

Deer Lodge people did what they could to help each other. Even the owner of the Orpheum movie house took films to the prison on Sunday and gave fifty passes a week for the poor so Charlie Chaplin, Douglas Fairbanks, and Mary Pickford could distract for a few hours.

"Is it our turn now?" The girl was at her desk, leaving her little brother fidgeting, eyes following his sister, even the bunny restless on his lap.

"Do you have an appointment?" Geneviève already knew the

answer.

The girl's eyes fell. "Can I make one now?"

"Yes, but I'm not sure if the doctor can see you unless it's an emergency."

The girl thought for a while, then whispered in Geneviève's ear.

"It's not for me." The girl turned back to check on her brother whose head dropped as if heavy, his little hands folded on his lap, the rabbit secured beneath.

"He doesn't talk anymore." The girl touched her throat. "His name is Caleb."

Caleb. She knew that name. Caleb Mason. She had helped deliver this perfect child. One Sunday, only a few months ago, prayers were offered for his family. Something about a tragic farm accident.

Doctor Briggs came in, surveyed the waiting room, and sighed. Geneviève could see he was falling behind. He took his oath and his responsibilities too seriously, spending much time counseling his patients.

"Caleb and his sister are here." She whispered the message as the little girl watched closely, having returned to her brother. "They don't have an appointment."

Doctor Briggs motioned Sarah over to him. "What can I do for you, Miss Mason?"

"Can you give Caleb something?" Sarah's soft voice was almost musical. "To make him better?"

Doctor Briggs bent down on one knee to look the little girl in the eye. "What's wrong with him?"

"Nothing's wrong with him." Her voice was defensive. Her eyebrows knit. "But he doesn't talk anymore." She touched her throat. "Maybe it's sick?"

The doctor rubbed his chin. He was always so good with children. Geneviève wondered what he'd say.

"Can you come back tomorrow? With your mother? First thing in the morning? 8:00 a.m. sharp?"

"That will be my *appointment*?" The girl's eyes brightened.

"Yes, Sarah, but bring your mother."

The next day, at 7:45 a.m., there were three in the waiting room.

The very same office in which the redheaded Siobhan had delivered her son. Now, Siobhan sat next to Sarah, who sat by the little boy. Oh, to be that mother.

"When did Caleb stop talking?" the doctor asked when they moved to his office. Caleb sat on Dr. Briggs's wooden desk, and Sarah stood nearby, holding his hand.

The boy was silent, the center of it all, everybody talking about him as though he weren't there. He focused on the bunny in his hands.

"A few months ago." As a scribe, Siobhan noted all comments.

"Does he ever choose to speak?"

"I haven't heard him speak since his father's death." Siobhan turned to her daughter. "Sarah?"

Sarah shook her head no.

"How much talking did he do prior to the accident?"

"He never *stopped* talking. I could open a book and he was almost reading it aloud with me." Siobhan's face brightened at the memory. "He sang a lot, too. He is a very bright little man." Siobhan smoothed a cowlick on the back of Caleb's head. Caleb squirmed as if uncomfortable with her touch and Siobhan turned back to the doctor.

"And we know his birth was quick. Uneventful. No trauma." The doctor's voice drifted off. "Has he ever had an injury to his throat? A prolonged illness? Hearing difficulties?"

"Caleb?" Caleb looked quickly to Siobhan and then to Geneviève with the bluest eyes she could remember. Siobhan had proved her point. "No. He's been a very healthy boy."

"I'm sorry to have to ask this, but when did your husband pass?"

"Sarah, why don't you take Caleb out, please." Geneviève lifted the boy, surprised at how light he was, from the desk and set him on the floor, then Sarah led to the waiting room.

"Yes. The timing is no coincidence. He saw . . ." Siobhan hesitated. "He saw his daddy. He witnessed the whole event and hasn't communicated since."

"And what about you, Siobhan?" Dr. Briggs turned his full attention on her. "How are *you* doing?"

"As best we can." She turned the personal into the plural of family, as so many mothers were wont to do. "But even before, we weren't keeping up," she admitted. "We lost the farm."

Geneviève excused herself to check on the children as Doctor Briggs and Siobhan murmured behind closed doors. She sat at her desk but found it difficult to concentrate on anything except the two youngest, orphaned patients. When she heard a soft knock, Geneviève brought the children back in. Doctor Briggs checked Caleb's ears and heart rate and hammered his knees. Nothing changed the little boy's expression.

"I fear that the wounds he experienced are not physical."

Siobhan nodded, frowned, and pinched back her tears. Sarah gazed up at her and squeezed her mother's hand.

"It will take time. Or perhaps a change of scenery. But there's nothing I can prescribe."

Sarah pulled her brother close. That little girl was remarkable. Geneviève wondered at her strength.

"There's no way to treat this? Nothing I can do?" Siobhan set her blank notepad down.

"Not that I know of. Not here in Deer Lodge." Doc Briggs seemed to be searching for something of hope. "But I'm also concerned about his weight. Has he been getting enough to eat?"

Siobhan's face fell. "I'm trying, but he doesn't eat much now."

"He's small for his size. Underweight. I'd like to see him again next week and check on his progress. That's something you can do in the meantime."

Siobhan frowned, and Geneviève wondered how much food there was at the Mason's.

"Time. Time heals many wounds." Doc Briggs's eyes were gentle, wise, so soft.

Siobhan looked to her son and her back straightened, as if fiercely proud. Sarah took the little boy's hand in hers, a beautiful trio.

"How *much* time?" Siobhan raised her chin.

"I don't know, Mrs. Mason. I don't have any firm answers."

"Would you have something for me to read? Anything about the voice?"

Doctor Briggs tilted his head thoughtfully. Geneviève was surprised by Siobhan's persistence.

"Let me look, Mrs. Mason. I'll have more answers at your next appointment."

Siobhan bit her lip as she fumbled for her coin purse.

"Mrs. Mason, I'm going to do what I can. But I won't take any payment."

"And *I'm* going to do what I can. But I must pay."

"Well then, since we're working together, I can't charge my usual." Doctor Briggs touched her notebook. "Take notes on everything you read. I have much to learn."

Geneviève studied the child, his dark brown hair, his tiny hands. The sister who loved him, the mother who wanted him whole. Why was the world so hard?

Chapter Forty-Five
Siobhan

The voice is a sound caused by the soul
by means of the repercussions of the air,
made in the throat with the intention of signifying something.
—Aristotle

Deer Lodge
July 1931

Samuel and Paul ran in a pack of boys through the alley, in the suffocating, dry Montana heat. Yet another day without rain. Where they got their energy, Siobhan could never figure.

"I am Count Dracula!" she heard from the street below, the boys imitating Bela Lugosi from that horror movie she would never let them see. They chased each other up and down the fire escapes, taunting one another.

Caleb watched the older boys playing outside the window. There was no one his age in the alley and besides, all the games Siobhan had previously encouraged, even played with them, needed his voice. Hide and Seek. Simon Says. Red Rover. Tag.

A can, packed with rocks, clattered in the back alley. Kick the Can was a good game for poor folk, just not for the silent. Besides, the boys liked the game because it had a jail. That was something they could all relate to.

Caleb watched Paul from the window, but when Siobhan joined Caleb at the window, he seemed to shrink inside himself. Below, Paul put the painted can in the middle of the alley, closed his eyes, then began yelling. "One, two, three, four, five, six . . ." Siobhan knew that if Caleb were talking, he could count to at least forty. Suddenly, when Paul reached fifty, he spun around and moved stealthily through the alley, hunting for his friends. He tagged one boy behind an auto and another on the fire escape, still another in a door frame. Each tagged victim was sent to jail but could be released if any of the remaining players kicked the can. Caleb tensed, his eyes flitting to each hiding spot, knowing where each kid hid, unable to signal a warning.

Samuel remained in the field, small, fast, and able to kick the can with ease. Then, suddenly he held up Caleb's stuffed bunny. Caleb stiffened. Why did Samuel have Caleb's favorite toy?

Samuel twisted both of Mr. Bunny's ears around Mr. Bunny's neck. It was supposed to look like a bow tie but for Siobhan and Caleb, it was a terrible reminder. Samuel had no idea what he was doing. An innocent prank turned vicious.

Caleb made some sort of choking sound and then banged on the window. Siobhan yelled. "Stop it! Stop that right now!" All at once, she was crying in her screams. "That's Caleb's toy. Don't do that!"

Samuel looked up, shrugged, and headed upstairs with the bunny hanging limply by his ear.

"Sorry, Caleb. I was just having fun."

Caleb stared out the window.

"Look. Mr. Bunny is all right. See his ears?" Samuel had one of Bunny's ears in each hand, dangling him above Caleb. If only Samuel knew. Caleb regarded the once-cherished toy and shook his head slowly, then harder, and with increased vigor until Siobhan was sure he would snap his own head off.

Caleb escaped out the window and sat on the fire escape where Sarah and he often spent the morning reading a book.

"Let him be alone right now, Samuel."

Caleb's feet swung slowly, he rested his arms on the railing and lay his head on them like a pillow. What was he thinking? If only she could reach him. Time would tell, but when? There was nothing physically wrong with Caleb. How could she reach the three-year-old witness and help him talk?

"Caleb, I brought you something."

Caleb turned slowly, his eyes dim. There was no excitement or anticipation.

"I brought your rabbit. Mr. Bunny is fine. He was missing you."

Caleb rested his head back down on his arms, unresponsive to caring for the toy rabbit.

Siobhan put her hand on his head, his hair warmed and dampened by the sun. She saw him stiffen and move his head ever so slightly away from her. This time she didn't retreat, she ran her fingers through his hair the way he'd always liked. She stroked her hand across his back the way that could help him sleep when he was anxious.

"Hmmm hmmm," she hummed the lullaby that was their nightly ritual. "Caleb, try humming. Think of something that makes you smile." She continued humming. "Touch your throat right here and you can feel a buzz. Try *Nnnnnnn*, see if you can feel it."

She demonstrated and touched her throat and then brought his hand to her throat to feel the vibration. He cringed.

"What would Bunny say?" She stretched the toy through the bars and in front of Caleb's face. "Hmm, I see Caleb." She jiggled the rabbit, its ears flopping freely. "Caleb, can you say, 'Hmm, I see Mr. Bunny'?" She paused. "Hmm. Or try *Bunnnnnnnnny*." She extended the N sound. Then she sang the words to their lullaby.

Sleep, sleep, grah mo chree,
Here on your mamma's knee

She tried to pull him up to her knee. Though he was nearly trapped with her on the escape, he had moved as far from her as physically possible and was clutching the bars. Why did he fear her so? Or was he terribly angry? Was it her?

"Caleb, I'm so sorry. Not just about Mr. Bunny, but about everything." She hoped he'd look at her.

"You saw something terrible, and I wish I could get a big eraser and erase it from your mind. Mommy saw it, too. I couldn't help Daddy. I tried, Caleb. Mommy tried so hard." Siobhan willed him to cry, to acknowledge their shared story, to forgive her.

Caleb moved his hand to the metal floor where he sat. Siobhan put the bunny near his hand, but he moved so quickly the rabbit fell to the ground far below. Siobhan gasped and Caleb froze. But still no tears. "I'm sorry. I didn't mean to scare you. Should I go get Mr. Bunny?" Caleb slowly shook his head.

"Caleb, it was too late." She choked out the explanation. "I got there too late. I'm so sorry. I tried my best, but Daddy is in heaven. Maybe he's looking at you right now, hoping you'll talk to God again and that he can hear your sweet voice.

"Angels are guarding . . ." And she looked far out to the mountains beyond. The sun was going down, and she knew what that felt like. She was running out of ideas and time. Maybe he could never forget. Maybe he could never forgive. Maybe she just wasn't good enough. Maybe there was someone else who was.

She finished her song in a whisper of doubt.

"And they watch o'er thee."

Chapter Forty-Six
Geneviève

Deer Lodge, Montana
July 1931

"Siobhan Mason brought her son back." Geneviève sat down across from William, who lowered his paper slightly.

"The widow? The one whose husband died in March?"

"Yes." Geneviève smiled softly, touched that he remembered. His mind usually seemed too full to recall the seemingly insignificant details she brought up. "Her boy still isn't talking. Dr. Briggs doesn't know what to do."

She tapped her hand on her lap and waited.

"Are you suggesting something?"

"I don't know."

"There are a lot of people that need help in these times. We can only do so much, Geneviève." William sighed. She sensed his weariness.

William had changed. At first William believed he could make a difference. After the investigating committee wrote its findings that the prison was unsanitary, unsafe, and unacceptable, William was hired as prosecuting attorney. Now he was putting men in the very place he abhorred.

"I just think that the little boy has been through a lot. He is so thin." She smoothed her hands along the burgundy velvet settee.

William set the paper down and smiled. "Make sure they have groceries and take them a few meals. You're such a good cook, that'll help the little fellow." Then he frowned. "Does she have a job?"

Geneviève shook her head and William got that look he had whenever he was coming up with a plan.

A week later, Siobhan returned to the office, this time with all four of her children. Though the Ellises had anonymously supplied them with food, the gaunt look on Siobhan's face had deepened, her pregnancy a strange protuberance on her bony frame.

Still, Siobhan's chin was high and graceful. With Irish accent, Siobhan didn't sound like most of the Deer Lodge old-timers. While in the doctor's office, waiting, Siobhan read from *The Wonderful Wizard of Oz* and Geneviève found herself mesmerized by Siobhan's lyrical voice. Not having read the book herself, Geneviève wondered about the talking characters.

"Oh, I see; said the Tin Woodman. But, after all, brains are not the best things in the world. Have you any? enquired the Scarecrow.

"No, my head is quite empty, answered the Woodman; but once I had brains, and a heart also; so, having tried them both, I should much rather have a heart."

"I'd rather have brains," the older blond boy interrupted.

"You're already smart, Samuel." Siobhan rubbed the boy's head and hugged him close.

"Did something happen to Caleb's brains?" Paul asked.

"Caleb is very smart, and he has a heart, too!" Sarah said, taking up his cause and pulling the little boy close to her, a perfect imitation of Siobhan and Samuel. Geneviève noted then that Caleb never sat by his mother, instead always under Sarah's protection.

"So, tell me what is better." Siobhan closed the book on her finger and turned right and left, addressing all four. "Brains or a heart?"

"I think you need both." Sarah answered with a definitive nod of her head, her strawberry blonde curls bouncing with authority. "You need to have brains to know how to use your heart and if you don't have a heart, your brains could get you into trouble and you might be mean." She stared at her two older brothers and they lowered their heads. Geneviève hid a grin at the little girl's scolding.

As Siobhan resumed reading, the children leaned in, and Geneviève found herself straining to catch the lyrical singsong voice and story of a yellow brick road and the four friends.

Although the mute boy never answered Siobhan's questions, she sometimes asked him to point out a word and he would find it on the page. The child was smart.

Geneviève made a mental note to find out more about toys and clothing. Perhaps there was something she could give to the children. They were all clean, but their clothing was too small, too short, too thin. Both Caleb's shoes had holes in them, and his shirt was faded and torn at the sleeve. The knees on his pants were patched how many times? He wore no socks. Her heart went out to the hand-me-down child.

The two older boys were restless. Which was older? They didn't look anything alike. One blonde and skinny, the other muscular and olive-skinned. Caleb was the only boy that looked like Jack.

Geneviève would have liked to get to know Siobhan if everything were different. If they could sit down over tea and talk while their children played together. There was something in her that made you want to be her friend. Geneviève would have told Siobhan about the babies that didn't live. About the many times she had been a mother without a child. Siobhan would listen with her head and her heart.

The doctors in Missoula had explained that Geneviève's last baby was as small as a pea. And yet she bled, and bled, and it wouldn't stop. The doctor said there could be no more children after that. William and she grieved together. That was when William determined he'd run for office.

When Doctor Briggs came out of his office, Siobhan rose, and Caleb and Sarah followed, a pattering of feet on the worn hardwood floors.

"I'm going to start working at the prison soon," Siobhan began. "And I believe I may have you to thank. And someone brought us some meals."

"Well, I wouldn't know about that," Doctor Briggs answered. Geneviève turned away and smiled but admitted nothing. William had pulled strings for her job, and she had made sure the family was fed.

"No heavy lifting in the prison, Siobhan." Dr. Briggs shook his head. "You have a little one to take care of." Geneviève shuddered. Which little one? The doctor frowned as soon as he saw Caleb. He was thinner than the week before. "Caleb lost a pound since the last appointment. I don't like to see that in a child so young."

"He doesn't eat very much," Sarah explained.

"Your little brother needs to eat everything he can. Can you help him with that?" Sarah nodded.

"Now about my research." Doctor Briggs continued, "I can't find any case studies on this particular condition or a prognosis for how long it would take Caleb to speak."

"Would anything *shorten* the duration?"

"There is something called elective or selective mutism."

"You're saying he's choosing not to speak? *Aphasia voluntaria.*" Siobhan said the words softly, showing him her notepad.

"Yes, that's another term for it."

"Is there a treatment plan for aphasia voluntaria?"

"I read something about speech therapy . . . speech *correctionists.*" The doctor tapped his pen on his clipboard in rhythm like a heartbeat and Siobhan recorded the words on her notepad. "But there's nothing like that here in Deer Lodge." He ceased his tapping and shook his head. Siobhan slowly set her pen down and searched his face. "A bigger city. A research hospital. But I'm not certain." She wrote something on her notepad. "I know it's not what you want to hear." His voice faded. "There may be other doctors. Other people. Other places . . ." He frowned and shook his head.

"I'm not sure that there's anything I can do here, Siobhan. It may just take time."

Chapter Forty-Seven
Siobhan

*There is often a good deal of the child left
in people who have had to grow up too soon.*
—Willa Cather, *O Pioneers!*

Deer Lodge, Montana
July 15, 1931

It was high time for the boys to be home and now she'd have to go looking for them and she had but an hour before work. The four needed to settle in for dinner.

Siobhan ran down the dusty street. Still no rain, just the same dry heat.

"Have you seen Samuel or Paul?" Siobhan stood below the prison turret and called up to the guard, thirty feet above. Gerald manned one of the tower lookouts and went to her church.

"They were over by the Hotel Deer Lodge!" Gerald pointed down the street behind her. "Then I saw them running down to Keystone!" Did Gerald know the goings-on in the yard as well as he did the streets of Deer Lodge? Nevertheless, Siobhan was thankful for the lookout. It was difficult keeping up with four kids.

Asking the whereabouts when her boys were little was almost cute. It kept them away from trouble. But now that they were eleven and twelve, she was worried they were causing it. When school let out, the boys ran wild. Too young to secure a job, and with no male role model, they sought out excitement. What would happen when the baby came?

Though having a prison in town was a stark reminder that people made mistakes, it also numbed some to depravity.

Samuel and Paul had found other fatherless boys with too much time and too little supervision.

Dust blew across the sidewalk, and she brushed her fingers through her hair, marching to Keystone to find out what could be so interesting to two boys with no money.

The bells jingled on the door, but thankfully no one looked up. Not the man standing by the cards or Mr. Findley at the counter chatting with Paul.

The radio blared an old Irving Berlin tune Siobhan recognized from the last prison concert she'd been to with Jack. "A Pretty Girl is Like a Melody." Why did everything have to be such a reminder of him? Siobhan closed her eyes and took a deep breath. The shop smelled of vanilla and sugar and unaffordable sweets.

Siobhan moved slowly through the store until she spotted Samuel filling his pockets. She felt her face heat up. Oh, if Jack were there, he would be so disappointed. Well, she'd get this sorted out. The treacly sweet aroma of vanilla ice cream and chocolate made her stomach turn as she approached the counter.

"Good day, Mr. Findley!" Paul's head whipped around at the sound of her voice; Samuel slunk around the end of the aisle.

"It's good to see you again, Mrs. Mason." By the look on her boys' faces, they didn't feel the same.

"For so many years, you've helped my family, and today is no different."

Samuel emerged, his eyes wary, occasionally glancing over to Paul.

"Samuel has something to pay for." She motioned to Samuel. "Samuel, why don't you empty your pockets?"

"But . . ."

"Now." Her words were quiet and calm, but firm. "Samuel, put it all on the counter and pay Mr. Findley for what you owe." Fred Waring and the Pennsylvanians began, ironically, "Little White Lies." Mr. Findley shut off the radio. Siobhan tensed her body against the wave of nausea.

Samuel retrieved his stolen merchandise, slowly laying it across the glass counter. There was no hope of paying for all that he had taken.

"I was just . . ."

"Yes, Samuel?"

Now was when she hoped that something good could come from their deceitful behavior. An apology. Would Paul let Samuel take the brunt of their plot? Would Samuel tell on Paul? Just what kind of brothers were they? The two exchanged glances as Mr. Findley rang up the bill, nervously looking toward Siobhan with each additional item.

"I can't pay for it." Samuel turned to Paul, his eyes begging for help. "Paul?"

Paul stared down at his shoe.

"Well, then, I'll just put it back," Mr. Findley suggested, nodding to Siobhan who shook her head.

"Thank you, but no. These boys did something wrong. They will pay for it." Now her voice had an unfamiliar bite. *Pay. Pay for it.* She didn't like how she sounded, but who else was responsible to teach them the lesson? She needed Jack. Jack would have known what to say and what to do. She didn't know how to be both mom and dad.

"But, Mom, we don't have any money."

"Really, Mrs. Mason. These are terrible times, and with your husband . . ."

"No!" She slapped her hand on the counter. "That is no excuse." Then added more gently, "Thank you. They will work something out."

The four stood at the counter in a standstill. It was then that the man by the cards stepped forward. Though she didn't know him, he felt strangely familiar. She bit her lip and closed her eyes. This was awkward and embarrassing, and she felt lost and alone and didn't know how long she could hold down her roiling stomach. Her eyes lifted from the checkerboard floor then back up to the hanging lights. She would stand tall.

"Good evening, boys. Your names are . . . ?"

"Shake hands with the gentleman, boys," she instructed, encouraging them forward with a tap on each back.

"Samuel."

"Paul."

"I'm Mr. Ellis. I work at the county courthouse. My job is to put people over *there*." He pointed to the prison. The boys' eyes almost sparkled. She knew they thought of it as mysterious and forbidden and thus more alluring.

"Would you like to visit it sometime?"

Her boys' eyes widened. This was turning into a grand day for them and not at all what Siobhan had in mind. She nearly interrupted.

"So much to see. Two men to a room. Each cell is about six-by-eight, and you get a bucket for a toilet and metal bunk beds that hang from the wall. Of course, it smells kind of bad and sometimes pigeons fly through the halls." Mr. Ellis's face wrinkled slightly, then he shrugged as if that were nothing.

The boys squinted as if skeptical and looked at each other.

"Those windows over there? Street side? They're broken, so it gets a little chilly in the winter. And then there's the hole." Mr. Ellis's voice got quiet and the boys leaned in. "You don't get any clothes. Just bread and water and you're chained to the handrail on the wall."

"Nah!" Paul said at last. "You're just joshin' us."

Even Mr. Findley looked appalled.

Mr. Ellis blinked but denied nothing.

"Sometimes you're let out of your cell to pace the yard. You can see the sky and the mountains, but that's about it."

The boys stared down at the floor.

"I could introduce you around. There are people in there for murder." Siobhan thought she saw Samuel wince. She almost felt sorry for him. Almost. "And there are people in there for stealing." He paused and looked first at Samuel and then to Paul. "I make sure that boys that do what you did today go into that place and stay there until they learn never to do it again."

The boys inched toward Siobhan, one on each side of her.

"Seems like I've witnessed a crime here today," he concluded, standing to his full height, an imposing figure. Then came the repentance. "We're real sorry."

"We won't do it again."

"You're going to need to pay for what you did." He echoed Siobhan's words. "Have you ever heard of the 'Bad Boy Law'?" Siobhan frowned. Was he making this up? She leaned against the counter, battling a wave of nausea.

"Parents are responsible for the crimes of their children under sixteen. Your mom has to pay for your thievery."

Paul and Samuel peeked up at their mom, who was buoyed by their repentant faces.

"Sorry, Mom."

"I'll never do it again."

Paul glanced down the road toward the prison and shook his head at Samuel, who looked as if he was about to bolt.

The man took money from his pocket and placed it on the counter. "This cover it, Henry?"

"That'll do."

The boys frowned and looked at each other. "Now, you're going to need to pay me back." They shifted their feet back and forth. Siobhan wondered what it would be like to owe Deer Lodge's prosecuting attorney. He knelt and whispered something to the both of them. Too softly for Siobhan to make out, but she did recognize the relief in her sons' eyes. And was there excitement as well? As he stood, he finished the negotiation.

"I'd say that would cover it. If you start now, you might be able to finish by Thursday."

The boys eyed the street, looking like they wanted a head start.

"And if you're done by Thursday, and the job looks really good . . ." He tapped the stool at the ice cream counter and spun it. "You can sit here and I'm going to buy you a float."

Samuel, whose eyes had filled with tears in fear of permanent banishment to the castle across the street, nodded and Paul pulled him toward the door, which jingled as they left.

"Now, Mr. Findley, can you put all that back on the shelf and in its place? I'm sure Mrs. Mason would like to pick out a few things more suitable for her household."

Eight cents for a loaf of bread. Eleven cents for a pound of hamburger. Eighteen cents would buy a dozen eggs. Ten cents for a gallon of gas.

"I haven't started my job yet. I can't repay you."

"No, the boys are doing that right now. The streets will be cleaner for it." Then he took one of the peppermints off the counter and handed it to her. "You look like this might help."

Chapter Forty-Eight
Siobhan

The thing that irks me most is this shattered prison, after all.
I'm tired, tired of being enclosed here.
I'm wearying to escape into that glorious world,
and to be always there: not seeing it dimly through tears,
and yearning for it through the walls of an aching heart,
but really with it, and in it.
—Emily Brontë, *Wuthering Heights*

Deer Lodge Penitentiary
July 15, 1931

That night, Siobhan stood at Tower Number Seven of the Montana State Penitentiary and waited for the key to be lowered. With her back to the massive castle and its oppressive turrets and six hundred caged prisoners, she could barely see her family's little apartment off in the distance. She wished that her children could look out and find her standing in front of the gate. She waved, though she knew they couldn't see her and doubted they were watching. The boys had always pretended it was Robin Hood's castle and Sarah had told Caleb stories of princes and princesses. "Where's Rapunzel?" Siobhan could remember her asking.

As the night matron, she would take over Johanna's shift. Johanna's husband was ill. This job might be for a few months or even be permanent.

A guard met her outside of Tower Seven, then a strange procedure followed with keys being raised and lowered in order to gain admittance to a dark, wet vestibule and finally into the yard. Together, they walked the yard, names and prison numbers scratched into the bricks. Then, a third gate and into the narrow exterior surrounding the women's prison, where if she looked straight up, she could see the sky, but nothing else. A fourth door let her inside.

When the door to the women's section clanged shut, she never anticipated the feeling of being trapped. What did these prisoners feel when they began a long sentence? What if Siobhan were never let out? What if her boys one day would land in a place like this? She couldn't let that happen. She wasn't the mother she was when Jack was alive. Pulled in too many directions, she felt like nothing to everyone. Everything in her wanted to escape.

In Charlestown, she would have run across a bridge. From Boston, the train had taken her here, where there was somebody who loved her and was honest and true. But now she was in jail, imprisoned by the choices of the men she loved.

The women's prison was small and stuffy, with wet dark brick and a wood ceiling. Years ago, investigators deemed the prison unsafe and declared it should be shut down, the conditions too dirty and unsanitary. A moldy odor persisted, sometimes slightly masked by cleaning solutions. She tiptoed across the rotting floors of the decaying foundation.

Time crawled with the monotony of the hours. There were six women prisoners. Soon, she began hearing their stories. Most were prostitutes, and some had done something unmentionable. She would have sworn none of them could have killed their husband or stabbed their employer. But prison officials cautioned her not to believe their stories of innocence.

Besides, she knew the truth. Innocent people can do terrible things.

Chapter Forty-Nine
Geneviève

Deer Lodge, Montana
July 16, 1931

Geneviève was surprised when Caleb appeared at the office alone. Caleb didn't sit down but motioned for her to follow. "Doctor Briggs is away at the prison."

He continued waving for her to come. To follow.

"What is it, Caleb?" *Those blue eyes. Those perfect blue eyes that must have been like looking into Jack's.* He was such a small three-year-old. So vulnerable.

"Are you all by yourself?"

He nodded and kept waving, finally he came behind her desk and took Geneviève's hand. His hand was warm and soft and so small.

The little boy's fingers felt good in hers as he led her out of the office. He trusted her. He needed her. She could have walked up and down Main Street all day. She could have left her job and pretended that this was her boy, her son. That he was one of her many babies with hands too small to be held. He led her behind the Keystone Drugstore, down the alley, and through a door and up the stairs.

The Mason's apartment, though stifling hot, was as tidy as she would have expected from Siobhan. Curtains made from flour sacks. One small table, two chairs and a bench, one unmade bed in the front room area with a pile of disheveled boys' clothing next to a crib. Peeking into the doorway, she could see a double bed where Sarah lay. The girl called out in a raspy voice, reaching for Caleb who took her hand. Geneviève felt Sarah's forehead and it was burning up. Where were the boys? Why were Sarah and Caleb alone?

Geneviève threw open all the windows that could be unstuck, then searched for a pitcher in the near empty cupboards. Geneviève took off Sarah's cotton nightdress and gasped. Sarah had half an arm. How had she never noticed? She placed a cool washcloth on her forehead and rubbed Sarah's face and then down her whole arm and to the three fingers on the shorter arm. She felt the tears slip down her cheeks; the girl was the most beautiful angel she had seen. Geneviève quickly wiped her own face with a nudge of her shoulder. She'd seen far worse and remained tearless. Why was she weeping today?

The little boy sat at attention, holding Sarah's little hand. It fit perfectly in his own.

"Honey, I think you should go over there." Geneviève nodded Caleb away from whatever Sarah had. But Caleb shook his head insistently. When would his mother come home?

"Did you know that you can listen to your heart better with a piece of paper?" She rolled a sheet of paper from her purse and placed it on Caleb's chest. He in turn took the tube and listened to Sarah's heart.

Time passed slowly with two silent children. At last, the door clicked opened and shut and Siobhan's eyes widened as she rushed to Sarah's bedside.

"What is it? What's wrong with her?"

"Whatever she has, you shouldn't be near her. It wouldn't be good for your baby." Geneviève gave her the wet washcloth. "Where are the other boys?"

Siobhan stared out the window. Geneviève felt the weight of realization. The boys didn't have their farm chores and their father's supervision. If Siobhan was away, Caleb was alone with Sarah. School would begin in another month. Caleb wasn't old enough. And then there was going to be another baby. What would she do?

Siobhan wouldn't leave Sarah. To be safe, Geneviève suggested Caleb stay with her at the office by day and the Ellis's home by night until Sarah was no longer contagious. She was hard to read, but Geneviève saw that even though reluctant, Siobhan seemed relieved, hopeful.

Each day, Caleb sat near her desk and whenever she was free, she'd read to him or tell him stories. He wore her stethoscope when it wasn't in use and enjoyed placing it to his chest and closing his eyes as he listened. She brought treats but saw what Siobhan would not tell her. The boy picked at his food. Around the Ellis dinner table, she tried to entice him with the best foods and cream-topped milk, but he would eat little. At night, she had to help him up the stairs to the bedroom in their home, his frail frame asleep on the twin daybed she had hoped would one day be for their own girl or boy.

Doctor Briggs wanted to admit him to the hospital. He was gaunt, unsteady on his feet, and he needed more fluids. Geneviève was sure this isolation would make Caleb worse. Or was she just being possessive and selfish?

After Caleb had been with them for almost two weeks, the Ellis's home had a new rhythm and heartbeat. Each morning, Geneviève made eggs and pancakes or waffles, decorating them with blueberries or strawberries. When Caleb was too weak, she stayed at home with him, and she read stories. On his good days, they went to work together, and he sat in a chair nearby, looking at her books, then she carried him home at the end of the day. At home, he helped set the table while she made dinner for the three of them.

Sometimes, they listened to a new children's show called *Little Orphan Annie*. She waited for laughter from Caleb, but there was little reaction. After an evening of stories and games, William carried Caleb upstairs and tucked him into bed. Geneviève then stayed to read to him until he fell asleep. Caleb liked it when Geneviève read from a collection of comic strips she had found about Pip, Squeak, and Wilfred. Caleb so loved his Wilfred rabbit, she found the comic strip and read it in a British accent, which made Caleb smile.

She had a different voice for Pip the dog, Squeak the penguin, and Wilfred the baby rabbit. Wilfred ran away and wrote to Pip and Squeak, "*Good bi, I'm off to cee the world.*" That seemed to concern Caleb until Wilfred returned and was hugged by his mom and dad. Sometimes, he borrowed her stethoscope and checked Wilfred's heart rate, seemingly unconcerned that it couldn't sound like his own.

At the end of every day, on the porch of their Victorian, William opened the front window and listened to *The March of Time*. Then they reviewed patients and clients. Though the house was still too big for the three of them, it was starting to feel like a home.

That night was no different. A slight wind blew across their front porch, cooling them after the long sweltering day. Geneviève could hear the radio still playing and the voice of someone she didn't know but felt she did because he so often joined them in their living room. Was it Lowell Thomas? His voice sounded weary of unemployment, and the blame for President Herbert Hoover and the discussion about Al Capone. Geneviève went back inside and twirled the dial until she found what sounded like Guy Lombardo's orchestra. "As Time Goes By."

"What happened at the trial?" Geneviève asked when she returned.

"Dolly Baker? She's in jail." William turned to her. "What? You don't look happy."

"She's a nurse. I find the whole thing troubling." Geneviève fanned herself.

"That I put her behind bars for possession of cocaine and morphine? Or that she was a prostitute known as Mouser?"

"That she was a *nurse*. What happened to her? What went wrong?"

"She'll be out in a year." William sounded defensive. "You'd be more troubled if you knew what the women's prison looked like." William scratched the back of his neck and frowned as if in pain. "But you can't rescue everyone, Geneviève."

Geneviève could only rescue one.

Geneviève worried about Caleb as if he were her own. What would happen when school resumed? Even if Siobhan left an eight and three-year-old at home, something like this could happen again. And what about the baby on the way? Could one child be rescued?

A solution deep in her womb was taking shape. Geneviève knew that Siobhan had no answers but that she loved that boy more than she loved herself.

She didn't tell William about that day, when she had walked Caleb home after work, she had heard Caleb's name and turned to see Sarah on the street corner. Geneviève had picked Caleb up and ran. Why did she do that? What was she hiding from? Once at home, Caleb stood looking out the window, as if waiting for someone.

He needed medical care elsewhere, she convinced herself. A fresh start.

"No, I can't rescue everyone. But we could help *one* person."

"Do you know what you're doing?"

"I love him."

"But he has a family. He *has* a mother."

"She's afraid for him. He's sick. We could help him start over."

"What if he gets worse?"

"He could get worse by staying here in Deer Lodge," she pointed out, and then braced herself to continue. "So could you, William. This place isn't good for either of you. Or me."

William lost his stern legal face, obviously shocked by her words. She had caught him off guard. She didn't tell him that Siobhan had once said, "Can you help him?" And they both knew that helping him meant more than Siobhan could articulate.

"You have the wrong job and it's making you miserable," she accused. William opened his mouth as if to protest. "You want to solve problems, not punish."

William Charles Ellis was unusually speechless. He'd never prepared answers to the interrogatories of his wife.

"Starting over can be good. Saying goodbye to say hello." She quoted his long-ago phrase.

She knew William loved Caleb. She also knew he had the wisdom of Solomon and that there were two mothers and only one baby. William leaned forward and spoke with an intense quiet.

"I'm not taking a child from his mother."

Chapter Fifty
Siobhan

*The sounds of people drowning
are something that I can not describe to you,
and neither can anyone else.
It's the most dreadful sound
and there is a terrible silence that follows it.*
—Eva Hart, Survivor of the Titanic

Deer Lodge, Montana
July 21, 1931

The first time Siobhan and Sarah saw Geneviève Ellis holding Caleb's hand and walking him through town, Siobhan had to run around the corner, where she clutched herself. It was all so very wrong.

"There's Caleb!" Sarah said, running to see her little brother. Siobhan ran after her.

"No, Sarah!" She caught her by the wrist, and she realized her grip was too strong. "Not right now."

"But he's my *brother!*" Sarah stood in the middle of the street, telling the truth. "I want Caleb back! I'm all better!" Caleb had been with the Ellises for two weeks now. Siobhan had given away Sarah's brother, the doll she'd had from birth.

"Caleb is sick." Siobhan needed to buy more time. Time for her to figure out a plan and time for Caleb to heal under a nurse's care.

"You didn't send me away when I was sick." Sarah took her short arm from its pocket, as if making a point with her three fingered hand. "Mommy can't make Caleb better and Daddy isn't here anymore." What else could she say to make her eight-year-old understand? Sarah was healthy now and missed her brother, but with Siobhan's new job and the boys running around and Caleb's weight loss, she needed help.

"Everybody is going away, and I just want Caleb. Get Caleb back, Mommy!" Siobhan knew Sarah hated her for what she'd done. The absence of her brother had made Sarah a sad version of herself and her older brothers were of no consolation. She was the only girl in a strange apartment that was not home.

"Caleb is with good people." Siobhan vowed not to cry in front of her daughter or the small crowd gathering on the sidewalk. She was supposed to be strong, but this was too much. *God help me.*

"I shouldn't have gotten sick. It's my fault. Caleb is gone because of me!"

"No, he's not."

"When do we get him back?"

"When he's better."

But she feared that staying in Deer Lodge, Caleb would never get better. The Ellises could do for Caleb what she could not and that made Siobhan both sad and jealous. If she took Caleb back to their apartment, could she make him whole? Could she keep him healthy? Did he hate her like his sister did?

There was a thousand-foot-long boat built in Ireland by Irish builders. Its name was the Titanic. Siobhan was ten when it sank. It had enough lifeboats for half the number on board. It couldn't save everyone. *Women and children first.* That's what she remembered. *Women and children first.* It didn't have the resources to save everyone and neither did Deer Lodge.

Millie had helped once, even twice, but she couldn't go back. The church had also assisted, but very little could keep her family together when the whole town was sinking under the weight of the depression and this godforsaken drought. Deer Lodge was a community, but it was a community of families struggling to stay fed.

There was no doubt she was drowning and there weren't enough lifeboats.

Chapter Fifty-One
Erin

Priest Lake, Idaho
July 25, 1981

Erin drove out of Spokane on the winding wooded roads to Newport, where she picked up groceries, then drove through Priest River and Nordman, the one-store town, and turned off on Reeder Bay Road where she caught a glimpse of Chimney Rock towering above. When the kids were little, they'd compete for the first sighting of the pink rock on the mountain on the other side of the lake.

She passed cabins and campsites, arriving to Hagman Road, and Grandpa's cabin on Copper Bay. The cabin was a home away from home, an escape. Her family had grown up hiking, huckleberry picking, canoeing, or inner tubing on a big old Goodyear tire tube. Grandpa had started the kids waterskiing when they were four and now all three could slalom. Grandpa and Geneviève had both skied into their seventies. It was the Ellis way.

Erin opened her car door and drew in a large, sweet breath of sun-warmed evergreens. The water was rippled. Gentle waves lapped the shore. Too rough to ski. A pink glow clouded the mountains. Chimney Rock. She was home.

Home had changed over the years; they built a boat shed off the water, upgraded the dock, added a floor and additional bathroom, and now the side door of the original cabin opened to a large contemporary family area with a modern kitchen, and a window looking out over the picturesque lake.

Erin opened the back door to the original tin-roofed log cabin, her favorite part of their retreat. A huge map of Priest Lake hung over the fireplace. She set her bags on the black iron stove that still worked when they wanted to heat water. Ike, the moose head guarding the door, which they decorated for every season, still wore tinsel from Christmas. She'd swap out a huge bowl of popcorn into its open handlike horns to humor her daughter.

Erin and Claire shared the love of the original homestead. Claire could trace their history from her great-grandparents to Grandpa and Geneviève, to her father, and now to herself by the photographs covering the pine walls recording decades of family vacations. They were all a part of this place and its beauty, and a part of every person who had spent summers here since the early 1900s.

Geneviève had an eye for creating a cozy, warm, homey space and had decorated the cabin tastefully, with beautiful quilts, throw blankets, curtains, and comforters.

Erin stocked the fridge and started her homemade chicken soup. Ever the Billy Joel fan, she cranked up the music and sang and danced to "It's Still Rock 'n' Roll to Me" while the aroma of chicken and onions filled the cabin with a hearty warmth and what she hoped would be comfort food for her girl.

"Mom!"

Erin startled and gasped.

Claire turned the music down. "Sorry, didn't mean to scare you!"

Erin threw her arms around her daughter. "Claire!"

"You sure know a way to a daughter's heart."

"Billy Joel or the soup?"

Claire smiled slightly. It was a start.

"I packed your suit and some of your things. Why don't you go out on the dock until supper? I'd say, 'go jump in the lake', but I don't want you to take it the wrong way."

Claire headed to the dock. A storm was brewing and soon it would come full force from the south to the north. Their small bay was somewhat protected, but the wind, waves, thunder, and lightning would give them a show like nothing else.

With supper on the stove, Erin joined Claire on the dock. She lay back and closed her eyes, taking in the warmth. The wood was rough against her back, but she spread out her arms to the sun. It was hard to imagine a more beautiful and undiscovered location. "Folks stop and stay at Coeur d'Alene or Pend Oreille, Hauser, or Hayden. That keeps us safe!" Grandpa said. He called the inferior distractions "lake decoys."

A slight breeze forecasted they couldn't stay out much longer. Then the wind picked up, as it was so apt to in the Selkirks, and a shiver fluttered across her. They walked back up the dock and washed their feet at the outdoor spigot.

Erin lit tall candles stuck in wine bottles on the kitchen table and set out a loaf of soda bread and the pot of soup. "Now tell me about it," Erin said, ladling chicken soup into heavy crockery bowls.

"Mom, just for tonight, can we not talk about it? I just want to eat dinner and go to bed." Claire sighed. "I just feel tired and sad."

"It's going to be a big storm. That ought to help you sleep."

"Maybe I'll be able to actually see what I'm feeling."

Erin nodded, reached across the table and held her hand.

The wind grew stronger; they had to shut the windows. The storm ripped down the lake, bringing thunder and lightning, stripping branches from trees and splattering the glass with rain pellets. Claire and she got up and watched it, as if a movie played on the front cabin window, finally falling asleep together on the two couches in the living room.

They both could always sleep through a storm. Erin believed there was something about the wind and the waves, the crack of lightning and roar of thunder that made her feel safe. As if something more powerful than anything inside of her was in control.

And now, that realization was the hope she held for Claire.

Chapter Fifty-Two
Siobhan

I think you are wrong to want a heart.
It makes most people unhappy.
If you only knew it, you are in luck not to have a heart.
—L. Frank Baum, *The Wonderful Wizard of Oz*

Deer Lodge, Montana
July 25, 1931

The walls of Mr. Ellis's office were lined with sections of books, muted shades of green, burgundy, and black. If Siobhan just stared straight at the library, she could say the words she had prayed and practiced.

"I have to do what's best for him and staying here is not."

"You're going to leave?" Mr. Ellis's face dimmed. Siobhan took heart that he was saddened by the prospect. Maybe it meant he didn't want Caleb to leave. Maybe he loved him as much as she did.

She took a deep breath and said the three difficult words. "No, *you* are."

"I beg your pardon?"

"Consider this. Caleb has seen too much. He needs help. I want to be that mother who has done good by him and I have a chance."

William Ellis said nothing. She tried to gauge a reaction, but she didn't know him well enough. He was like a great Pharaoh living in his castle on Milwaukee Avenue. But she hadn't known what he was really like until that day in Keystone Drug, when her idea was conceived.

"Do you know what I'm saying?"

"I don't know how to answer."

"Geneviève loves him. I hope you do, too." Her voice was flat, monotone. She just had to get it out. She loved him. Jack had loved him. Now someone else could, too.

Only that morning after leaving the prison, Siobhan had gone to Geneviève, ready to take Caleb back. But as she stood on the front porch of the Ellis home, Siobhan couldn't look at Geneviève. She really didn't think she could do it. Caleb had everything there. He had a future. And she was so tired. So exhausted. She had asked the only question left to her. "You love him, don't you?"

"You're tired. You need time to think."

And then the words formed. Words that she had never anticipated. "You could love him like a mother, couldn't you?"

Geneviève's face clouded. Siobhan couldn't tell what Geneviève was thinking because she was so conflicted between wanting her to love Caleb and wanting her to deny him.

"I love Caleb like a mother, but I am not his mother."

Siobhan exhaled. She appreciated Geneviève's honesty. No, Geneviève was not his mother, not while Siobhan was alive, but one day William could be his father. In the meantime, Caleb might get the help she couldn't give him.

"Mr. Ellis, I've spoken to your wife. Geneviève's rescued my son. I need you to take him. To keep him."

"Now, Mrs. Mason, I can't just take a child."

"Hear me out. We'll do it all legally. You can handle the paperwork. It'll be an adoption. But the one thing is—you can't stay here." Siobhan wrung her hands. This was the hitch. "Do you understand? Go where he can get help. Only you can do that for him. You have to let him start over." And then more desperately, she added, "Sometimes people need to start over."

She held back the tears. She'd started over in Boston when she hadn't wanted to. She'd started over in Montana when she did want to. Now, starting over meant giving up her child when she didn't want to. But didn't Caleb deserve a better life?

The clock ticked in the background, the only sound. Documents lined the wall. He was important. University of Virginia. That was a long way away. Maybe he'd take her boy there. She turned her eyes upward to keep the tears from rolling down her face.

"I just don't think I could do that. To him. To you." William Ellis shook his head.

"What about Geneviève?"

At lambing season sometimes when a baby was orphaned or rejected, Siobhan tried to graft the bummer lamb to a mother who had just delivered a stillborn. Sometimes the lonely mother would accept it. Was that what she was doing?

He closed his eyes but still shook his head. Siobhan bit her lip. Should she tell him? Would this confession taint a fresh start for Caleb, or would the confession convince William of the urgency? What if her confession made him reject Caleb? She wasn't sure if she wanted her plan to work or to fail.

"With time, Caleb will get better." William said, confirming the necessity of her decision.

"Mr. Ellis, you don't understand." Then she made him understand. She made him listen to what she had told no one else, about how Caleb had seen Jack in that barn, and now seemed to be dying with that memory.

If she had wondered if William could be compassionate, that he could love her son, that he could care about both him and her, now she had no doubts. The catch in his voice. The softness of his tone. The tears that didn't flow but were caught in his words.

"Please, Mrs. Mason, Siobhan, I'm going to have to think about this. I need time."

Chapter Fifty-Three
Siobhan

The sorrow that lay cold in her mother's heart . . .
converted it into a tomb.
—Nathaniel Hawthorne, *The Scarlet Letter*

Deer Lodge, Montana
July 26, 1931

Time. If only time would offer one viable solution, she'd take it. As Siobhan took a seat at the diner, she wondered how long Millie would have a job. With almost twenty percent unemployment, few Deer Lodge residents had the means to dine out. Someone had sprayed a table with vinegar, and the smell of grease and hamburger made Siobhan queasy, but she had to talk to Millie. The barstools at the counter were empty. Millie had a break and sat across the table from her.

"You said he needed help," Millie questioned why Caleb was still with the Ellises.

"Not the kind I can give," Siobhan tried to explain without giving the full reason. "Or afford. Nothing a child could get in Deer Lodge. He keeps losing weight. The only person he will stay with is Sarah and she's got to go to school. Sometimes I work days, sometimes nights. I don't know what to do. I can't leave Caleb alone."

"And Jack's family?" Millie got up and poured Siobhan another cup of coffee. Siobhan took a long breath. She could hardly stomach the drink, but its earthy dark aroma reminded her of Jack.

"Jack left West Virginia almost twenty years ago. I would never find his relatives. And he left for good reasons. I don't think they could help us."

"It's amazing he was such a good dad."

He was a good dad. *Was.*

The gramophone played instrumental jazz in the background. Millie liked the sassy sound of a trumpet, saxophone, and piano. Thankfully, music without words. Siobhan couldn't think when people were singing.

"I'm sorry." Millie's voice sounded deep and dark like the music she loved.

"No, you're right. He was a good dad. I wonder if he knew that. Oh, Millie, why did he have to leave us?"

"There was a time I told you to look forward. It's that time again." Millie took Siobhan's hands in hers.

"I have to save Caleb. Or one day he might end up like his father." Siobhan shook her head back and forth, digging her fingers into Millie's palms.

"Oh, Siobhan! Why would that be so terrible?"

Siobhan took a deep breath and clenched her stomach over the wave of nausea. Was it the smells or her empty stomach?

"He's starving and quiet. There's no life. He's detached himself from me." She got it out and then bit her lip against the next roll of her stomach.

"Siobhan, he saw his father's death. He can survive that."

Siobhan closed her eyes. He'd seen much more than that.

"You don't send a child away just because he witnessed an accident, Siobhan. What kind of mother does that?" Millie pulled her hands away.

Millie was her best friend. She could tell her, admit there had been no accident. Millie should know. Millie would help her figure out what to do.

"I won't say he'll get over it. People never do, but it's no reason to give up on him." Millie's hands pleaded her case.

"I'm not giving up on my son!" Siobhan pounded the table and her coffee spilled. "There's nothing in me that is giving up. I'm trying to save him!"

"Well, I don't understand that kind of salvation." Millie pulled a cloth from her apron and wiped up the mess.

"He saw something . . . more." Siobhan began in a choked whisper, then let spill the words she vowed she'd never tell another human being except William Ellis.

"Jack? No, Siobhan, No! No!" Millie shook her head violently.

"And he saw me cut him down."

Millie's eyes widened, then she bowed her head on the table.

"Don't tell anyone, Millie. Ever. Do you understand?"

Millie finally lifted her head, her eyes so dull, they frightened Siobhan. She needed someone to have hope. If Millie didn't? . . .

"Siobhan, I am so . . ."

"Don't say that. That's not what I need to hear right now."

"What you've *borne* in the last months."

"I *know* what I've borne," she spat angrily. "And I know what's coming and I'm willing to fight for it. But I think that maybe the best way to fight is to do right by Caleb. He needs somebody. Somebody who can save him. Somebody *else*." Siobhan couldn't tell. Did she sound like Moira or was she Brigid?

Millie took her hand. Millie's silence meant she had no solution and recognized the pieces were coming together and even *she* could not deny what was best for Caleb.

"At church I heard about a terrible time when they were killing all the babies." Siobhan's voice was soft but steady. "And I thought of my babies and how I didn't want to lose any one of them, but I knew I couldn't take care of them all." She drew in a long slow breath. "And I wondered about my boy. How would I keep him safe when he has no voice? Or keep him alive when he won't eat?" Now she looked at Millie. This was the part Millie had to understand.

"The reverend said Miriam put the baby in a basket and hid him in the river." Siobhan stared out the window as if seeing the scene. "What was that girl thinking? Why?" She paused and swallowed. "But then, the Pharaoh's daughter drew him out of the water, and he was saved." Her voice was barely a whisper. "His mother gave him up to save him."

Where was Moses's father? Did he have a say? What would Jack think of her? She'd never know, but she needed Millie to understand. Millie listened and nodded her head, tears unfamiliar to Siobhan rolling down her face. At last, she spoke. "When you got off the train, I thought you wanted a job."

"I didn't know what I wanted. I was lucky I found you."

"I wasn't so sure you thought that."

"I didn't at first. I wasn't certain about you and Jack."

"Are you asking if Jack ever frequented Kate's Place?"

"No. I'm asking if you and Jack were close."

"Oh, Siobhan, how can I convince you?" Millie took Siobhan's face in her hands. "Jack was a friend. He was fiercely loyal to Annabeth and when she died, he was lost. There was a night he was in the bar. I was there." Siobhan looked down. Did she want to hear this or not? "He had the baby with him, and he was so scared. So, I took care of the baby for an hour. I just let Jack stay there alone. He needed something. When I returned, he wanted to talk. But I knew that he shouldn't. Not with me. So, I kept the baby in a basket on the seat between us." Siobhan was touched by the unnamed baby being a sort of chaperone. "But then when you came to town not a day later, I don't know if I could say it, but it was like an answer to a prayer. His."

"I don't know why I asked."

"For some reason, you needed to know. But you have to trust that he loved only you."

Chapter Fifty-Four
Siobhan

The years seemed to stretch before her like the land;
spring, summer, autumn, winter, spring; always the same patient fields,
the patient little trees, the patient lives; always the same yearning,
the same pulling at the chain—until the instinct to live
had torn itself and bled and weakened for the last time,
until the chain secured a dead woman,
who might cautiously be released.
—Willa Cather, *O Pioneers!*

Montana State Penitentiary
July 30, 1931

When was the moment someone committed a crime? What made someone step outside the rules? In the darkness of that night, Siobhan observed that the five sleeping prisoners looked like innocent children in their beds. Their thoughts could be dreams of when they were younger and free. Nobody was imprisoned in slumber.

The sixth prisoner, twenty-four-year-old Dolly Baker had just been sentenced to a year in prison and a five-hundred-dollar fine for being caught in possession of cocaine and morphine. And yet Dolly had been a nurse at the State Sanitarium in Galen. What came first? Her drug addiction or walking the streets of Butte, Montana as the prostitute known as Mouser? Now Dolly added to the wretchedness of this place as she fought to escape the horrors of withdrawal. Sleep could not free her from her pain. Siobhan wished she knew how to help her.

Sometime before dawn, even before the door opened, she heard the jangle of the four keys it took to get in and out of the prison. It would be Johanna and the guard. She would have thought it musical any other day, she was free!

But then she remembered one woman's story of captivity and the nun with the keys. *Those keys. Those bars. The one who told her the story. Brigid. What had she inherited?* She was becoming her mother. They both made choices that imprisoned them. Siobhan swallowed. She had already given her son away. What kind of mother was she? Brigid or Moira?

Moira. Oh, how she loved Moira. But hadn't Moira given her away, too? She never wanted to be given away. Caleb hadn't wanted to be given away. She hoped it wasn't too late.

"Are you feeling all right, Siobhan?" The woman draped her sweater over the back of Siobhan's chair. Siobhan could now leave.

Siobhan followed the guard out as quickly as he could reverse his path and unlock the gates. Could she keep reversing and unlocking the past? When they got to the last lock and key, she ran toward freedom and never looked back.

While her children slept, Siobhan returned to Jack's farm where all the pieces of their past awaited somebody with enough money to bring the homestead back to life.

Their old automobile remained on the property. It was unclear whether it was to be sold or whether it would just die a slow death on the farm . . . she could take it. If it was stealing, then God forgive her, but she needed a way to get her family out of the prison that was Deer Lodge.

From there, she headed to the Ellis's home on Milwaukee Avenue. She glanced up to Caleb's room. The curtains were drawn, he was still asleep.

She knocked. Caleb usually stood at the window looking out. Not today. No one came to the door. "Hello! Hello!" She tried the lock and then pounded. Couldn't they hear? "You can't keep him from me!" She pounded repeatedly until her knuckles were torn. Finally, she ran to the hospital, and threw open the office door, panting and out of breath.

Dr. Briggs was the only one there.

"Where is she? Where's Geneviève? Where's my son?"

"I don't know, Mrs. Mason." His face was serious and sad.

Siobhan staggered and sat on the bench. It had happened. The paperwork and the signatures and even the leaving. This was exactly what she asked for. This was what she *begged* for William and Geneviève to accept. Not anymore.

She wanted Caleb back.

Chapter Fifty-Five
Geneviève

Missoula, Montana
July 29-August 2, 1931

Each day Caleb spent at St. Patrick's Hospital in Missoula, Geneviève grew more anxious. Not over Caleb's health, which was stabilizing. But what about Siobhan? How could she let him go? Was Siobhan feeling regret or relief? What about Caleb's older brothers and sister? Had she stolen a child from a desperate mother? Everything had happened too fast, and they had run off without a goodbye.

William had said he was ready to consider leaving Deer Lodge. He told her to pack enough for the summer months; their belongings were being shipped to William's parents in Spokane. Geneviève had no idea what had transpired, she only knew she once again felt something akin to the flutter of pregnancy. The heartbeat of another mother's child; there was hope and life outside her womb. The Ellises would be a family and Caleb could forget whatever silenced him.

Geneviève had packed a few articles of Caleb's clothing, a special coin, his furry rabbit, and some pictures Siobhan had given, which Geneviève had hidden away for now. That was the only reminder of his family.

Their only goodbye was to Doctor Briggs, not only her employer but her friend. She needed him to understand. But when she started to explain he was quick to interrupt.

"I don't want to know where you're going."

"I have all the papers. It's a legal adoption." William opened his briefcase, but he was not yet convincing as a defense attorney.

"She asked us. She *begged* us," Geneviève defended.

"I know." Doc Briggs rubbed his forehead, pinching it as if he had a headache. "And maybe it's the best thing for the little fellow. But if Siobhan comes to me, I don't want to be able to say where you went. I don't want to be in the middle of this. Ever."

This was what Siobhan said she wanted, and yet was Siobhan thinking clearly? This was a critical juncture in all their lives. If they had made a terrible mistake, it could be rectified still, Geneviève thought.

But what of herself? She loved the child and thought of him as *her* child. Caleb was as much a part of her as the babies who had never survived outside her womb. But still, his umbilical cord had been attached to another mother.

Now Geneviève held the phone, the cord draping downward. She didn't know exactly what she would say but she just knew something had to be said or her tortured feelings would rip her apart.

She knew the number by heart and was put through to the hospital. An unfamiliar voice answered. Of course, he would have hired another nurse.

"Is Doctor Briggs available?"

"I'm sorry, he's with a patient."

What could she do? It was long distance. She had no other phone to use and they were leaving tomorrow. She needed to speak with him.

"Could you interrupt him? Just this once. I used to work for him and . . ."

"Dr. Briggs, there's a woman to speak with you." The woman's voice was suddenly muted. Geneviève closed her eyes and waited until she heard his voice, then sighed a prayer of relief.

"I'll make this quick. Dr. Briggs, I need to speak with Siobhan."

"I don't know how to help you, Geneviève."

"What do you mean?"

"She left town two days ago. They moved."

"Where? Where to?"

"I don't think she knew. But the apartment is cleaned out and their automobile isn't there. No forwarding address. They're gone."

Geneviève dropped the phone in shock. It was final. She had tried. She picked up the receiver and hung it back up. Caleb was theirs.

Chapter Fifty-Six
Siobhan

We come and go, but the land is always here.
And the people who love it and understand it
are the people who own it—for a little while.
—Willa Cather, O Pioneers!

Priest Lake, Idaho
July 31, 1931

"Help me get this down the stairs." Siobhan had emptied Jack's bookshelf and boxed her library. The boys were wide-eyed, and their hair stood straight. It was a cloudy day, but it would not rain. It would never rain. The three struggled to carry the bookshelf down and hoist it to the roof of the auto, securing it with rope by fastening it through the open windows.

"But what about Caleb? We have to get Caleb!" Sarah rubbed her eyes and surveyed the suitcases.

Siobhan stood and faced her with the truth. "I don't know where he is, Sarah. They've left."

Sarah screamed. "They can't take him! He's ours!" She threw her arms up in the air, unevenly reaching for something.

What could Siobhan say? It was the truth. But he wasn't "ours" anymore. He was the quiet little boy, just a memory, who would never grow up in their minds. She would always see him as the three-year-old son she'd never said goodbye to.

Sarah frowned. "Then we can't leave!" She sat on a suitcase, proving her point. "We can't go without him."

"Staying here won't bring him back. But maybe if we . . ."

"Where are we going?" Samuel piped in.

Siobhan couldn't answer quickly enough to convince them she had a plan.

"You don't know where we're going, Mam?" Paul was too observant.

"I don't wanna leave here," Samuel announced. "I have friends."

"This place isn't good for us. We need to start over." She let that linger, waiting for an argument.

"But remember when our cat jumped on that truck and went far, far away and she found her way back? What if Caleb comes back? We won't be here." Sarah, always thinking of the lost ones.

"When we get to our new home, we'll send letters with our new address. But in the meantime, Sarah, Caleb is with good people and getting stronger." She said that more for herself than for Sarah. She'd never tell Sarah that she'd begged the Ellises to take him.

"I could have taken care of him and helped him!"

Siobhan knew with increasing certainty that losing Caleb meant she'd lost Sarah as well.

"Pack your clothes while I pick up a few things at the store."

The town was waking up and businesses opening along Main Street. This was goodbye but it didn't seem real, especially since she didn't really know where she was going or what they would do. She only knew they had to get out and start over.

"I'm leaving," she said to the grocer, as she purchased a few items that would get them through the next few days. Saying it aloud made her feel it was allowed.

"We're leaving," she said to Fred, who manned the counter at Keystone. Each time she said it, her fear lessened, as if she weren't carrying a terrible secret burden.

"We're leaving. We're leaving. We're leaving."

But when she told Mr. Rovang of Deer Lodge Bank and Trust, he frowned and shook his head.

"Siobhan, I'm so sorry about everything."

"We're starting over." She brushed him off.

"Will you be closing Samuel's account?"

Would she be closing Samuel's account? A strange and heavy numbness spread through her. *Samuel's account?*

"Jack told you about it, didn't he?"

Siobhan couldn't talk. Was this what it felt like to be Caleb? Unable to form words?

"Are you feeling all right, Mrs. Mason?"

What else had Jack hidden from her? Why didn't she know about the account? She wanted to be angry, but how could she be mad at someone who was dead? Someone so alive in her mind? Someone she so loved?

"Sit down on the bench. I'm going to get you a glass of water." Siobhan surveyed her town with the eyes of someone who no longer lived there. People coming in and out of the stores. The large windows. The brick buildings. The prison castle. This was not her home.

By the time he returned, she knew what to say.

"How much is it?"

"I know what you're thinking, Siobhan." He sat beside her and handed her the cup of water. "Not enough to save the farm. Just a little nest egg. A start for Samuel. His grandfather deposited it at the boy's birth, when he came for Annabeth's funeral. When things were bad, I reminded Jack he could use it, but Jack wouldn't touch it. So, I didn't bother him about it."

"I'm leaving. I'll need it."

He handed her the paperwork and the cash he'd already withdrawn. "That's what I thought. This will give you a little help."

Crossing Montana with its mountains, valleys, undulating hills, and rivers kept the boys' interest. When Siobhan tired, she let Samuel and Paul drive the long open stretches where they didn't have to shift gears. One boy put his foot on the gas while the other boy steered. Sarah pouted in the back seat. Each night, they camped out by the car. She told them it was called car camping. The boys thought it was wonderful, but she was uncomfortable.

She purchased a map after Samuel repeatedly asked where they were going, then instructed the three to trace their fingers along the roads and name the towns they drove through. Having a map provided the children with purpose and a plan. From Deer Lodge, they headed north to Garrison, Gold Creek, Jena, Bearmouth, Nimrod, Baird, Iris, Clinton, Bonner, and then Missoula, the first large city her kids had ever seen. And the first place they had to make a major decision.

"Which way, kids? North or West?"

"One way looks shorter, Mam!"

"But is it as interesting?"

"There's a town called Paradise!"

"I see *Hellgate!*"

The children scanned the map and fought over seeing Flathead Lake, the biggest piece of water in Montana, or heading west where it looked like Idaho was full of lakes.

"There's a town called Butte!" Samuel blurted out, pronouncing it as a swear word.

"That's *Butte*," his sister corrected. One of the first words she'd spoken in the last few hours.

"Look, there's also Athol!"

"Paul, that's not nice." Siobhan hid her smile.

"It's just the name of the town!" Paul defended, shaking his head.

"And the North Pole!" Samuel squealed.

Having a map felt different than all the other journeys she'd taken. Opening the new Idaho map both terrified her as they moved farther away, but also gave her a sense of purpose.

"Look at all the blue spots. This Priest Lake is near Chimney Rock. Can we go there? I want to see a chimney in a rock!" Samuel started bouncing on the seat again.

"No, that's way too far." Paul yanked the map away. "I wanna get to Washington."

"There's a place called Hope." Sarah tapped the map.

Siobhan took a deep breath. She couldn't help but smile at the irony. "That sounds like an interesting place."

"It's near this really big lake. What's C-O-E-U-R D-A-L-E-N-E?" Samuel spelled. "How do you say that?"

"Hmm. I don't know. You got me stumped."

"I thought you could read anything!" Sometimes Samuel expected perfection.

"Not if it's in another language."

"Some people talk with their hands." Sarah spoke a simple truth.

"Yes. That's called sign language."

"It's for people who can't talk. But other people can learn it so they can *hear*." Siobhan knew what Sarah was trying to say. *We could have listened to Caleb!*

"Or pend oreal?" Paul tried to sound out the word, as if he knew his mam needed them to change subjects. "P-E-N-D O-R-E-I-L-L-E. That's another really big lake."

"I wonder who named that lake?" Siobhan turned her head to ask the question.

"What are we gonna name the baby, Mam?" Samuel continued bouncing on the seat with excitement.

"Oh, I don't know. I haven't thought much about that yet. We have months to decide. And stop jumping up and down."

"How about now, Mam?" Paul's voice was more serious. "Let's pick some names now."

Siobhan sighed. They knew Jack wasn't here and that he named the boys and Siobhan named the girls.

"What are some Irish names?" Sarah asked softly. Her name, Saraid, had been misspelled and mispronounced. Did she really still want a little sister to share in that tradition?

"Catriona, Colleen, Deirdre, Fiona, Niamh, Rhiannon." Siobhan paused. "I almost named you Saoirse." She dwelt on the softness and repeated the name. "*Seer-shah*."

"That sounds pretty, Mam." Sarah sat back and mused.

"Yes. And it means *freedom*."

"Saoirse," Sarah repeated. "Then all the girls' names would start with the same letter!" Sarah seemed tickled at that realization.

"Sarah, why don't you name her if it's a girl and the boys can name their little brother."

"What do our names mean?"

"Samuel was much prayed for by his mother Hannah, so she dedicated him to the Lord and a prophet raised him in the church."

"That doesn't sound like much fun." Samuel kicked the back of her seat.

"Nonsense. He heard God speak to him three times and later

became a prophet."

"What about Paul?"

"Paul did dreadful things but later he changed and preached everywhere. Even in prison."

"That doesn't sound like much fun, either."

"It's not really about fun, boys. They were strong and brave men."

"What about Caleb?"

She wasn't expecting the subject to return to her youngest and it made her sad, but she had to answer.

"Caleb was a spy."

The boys made groans, as if they wished they had his name.

"He was a good spy. He was supposed to check out and see if the new land was all right." She stopped. Was Caleb's new land all right? "And it was a good place and so he and Joshua said the Hebrews should follow into the land. And because he did that, his children and grandchildren would get to live in that good place as a reward."

No one said anything. Were they drawing the same parallels she was?

Siobhan ended that discussion as she focused on the incline of the pass between Montana and Idaho. The auto was old, she needed it to make it to wherever they were going. Where would that be? She began feeling queasy and her stomach ached, cramping at the thought of everything before her. She knew they needed to stop even though it wasn't night.

"It's Lookout Pass! Can we stop, Mam, can we see if there's something there?"

"We'll stop when we get to a town. We need to get to a town."

This was the highest point. It had to be climbed. She'd find a good place after that.

Sweat beaded on her forehead and her arms shook with chills. The seat felt wet and in looking down she saw blood. *No. No. No.*

"It's not night yet, Mam. Why are we stopping?" Paul had the map spread before him and had marked places to stop. Cataldo or Coeur d'Alene.

"I need to see the doctor." Siobhan pulled into a lot at the outskirts of Kellogg, next to the small hospital, and then threw a blanket over her seat. One step. Two steps. She doubled over with cramping. She took a shallow breath, taking in the scent of evergreens, rich, pungent, earthy.

"Mam? What's happening? You got blood on you."

"Go set up for the night, Paul. I'm only going right there." She pointed to a building which seemed to swim in front of her. She had to get there. It couldn't be more than twenty steps.

"I'll get you there, Mam."

"But then you have to go back and watch your brother and sister."

As soon as she was admitted to the hospital, Siobhan sent a worried Paul back and the nurse took over. The entrance smelled strange to Siobhan. The pine smell gone bad. Siobhan turned suddenly and vomited. The next thing she remembered was laying on a table.

"The baby is coming." The nurse spoke softly.

"It's too soon," Siobhan whispered, tears streaking down her face. If she explained that it was the wrong time, she could make it all stop.

"Sometimes these things happen."

"But it hasn't happened before."

This would be the last child of Jack and Siobhan.

Within minutes, something slipped from her. She felt little pain, only loss and grief.

"The cord," the doctor whispered to the nurse. "Around the neck."

"What happened?" Siobhan grabbed the nurse's arm. "What's going on?"

"You've had a miscarriage."

"That was it? That was all?"

"You couldn't be more than four months along."

"Five. I don't hear anything. What's happening? What about my baby?"

"It was too small to live. It's not alive."

Miscarriage. *Miss. Carry.* Everything about it pointed the finger at her. She had missed. She had failed. Like a mother carrying a newborn and walking across a room and suddenly dropping her baby. It was the mother's fault. She had mistakenly carried it. And now she would miss this child. Oh, how she would miss this last baby.

Or was it *stillborn*? What was the difference? This baby was still born despite all obstacles. Why couldn't it live? It had been kicking inside her just days before. What had happened? *Miscarriage. Stillborn.* Such awful words for a baby who never took life outside her womb.

"I want to see it. What is it?"

"That's not what we do."

"But I want to see my baby."

"We don't think it's best."

"*I will see my baby.*" Siobhan punctuated each word. She couldn't remember a time she had sounded so quietly forceful.

The nurse and doctor exchanged glances.

"I will see my baby." She clenched her teeth. "I will see my baby."

The doctor nodded and then whispered something to the nurse and left the room.

"You said something about the cord. What about the cord?"

"I'll take care of it. Sometimes it wraps around the baby's neck." The nurse turned her back.

A cry of anguish escaped Siobhan. What had she done wrong? How could that happen? How could her own life strangle out the life of her child? Had she strangled the life out of her husband, too? *The sins of the father.*

She watched the nurse fold a baby blanket once, twice, then a third time. The nurse frowned, then set it aside in favor of a small diaper which she folded in half, then carefully placed a tiny, pinkish-blue object in the center. She set the package in the crook of Siobhan's arm.

"She's so tiny!" Siobhan gasped. She had never had a doll this small. The baby could fit in the palm of her hand. Everything about her was perfectly miniature. "Oh, honey!" The mother cried out. "I'm so sorry!"

The nurse turned away and began putting away soiled cloths and instruments.

"We love you. You have brothers and a sister who love you." Siobhan spoke as if the baby was listening. But then she wondered if the baby really was listening. Just not to her. She was sitting on her daddy's lap. Jack would recognize her. In Siobhan's mind, the baby looked just like Jack.

Angels are guarding

And they watch o'er thee.

Siobhan touched each toe. "One, two, three, four, five." Then she ran her finger along the inch-long arm and kissed her baby's forehead, its tiny eyes that would never see the light. Then finally, she exhaled warm air on her as if she could breathe life into her daughter.

Siobhan walked out of the hospital, back to their little campsite, and their Ford despite the nurse putting up a fight about her leaving so soon. Siobhan had won. She had three children living out of an auto and they needed her.

"Mam!" Samuel ran open armed to her and Siobhan put out her hands to stop him short.

"Be gentle. Slow down. Samuel."

"Are you better now? Mam?" Paul set the bread and jam aside, obviously their breakfast or lunch, and traced his foot in the dirt nervously.

"I will be all right." She scanned their picnic place. "Where's Sarah?"

"She won't get out of the auto. She's afraid. Afraid you left her."

"And people say terrible things about her." Samuel added.

Siobhan had taken for granted their Deer Lodge familiarity and not anticipated the stares Sarah would now face and learn to live with.

Siobhan opened the door, tucked herself in the backseat, and put her arm around Sarah, suddenly wishing she could have brought back Sarah's baby sister for her to love. "I missed you."

"Me too." Sarah nestled herself beside her mother and Siobhan closed her eyes. She tried to remember what it felt like when the baby kicked. She could have had two daughters. Oh, how Siobhan wanted this baby girl. More than anything. And yet, was it possible she could feel both longing for her child and the freedom that she was not responsible for another life? She was drowning in both guilt and wanting.

"I'm sorry, Mam." Siobhan didn't ask why Sarah was sorry, just took it as reconciliation.

Leaving this town, a hollowed shell, was even more difficult than leaving Deer Lodge. This move didn't wipe out the memory of the past, it wiped out the potential memories for the future. What would this baby girl have become? Siobhan missed what could have been.

"What is it, Mam? What happened?" Samuel rested his hand on her shoulder as she drove them out of town.

"Do you feel bad again?" Paul studied her face; she knew it was now covered in tears.

"We can drive for you!" Samuel offered.

What could she say? How could she tell them she'd failed yet again?

"When I was in the hospital, the baby came early."

"What? Where is it?" Sarah jumped up in her seat. "Did you leave it there?" Sarah's voice was angry. "Go back and get the baby!"

"I can't." Siobhan clutched the wheel. "The baby didn't live."

Sarah started crying but that didn't stop her choking through questions.

"Why not?"

"I don't know."

"Who broke the baby?" Samuel asked.

"Nobody broke the baby. It was just too little. Too young to survive."

"Then why did it come now?" Sarah's voice was now frail.

"I don't know." And then it seemed none of them knew what to say. She would have thought that the interrogation would have hurt, yet with each question the weight was lessened, as she shared her grief. "I don't know what happened." She shook her head. She had no answer. They had to know that.

"Do you know if it was a boy or girl?" Sarah leaned over the front seat and Siobhan could feel her warm breath on her neck.

"It was a girl. And now Saoirse's in heaven with Daddy."

"What did she look like?" Sarah's wet face was almost touching her own.

"She was very tiny. She could fit in the palm of my hand." Siobhan lifted her empty palm as if she could see the baby and then Sarah did the same. "She was smaller than your Raggedy Ann. And she was very beautiful."

"I didn't get to see her! I didn't get to say goodbye."

"No, you didn't."

"I didn't say goodbye to Caleb either." Sarah sat back in the seat.

"No, honey, you didn't."

"*Never say goodbye because goodbye means going away and going away means forgetting.*" Siobhan was surprised Sarah had memorized that line. The boys had thought themselves too old for *Peter Pan*, and yet as Siobhan read from Antonio's gift, they slashed with sticks as pirates and her own Wendy Girl had held Caleb close.

"I will never forget!" Sarah shook her head angrily.

"She didn't have a name!" Sarah's voice pleaded for the baby they'd left behind.

"Yes, she did. I wrote her name down on the paper, Sarah, so she'll always be remembered. Just what you wanted for her, honey. Our little *Saoirse Hope Mason.*"

That night, Siobhan just kept on driving, even into the night, unsure where to stop for rest, the children asleep in the back. At last, she pulled over at the side of the road and fell asleep.

As the sun rose, she saw an expansive, placid blue lake surrounded by mountains, barely a line of demarcation between, except a foggy mist hovering above the shiny water. Before her, the water hugged the white sand beach in the early morning sunrise. She watched the scene change; the sun sparkled on the surface like jewels, glistening stepping-stones leading to one shimmering diamond. This was a gift.

She stripped off her shoes, and the cold moist sand chilled the soles of her feet and the places between her toes. She shivered in the cool morning air but still took off her sweater and then her shirt and skirt until she wore only the slip beneath. Leaving the discarded items behind, she ran toward the water and then stopped when her feet were immersed.

Deeper and deeper she walked, feeling the cold explore every inch of her body until she was up to her neck. She scooped a handful of water and let it fall from her hand like rain, the droplets sweet and gentle music in the quiet morning. No more drought.

She wanted Jack there to hold her. With him, she could float. She needed him. How could he leave her? "Trust," she heard him say, his lips behind her ear, as he ran his hands along the curve of her back and lifted her to safety.

She spread her arms and trusted. She took a huge breath and began sinking but she did not fold her body. She felt the inner panic but waited as she slowly lifted. She took another breath and held it, finding that it was easier when she was very still. Then she tipped her head back, spread her arms, arched her spine, and floated. She could almost feel Jack's hand on the small of her back.

How long could she lay there, the sun warming her face? The world was so far away and this reality so peaceful. So quiet. How silent was everything she had to face.

"Mama!" she heard at last, and her body folded and collapsed. She was now deeper than where she could stand. Her children ran along the shore, calling for her.

"Mama! Mama! Mama! Mama!" Did they need her? No. They could swim. She could sink or she could float. She had learned that from Jack. On many a weekend at Rock Creek, Jack had taught them all to swim. They all knew their strokes.

All but Caleb. She panicked. Jack hadn't taught Caleb to swim. Siobhan thrashed about. Jack had called it treading water, but she felt like it was drowning. Suddenly, her foot touched the ground and she bounced upward and jumped forward until she could stand. Dripping wet, she slogged toward the beach, her slip clinging to her skin.

Samuel and Paul jumped in the water and began wrestling, then rode on each other's shoulders, splashing their sister unmercifully. Sarah finally joined in; though a tiny bird with a broken wing, she could wrestle with the best of them. Paul picked her up and threw her in the air much to her squeals of delight. Samuel swam laps around them. The smaller of the two boys, he smarted under Paul's physicality.

She studied the map: Lake Coeur d'Alene, Idaho. It looked like a French word. She didn't know how to pronounce it but imagined it must have a beautiful sound and lovely meaning. She was close to Washington state, her destination nearly fifteen years before; only thirty-two miles from Spokane, Washington.

Sarah ran out of the water and stomped her foot in the sand. "Caleb doesn't know how to swim." Sarah, the little mother, knew. Her voice accused in the same way Siobhan's conscience had. Siobhan had tried to save Caleb, but she grieved that she had perhaps done the wrong thing. Everything within her wanted him back, but she had no idea where he was. She could drive day and night, but she might be moving farther from him.

There was a part of him that would follow them everywhere they went. Now Siobhan had to hope that someone else would teach Caleb what he needed to know. To teach him to float. To swim. She had to take reassurance that William was now his father and that Jack had abandoned that privilege. This was not her fault.

Chapter Fifty-Seven
Erin

Priest Lake, Idaho
July 1981

After the storm ripped through the Selkirk Mountains, Erin awakened to a bright and clear morning, inspired to make her favorite Belgian waffles topped with huckleberries and whipped cream. The sweet, sugary-vanilla aroma filled the cabin and Claire poked her nose up from under the blankets.

"You're too good to me," her daughter groaned with a yawn.

"Good morning!" Erin called out gaily. "Just look at that sky cleared from last night's storm. But there are a lot of trees down. Luckily, we didn't lose power."

"I fell asleep in the middle of it all." Claire took a seat at the table.

"You're used to these storms, I guess." Erin poured the orange juice. Claire took a sip of hot cocoa. Erin knew that yesterday was coming.

"It was stupid of me to try."

Erin poked a thick circular waffle on her own plate and then one straight off the griddle for Claire.

"Dad was right. Digging into the past made everything worse for everyone." Claire spread butter, huckleberries, syrup, as well as whipping cream over her waffle.

"Maybe GinnaBee was right, too. Sometimes we don't need to know the whole truth." Erin didn't agree but made no comment.

"Aria looked so confused and hurt and I don't know what else. She just plain didn't want me there."

"That must have been hard." Erin licked the huckleberry sauce off her thumb. "I'm so sorry, honey."

"Now, I don't know what to do. Now, I'll never know." She frowned and shook her head.

"We're your home. We're your family. We love you."

Erin poured herself a cup of tea. Orange Spice. The smell of Christmas in July.

"She probably hates me. She was going places. And then me."

Erin held her tongue.

"And one more thing. She has kids. There were other children in the backyard, Mom!"

Oh, Aria, what was wrong with your own daughter? You could have opened the door, as well as your heart.

Claire picked up their cups and moved to the couch and Erin followed. They could finish breakfast later.

"What is it you really want?" Erin curled up in the wingback by the fireplace.

"What I really want is an explanation. No, what I really want is for her to want me. Maybe for her to say what she can't—that she wishes she had *kept* me." Claire paused and took a deep breath. "Did she love me? I mean, if it had been legal, would she have had an . . ." She couldn't even say the word. "Would I be alive if she had the choice?"

Erin swallowed hard. That would have changed all their lives.

"Mom, do you think she gave me up because she loved me? Or because she couldn't do anything else?" Claire lifted her palms as if in question. "That's a really big difference." Claire sighed heavily. "I want to know she's a good person."

"She might be a good person and still do that."

"Well, her record says otherwise."

"You're judging her too harshly. She did a wonderful thing in giving birth to you."

"Mom! Don't you hear what I'm saying? She had me because the other option was illegal. She didn't make a choice for me out of love like you did!" Claire's words turned her Erin's stomach. "She didn't have a *choice!*"

"She did." Erin sounded monotone.

Claire eyed her strangely.

Erin paused and took a deep breath, gulping the last bit of air from the room. "Even back then, a woman had a choice. It was just more difficult."

Claire shook her head back and forth slowly as if indicating Erin shouldn't continue.

"I know from experience."

"What?" Claire's voice held disbelief. "Mom!" Her voice quivered. "Mom?"

Erin knew she was about to hurt her daughter.

"Just getting to walk in a high school graduation gown was a big deal. Then it took everything to put me through college. I thought I had one chance."

"And you graduated." Claire sounded like she needed to hijack the story.

"I did." Erin stopped. "But in my sophomore year of college, I got pregnant."

Claire winced and she chewed on her bottom lip as the tears welled in her eyes.

"I didn't tell my family. They'd have said the only gown that mattered was the wedding one."

Claire shook her head slowly, as if she could make the story go away. But Erin continued, bringing to life her twenty-year-old self.

"I'd have lost my scholarship and if I didn't finish, I doubt any of my younger brothers or sisters would have."

"And the guy?"

"Just someone I dated briefly. I would never have married him and that's what people did back then."

"But the *baby*?" Claire's voice trailed off as she now cradled the pillow in her lap.

"I didn't make the choice your mother did."

Claire was strangely quiet.

"What are you thinking, honey?" Erin asked at last.

"Grandma was right. Sometimes you don't need to tell the whole truth."

"Claire . . . I . . ."

"You didn't *need* to tell me. I didn't want to know!" Claire stood. "Especially right now!"

"I love you." It was the only thing she could think of to say.

"What about the *baby*, Mom?" Claire's voice was saturated with sadness. "Did you love it? And what about Dad? Does he know?"

"I told him before we were married."

"That baby . . ." Claire stopped and restarted. "That baby was *my* older brother or sister!" Claire wouldn't look at her. Very softly, she added, "It was *illegal*."

"I'll never forget what I did. And I don't know that I will ever forgive myself. When November comes, and I think about his birthday . . ." Erin stopped. "I've done a lot of crying over that day." Erin's eyes were dry now.

Who would or could speak next after the storm?

"But when you came along, I thought if I could rescue you, I felt like I was redeeming my bad decision."

"I was a *replacement*?"

"No one could replace that baby."

"Fetus?" Claire suggested, a wounded edge to her voice.

"*Baby*," Erin corrected. "And yes, I did love that baby. And *no*, you were not a replacement. You were a gift."

"Would you do it over again? The *abortion*?" Claire finally articulated the word.

"How can I answer that?" Erin's face dampened with tears. "No, I could never do it again. But if I hadn't, you wouldn't be here now."

Claire rubbed her forehead.

"I hope you can come to . . ."

"To forgive?"

"No," Erin said quickly. "Because it's not yours to forgive." Her voice was stern. "Maybe to understand," she added, softer.

"You must have felt better when that court decision was made."

"Making it legal didn't make it moral."

Claire's face softened at Erin's admission, and she wiped her eyes.

"Your other mother probably had a choice, and she made a better one than I did." Erin folded her hands in her lap. "I know your feelings about me have changed, but now maybe your feelings about *her* should, too."

Erin stood as Claire picked up her suitcase and packed the few articles she'd removed the night before. She zipped it shut.

"Where are you going?" Erin reached for Claire.

"I don't know. I wish I could go back to when I didn't know anything." Claire lifted her overnight bag and, as she left, gave Erin a weak hug.

Chapter Fifty-Eight
Anna

Arlington, Washington
July 25, 1981

Anna had thrown open the door expecting to catch Aaron ringing the doorbell and running away. Instead, she startled to find herself looking in a mirror.

"Hi. My name is Claire. I hoped we could talk."

Talk. Talk. Anna's lips tightened and then smoothed back and forth as if she had just applied lipstick. *What could she possibly say?* Her mind raced with questions. Of course they should talk. But there was no way she could allow Claire into her life now.

"I can't," Anna said at last, shaking her head. There was a catch in her silken voice. "I just . . . can't." Her knees felt weak. She would faint. She clutched the doorknob to steady herself.

"I just want to get to know you."

"I just can't." Anna tried to close the door.

"Wait. Please." Claire pleaded. "Take this." Claire slipped a package into her hand.

"I'm sorry." Anna said. "I'm so sorry."

The door clicked shut and Anna held the package as she pressed her head against the door and cried.

Chapter Fifty-Nine
Geneviève

Priest Lake, Idaho
August 1931

William determined they'd return to Spokane, Washington, and to his extended family, but the doctors said Caleb needed a place where the three could be alone. Together as a family. If Caleb spoke again, it would come from quiet and peace, not chaos and confusion.

"Priest Lake," William said at last, and Geneviève raised her eyebrows in a tease.

"It really exists?" she asked. William had vacationed there every year of his childhood and yet he'd never taken her. It sounded like the stuff of magical dreams.

William had stayed at Forest Lodge, a resort at the north end of the lake where the thoroughfare connected with Upper Priest Lake. "Spitting distance from Washington, Montana, and Canada." He had told fanciful stories of a famous actress Nell Shipman who brought a menagerie of zoo animals and a film crew to produce movies in the winter of 1923.

William's grandfather had homesteaded on the west side of the lake, which he and William's dad turned into a fishing cabin. But to get there would be an adventure. Was Geneviève game? She'd relished the change of scenery. Hadn't this Virginia girl traveled to France and Spokane and Deer Lodge?

The three took the train to Sand Point, where they bought a car and drove to Coolin on the south side of the lake, spending the night at Handy Bungalow near the Leonard Paul Store. The first few days, Geneviève played with Caleb on the beach, building sandcastles and filling buckets of water and pouring them out, reading to him anything she could find at the store where she also bought the occasional ice cream. Ever since the day she'd learned Siobhan was gone, Geneviève had determined that she would prove worthy of Siobhan's choice and the entrustment of her child. Caleb would be strong and healthy. All their lives depended on it.

While Will and his dad continued work, Geneviève and Caleb took Sam Byars Steamers to Elmer Berg's Shady Rest Resort, moving farther north and closer to the cabin.

The journey up the nineteen-mile lake took half the day. Geneviève marveled at the beauty of this pristine jewel. Originally called Kaniksu Lake, it later became Priest Lake, after the Jesuit missionaries who settled at Kalispell Bay in the mid-1800s. Everything felt like a tremendous adventure, and she hoped Caleb felt the same.

After five days at the resort, William came for the two, and they boarded another steamer to see their summer cabin.

William narrated the journey, labeling the bays, pointing out features in the forested Selkirk mountains, and explaining the history of various islands. Geneviève liked this version of her husband. Relaxed, content, so happy.

"Here we are!" William jumped out and secured the boat to the dock. Geneviève lifted Caleb into William's arms and then stepped onto the dock and ran to the sand, immediately kicking off her shoes. The sand was hot beneath her feet, the mica diamonds twinkling in the sun.

"There's Chimney Rock!" William pointed out a rocky protuberance on the opposite side of the lake. A warm wind blew her hair in her face, the water lapped at the shore. But all else was quiet. They were following doctor's orders: the Ellises were now intimately enclosed in a quiet beauty. This was a place to build a family. To heal. She inhaled the rich aroma of evergreens, campfire, warmed sand, and something she couldn't yet place—but it smelled like home.

The log cabin became just that; with its green tin roof, icehouse, and outhouse back farther in the woods. She carried their water from the lake and feasted on the fish William caught, then cleaned and fried. He could name each one: cutthroats, Dolly Vardens, kokanee, and mackinaw.

William taught her to collect mushrooms. The morels and chanterelles would be difficult to find during the summer, though not the aspen bolete, with a dark red cap, a white stalk, and a black dusting. He said she could find them beside roadsides and trails, but to check with him before eating. She was a nurse, but their remote location would not lend itself to medical intervention, and that troubled her.

Huckleberry season had arrived, Caleb and Geneviève picked daily. Bears were a constant fear. Geneviève had been forewarned to call out and make noise. But what of Caleb? What if he wandered too far off the path and she couldn't find him?

"You're the bear guard. If you clang these pots together, the bears will know not to come near. And if you can't find me, then just bang the pots and I'll come."

Geneviève cooked on the wood stove. The coal oil lamp and Coleman lantern kept their cabin lit until with the soothing patter of rain on the tin roof, they fell into a deeper sleep than they had ever known.

A wide-nosed moose head that seemed to be smiling hung over the door. Furniture was minimal, a wash basin dresser, an oval mirror over the stone fireplace, one double bed, and a single that had been brought from Spokane. The fireplace was made of stones collected from the beach and the mortar was beach sand and blue clay mined from the thoroughfare.

The cabin sat on an almost-bay at the narrowest point of the lake where William said he had swum across every year as a youth. A storm could whip up on the lake and leave just as quickly. Their bay was safe. From the front window she could see their beloved Chimney Rock standing guard. Everything about this place felt perfect; here they felt like a family.

Caleb and his dad would go out in the little fishing boat. She supposed William was talking to Caleb, but perhaps they sat in silence. They once journeyed to the cabin of friends on Eight Mile

Island. Sometimes they skipped rocks on the shoreline.

William seemed to have returned to his youth and an enthusiastic vigor she hadn't seen since early on in their marriage. Now he was coming home at last in so many ways.

And still Caleb remained silent. Was he mute because Siobhan willed him to be? Because the two shared an accident Siobhan wanted Caleb to forget? *Don't talk about Daddy.* Or was Caleb quiet because Geneviève willed him to be? *Don't talk about Mommy.* Did Caleb comprehend that Geneviève wanted him to be hers alone? That she didn't know if she could ever bring out the photos Siobhan had given her?

Geneviève and William were now Mom and Dad even if he couldn't or wouldn't call them that. Caleb had a new last name and so Geneviève suggested they give him a new first name as well. One of the nearby bodies of water to the south was Chase Lake. Geneviève liked that. *Chase. Chase William.* The reversal of William Charles. The farm accident that damaged Caleb Andrew Mason brought her Chase William Ellis. This would mean a fresh start.

The days grew warmer. William said these were the peak weeks to be at the lake and then the evenings would cool. Their days had a rhythm of reading, fishing, cooking, playing in the sand. But the clock was ticking toward fall, and William's career, and where they would next call home.

One afternoon, Geneviève stepped out on the sandy beach with Chase and watched as William headed down the long dock with hammer and nails to fix a loose board that squeaked each morning when the waves washed on the beach. A few extra nails would bring them an extra hour of quiet. The sun was setting, and the water darkened.

For a moment—just a moment, she lay down on the warm sand and took in the last of the sunshine. She first heard the splash. Too loud for a fish. She heard her husband's voice but her son's name.

"Chase? Chase?" William called out.

There was no response. No panicked voice. No crying. Just silence. As she ran to the dock, her husband dove in, treading water as he called out for Chase. William's arms thrashed the water as he screamed. It was quiet only when he dove.

She heard herself fill the silence with screaming. Each time William resurfaced, she hoped to see him carrying Chase and all she could think was that they had lost another child. Another child had slipped away. That she didn't deserve to be a mom. That there was something inherently wrong with her. She had not watched the boy closely enough.

"William, do something!"

William dove again and began swimming in larger circles around the dock, coming up for breath and diving back down and swimming deeper. Geneviève threw off her dress and shoes and dove into the water and swam beneath the dock where it was especially dark. Her father had always warned her never to swim under the dock. Had Chase tried to come up for air and found a wooden lid? As if in a coffin? Was he caught or trapped? She had never felt such fear, grief, guilt.

"Chase!!!! Caleb! Chase!" Could he hear her voice? She couldn't hear his.

At last, William surfaced, carrying the boy toward the beach. Geneviève ran in her wet slip and bare feet as they laid him on his stomach. Geneviève turned Chase's face to her and slapped his back until the boy spit up water onto the sand. William carried him into their cabin and Geneviève grabbed blankets.

"Put him by the fire!" They were much too far to get immediate medical attention. It was up to her.

"We just got him. How did we let this happen?" William was desperate. "What kind of a father am I?" William stripped the boy of his wet clothing.

"Shush, shush," Geneviève said, half to reassure the child and half for William's sake. She was so afraid William would return the boy now. But then again, maybe they *should*. Maybe Chase was better off with his real mother and family. Maybe living in a silent world was safer. Maybe they didn't know how to raise a little boy. Oh, Siobhan! What had they done?

She stroked Chase's cheek and hair and wrapped him in the quilt

Will's grandmother had made, bringing the boy close to her body. William returned with Chase's pajamas, the ones they had bought in Missoula. A replacement for the ones they had left in Deer Lodge.

"Chase . . . my Chase . . ." Geneviève said, rubbing his body, as she pulled the flannel pajamas over his cold limbs. Then she clutched his little body close to hers. The fire warmed them both. William sat at Chase's other side and the two embraced him.

"He needs a dog," William said at last. Unexpectedly.

"What?" Geneviève laughed. Her husband always had a solution for everything.

"He needs a dog!"

"Where did this come from?"

"I had one growing up. Every boy needs a dog," William rationalized. "The dog could be his voice."

"Whatever you think," she concurred, then whispered, "I love you," in her husband's ear. And then in her little boy's, who suddenly felt more her own than ever before. "I'm so sorry, Chase! That must have been so scary."

Silent tears streaked down Chase's face and she had to wonder if they were for his underwater terror or for being moved to a strange cabin in the middle of nowhere with people he barely knew, and a new name imposed upon him. In his fear, did he want to cry out "Mama" for that other woman? Were William and Geneviève terribly selfish in taking him away? Should they return him to . . . to what?

"Oh Chase . . . Chase . . . Chase . . . we love you so much. You are our little boy. We don't want you to be scared or sad. We are so sorry. So sorry for *everything*."

She squeezed him tight and her tears wet his face. He was crying, too. They were communicating something about the same event. She hoped her *everything* could be understood. Her apology could be taken on so many levels.

Chapter Sixty
Geneviève

Priest Lake, Idaho
August 1931

"You can pick any one of those puppies, Chase," William said, laying his hand on the boy's shoulder. "The two puppies going to farms have been removed from the pen, so which one do you want?"

Geneviève had never seen an English Shepherd before. They were like a hardy farm collie, like Lassie, except with a wider nose. Geneviève watched Chase circle the pen.

"The ones who are brown and white will turn redder," the farmer explained. "The brown ones with black are the shaded sables. The ones who have no black are the clear sables. Like that golden one over there."

Chase first gazed up at William with his head cocked and a furrowed brow. Then he turned to the pups crawling around the whelping pen. With his hands clasped behind his back, he surveyed the litter. A few nearly escaped the wall. One hung back beneath the pig rail in the corner, two were sleeping, and one was investigating the other puppies.

Chase pointed to a pile of puppies at play.

"Which *one*?" his father asked him, tempting him to speak.

Chase pointed to a quiet little puppy in the corner cuddling with a tricolor. It seemed relaxed, as if it knew it had been chosen. Chase's puppy had a beautiful red and white coat and a star across its forehead.

"That's the one, Chase?"

Chase nodded his head affirmatively.

"What do you want to *name* it?" William bent down to look Chase in the eye.

Chase looked up at Geneviève.

"Any name you like, honey!" Geneviève smiled encouragingly.

"What would you like to call the pup?" William asked again, but there was an edge to his voice. "You should name your dog,"

"Maybe Chase wants to think about it, William. Take the puppy home and see what it's like first."

"When you say the name of the puppy, then we can bring it home." Why was William so firm? So insistent. "Say the name of the puppy and we can go home."

"William! Don't do this."

"How can he call for his dog if it doesn't have a name? Or if he doesn't have a voice?"

"Don't push him, William."

"Geneviève, I think he can talk." William leaned toward her. "He just needs a nudge. An incentive."

"Not now. We don't have to go this fast." Geneviève pulled William aside and whispered in his ear. "He'll come around in his own time. Make him feel safe. Loved."

William watched the boy. Geneviève saw more love than anger in his eyes. She hoped the boy did, too.

"All right, buddy. Let's get inside the pen and play with them." William lifted Chase over the rail and the three were promptly attacked by jumpy puppies chewing on shoelaces and nipping at pant legs. Geneviève laughed at the activity, but Chase cowered when the pups began biting his sandals and bare toes. William picked Chase up and held him as the pups piled around them. When the pups finally grew bored and chased one another around the pen, Chase's little sable pup left the pack and wandered over to Chase, who hesitatingly petted its head.

"Cross your legs and sit on the floor, and you can hold it." Geneviève picked up the puppy, kissing it on the nose before she placed it in

Chase's lap.

The boy stared wide-eyed at his treasure, seemingly surprised that the puppy would stay with him.

"Well, I think it's time to take your little fellow home."

"I think it's a *girl*, William," Geneviève corrected with a laugh.

"I guess it's kind of important to know if it's a boy or girl before you name it!" William said, shaking his head.

The puppy licked Geneviève's face and she laughed at the warm pink tongue. Chase smiled in a way Geneviève hoped would one day turn into a laugh.

"In Australia, they call a female *sheila*," William hinted. "Or maybe you should name her Star for that white marking on her forehead?" But Chase shook his head. "What about Ruby, since she's reddish? Or maybe Otis?" He teased and Chase frowned.

"William, we have a lot of time to think about names. Let's see what she's like first."

Her husband knelt eye level with his son. "You picked a really good pup. I think you probably picked the best little girl in the bunch."

Did Geneviève imagine that Chase smiled?

"When I was a little boy, I had a puppy, and she was my best friend. She was the top dog of the bunch, just like your puppy." William petted the white collar rough on the little girl. "Her name meant fair and good. And that puppy *was* fair and good, and she was mine. All mine."

Geneviève felt she'd known William's only dog through the many photographs. One where he held Bonnie proudly in his arms, another with William in a Boy Scout uniform and Bonnie standing at attention beside him, and then William in his graduation gown bending over a full-grown dog who gazed up at him with cloudy, older, and wiser eyes.

"And my puppy was named Bonnie. Because she was a bonnie lass."

The puppy chewed on Chase's shirt and her son tensed with fear.

"She's just trying out her new teeth," Geneviève explained. "She won't hurt you, honey."

The puppy turned and her tail swished Chase's face and the three laughed. Geneviève liked what she saw. William was warming to the idea of this quiet boy, and the puppy was drawing them together as a family.

Then the puppy wriggled free and moved to the other side of the pen. Chase motioned for it to come back. He clapped his hands and waved at the puppy, who sat back on her bottom and gave a small bark, as if teasing them. Chase looked to Geneviève and then to William, then Chase again motioned for the puppy and waved his arms. But the puppy only whimpered slightly and barked.

"Bonnie!" the boy said softly. "Bonnie!"

Geneviève gasped slightly, a catch in her voice, as she called, "Come, Bonnie!" reaffirming Chase's name.

When the puppy loped over to Chase, William smiled, swallowing suddenly. "Bonnie it is, then," he said ruffling Chase's hair.

Chapter Sixty-One
Geneviève

Spokane, Washington
August 1931–1933

William spent every remaining summer day helping Chase train his puppy and giving Chase swimming lessons. Chase was frightened and yet brave and by the end of August, he had learned to do the crawl, tread in place, and float on his back. And Bonnie? She could now heel, sit, and stay.

When the leaves began turning, the lake chilled, the stove and fireplace were needed in the morning and evening, and Will began talking of returning to law.

At the end of September, they moved to Spokane, Washington where they bought a house on South 33rd Avenue and William hung out his shingle.

Chase's words were slow in coming, saving them for the most important moments or for his dog. Boy and dog were inseparable, and Chase talked in hushed whispers to his beloved pet. Bonnie was his sole companion and counsel. Geneviève had no idea what Bonnie heard, but whatever it was, her counsel was healing, and so Geneviève loved that dog almost as much as her son.

Geneviève read everything she could about people suddenly silenced. A stretcher-bearer in the trenches came home with haunting hallucinations of soldiers screaming out in pain for help he couldn't give without risking his own life. He was debilitated by the memories. Unable to quiet the voices, he silenced his own. Absent of soul meant absence of sound. His treatment involved improvised singing of the sounds he remembered. Geneviève had no idea of what had happened to Chase, but if she could only get him to voice it.

Geneviève learned that speaking and singing involve at least a hundred muscles operating fifty to fifteen hundred times per second, and at a faster rate than almost anything else a person does. Who knew that the voice was such a unique fingerprint?

There was so much technical and medical jargon that she'd share with William at night on the front porch, when they talked about their days while Chase slept in his room at the top of the stairs. Who knew that to express a feeling involved abdominal muscles, respiratory system, lungs, vocal folds? But was this a scientific and mechanical-like maneuver Chase was silenced by or was it something else?

Though William started as an attorney with his background from Deer Lodge, it wasn't long before he was running for judge. Their lives were changing.

Chase turned five and he ran away. When Geneviève couldn't find him or Bonnie, she thought he must have fallen asleep somewhere in the house. Then she tried his friends' houses, but no one knew where he was. Geneviève drove their Chrysler around town, hoping to find her lost boy. *The only thing we have to fear is fear itself* ran through her head. Though Roosevelt's inauguration had little to do with her, she understood that kind of fear.

Geneviève found Chase on the front porch of a home four blocks away, sitting on the top step of a white bungalow, his elbows on his knees, his face in his hands, Bonnie resting at his feet.

"Chase, I was so worried about you! Why did you go away?"

"I don't know."

But three days later, he was gone again and so she immediately drove along the same tree-lined street, to the same bungalow on Manito Boulevard, where she found him rocking in the swing on the porch.

"Chase!" she called out from the open car window, before opening her door. "I've been worried about you! You can't just leave like that." Her voice was brisk. She took a deep breath before she joined him on the swing. "Why did you come back here?"

"I thought this was the way home."

He didn't stop looking. The third time he went missing, he explained, "I need to see who lives here. Can I see who lives here?"

"Chase, we can't go knocking on their door. Besides, I don't think they're home. They would have heard you."

She took his hand and they headed back to the car.

The next Saturday after breakfast, Chase disappeared again, and this time William accompanied her to the house on Manito Boulevard where they found him on the bottom step, gazing out at the world. Bonnie ran to greet them.

"Chase, why are you here?" William sat down next to him.

"You can't just keep running back here!" Geneviève scolded, tears brimming in her eyes.

William touched her arm and she turned away.

"Chase, do you know why you keep coming back here?"

"No, Daddy," he answered, looking down at his shoes.

"You like this house?"

"I don't know."

William leaned back against the step. Relaxed and yet in deep thought.

"Could we see who lives here?" Chase asked at last, looking up, his blue eyes pleading. Geneviève knew William would be rational.

"It might be nice to say hello." William patted Chase's head. Geneviève's mouth dropped as the two climbed the steps, but she held back. "Do you want to knock, Chase?"

Chase shook his head and so William rapped loudly on the door.

The door opened to reveal a woman in the frame of the doorway. From her view, Geneviève figured her to be in her late sixties. She was joined by a man who Geneviève assumed was her husband.

"We were just in the neighborhood admiring your flowers out front. Beautiful garden. And my little boy likes your house."

"Well, aren't you sweet," the lady said, bending down and smiling.

"My name is William Ellis and I'm running in the next election. I'd love to have your vote." William extended his hand. All the while, Chase looked from the woman to the man and back again, a worried look on his face.

"You don't look like my mommy," he said at last.

And the older woman laughed. "No, your mommy is so young and pretty." The woman nodded to Geneviève at the base of the steps. "We'll think about the vote." The older man shook William's hand.

But Geneviève's heart hammered. She thought by now she was his mommy. If Chase was still looking, what was wrong? Something about this house was a reminder of home. What was lacking in theirs?

Was it really an adoption or had they stolen a child who belonged with someone somewhere else? But he belonged in her heart, didn't he? He was their home. He was the center of their marriage and their family.

William took Chase's hand and they left. Geneviève couldn't say anything. Nor did she ever speak about that house. Chase never again ran away to Manito Boulevard.

Not everybody understood her son. She hated the word dumb and that teachers described Caleb that way. Chase was not dumb. He could work with his hands and read silently, and he spent hours fishing with his dad. As a family, they enjoyed listening to *The Lone Ranger* and *The Shadow*. Chase seemed fascinated at how the words came out of the radio and laughed sometimes at the comedy of Jack Benny.

Geneviève had to admit there was no better sound than a child's giggle and that Chase's laughter was worth the wait. If Chase had much to say, he only shared it with those closest to him; his words were savored.

But their local Jefferson Elementary wouldn't take him. They said they didn't have the resources to handle a "special" child like Chase. He was special all right; they just didn't know! Many kindergarteners were still counting Cheerios, threading Fruit Loops on a string, but her boy was reading, albeit to himself.

Then again, having him home for another year was appealing to Geneviève. She couldn't imagine the loneliness she'd feel when he started school.

One night after Chase had fallen asleep, Will and Geneviève listened to Roosevelt's fireside chat on the front porch, a wind cooling the night just enough to necessitate a blanket. The leaves would soon turn. Another change of seasons. "They say we should wait—consider putting him in kindergarten next year." Geneviève approached the topic gently.

"They? They don't know him like we do. Go back." William was firm. "We've paid our taxes. He's five now. If he waits any longer, he'll be so bored, they won't want him in their classroom. He's ready, Geneviève. This is the best thing for him." Deep down, she knew William was right.

Chase and Geneviève returned to Jefferson Elementary and sat across from the principal in hard wooden chairs. Chase's feet swung shy of the floor; his hands folded quietly in his lap.

"How old are you, Chase?"

The boy raised his hand slowly, five fingers stuck together like a little army.

"Would you like to go to school this year?"

Chase shrugged his shoulders.

"He would like to make friends and continue learning." Geneviève glanced from Chase to the principal.

"Chase." The man stared at the little boy. "Do you have a pet at home?"

He nodded and smiled shyly.

"And what's its name? Is it a dog?"

Chase nodded again and then his eyes flicked up to his mother.

"Bonnie. She's an English Shepherd. Chase plays with her all day."

"Mrs. Ellis, I can't imagine how this is going to work. You can't go to kindergarten and speak for him. I can't assess his social readiness when he doesn't talk. I don't know his ability level. Can't you see that another year at home might help him socialize? He'd only be six then."

Geneviève fingered the strap on her purse. Chase's eyes kept flitting to the table, to a *National Geographic*. On the cover was a bird as colorful as Captain Hook. As she reached across him to take away the distraction, she suddenly had a change of heart and opened to the middle.

"Chase, why don't you read this for me?" She pointed to the sidebar. "You always like stories about animals."

Chase frowned and bit his lip.

"Please, Mommy likes it when you read."

The principal peered over his glasses skeptically.

Geneviève placed her finger over the start of the first full paragraph as Chase struggled with the strange spellings and pronunciations, sounding them out creatively.

"The Matschie's female tree kangaroo carries and nurses her joey in her pouch. Adults live in the trees eating leaves. These furry marsupials can only be found in . . ." Chase frowned but attempted each word as it appeared to him. "Papua New Guinea's Huon Peninsula." Geneviève bit her lip at *Pahpooah noo goowineea*.

She didn't look up but could see out of the corner of her eye that the principal's look of doubt was turning to amazement. "What's this, Chase?"

"Den-dro-la-gus mat-schiei."

"But what is that?"

"You mean, like its name?" Chase looked up at her.

Geneviève flipped to another page, which revealed the Golfo Dulce poison dart frog and a baboon-like monkey, a gelada. Then a picture of a dromedary camel crossing the desert.

"Could the kangaroo live here?"

Chase shook its head.

"But why couldn't the kangaroo live here?" She flipped a page. "Or what about where this red-eyed tree frog lives? Could the kangaroo live there?" She turned yet another page and pointed. "Or what about this poison dart frog? See where he lives? Could the kangaroo live here?" Chase kept shaking his head and she started to realize she sounded like her husband in court.

"Why wouldn't the marsupial live here or here or here?" She pointed to pages all over the heavily illustrated magazine. She watched the principal. Surely, he understood her boy was smart.

"It . . . it . . . it . . ." Chase stuttered and shook his head in frustration. "Mrs. Ellis, I don't think you need—"

"Let him talk!" Geneviève interrupted. Chase's lip was quivering. His eyes were glassy. What was she doing? Why did she have to prove herself or Chase to somebody who didn't care about him the way they did?

"It's not . . ." Chase kept trying, frowning as if the effort hurt his head. "It's not . . . it's not . . ." Then she realized he did want to say it, but he lacked the word. "It's not his d . . . d . . . dirt."

"*It's not his dirt,*" the principal echoed, exhaling as he sat back in his chair. "It's not his dirt."

"You're right. It's not his *habitat.*" She put her arm around him and with her other hand pointed out the word. "Habitat. That's where he can eat and sleep and find food and shelter and protection. It's his home, Chase. It's his *home.*"

Chapter Sixty-Two
Siobhan

A decade of selected letters to Antonio
Dated August 1931–December 1941

August 10, 1931

*D*ear Antonio,
I have a new address in case you still want to correspond. After all these years, I finally made it to Washington. It's quite different from Montana.
- Siobhan

August 30, 1931

Dear Antonio,
Thank you for the book. I've gotten a job at the Northshore School District main office where Sarah and the boys attend schools. It's walking distance from our apartment. I enjoyed Hitty, Her First Hundred Years *and see that it won the Newbery Medal last year.*

Very unusual to have a doll's point of view. Because the doll talks about moving all over the world, it seemed to help Sarah think about her great move. How sad that the doll is separated from her owner. Sarah once had a toy bunny she played with.
- Siobhan

October 4, 1931

Dear Antonio,
Thank you for The Swiss Family Robinson. *We read that as a family, too. Sarah misses home and so much more. She is a kind and imaginative soul but is often teased by other children.*

You underlined "It was one of those happy days that God grants us sometimes on earth to give us an idea of the bliss of heaven." I trust that means you've experienced one of those happy days. It rains here a lot but is green like Ireland.

I see you're now living in Europe. I hope that means you're still studying!

- *Siobhan*

December 4, 1931

Antonio,

Sarah and I both thank you for A Little Princess, *though she hasn't let me read it yet. She comes to me with questions. (It's a long book!)*

How could you know that Sarah means princess and that my Sarah could so relate to Sara Crewe? You're so clever. She immediately pointed out that someone had written in the book. (She knows we're not supposed to do that!) She shared with me all the sentences you underlined. She especially liked: "She did not care very much for other little girls, but if she had plenty of books, she could console herself." I wasn't sure what to say about that. She came to me again, when Sara Crewe's father dies and the children at the boarding school tease her. This was your best book choice ever.

You did not underline this sentence, but Sarah did. "Perhaps there is a language which is not made of words and everything in the world understands it."

Thank you for caring about Sarah.

- *Siobhan*

April 7, 1932

Dear Antonio,

You spoil my girl. Two books in a row! I must admit I read The Secret Garden *before she had a chance. I didn't mark it, but I copied one line to remember. "She made herself stronger by fighting with the wind." That's what happens, doesn't it?*

I need summer to come. Unlike Montana, it rains here every day. I need to see the sun and have my own little plot of ground and grow something and know it will live. More than to survive but to thrive.

- *Siobhan*

June 15, 1932

Dear Antonio,

School is almost out for the year. Can you believe it's been thirteen years since you handed me my first book? A Farewell to Arms *was difficult. You underlined: "The world breaks every one and afterward many are strong at the broken places." Do you agree with that?*

I see you've moved again! I am guessing this time you're teaching. Professor Savelli! I wish I could be in your classroom. I can still see you walking across the beach at the North End. I'm still sorry I laughed.

- Siobhan

November 7, 1932

Dear Antonio,

Harriet Beecher Stowe was quite a fascinating woman! Thank you so much for her amazing book. I wrote this line on a card and posted it on my mirror: "I am braver than I was because I have lost all; and he who has nothing to lose can afford all risks."

Antonio, she was so strong. She, too, had a little boy named Samuel and she lost him very young. I have to wonder how much of her heart is in Uncle Tom's Cabin.

"No tear dropped over that pillow; in such straits as these, the heart has no tears to give—it drops only blood, bleeding itself away in silence."

"Any mind that is capable of real sorrow is capable of good."

"The longest way must have its close—the gloomiest night will wear on to a morning."

I like that you've sent so many books by women. That line: "Could I ever have loved you, had I not known you better than you know yourself?" Antonio, sometimes I think you know me better than I know myself!

The high school needs an assistant librarian and so I'm going to apply.

- Siobhan

April 10, 1933

Antonio,

I haven't heard from you and was afraid my letter might have been lost so I wrote again. I hope that you are safe. I went back to one of our first books. I still love Willa Cather the best. Maybe I'm feeling nostalgic, but I was remembering times when we sat in the Boston Public Library reading O Pioneers!. I bought my own copy and underline as I read. Maybe I should send it to you when I am finished? Or at least some of my favorite quotes.

"Everywhere the grain stood ripe and the hot afternoon was full of the smell of the ripe wheat, like the smell of bread baking in an oven. The breath of the wheat and the sweet clover passed him like pleasant things in a dream."

That was just like how it was in Montana. Some days I miss the land.
- Siobhan

March 14, 1934

Dear Antonio,

How thoughtful of you to send another Willa Cather. What a beautiful title: The Song of the Lark. Interesting how the girl leaves home for the big city to discover her voice. The sacrifices she makes! Opera. I would love to hear her sing. Imagine how beautiful she must sound!

You only underlined one phrase, but I underlined many. Here are two.

"People live through such pain only once. Pain comes again—but it finds a tougher surface."

"There are some things you learn best in calm, and some in storm."

I think sometimes you hear discouragement in my letters. I'm sorry if this weighs you down. You're probably in much more difficult circumstances than I. Today is a difficult anniversary. The one phrase you underlined gave me great encouragement. The lark's song will be mine!

"He knew he would always remember her, standing there with that expectant, forward-looking smile, enough to turn the future into summer."
- Siobhan

June 1, 1934

Dear Antonio,

When I said I needed a distraction, you didn't need to send me a thousand-page novel. I appreciated your warning at the beginning of War and Peace about there being too many places with tension and your advice for me to read it "blind." That is a challenge keeping track of five

*different families, so I made a graph. You would have been proud. Do
you ever teach that to your students?*

*I confess that I haven't finished it yet so I will need to write again. I
stop many times to think about what Tolstoy writes.*

*"Man cannot possess anything as long as he fears death. But to him
who does not fear it, everything belongs. If there was no suffering, man
would not know his limits, would not know himself."*

*The children are all growing up and are doing well. I have two in high
school now.*

- Siobhan

July 17, 1934

Dear Antonio,

I am still working on War and Peace, *but I thought I'd write anyway
because it's taking me a while to finish.*

*You underlined: "We love people not so much for the good they've
done us, as for the good we've done them." I wish I could talk to you
about that. I'm plodding ahead, though!*

- Siobhan

August 25, 1934

Dear Antonio,

One short children's book is too quick of a read compared to War and
Peace! *But really,* The Little Engine that Could? *I think you mock me!
We're getting ready for another year of school. By the way, it may be a
classic, but none of my children are that young! You tease!*

- Siobhan

March 2, 1935

Dear Antonio,

*Alice's Adventures in Wonderland was a much better choice,
although the boys thought it silly and wouldn't listen to me read it.
Sarah is a bit like me and captured funny sayings after each reading. Her
favorite character was the Cat. Now whenever she has an opportunity to
be philosophical, she quotes Lewis Carroll.*

*"It's no use going back to yesterday, because I was a different person
then."*

"If you don't know where you are going any road can take you there."

Look what you started!
- Siobhan

November 4, 1936

Antonio,

I am sorry I didn't write for so long. This has been a very difficult year. I really wanted to like To the Lighthouse. *I wanted to love it because I love lighthouses and I miss Loop Head. But it was vastly different, since it was all thoughts and observations. No action or talking. Very strange. Is that how Virginia Woolf always writes? Thank you again for another female author.*

I still collected phrases that resonated with me, and I see that you underlined only one phrase and put in a question mark. "Friendships, even the best of them, are frail things. One drifts apart."

Let me reassure you, Antonio, our friendship is not frail, and I hope we will never drift apart.

I promise to be more faithful in my writing.

I share this one long sentence because I have known this truth.

"She had known happiness, exquisite happiness, intense happiness, and it silvered the rough waves a little more brightly, as daylight faded, and the blue went out of the sea and it rolled in waves of pure lemon which curved and swelled and broke upon the beach and the ecstasy burst in her eyes and waves of pure delight raced over the floor of her mind and she felt, it is enough! It is enough!"
- Siobhan

February 13, 1937

Dear Antonio,

I think that Zora Neale Hurston likes the ocean, too, when she writes, "Love is like the sea. It's a moving thing, but still and all, it takes its shape from the shore it meets, and it's different with every shore." Thanks for the warning that Janie and Teacake would not end out well. I read the ending first. He loved her enough to sacrifice his life for her! This was a beautiful book and one that I will read again. Honestly, Antonio, nobody has more variety in their library than I!
- Siobhan

December 30, 1937

Dear Antonio,

Thank you for the fascinating tale, such a beautiful Christmas gift. We loved The Hobbit. *I hope there will be more from this J. R .R. Tolkien. If we stacked the first letters of our names, you would be A. M. Savelli and I would be M. S. K. Mason. I still wonder about your middle name!*

"There is nothing like looking, if you want to find something. You certainly usually find something, if you look, but it is not always quite the something you were after."
- Siobhan

June 15, 1938

Dear Antonio,

I loved Our Town. *You've never sent me a play before. How lucky you were to be able to see its Boston premiere at the Wilbur Theatre, but I cannot believe it was so poorly received and that people were walking out!*

I take to heart that it is doing so well in New York City. Maybe one day I might be able to see it. And to think that you and Thornton Wilder are contemporaries!

This is one of my favorite quotes:

"We all know that something is eternal. And it ain't houses and it ain't names, and it ain't earth, and it ain't even the stars . . . everybody knows in their bones that something is eternal, and that something has to do with human beings. All the greatest people ever lived have been telling us that for five thousand years and yet you'd be surprised how people are always losing hold of it. There's something way down deep that's eternal about every human being."

Emily was a beautiful character, but I wish her family could have seen that she was there and heard her wise words. I guess that's what we all need to do. Stop and live life. But sometimes it's hard when so much is happening.

"Oh, earth, you're too wonderful for anybody to realize you."
- Siobhan

September 12, 1938

Dear Antonio,

I didn't like The Yearling *and you never warned me what was going* to happen. *That was not a happy children's book. The mother wounds the boy's deer, forcing him to kill it? Then Jody runs away? I hated that. You deserve only a short letter for that novel. "Now he understood. This was death. Death was a silence that gave back no answer." That was terrible.*

- Siobhan

June 14, 1939

Dear Antonio,
You underlined only two phrases.
"It was her habit to build up laughter out of inadequate materials."
"Her joy was nearly like sorrow."
I must admit they were the two best lines from The Grapes of Wrath. *Prison, Dust Bowl, Foreclosures. I think you know more about my life than I have revealed. Did you know that John Steinbeck had trouble finding a title for the book, but that his wife suggested the line from "Battle Hymn of the Republic"? I wonder how many titles are inspired by songs.*

- Siobhan

December 30, 1939

Antonio,
I saw the movie The Hunchback of Notre Dame. *I was terrified and clung to my seat.*

I confess I should have read the book first, but Maureen O'Hara was so spectacular and Charles Laughton so handsome.

I'm going to read it now. You don't have to send that book because I checked it out from the library, and I promise not to underline or bend a page.

I haven't heard from you for a few months. I know that much is happening in Europe and your address always changes. Antonio, stay safe, please. Please stay safe.

- Siobhan

August 17, 1940

Both boys decided to forgo their college courses and enlist before the draft on September 16. I tried to dissuade them, to no avail. Now, I address dozens of envelopes at once and write as often as I can. Paul and Samuel write back because they want to hear more. Does that sound

familiar? I learned it from you! The letters draw a line from me to them.
Have you heard of the Anderson family? One mother lost four sons in
the Great War, and John and Margaret Smith lost five sons! That is what
I fear. Wherever they are, I put a pin on the map in my kitchen. Samuel
is in the Navy and Paul is in the Army.

I'm suggesting a curious read. George Orwell is a fascinating author.
Here's an example of his work in Coming Up for Air. *(Isn't that a great*
title?)

"The past is a curious thing. It's with you all the time. I suppose an
hour never passes without your thinking of things that happened ten or
twenty years ago, and yet most of the time it's got no reality, it's just a
set of facts that you've learned, like a lot of stuff in a history book. Then
some chance sight or sound or smell, especially smell, sets you going, and
the past doesn't merely come back to you, you're actually IN the past."

Sarah is dating a young man and I think they will marry. I'm taking
classes at the University of Washington. (I guess you could call me a
Husky.) I'm one of the older students, though there was a graduate
student who tried to ask me on a date. I am taking Physics, Anatomy,
and even a Music Theory course! My coursework is interdisciplinary,
nonmedical and medical. I love learning about the disordered aspects
of speech. Orwell would approve. "Perhaps a man really dies when his
brain stops, when he loses the power to take in a new idea."
- Siobhan

October 6, 1940

Dear Antonio,

That book All Quiet on the Western Front *was a painful reminder of*
my brothers and everything about the Great War. Did you think about
your brother Luca when you read it?

There are fronts in every battle, but I hope my sons are nowhere near
any of these. "Why do they never tell us that you are poor devils like
us, that your mothers are just as anxious as ours, and that we have the
same fear of death, and the same dying and the same agony—Forgive
me, comrade; how could you be my enemy?"

I knew you understood what I was thinking. Why do people fight so?

Classes are going well. I am in the Speech Division of the English
Department. Isn't that ironic? Though I love the study of literature, I

have found the study of voice and treatment so practical and rewarding. If you can find it, read this article from "A Comparative Study of Speech-Defective Children." It's written by James A. Carrell, the director of our UW speech clinic. My classmates and I travel throughout the rural areas with our speech clinic making speech therapy recommendations. I find this very rewarding while I wait for my sons to come home.
- Siobhan

January 5, 1941

Dear Antonio,
Dublin has taken hits in this war. Ireland can remain neutral and still get caught in the evil of war. Though it seems so far away, County Clare is still so close to my heart.

Thank you for Little Women. *It's nice to have a book that's not about war, although it does give us a look at the Homefront when Father goes off to war. I read it to Sarah, and we enjoyed that time together, which will be less frequent now that Sarah is married. Although, Lars is away so much, she may still want her mother nearby!*

The two are as poor as church mice, so I laughed when I read: "I have nothing to give but my heart so full and these empty hands." And Jo's romantic response, "They're not empty now." Lars and Sarah are so young, but they are friends. I think of that other line by Cather: "I think we shall be incredibly happy. I haven't any fears. I think when friends marry, they are safe. We don't suffer like—those young ones."

The wedding was simple. I wish Paul and Samuel could have been here. Lars is a good man, but not who I would have chosen. They love each other. Their lives will be challenging but that is not always bad. Like Louisa May Alcott says, "I am not afraid of storms, for I am learning how to sail my ship."

Speaking of ships, Samuel is in Hawaii, on the USS Nevada. *I'm so glad he's nowhere near Europe! He writes about how beautiful the harbor is and how warm the weather and how delicious the tropical fruits. Meanwhile, it's rainy and cold here!*

Writing to you has been good practice for my college essays. It's all quote and explain. State, restate, and restate it again. My professors say

I'm particularly good at analyzing literature!
- Siobhan

March 24, 1941

Antonio,

The Jungle *is a very odd book. Who would have thought I'd learn so much about Chicago and the meat packing industry? There is one very funny line in that book, and I will remember it whenever things get hard (or hot). "She was standing upon the brink of the pit of hell and throwing in snowballs to lower the temperature."*

I'm now assisting at the UW Library and my tuition is waived! I'm not saying that so you'll stop sending books, I'm just being honest. Besides, I much prefer books you've written in and being able to fold the pages or underline places I want to return to. Books are my friends and when I open them, I want to know I've come home to something familiar. If there were a degree in reading, I would have mine now! The Division of Speech is no longer under the English department. We are our own Department of Speech. I'm chalking up the credits for a bachelor's degree.
- Siobhan

October 15, 1941

Antonio,

How did you celebrate your 38th birthday? Are you surprised I remembered? I can still remember your mama's meatballs and a very hearty meal in Boston on your seventeenth birthday!

Last week, I went to a party at Lars's family home in Ballard. They are all fishermen. So, guess what we had for dinner?

The men of his family are happier on sea than land. (I think the women are happier when the men are at sea, too.) But not Sarah. She's lonely much of the time. And we both miss Samuel and Paul. I have no patience and too much time to worry. Sometimes I'm not sure what to do with my fear.

"The strongest of all warriors are these two—Time and Patience."

That was from War and Peace. *Remember? You must have war on your mind. No more books on war. I live it in my mind every day.*
- Siobhan

November 5, 1941

Antonio,

Sarah is expecting a baby. This will be my first grandchild! The baby is due sometime in February or March.

Antonio, on some things I've been silent, but you have probably read between the lines. You've always been so good at that. You must know I am a widow. I have raised my children the best I know how, and reading has been important in all of our lives. Thank you for the library of education you have given my family and me. Over two decades worth of books!

I am curious how your address changes so often! Sometimes words are blacked out and it takes a long time before I hear from you. Stay safe, my friend.

- Siobhan

December 14, 1941

Antonio,

Last week a man got out of a car wearing a military uniform. I didn't want him to come to my door. I wouldn't answer his knocking. If I didn't answer, then I wouldn't know . . . which son? Where? And if I didn't know, then someone would still be alive. But he kept knocking and then he rang the doorbell, and I hid. Antonio, I hid! I kept one son alive just a little longer by avoiding the notice.

How do these men deliver such news?

I didn't want to hear it alone. But then I realized that not knowing who had died meant I could only grieve for myself. The futility of that! I opened the door and he turned around and came back and said he was sorry and handed me an envelope and told me my son had died for his country and I asked him which son and he said, "Samuel Jacob Mason."

When Pearl Harbor was bombed, it emptied my soul.

I cannot write or talk about this without crying. There was a line from War and Peace *that sticks with me, and I question it. "It's all God's will: you can die in your sleep, and God can spare you in battle."*

Why didn't he spare Samuel in battle?

- Siobhan

Chapter Sixty-Three
Siobhan

Of course, in a novel, people's hearts break, and they die,
and that is the end of it; and in a story this is very convenient.
But in real life we do not die
when all that makes life bright dies to us.
—Harriet Beecher Stowe, *Uncle Tom's Cabin*

Ballard, Washington
December 21, 1941

The grief in losing Samuel was raw as Siobhan and Sarah entered the holidays. But Siobhan held out the hope that there would be a bright spot in 1942, the birth of Sarah's baby. Not a replacement for Samuel or Caleb, but a child to love. Siobhan enjoyed spending time with Sarah in her tiny apartment frugally decorated with homemade ornaments and hand-sewn Christmas stockings.

"I talk to him and sing to him," Sarah admitted, her hand cupped around her growing belly. Sarah rocked back and forth in rhythm to the music on the radio, sounding just like Billie Holiday. And when she joined in with The Andrews Sisters, Sarah could sing any of the harmony parts without music. "He's my little Boogie-Woogie Bugle Boy!"

"And you're so certain it's a boy?"

"No, but I have to think of him as someone. And for some reason. I like to imagine him a *boy*."

Siobhan hoped that when Sarah had a baby of her own, Sarah might forgive Siobhan for giving away Caleb and heal the festering wound of Caleb's absence. But then again, it might make the new mother question how Siobhan could have ever done that.

"Well, it would be easier to think of any child as a boy, since you had three brothers." *Three. Had.* Samuel was gone. And the unspoken third.

"Silent Night" followed, and Siobhan closed her eyes to shut out the sad memories.

"Mam, don't you ever think about him? Wonder about him? We could probably find him if we tried. We could look for the Ellises." Sarah frowned and rubbed her forehead, groaning slightly.

Siobhan didn't answer, surprised Sarah remembered their names.

"My head hurts so. And my neck, too. Could you rub my shoulders, Mam?"

Siobhan pressed her fingers against Sarah's temples, then massaged Sarah's neck and shoulders.

Her daughter clutched her stomach and leaned forward. "I thought the nausea would go away after the first few months."

Sarah wasn't warm to the touch, but she was perspiring. She leaned back and her hand covered her belly, one arm cradling below, the smaller hand tucked above, and closed her eyes. "When he kicks, I know he's mine." She paused. "You had to feel that way about Caleb. That he belonged to you."

"Sarah, I can't go back. Don't you think it hasn't torn me up every day since?"

Sarah stretched her legs in front of her.

"How long have your ankles been like that?" Siobhan asked.

"It's just water. My girlfriends tell me that happens. I'll ask about it at my appointment on Monday."

Siobhan pressed her hand on Sarah's chest and felt her heart racing. "We're going now."

She didn't want to be right, but the doctor immediately confirmed it. They'd take the baby now, ready or not. Siobhan paced the halls, wondering how her daughter would handle the ten percent chance of her baby's survival. Sarah was about to be robbed again.

"You can see her but just for a minute before her surgery. She's been calling out for you." The nurse directed Siobhan back into the room.

"She's been calling for me and you didn't get me?" Siobhan could only imagine what Sarah might have been feeling. Sarah wanted and needed her, and Siobhan hadn't been there.

"The room goes in and out of focus." Sarah stared straight ahead as if she didn't recognize Siobhan, her breathing short, her face and hands now swollen.

"I'm here. I love you, princess." Sarah was nearly incoherent, but Siobhan could hope she heard.

The nurses cleaned her daughter and prepared to wheel her away. A new doctor explained the urgency.

"We have to take the baby now no matter what or we'll lose them both."

"It's too early. She'll never make it."

"Yes, it is. But it's the only way we'll save the mother."

Sarah would never forgive herself when she found out her baby was gone.

"Placental abruption. She's bleeding heavily," someone in white announced.

Sarah's arms and legs suddenly went stiff, and she thrashed back and forth.

"You need to leave! Now!" The nurse moved Siobhan out of the way as they wheeled Sarah to the emergency room. Siobhan turned back to see her daughter's legs and arms jerking and the nurse placing a wooden spatula between her teeth.

"Sarah!" Siobhan shouted as a swarm of medical staff surrounded the bed. How could they take Sarah away from her?

"Mrs. Mason, you need to leave!"

Leave? She could never leave her daughter. She left one child. She had let another slip from her body. And another had been taken by war. Never again.

Chapter Sixty-Four
Anna

Arlington, Washington
July 25, 1981

Anna couldn't believe she'd let Claire go. She pressed her body against the door in case Claire tried to push it open again, then found the barrel bolt and slipped it into the cylinder. *Locked. Closed. Sealed.*

The air had been sucked out of her chest. *I thought those files were sealed forever.* Slowly she slid down the door, until crumpling onto the floor. She had locked her daughter away from everything. Everything except her heart.

Anna opened the envelope and read the note inside.

Dear Aria,

As early as I can remember my parents read this book to me. I'm sharing it with you now. Anna began reading the homemade scrapbook.

Our Baby's Story

Once upon a time, a little baby grew in her mommy's tummy. At the same time, the baby also grew in another mommy's heart. The birth mommy loved her baby so much that when she couldn't take care of her, she gave her to Chase and Erin Ellis to love. That's adoption and it's very special because it means a baby is chosen and loved by two families. Chase and Erin Ellis named their baby girl Aria Claire, and said she is the best thing that ever happeneded to them. They are a very happy family.

327

Her daughter had a name. *Aria. Her name. Aria.* Her daughter also had a family, and she was loved.

Everything Anna dreaded and everything she longed for had just happened. Claire wanted to know her, and she had to admit she wanted to know Claire. That tall, beautiful redhead with green eyes looking at her so earnestly. Claire was a picture of herself, before what happened so long ago.

So long ago was now almost twenty-two years . . .

That awful night, when she'd awoken dizzy, confused, and lost. Shivering.

Her vision was blurred, and her head hurt, as if she had been hit. Hard. She had closed her eyes against the pain and rubbed her head to find bits of pine needles stuck in her hair. Why was she cold, shaking? Wasn't it summer? The rocks felt sharp beneath her, cutting into her stomach.

Why was she uncovered? She tugged her dress back down below her hips. She opened and closed her eyes to see if she could focus on anything. Something pink. Her panties were just beyond her reach. Where was she? What had happened?

The last thing she could remember. What was it? A song? She'd been singing, wearing a wig, breeches, a vest. She was singing about love.

She could hear a B flat ringing in her head. Perfect pitch. The sound of a fluorescent light bulb in the practice room. She hummed the note. She hummed it again. Or was it all in her head? Did her song start on a B flat? What was that note? She could almost hear the note resonate in the rehearsal room, accompanied by the cacophony of voices in differing tempi, pitches forming a strange choir.

Why was her face on the pavement? Had she fallen? The thought of standing nauseated her. Something was horribly wrong.

She rolled over on her side and stuffed her panties in her pocket. Unsteady, she pushed herself up, shivering uncontrollably, nausea rolling over her. Where was she?

The general numbness gave way to pain as she began walking. She felt sore and bruised, inside and out. She tried to read the street signs, but everything felt unfamiliar. At last, she heard the chime from the church near the university. Bells. Bells. Bells. B flat bells led her home.

Once in her dorm room, she turned on the one small light by her bed. She was unable to stop shaking. She peeled off her dress and threw it into the garbage can. Her roommate turned over at the sound. Aria froze, hoping Shauna was still asleep.

"Aria, what happened to you?" Shauna asked suddenly, raising herself up on one elbow.

"What do you mean?" She ran her fingers through her gnarled hair.

"Look." Shauna's voice was low and flat. "Look at yourself in the mirror." She pointed, her finger shaking. "Turn around."

Bruises. Scratches. *Names.* There were names etched in pen on her backside. With her fingertips, she could feel the grooved red tattoos, left by somebody who knew what happened. A lot of somebodies. Names of people she didn't know or remember.

"Aria! Don't!" Shauna yelled. But it was too late. Aria locked the bathroom door and turned on the shower, to wash it all away as Shauna pounded on the door.

She clung to the showerhead as the water streamed over her face. *What do I do? What happened to me? I have to get clean!* At first, she screamed without sound. Then suddenly she let it out and sank down the wall tiles until she crumpled into a heap on the floor, dirty soap suds circling the drain.

Block it all out. Block it all out.

An image of the fresh libretto floated free. *Le Nozze de Figaro.* Unmarked, clean, a few erasures. A new role. What note did "Voi Che Sapete" begin on? Was it a B flat? The words . . . the translation. *What do these feelings mean? Could they be love? My heart flutters, I tremble . . .*

The opera was described as recounting a day of madness. Was she now going mad? The stage lights were warm, and people clapped for her Cherubino. Hadn't there been a standing ovation and flowers? Her voice teacher was crying. She had made her happy. Aria had been happy.

Then there was the dressing room. She had lingered longer than any other performer, one by one pulling out the wig pins that poked her scalp. Her hair had tumbled down in long auburn coils and she massaged her head with relief. Too tired to bother with removing her makeup, she took off her costume and slipped a thin summer dress over her head.

She remembered that much.

Then, she'd tiptoed back onstage for one more look at the concert hall. The opera was over but there would be other roles to play. This production had given her the recognition her voice teacher had predicted. "Aria's mezzo-soprano voice fills the hall with a warmth well-described by her beautiful name," one reviewer had written. She was eighteen and just beginning her college career with an opera fellowship. There were so many more performances to come.

Of course, there were the after-parties, which her friends had long ago given up inviting her to. "No, I'm tired. Next time." That's what she'd always said.

The heavy side door to the alley had clicked shut behind her. She was so strangely tired, she thought about a taxi, but the night felt soft and warm, the walk would do her good. She remembered the bells. She counted. There were twelve. *Just like Cinderella.* She had laughed. But that was all she remembered.

Aria stayed in her room for three days, unable to get out of bed, skipping her classes, barely eating. The names could be out there. The names would find her. Whoever they were.

She couldn't rehearse in the practice rooms where the fluorescent lights buzzed in B flat. Where she felt unprotected, her back to the door, unsure someone was looking in the small window while she played or sang over the sound of a warning. All alone. And that B flat. Always that B flat ringing in her brain.

When she'd finally ventured to the cafeteria, she feared she'd meet an unfamiliar face—one who seemed to recognize her, so so she wrapped herself in a large sweater, kept her head down, and slunk around invisibily. The names could be *anywhere,* so she would be careful *everywhere.* When her voice teacher called to find out about the missed lessons, she explained she was sick. And that was the truth.

"Whatever they did to you, you need to report it," Shauna had said.

But Aria had been hurt by the names once. She would not be hurt again.

The blue and red bruise on her forehead where she had either fallen or been hit turned purple and then yellow. Most of her injuries were hidden with clothing, but she hurt in private places that no one would ever touch. To relive all of that? Never. She felt like damaged goods.

When Aria dropped out of school and moved home, she lost her college scholarship and the opera fellowship. She would never tell her mom what happened—not after everything her mother had done for her. And her father? He would be horrified. She was Daddy's girl. He couldn't know.

Why had she lingered at the theater? Why was she one of the last to leave? Why didn't she go to the party with everyone else? Now her life was changed by the names. It would always be about the names. Who could she trust?

Her mother wanted her to talk to someone. But she sat staring at the counselor, unable to form the words the counselor said would help her heal. For a time, Aria thought it would be better if she were not alive. If she didn't eat. She had trouble sleeping. She felt neither joy nor pain.

Eight weeks later, when she realized her missed periods and nausea were not the result of insomnia and stress, even then she withheld the truth. She would not force the horror of the event on her family. So, she told them it was an accident, a mistake, a one-night stand. She thought about not having the baby, but it seemed so unfair to an innocent child. If she herself could die, it would be better for everyone. Avoiding pain for others meant consequences for herself.

The birth was a reminder of everything she couldn't remember about that night. Contractions. Such a strange word. The process of becoming smaller. Indeed, she felt small and helpless. Her abdomen hard, the dull ache in her back, the undulating pain. Hours and hours. A doctor asking her mother about violence. Complications. Spreading her legs. A hospital gown with no back. The lower back pain. Her blood pressure spiraling out of control. The gloved fingers inside her. The screaming. The tightening. The speculum. The tears. The pushing and the pulling. The tearing and the burning. And then the emptiness.

Chapter Sixty-Five
Anna

Arlington, Washington
1960–1970

A ria. Anna. Two letters changed and she had a new name and a new identity. It looked so similar yet sounded so different. Safer. No one would ever find her or remember her. She transferred from Vocal Performance in New York City to Music Education at Central Washington University in the middle of Washington state, where the wind blew all day and night and where she could only hope no one knew her. She found a practice room with a lock and covered the window with paper. She was invisible. Graduation couldn't come soon enough.

A teaching job opened in a small district with one elementary and one high school situated at the foot of the mountains and safely tucked into the heart of a community where she could teach without fear. Darrington, Washington would be a safe haven.

She filled her classroom with drums, recorders, music games, rhythmic dance, and songs. Always folk songs. She remembered the Irish tunes her mother had sung to her and now her students' echoes pleased her.

"You could sing somewhere," fellow teachers encouraged in the faculty room. "There are a lot of singers out there who don't sound as good as you do. Have you ever thought of auditioning for the Whatcom Chorale or even the chorus for the Seattle Opera?"

Her stomach tightened. The anxiety, the fear.

The principal of Darrington Elementary was Ben McMahon, whom the students lovingly dubbed "Mr. Mac. The Seattle native had earned a masters and then a doctorate. Darrington staff anticipated he wouldn't be long at their little elementary school but move quickly up the ladder.

"Dr. Mac's a catch." It was impossible for older, matchmaking staff not to tease. Anna and Ben were the only two faculty members under thirty. *Benanna,* they'd joke.

Ben asked her out on December 7. She would always remember because it was a day that would live in infamy. So taken aback, she had no way of saying no; much to her surprise she said yes. He didn't have big plans, he had lost a bet with the fifth-grade class and asked, would she help him make cookies for twenty-five kids?

With last year's school yearbook open on the kitchen table, they drew faces, clothing, and hair for each gingerbread child. Bing Crosby and then Julie Andrews sang Christmas carols in the background.

"That's Kevin," Ben pointed out. "Put a soccer ball at his feet." Anna cut out a small circle and squished it on Kevin's foot. "Angela plays the guitar," she pointed out, as Ben went to work on it. "Jimmy likes trains. Maybe a conductor's cap?" Then she worked on one with dark hair, two dots of brown for eyes, and a gentle smile. She colored in socks, navy blue and red, Gonzaga University's colors, and dressed the gingerbread man in a basketball uniform with the number one on it, adding a colorful tie swung over his shoulder.

"That's what I look like?" He laughed. "Now you're fair play."

Ben turned his back on her and like a woman having her portrait done, Anna fretted over the results. He kept adding more and more dough, until he finally stepped back and revealed not one gingerbread lady, but a woman surrounded by five little figures with their frosting mouths singing a perfect *O.*

"That's you," he said, smiling. "Always surrounded by children."

Theirs felt like a simple friendship. It was enough for Anna, and she hoped it would be enough for Ben. It was difficult to imagine what would happen professionally if they started dating and then broke up.

But winter slid into spring and friendship warmed into something much more. Ben had told her more about himself than she had shared about herself. She knew why he had become a teacher and how he hoped to help kids through the things he had struggled with. The things he wasn't proud of. Still, each evening when he drove her home and gave her a lingering kiss, she wondered if it were their last.

On the final Friday evening before school began, they made shrimp paella together, he helped her cut out decorations for her classroom, and then they sat on the deck as they had so often that summer. It was a warm evening lit by the stars, but a cool breeze came off the mountain and she shivered.

"There's something that makes us perhaps impossible." She cleared her throat, her heart pounding with the finality of what she was about to say. Why had she put in the perhaps? Was it to soften the blow for Ben? Or was it for herself? Could it be she was still holding out hope?

"I'm listening. Talk to me."

Sitting on the lawn chairs in the dark, she couldn't see his face and that made it easier. Her teeth chattered not so much from the chill but the fear.

"Let me get you a blanket." As he walked back inside, she contemplated what would happen when he knew the truth. She hid her tears as he spread the blanket over her. In bits and pieces, for the first time, she let out her story. He listened quietly, making it easier for her to reveal her secret. It was still unbearable and yet a cathartic unburdening. Then she got to the part about the pregnancy and she started crying. How could she tell him the rest? How could she confess she'd given up her own baby? Her daughter was still out there somewhere.

"And what about the baby?" He wanted to know but she didn't want to tell.

"I . . . I lost the baby." That was the truth. Sort of. Then her crying turned to hiccupping sobs. "I'm so sorry, Ben."

"Why do you keep saying 'I'm sorry'?" He slapped his armrests and threw his head back. "I'm angry. I'm hurt." He ran his fingers through his thick hair. "So angry at *them*. And so hurt for *you*."

Those were nice words, kind words. Words anyone could say. *Should* say. Ben shook his head back and forth as if in disbelief.

"It's so wrong, Anna. All of it." Then more softly added, "You've never told anyone?"

"No," she whispered. "I'm so ashamed."

"Why? It's not your fault." He reached over and took her hands in his. "You have to know that. They should be in prison for what they did!"

Anna dropped her head back on the chair, suddenly exhausted.

Ben reached over and pulled her toward him, so her face was on his chest, and he stroked her hair like her father had done when a movie seemed too scary.

"I can't believe I'm the one you told." When he released her, he gently traced the tears away with his finger.

She thought about her doubts, how she'd always avoided relationships. She felt so vulnerable and exposed. What could she say?

"I know you need time to think."

"I do . . ." He frowned, and his knee bobbed nervously. "It's hard to know what to do." And then he got up and paced the short length of the deck.

"I have a gift I was going to give you. Later. But I want to give it to you *now*." He seemed to be wrestling with himself, talking through his options, but in the end, he offered nothing.

"It's all right, Ben," she said, releasing him from any commitment. She recognized his gentle way of letting her go and she'd give him the permission.

When she stood to leave, he did give her a hug, but she was certain everything was different.

"Goodbye, Ben."

Chapter Sixty-Six
Geneviève

Summer Meadows
Spokane, Washington
July 26, 1981

ummer Meadows. Summer Meadows. They called it Summer
Meadows and it was summertime, but the place felt unfamiliar
and not like home. And where were these meadows? It certainly
smelled like flowers, but she was certain the scent came out of a spray
can. So many old and sick people, and she didn't know any of them.
She thought perhaps she should be at the nurse's station or checking
heart rates. Where was her stethoscope? *Nurse Geneviève.*

"She's having such a good day," Nurse Lily exclaimed. "So talkative
and chatty about the past."

Geneviève set aside her word search and looked up. Somebody was
there. Such a pretty girl. That red hair. She knew she loved that person.
Some feelings never changed.

"Hello GinnaBee!"

GinnaBee. GinnaBee. GinnaBee. That was a good name. That was
her name. Her first grandchild had given her that precious name.
Claire.

"Claire!" She waved. It was always good when she could remember.
Claire sat near her. Something was wrong.

"You look sad."

"I am, GinnaBee."

She was doing good today. Today things were clear. She could move around in the office of her mind. She could talk about the past, possibly even the present. She would hold on to that for as long as she could. Her thoughts got so easily twisted by neurons and synapses and whatever else happens to a brain with Alzheimer's. How she loathed that diagnosis.

"How long have I been here?"

"Just a few days, GinnaBee. Do you like it?"

She hated it. But what if most of the time she didn't even know she hated it? Just moments like this when she wasn't in her home or her cabin. Or when she remembered that William was gone. Or when she wasn't living with her son Chase. That's when she hated it. Maybe it was better not to remember the past.

"It's not home; but I don't know where home is anymore. I don't remember."

"I'm sorry, GinnaBee."

"Me too." Claire took her hand, so she continued. "One day, I might not remember you. But I will remember that you loved me. So, remember I love you, too. Always."

"We'll always have that." Claire squeezed her hand.

"I just don't want to be such a burden." Her head fell. "But then again, most of the time I don't remember that I am." She chuckled.

A woman strolled into her room and began to climb on her bed.

"That's Mrs. Miller. She gets confused sometimes."

A nurse scurried in after her. "Eleanor, this isn't your room. Let's go down the hall."

"Sorry," the nurse mouthed as she escorted Eleanor out the door.

"I brought you something." Claire pulled her old tape recorder from the paper bag. "I painted PLAY green and EJECT red. Sort of like stop and go. That's all you need. I'll show you how to take the tape out and put it back in."

GinnaBee punched the green button. She immediately recognized the tune and swayed to the music. "Sweet Georgia Brown," she sang, not remembering any of the other words except the title. The clarinet scatted above, and she was back in the ballroom of the Davenport Hotel.

"It has all of your favorites. Glenn Miller. Count Basie, Benny

Goodman, Louis Armstrong. Duke Ellington."

A slow smile of remembrance stretched across her face.

"We used to dance." William was there laughing with her. His arm extended showing off her beautiful new dress. It was emerald green.

"Yes. You and Grandpa were really good. But don't show off too much here at the Meadows or you might knock a few people over!"

GinnaBee laughed but went silent.

"Will you dance with me?" Her voice sounded so small.

Claire smiled and took GinnaBee's hands and lifted her out of the chair. GinnaBee put up her arms but Claire seemed confused. Claire forgot she had to be Grandpa. A new perspective.

At the end of their slow waltz, Claire lowered GinnaBee to her chair. GinnaBee smiled. She could dance. She closed her eyes in sweet remembrance. "Dream a Little Dream" played in the background.

"I went to the lake," Claire said at last.

GinnaBee sighed, opened her eyes, and pictured the cabin off in the distance.

"Let's go this summer. I'll break you outta here," Claire suggested, then laughed and GinnaBee joined in.

"A life of crime? Two for the road!" GinnaBee slapped her knee. *Two for the road.* Hadn't William joked about that once, too? *William.* She missed him. Where did he go?

"I don't know what I'd do without you, GinnaBee." Claire rested her head on GinnaBee's knee. "Sometimes I don't know what to do."

Geneviève closed her eyes and tried to think. Sometimes it was so hard. She held on to so much history and stories, and memories and wisdom, but she couldn't always find the drawer for it. And when she was gone, it would all die with her. What hadn't she told them? What hadn't she given them?

"My other mother doesn't want to see me."

Other mother. Other mother. Other mother. Something bothered her.

Claire gazed up at her suddenly. That look. What had happened? Did she say something? She must have said the wrong thing. Opened the wrong drawer.

Geneviève watched out the window; nurses pushed wheelchairs, a few seniors packed oxygen tanks as they scooted their walkers past the flower garden, a gray-haired woman sat hunched alone on a bench. Did she look like them? She didn't feel ninety-one. Inside, she was much younger. It was her mind that was old. So unfamiliar and unresponsive. So unforgiving.

"My mother is somewhere out there. I needed to see her—my other mother. I wanted her to like me. I wanted to like her, too."

Claire has another mother. Who is Claire's other mother? Siobhan. No, not Siobhan. But Siobhan is the other mother.

Geneviève could feel the ocean swell of her heart. She could look out and see a wave coming. It was so big she wasn't sure where to stand. Did she want to be toppled? Or did she want to ride the wave? Should she run for the beach or take it full on?

"I don't think it mattered to you that I was adopted, did it?" Claire asked abruptly. "I mean, you didn't treat me any differently from Biz and Ev. You loved me no matter what."

She liked the sound of her granddaughter's voice. A pleasing voice. So gentle. She would make a good nurse. Nurse. They shared that didn't they? Hadn't she once been a nurse? Where was her stethoscope? France. The frontline. The trenches. She stared out the window. No. There were no trenches today. Just meadows, maybe, if she could only find them. Claire kept talking and she kept listening. She stayed silent because it felt safe.

"I loved Chase, too," she said at last.

"I know, GinnaBee."

"He didn't talk."

"Dad still doesn't talk much." Claire offered her a glass of water with a straw. Geneviève could picture the little boy and she wanted to hear his voice. Why couldn't she remember what it sounded like? No. No. No. She didn't want to leave yet. She needed to remember. She wanted to share something.

"Tell me about when he was little."

She shivered. It was suddenly so cold.

"Are you all right, GinnaBee?" Claire draped a blanket over her lap.

Claire's hand was so close, she grabbed it. "He was so scared. It was hard." She clung tightly to her granddaughter's soft hand. Maybe if she held on, she could remember that other little hand.

"Really? When? How old was he?"

Geneviève could find that file drawer. She opened it. She could see him. She couldn't *hear* him, but she she he was there.

"Three. He was three."

"What scared him?"

She scrunched her face and shook her head. The memory. There was something.

"GinnaBee, does something hurt? Should I get the nurse?"

"No. No." That wasn't the truth. She did hurt. There was something wrong. Did she do a bad thing? Something bad happened. She didn't know what, but William did. It was all right. They had a son. But why was he scared?

"He didn't really know us at first." Geneviève's voice cracked. She could remember driving away. She could see how the lights in the town dimmed in the rearview mirror. Was that what a memory looked like?

Claire cleared her throat. Was she uncomfortable? Had Geneviève done something? Said something? Was she now that lady with dementia that she never wanted to be?

"He didn't have a voice." She shook Claire's hand; it was small and unscarred.

"Don't think about it, GinnaBee."

But she had to think about it. She had to work it out in her mind. There was another file in the drawer.

"Bonnie," she said suddenly. "Good and faithful."

"You liked that dog, didn't you, GinnaBee?"

"Bonnie was a good dog." She smiled at the memory. "Bonnie Lass."

"Yes, Grandma." Claire patted her hand. Why did she do that? That was what you did to placate someone.

"Bonnie was his first word. I remember that!" Geneviève nodded proudly.

"But I thought Dad was older when you got Bonnie. He wasn't a baby. Dad spoke that late?"

Yes. No. Didn't Claire believe her? What was so strange about Bonnie being his first word? "You don't believe me." GinnaBee's voice sounded like someone she didn't like. Was she angry?

Meadows. Hospitals. Trenches. It was all the same.

Claire sighed and peered out the window. Why was her granddaughter so sad?

"There was a storm yesterday, GinnaBee. The lake looked like an ocean. I love watching it from the cabin because I feel so safe."

Geneviève saw the dock. She saw the lake. She watched William's mouth move. The boy wasn't there. She couldn't hear the boy. Where was the boy?

"Something terrible! A drowning!"

"No, GinnaBee." Claire took Geneviève's hands and held them close to her face. "It was a beautiful storm. Everybody was safe. It's over now. It was yesterday."

Bonnie. Storm. Cabin. Yesterday. No, this was not about yesterday. This was about what happened a long time ago. What was in that file drawer? She wasn't at the cabin yesterday. Or was she? She shook her head. Everything was mixed up.

Claire was crying. "Oh, GinnaBee, I am so lost!" Geneviève felt the same. Claire leaned her face on Geneviève's knee, just like she did as a child. The cabin. Home.

Geneviève patted Claire's head gently, pulling at her hair like a soothing memory. She could hear a nurse wheel a patient down the hall, a doctor was paged, a beeping sound, a child crying. "William's dad built that cabin before the Depression. That's where we lived at first. When he came."

"When *who* came?" Claire's voice sounded like a music box. Sweet. Pure. Innocent. If only Geneviève could wind it up and listen to it every day.

"The boy. He almost drowned. He had no voice." Her hand froze at the memory.

Claire jerked her head up and studied her grandma. Claire was worried, too. "*Who* almost drowned?"

"That little boy from Deer Lodge."

"Oh, Grandma, I miss you so much." Claire laid her head back down on Geneviève's knee and squeezed her hand tightly.

I'm here. I'm here. Don't go. I'm here and you're talking to me, and I love you and I need to tell you something. How? Was he still little?

Where were Siobhan's photographs? Who was he? Where did he come from?

"The little boy . . ." There was something left but it was becoming jumbled. She wanted to finish, but could she?

"What little boy?" Claire asked. "GinnaBee . . . what little boy?"

Wind the music box. Listen and talk.

Geneviève focused on the moment. The one child in her mind. The boy. She closed her eyes and opened the file. But no matter what she did, she just couldn't remember his name. His other name.

"That quiet little boy," she whispered. "The one we adopted."

Chapter Sixty-Seven
Erin

Spokane, Washington
July 26, 1981

A silver strip of mist hovered over the hay bales on the fields leading away from Priest Lake. Like a mysterious ribbon, it would evaporate in the morning sun. Her daughter was somewhere ahead of her, leading her back to Spokane.

Erin turned on the radio. President Reagan. Saddam Hussein. The appointment of Sandra Day O'Connor. She spun the dial for music. Connection. That was what she wanted. Her family connected. When she arrived home, she found herself alone, until the garage door opened.

"Hello? Anybody home?" Claire threw open the door, then slammed it and dropped the keys on the kitchen table as she headed to the family room.

"Oh, I'm so glad you're back. I was worried," Erin said. "I got home an hour ago and you weren't here."

Claire's eyes were red. She just stared at Erin and shook her head.

"I thought you were always about full disclosure, 'Let's tell the whole truth.' But you're *still* hiding things!"

"Honey, we've been over this. I can't change what I did. Or what I did or didn't tell you. I can only say I'm sorry."

"Not *that!*" Claire's voice was full of pain. "You've always prided yourself on saying it's okay to be adopted, so why did you never tell me Dad was adopted? Why did I have to hear it twenty-one years later from *GinnaBee*? Was everybody in on the secret except me?"

Erin was stunned. There was no way it could be true. She could not have been married to a man for over almost thirty years without knowing the truth. Especially since they had adopted Claire.

Claire dropped to the couch. "You didn't know." Claire's voice was dull. Shocked. Erin could only look at her daughter. She felt a mixture of hurt, pain, curiosity, and as if she'd been slapped across the jaw.

"Dad never happened to mention it? Like maybe when you were adopting me?" Her arms opened, begging for an explanation. "What would be so terrible about telling me he was adopted? I mean, it's not like it's a crime or something. It's not like he was embarrassed about it, right?" Claire sounded bruised. "Do you think that maybe once when I was struggling with the whole thing he might have said, 'I'm kind of curious about my biological parents, too? Maybe we could both look together.'"

Claire leaned back, seemingly exhausted from her outburst.

"Maybe he doesn't *know*?" Erin asked at last. "Or maybe Grandma is *confused*? She's kind of an unreliable narrator right now."

"*Deer Lodge*," Claire stated. "Did anyone ever mention Deer Lodge?"

"I've heard Grandpa mention it before. I think it was a prison town." The garage door opened and closed. They both turned to look.

"Where have you two been all day?" Chase asked as he came in, twisting open a Wonder bag and popping two pieces of bread in the toaster.

Claire looked at her mother and they both waited. *For what?*

"How much do you remember about Deer Lodge?" Claire asked.

Chase cocked his head slightly and then turned to them confused. But there was something. A flicker of recollection.

"And just when were you going to tell me you were adopted?"

Chase opened the refrigerator and pulled something from the back.

"Dad! Is it true? What's going on?"

He closed the refrigerator, turned in slow motion, and set a beer on their gold Formica counter.

"Why didn't you ever tell me?"

Chase dug around in a drawer until he found the bottle opener, then popped the top. The stench of burnt toast seeped from the toaster and he pulled the slice out and threw it away. Claire and Erin stood waiting for an answer. Her dad walked to the family room where he collapsed into his recliner. His response was slow. Minimal.

"I don't know." His voice was soft but defensive. "Why should I? It wasn't necessary."

"Not necessary? When I'm adopted, too? That it might be important to *me*? That we had something in *common*?" Claire moved to the chair across from him, sinking into its worn comfort, tracing her fingers into the avocado and orange stripes.

"I told you that digging in the past could cause you pain."

"*My* pain or *yours*?" Claire paused but he didn't answer. "How could *my* searching hurt *you*? Are there other things? More things that also 'aren't necessary'?"

He didn't say anything, which seemed to defuse Claire's anger. "Why couldn't you tell me?" Claire's voice was so soft Erin could barely hear it.

"I'm not sure." He tapped the bottle rhythmically. "I think I was afraid."

"For *me,* or for *you*?"

"Maybe both." His voice held a kind of earnest, wistful quality she'd never heard before,

"About what? What is it?"

"Something I don't know. Just a feeling. Not about you. But you remind me of it all."

"Did it ever occur to you this was something we could have shared? Did you ever think that if you hid one thing, I couldn't trust you on others?"

"And how is it that after all these years, William and Geneviève never brought it up?" Erin added, suddenly feeling broadsided. "Was there a conspiracy?" She stood over Chase waiting for an answer.

Chase took another drink and shook his head.

"When we adopted Claire, wouldn't that have been a suitable time to talk about it?" She sat on the ottoman near her husband.

It was a long time before his words fell into the tense silence. Erin dug her toes into the carpet in frustration. Her feet looked a sickly color nestled in gold shag.

"Did you ever wonder why I was reluctant to adopt?" Chase said at last.

"What could *your* adoption possibly have to do with *Claire's*?" Erin then tried out a more empathetic, gentle voice. "Chase, you're my husband. Now I wonder what else is hidden."

"Sometimes, I do, too."

"What do you mean? Do you know why you were adopted?" Her husband's response was strange, his memories off-kilter.

"No. And I don't think I want to."

"How can you say that so quickly?" Claire piped in.

"I don't need to go digging up the past."

"Really, Dad, you might have brothers, sisters. After all these years why wouldn't you want to know? It makes me so curious!"

"Not everybody is like you."

"And maybe that's why I'd like to find somebody who *is*!" Claire stood and began pacing. "Dad—your parents. They might still be alive."

Chase shook his head slowly, frowned, and then exhaled like it was a bad memory.

"What is it Dad? What are you afraid of?"

Her daughter was pushing and maybe she shouldn't be. Erin had been married long enough to know that something was terribly wrong.

"I wasn't a baby. I still remember some things."

"What kind of a person gives up a little boy? And why?" Claire asked. Erin wondered if they really wanted to know that person either.

"I think I did something wrong."

"Dad, you were just a little boy!"

"There was something. Something happened and then I was sent away."

"What was it?"

"I don't know, and I don't think I want to remember."

"And so, after all these years, you don't want some sort of answer? Closure?"

"You've just blocked it out. For years," Erin said. "Until Claire."

"I reminded you?" Claire winced.

Chase was quiet. He was working on an answer. She knew his silence didn't mean Claire was the source of pain. Even she could not have answered right away. But neither could she hold her tongue. "You couldn't trust me with the knowledge that you were adopted?"

"It's not a matter of trust."

"What is it a matter of?"

"I don't know." He blinked. His eyes were glassy, clear. "Can't that be enough?"

Erin considered that idea. Maybe not knowing had to be enough.

He turned to his daughter. "You didn't bring me pain, Claire. But you made it hard for me to control the memories."

Erin reached out and put her hand on his leg. "And then it was more complicated. When we had Evan," she said softly. "When he was a little boy."

"I'd watch him and wonder. And have that feeling. A terrible feeling that I was responsible for something." His gaze fixed out the window as if he wanted it all to go away.

"Somebody knows their names," Claire said, and Chase nodded in agreement. "You could find your family." Claire bubbled with hope as she had at the beginning of her own journey.

But Erin had to wonder if Chase was Claire's replacement project and if this search would also end in pain.

"What if you don't do this, Dad? You'll never know. Maybe your story has a better beginning than my ending." She jumped up. "We could go to Deer Lodge! Somebody there might remember them. Or you."

Chase got up and started to leave.

"Don't leave, Chase."

"Something really bothered GinnaBee about the whole thing. I couldn't get any more information. I think we should just go to Deer Lodge."

"And do what?" he asked, turning back. "They'll think we're crazy. Way back in 1931, do you remember a family that had a little boy they gave away?" Chase imitated the inquiry.

"*Somebody* there is bound to remember. It's only fifty years ago. Somebody's still alive!" Claire sounded as determined to find Chase's mother as she had her own.

"I don't want to go back."

"Dad, you have to know."

"No, actually, I don't!" He sounded firm and decided.

"I don't get it. Every part of me needs to and I'm not even related."

"Well, we're different."

"Yes. We are. But if you understood your family, maybe . . ."

"No."

"Then I'll go alone."

"You can't do that, Claire." Erin didn't want a repeat of Aria's doorstep.

"Don't go." Chase's voice was unusually firm. Erin couldn't help but feel that whatever lay hidden was a terrible secret.

"I'll go with you," Erin blurted out, then stopped. "That is, if you want me. We could *run Erins*."

Claire smiled at the family joke. Evan had come home confused why Miss Polly said she was running Erins. Shouldn't she be running Pollys?

"I was hoping you'd say that," Claire admitted. It was a concession. A small act of reconciliation with her daughter. Chase left the room without a word.

An hour later, Claire spread out a map and pointed to their route. "Deer Lodge is in Powell County, Montana. It's almost three hundred miles away. The drive is going to take us about four and a half hours. It looks like it has a big state prison. Nearest big cities are Butte and Helena."

"Good job! You're quite the tour guide," Erin nodded. "This is going to be an adventure!" Erin knew the clock was ticking on Claire's summer. She had to be back at UVA by August 16, which meant she had two and a half weeks.

"Maybe we should take GinnaBee with us. She might be able to help navigate." Claire said, staring at the map.

"You were kidding, weren't you?"

"Well . . . I don't know. It might be fun. It might bring back good memories."

"Or bad," Erin cautioned.

"Right," Claire said. She folded the map, carefully returning it to its compressed size. "Hey, Mom. Thanks for coming with me."

"You're welcome." Erin smiled. "You may not have wanted to come along, but I felt like you needed me, and I'll take that for now."

If they could find Aria in one of fourteen high school yearbooks in Seattle, Erin figured they could find Chase's mother in a small town in Montana. They were a team.

Chapter Sixty-Eight
Anna

Arlington, Washington
September 8, 1970

Anna turned on the car radio to help face her first day back at Darrington Elementary. But when Aretha started singing "I Say a Little Prayer for You," Anna turned the dial and cranked the volume for "I Heard it Through the Grapevine." She couldn't spend her life pining over Ben McMahon and what could have been.

The front of the school was decked out with Ben's Welcome Back banner and a long red carpet, lined with the staff ready to greet the students.

Their discussion three nights before had changed everything. He barely acknowledged her when she took her place on the side of the runway; in fact, he left as soon as she headed for her classroom. Things would be so different this year. Uncomfortable. Was it too late to transfer?

The bell rang. Though she had greeted all twenty-three of her fourth graders on the red carpet—in fact, they had seemed unusually giddy for a first day, high-fiving her with enthusiasm—none of them showed up to her classroom. She went to the front office and it, too, was empty, as were the other classrooms. What was going on? The Rapture?

Music suddenly blared from the gym, leading her to The Temptations' "My Girl" and bleachers filled with students, teachers, and parents. As if on cue, they each raised a card, spelling out, "Will you marry me?" and breaking into excited laughter and cheering. Then the children, conducted by one of her former students, now a middle-schooler, began singing "Earth Angel" with that inevitable Valentine question.

When she turned around, there he was, Mr. Mac, in his first day of school navy suit and red tie—bending down on one knee, holding a small velvet box.

When the song was over, she'd never heard the gym so quiet.

"Will you marry me, Miss Hanson?"

To which she whispered softly, "Well I couldn't say no, now could I?" and then more loudly, so the crowd could hear. "Yes, Mr. Mac."

The cheers were louder than when the 0 & 9 Darrington High School basketball team won its first game. He dared to kiss her in front of everyone. Together, they'd be undefeated.

On their wedding day, she felt like a princess, especially when she wore her wedding gown to their honeymoon night at Snoqualmie Falls Lodge. Simple lines, classic style, silk. Little girls looked up and stared, couples smiled and nodded, a few cheered. Then they stopped at an overlook and asked an older gentleman to take their photo. Room service delivered a meal which they fed to each other in their king-sized bed, she still in her gown, he in a tuxedo, the tie now loosened, the cummerbund cast aside and his jacket hanging on the chair. His face had stubble she had never seen before, rough to her touch but so masculine.

"I . . . I'm afraid."

"Just let me love you."

He slowly unbuttoned the back of her wedding dress and watched as it slid to the ground leaving her in hose and lingerie. She heard his sudden intake of air and felt his arms enfold her.

"You're cold," he whispered in her ear. While he worked the fire, she opened her suitcase and fingered the white lace peignoir set her mother had given her when Anna was first engaged—when her mother explained what would happen on her wedding night.

Now with her mother's gentle words and a deep breath, she neared the hearth where the fire spat and crackled, feeling its warmth through the sheer lace.

"I waited for you, and you waited for me," he said, as if knowing her sadness and fears, then scooped her up and laid her on the bed.

In the firelight, she shivered as he traced her outline with his fingers.

He lay near her, and she nestled close, closing her eyes in trust. His soft, full lips met hers. His caress made it feel an ocean wave had taken her out to sea. Could anything be as intensely beautiful and satisfying? Drowning in his love, she felt so utterly exhausted, she fell asleep in his arms.

The next morning, she awakened to the sound of the shower and a man singing. He needed a few voice lessons. She smiled as she ran her hand over *his* side of the bed and giggled.

Last night, he had asked nothing of her, he had only given. And in the strength of his simple and patient love, she felt new. "Set me as a seal upon your heart," the minister had said in their vows. "For love is as strong as death."

She slipped out of bed and tiptoed toward his voice. The room was a misty fog, steam-filled and warm. Through the frosted glass shower door, she could see the form of a man. He was beautiful, and she felt more excitement than fear.

Swiping the mirror with her hand revealed hair still curly but tousled from the wedding stylist. The gown concealed little, the lace revealing the curve of her figure and hints of more. She shivered in the remembrance of his caress.

Anna slid the shower door open to see his muscular body stroked by the water in the way she wanted to do right then. He turned and watched as she lowered the thin silk straps off her shoulders, shedding her past sadness, and stepped into the shower.

Chapter Sixty-Nine
Erin

Deer Lodge, Montana
July 28, 1981

The drive to Montana was more beautiful than Erin could have imagined. The lakes of Northern Idaho followed by open spaces and countryside spread out to valleys and mountains and finally open sky and land as far as she could see. Music boomed, alternating between listening to Air Supply and Styx, and Erin belting along with Jerry Lewis's "Great Balls of Fire," and Buddy Holly's "That'll Be the Day." This truly was an adventure.

At last, they turned off in Deer Lodge and Erin could feel her heartbeat quicken, almost as if she were going back in time to a place she'd been before. This time they headed east instead of west. It was just a thought, but could this search for Chase's mom in some ways make up for Claire's unsuccessful reunion with Aria?

"Check that out! Grant–Kohrs Ranch." Claire pointed to the stately white farmhouse and barns, one of the first sites entering Deer Lodge, then swung her arm to the other side of the road, where there was a riding ring and grandstand. "And look! The rodeo is coming to town!"

A billboard advertised the upcoming August 1, Loggers Day held on the corner of Second and Cottonwood featuring Men's Cross Cut, Big Saw, Log Roll and Tug of War. Would Erin and Claire still be here by then or would their mission be completed?

And then a town Erin speculated could be the movie set for a 1930s Western. The Main Street store fronts were vintage, and nothing smacked of 1981. Erin was certain very little had changed since her husband had left, if in fact he had ever lived here.

"What. Is. That?" Claire's voice was monotone.

A large building taking up a city block in length loomed over Main Street with pillars on its four corners.

"That's the prison."

"Wow," was all her daughter could say as she exhaled. "That's ominous."

"But check out that movie theater! The Rialto. It's so old-fashioned! I wonder what's playing?"

"Everything looks like it's been frozen in time." Erin stopped at the post office and ran in to pick up a commercial guide before they continued. Claire frowned as Erin turned off Main Street and deliberately got lost in a few short blocks, marveling at the historic homes, but ignoring the derelict ones.

"Sitting here at the base of the mountains. Such a beautiful valley. But . . ."

"But what?" Claire asked.

"Don't you feel it?" Erin shook her head. "So much beauty. Freedom. And so much ugliness. Sort of oppressive."

They turned back up Milwaukee Avenue and Claire pointed to a house. "That's where I'd want to live."

Erin stopped the car at a beautiful Victorian and flipped through the guide. "It says that the man second under the warden lived here."

"Never mind." Claire laughed. "Okay, now we kind of have to stalk people GinnaBee's age."

"Maybe you were right. We should have brought her along," Erin teased.

Claire tilted her head and added softly, "I'm glad you came, Mom."

"Well, no one can 'run Erins' better than me."

Erin stopped at the bakery and ordered a soda. An elderly woman with a badge that read Dorothy was wiping down the counter.

"Excuse me. What's your favorite pastry?"

Dorothy pointed out the various types in the display case and described how they started baking in the morning and what was the most popular in Deer Lodge.

For once, Claire didn't roll her eyes. Erin had weathered her daughter's teasing about her chattiness and how she knew the name of every clerk in Spokane, whether they liked their job, or what was the best thing that happened to them that day. Erin's reasoning was that life was more interesting when she made friends.

Maple syrup and fried doughnuts and a sweet vanilla frosting aroma made the decision more complicated.

"Say, I have kind of an odd question. My husband used to live here as a little boy. Then he was adopted in 1931. Were you here then?"

Erin knew it sounded kind of suspicious. Ridiculous even. Fifty years ago?

"Do you remember anything like that?" Erin's smile maintained an innocent curiosity.

The woman then wiped the table and shook her head. Why would Dorothy give any information? Who were these two out-of-towners to her?

"Don't recall anything about an adoption. I was just a teenager back then, anyway."

"What did it used to be like? *Back then?*"

"The Milwaukee slowed its runs, I-90 bypassed us, then passenger service stopped in '64. Last year, the western extension was shut down and the rails torn up."

"Not much traffic, then?"

"You got it." She turned her back and walked away.

Erin followed the waitress with her eyes. "Now that we've started asking questions, maybe word will get out what we're looking for."

"Or lips will tighten." Claire leaned back in the booth. "We don't know the full story."

After wiping every Formica table in the restaurant, the woman slapped their bill on the table and leaned in. "There's a woman who works at the old prison, Patricia. She knows people from back then. Museum closes in an hour. It's worth a look. Lots of interesting things to see."

They paid without waiting for change and hustled toward the prison, where Erin purchased two tickets and, with brochure in hand, they prepared to take the self-guided walking tour.

"Look, since it's almost closing time, I can take you around if you want. Tell you about our museum here."

"I'm Erin and this is my daughter Claire."

"Yes. My name is Patricia."

Claire nudged Erin and smiled.

The tour began in the yard, a wide-open space of dirt and scrub grass. Then Patricia led them up the steps of a magnificent white building. But the inside had been destroyed. Erin imagined that the crusty shell had once been an impressive theater. Now the columns stood lonely and forgotten.

"This looks like it was amazing. What happened?" Claire asked.

"This is the W. A. Clark Theater." Patricia waved them toward the grand entrance, as if it were a ribbon cutting for its opening, but a long rope prevented their admittance.

"W. A. Clark?" Claire asked. "There's a man with that name who funded the law school building at UVA. My dad went there."

"Not surprised. His son was a turn of the century UVA law school graduate."

Erin and Claire exchanged looks that said, *Coincidence? Could this get any stranger?*

Patricia frowned, perhaps unsure whether she was being made fun of but continued.

"W. A. Clark Theater was the first theater for any prison. Such a privilege. It could hold a thousand people. Leather seats, no less."

"So, what happened?" Erin stepped up to the rope and surveyed the ruins.

"A fire. The prisoners had just seen *The Odessa File*. Remember that movie? An espionage thriller starring Jon Voight." Patricia sure knew how to make a short story long.

"After the movie was over, some of the prisoners were cleaning up. The state marshall suspected arson. You see, *privilege* isn't always *appreciated*. Probably a prisoner, a candle, a toilet paper roll thrown in where the wrestling mattresses were stored. Unfortunately, the stage curtains caught fire and it all came down."

"So unfortunate." Claire studied the hollow shell.

The three stood in silent homage to whatever it had once been.

Patricia shook her head. "I remember so many shows as a child."

"You cannot even imagine." Patricia shook her head. "I remember so many shows as a child."

"Here? *You*? When you were a *kid*?"

"The theater wasn't just for prisoners. Certain performances were for the public. They brought talent from all over the country."

"But *that*?" Claire pointed out a wooden structure.

"The gallows. They're stored here now."

"They hung people in the theater?"

"No, out in the yard. Only twice. And that was way back in the early 1900s."

Erin shuddered. The juxtaposition of theater and execution was a little disturbing.

"The Galloping Gallows could be dismantled and taken to another location for an execution," Patricia said it as if she was proud of the contraption. "The gallows were for two men who tried to kill the warden. He made a point of putting down riots. Then in 1959, there was a much larger revolt." Patricia shook her head as if she had been inside the walls. "I'm sure somebody will write a book about that someday." They continued across the yard as she narrated.

"There was a three-day standoff. I'll show you where a bazooka was shot at one of the brick towers. The inmates were trapped above. The riot ended in a murder-suicide. Such a horrible bloodbath."

She pointed at the scarred tower. "My dad used to work there as a guard." Patricia gazed up as if she could still see her dad at his post. Erin tried to imagine what that would be like for a little girl on Main Street to wave up to her daddy on duty.

"He was trapped in the prison during the standoff. But he was one of the lucky ones." They all stood respectfully silent. "Those were a long thirty-six hours."

Erin itched to ask questions as they toured the main facility, seeing the small cubicles, hearing the stories of rules, prisoners, and wardens. And finally, even the tale of Turkey Pete who had earned his name by selling off the prison's turkeys for twenty-five cents. Turkey Pete never stayed in his cell but was granted freedom throughout the prison and slept in the lobby. When he died in prison, they retired his cell as a shrine.

"You are full of so much information!" Erin flattered. Erin hoped Patricia knew as many details as possible about the residents from 1931.

Patricia glanced at her watch. "Yes, but it's nearly closing time and I have one more building I want to show you."

They trooped across the yard, where the flag still flew high, its metal chain chattering against the pole. From the center of the yard, they could see the mountains. Erin took a deep breath as the prisoners must have. Patricia pressed them forward and through a door in the wall.

"And this is the women's prison." The little structure had no yard. "There were never many prisoners here." Erin assessed the building. So small. Institutional. Gray. Run-down. A prison in miniature.

"The women prisoners, what crimes were they here for?"

"Oh, mainly murder and prostitution. Up until a decade ago, Kate's Place was still in operation, and I'm told Butte still has a bordello on Pleasant Alley."

"What?" Claire asked, and she would have continued had Erin not tapped her and changed subjects.

"I'll bet you might know William and Geneviève Ellis."

"Ellis? Can't remember that I do." Patricia led them back into the yard.

"It would have been around 1931. He was a lawyer, his wife a nurse?"

Patricia cocked her head and adjusted her glasses, as if that might help her focus on the answer. "1931? I'd be ten." She shook her head.

"Anybody else who might remember them?"

"You could call on a doctor that lives in town. Practiced at the hospital and even in the prison. Usually had a nurse, too. Doc Briggs. He must've been pretty young back then. He's retired now."

Patricia motioned her arm toward the metal door but turned around to survey the yard one more time.

"This old nineteenth-century prison just couldn't keep up with the number of prisoners and their mischief. Overcrowded, neglected and outdated." She spoke as if she had more sympathy for the building than its residents.

"What happened?"

"They built a new one in '77 on sixty acres just five miles from here. Closed this in '79." Her voice dropped low, as if she were talking about the death of a loved one.

"Just two years ago." Erin nodded in sympathy though everything about the institution cried out for reform or demolition.

The trains, the road, the prison. Everything seemed to have left Deer Lodge except Doctor Briggs. But what about Chase's mother?

"Doc Briggs lives on Pennsylvania. You could walk to his place. Big brick house."

Erin and Claire negotiated the cracks in the sidewalks. An assortment of cars lined the road, varying from models Claire was sure were 1940s vintage to 1960s junk. All were poorly maintained. Deer Lodge had obviously never pulled itself out of a sluggish economy.

Maybe the doctor could provide a name, but then again, what if Geneviève was truly an unreliable narrator? What if her Deer Lodge was a *deer lodge*? A place William had once gone during hunting season with a little boy. Maybe they were on a wild goose chase and putting Chase through hell.

Their knocking had obviously interrupted Doctor Briggs's dinner, calling him from a small table in his dining room, wearing a napkin tucked into the collar of his shirt. "Here goes nothing," Erin whispered under her breath.

"I believe my mother-in-law may have worked for you. Geneviève Ellis?"

"Ahh yes, I remember her." He smiled and scratched his head. "Not bad for a guy in his eighties! Worked for me way back in the twenties." The recollection appeared fond. That was a good start.

Claire's eyes widened. Erin felt like she could have kissed him if he wasn't wearing his dinner on his face.

"Do you remember her little boy?" Claire's question bubbled out and Erin steadied her arm to slow her down.

Dr. Briggs's face sobered. He hesitated as if unsure what to do with the question.

"Oh, that's too long ago for me to remember."

"Geneviève Ellis had a boy. Adopted. Right here in Deer Lodge."

"Yes, I think something like that might have happened."

"What about the boy's mother? His *biological* mother?"

"What about her?"

"Do you have a name?"

"Now you two are asking for information beyond what I can talk about." Doc Briggs smiled knowingly. "I took an oath. I took an oath of Hippocrates," which he began to quote, proving the strength of his memory.

"I understand, but . . ."

"Do you really?" he questioned softly but firmly. "I have patients who still live in this town and some that don't. I know what you want, and I'd like to be able to help, but this goes against who I am." He took off the napkin and wiped his mouth.

"We don't have a lot of time to find her. Maybe she isn't even alive."

"Yes, but if this person doesn't want to be found, then I shouldn't help you find her." He folded the napkin as if it finalized the end of their discussion.

Erin looked at Claire. Hadn't they heard that before?

"You see that prison out there?" Doctor Briggs pointed out the window.

Who couldn't see that prison? It was the proverbial elephant in the room. You couldn't miss the monstrosity.

"Plenty of people locked up there for a lot of reasons. Then there are those that are locked up here." He tapped his head. "They don't want to remember what happened to them. When they leave, they want to start over. Maybe this person needed to start over."

"What if her life is a prison because she doesn't know what happened to her son?" Claire blurted out.

The doctor scratched the back of his neck. "Look, it's not my place. And maybe it's no one's to tell you things like that." He considered Erin then Claire. "I mean, I see a wife and daughter, but I don't see the man. The son." He paused for emphasis. "Who is it who really wants to know?"

He had a point. Erin couldn't deny it. Claire was unusually quiet. What more could they say? Erin felt deflated.

"This person," Doctor Briggs spoke slowly and carefully. "She had a friend who might be able to help. Or at least she might know if she *should*. Her name is Mildred. Mildred Duncan. Her daughter Cora owns Cora's Cafe. They're closed for the day, but you could find them there tomorrow. Tell 'em Doc Briggs sent you."

Chapter Seventy
Erin

Deer Lodge, Montana
July 28, 1981

"Good job, Mom!" Claire high-fived Erin as they got back in the car.

"At least we know something happened here. But you know, Claire, his mother may not even be alive." That was the harsh reality. It could all be a dead-end street. Literally. If Doc Briggs was so old, what age was Chase's mother?

Erin parked the car on a nearly deserted Main Street in front of the stately brick building known as Hotel Deer Lodge. She was almost certain they were the only guests for the evening, and for some reason it made her sad. What had endeared herself to this quirky town, with the potential of possibility seemingly so out of reach?

"I've never slept so close to a prison." Claire shrugged her shoulders and laughed.

The lobby of the hotel doubled as a ticket office. "We've shared it with Greyhound since the railroad traffic slowed and shut down." The man behind the desk was matter-of-fact when Erin thought he should be apologetic. The hotel must have once been a work of art. Now on the front southeast corner, the structure had been reconfigured and occupied by a sporting goods store, and the northeast corner converted into a bar and diner. Claire turned in circles in the lobby, as Erin studied the large front windows, a big oak check-in desk, and a staircase with large oak newel post and banister. Then she closed her eyes and shut out the musty smell, faded paint over cracked plaster, marred and dinged woodwork and faded floors, to imagine what it might have been like fifty years before.

"Ma'am? Ma'am?" Erin opened her eyes. "We only keep rooms on the main floor now." Martin handed her the key to room 107.

Room 107 must not have changed much in the last decades. Or century. Claire set her overnight bag on the carpet and sat on the bed, sinking into a mattress with springs that sounded like they had long ago given up. "I'm glad they at least have a television."

Erin shook the drapes and threw them open to the sunlight. Dust motes floated in the rays from the setting sun. "Me too, because you do know what tomorrow is?"

"July 29th?" Claire shook her head. "Don't remind me. I only have another three weeks before I have to go back to school."

"Well, that too, I suppose. But it's Princess Diana's wedding day!" Erin took out her alarm clock and set it on the nightstand. "It starts at 3:00 a.m., so we better get to bed soon, so we can get up early and watch it."

"3:00 a.m.? Really? You want to get up that early for a *wedding*?"

"Of course I do. A royal one. This is one of those things we'll always remember." Erin attempted a British accent. "We will watch the royal wedding in Deer Lodge, Montana."

The next morning when the alarm went off, Erin bolted out of bed. "It's on in five! Wake up!"

"Arghghghgh. Nooooo." Claire groaned and pulled the blankets over her head.

"You said you wanted me to get you up. It's almost on."

"You are too much, Mom." Claire stepped into the bathroom.

"Ten, nine, eight, seven, six . . . Hurry up!" Erin encouraged. "Glue yourself to the telly! It's on!" Erin again tried on her best British accent. "Besides, I thought we'd have some crumpets and tea while we watch!" Claire straggled back in and tucked herself beneath the covers. "I'd make scones, but we don't have a kitchen and all I could find at that bakery were homemade donuts. So, my dear, it's high society in Deer Lodge, Montana."

Claire licked the frosting off a maple bar and took a bite.

They sat up in bed watching the carriage drive through the streets, with occasional glimpses of Princess Diana looking like she was taking a bubble bath of wedding white in her glass carriage.

"That's St. Paul's Cathedral. Thirty-five hundred guests. But there are more than six hundred thousand in the crowd and another seven hundred and fifty million like us, watching all around the world."

"Thanks for the play-by-play, Mom." The commentators gave them details, but as usual, Erin provided most of the chatter.

"I'll bet none of those carriage drivers have been on the telly before." At the next commercial break, Erin suddenly jumped out of bed. "I'm heating the water in the coffee pot. I stole a few tea bags from the restaurant."

"Hurry, she's about to get out!"

Erin returned with two paper cups.

"Look at the way she unfolds herself, Mom. That dress goes on for miles!"

"Well, actually, it's twenty-five feet long."

"She looks so princessy in those big sleeves. Wow. Maybe one day."

"That dress cost a hundred and fifty thousand pounds. Don't get any ideas."

"Ewww, this tastes like coffee-flavored tea."

"Then have another donut. Try the Bavarian crème. You'll get a mocha feel."

Claire whistled through her teeth. "That veil."

"It's a hundred and fifty yards in tulle! Makes her look like she's floating."

"What about your wedding, Mom? What was it like?"

"Small. We thought about eloping or going to a justice of the peace. We didn't have much money and since most of our friends lived near UVA, we had it at the UVA chapel. June 25th," Erin chattered on happily. "Grandpa and Geneviève gave us a West Coast reception in Spokane on the Fourth of July with fireworks and everything." Erin smiled in remembrance and Claire echoed her grin. Then Erin quieted to hear the royal vows.

"Did she just say his name wrong? That is so cute!" Claire giggled at the mistake.

"Charles Philip Arthur George, Philip Charles Arthur George. What difference does it make when you have that many names? Makes her human. Relatable."

"She seems so shy. Demure. She always keeps her head down but her eyes up. She's so young." Claire mimicked the look and Erin laughed.

"She is. She's younger than you are." Erin selected a second donut. "Here try this one."

"It's a modern-day fairy tale, Mom."

"I hope it ends happily ever after."

Erin turned the sound down, and then leaned back as if preparing to deliver one of her talks. "Celebrations are important. That's why we always celebrate birthdays at the exact time. I bet no May 18th goes by without your mother thinking about you." Erin waited to let that sink in. "Not a November 5th goes by and I don't think of him."

"Why do you always say *him*?"

"I just feel like it was a boy."

Claire stared at the ceiling and so Erin followed her gaze. It needed painting and repair. If Hotel Deer Lodge could only maintain one floor, it wouldn't be long before the hotel would close. So sad considering its history and potential. A Motel 6 would never have its character and charm.

"You accused me of thinking of you as a replacement."

"I know. I didn't really mean it. I'm sorry."

"No, don't. I just need to explain something." Erin turned to focus on Claire. "I wanted *you*. That didn't make me a hero. It was completely selfish. I wanted to be your mom, even if I might not be as good a mom as your real mom."

"She's not my *real* mom."

"You know what I mean. Or if there was a better mother out there. Didn't matter. I wanted *you*. I didn't just want a baby, I wanted you. I wanted to be a mother more than I cared about whether I'd be the best mother. It was selfish. Then when I got pregnant with Elizabeth, I could have told the adoption agency that we had a baby on the way. We could have pulled out and let some more deserving mother get you. Somebody who didn't already have a baby on the way.

"But you love that particular baby. Not a replacement. You love the one you're having or adopting." She stopped. "But I was selfish in a different way about that little boy. I never gave him a chance."

"Mom." Claire reached out and took Erin's hand. "Special Delivery. That was *your* idea, wasn't it?"

"I could relate to unwed mothers in crisis pregnancies."

"The Moses Project. Was that your idea or Dad's?"

"Dad's. He never wanted to practice law. He wanted to work in public policy or head a nonprofit. So, with Grandpa's help and contacts, they got The Moses Project started."

"Now it all makes sense. HOW. Such a great acronym. A vision for the homeless, orphans, and widows." Claire could hear her dad's motto articulated in her mother's fundraising speeches. "*HOW can you help?*"

"Your dad has a lot of heart, even if he doesn't have a lot of words."

"He has you to balance things out."

"It's for a worthy cause and I do like talking!" Erin admitted.

"And now for the morning paper. Where do you suppose we could find one in Deer Lodge?"

"Actually, that's a great idea. If there's a library in town, they'd have back issues of the local paper. Birth announcements?" Erin was building up steam, fueled by sugar, caffeine, and carbohydrates.

"Except nothing will be open yet. But we could just drive around until then?"

In silent agreement, neither packed their suitcase and they didn't check out. They were cautiously optimistic.

"I really want to find Dad's mom, but if we don't, I have to say the trip will be worth it anyway."

"I'll take that as a compliment, unless you just love Deer Lodge and not me?"

"Deer Lodge *is* pretty intriguing," Claire teased. "Now, let's go find the high school. We're pretty good at high schools!" Claire pulled out the brochure map and pointed to a photo.

"This says Betty Crocker was born and raised in Deer Lodge!"

"Who knew?" Erin said. "Nothing surprises me about this place." Erin shook her head. "You can't make this stuff up!" She followed the sidewalk lined streets of historic houses mixed with ones that probably needed bulldozing.

"What if Dad's mom knew her?"

"Or what if Betty Crocker was Dad's mom!" That set them both laughing.

"Not if cooking is inherited!" Claire shook her head and then added more soberly. "She's buried up there at Hillcrest Cemetery."

"RIP, Betty Crocker."

"No, *Janette Kelley.* That was her real name."

Erin pulled up to a three-story brick building surrounded by a dozen spruce trees and stopped the car. "This is Powell County High School. Home of Betty Crocker."

"Good thing she's not the mascot."

"Why does it look so familiar?" Erin studied the mascot of a little man on the front of the school.

"Powell County *Wardens!*"

"But he's wearing prisoner stripes."

"It's Turkey Pete, Mom. Can't you tell? I'd recognize that nose anywhere. Remember that guy in for murder? When his term was up, he didn't want to leave, so he spent the rest of his days in the prison."

"Just when you think it can't get weirder." Erin then pointed to a cute little Craftsman across the street. "The Woman's League Chapter House. What's that?"

"A literary club a few women started before the turn of the century."

"Sort of the earliest book group?"

As the town fanned out, the homes told a story of the decades and economics, changing from the 1880s to the 1920s, '30s, and then beyond when dollars and design ran out.

Erin and Claire loved the intricate Victorian homes, but even more, the Craftsman with porches that invited you in. Did they love this style because of their columns, piano windows and low-pitched gable roofs? Or was it the artistic detail of brackets, lintels and rafters? Or was it because it looked like home?

They left the neighborhood and headed down Main Street past the prison, past the train depot, and the roundhouse.

"Hey, Mum, why did you come with me?" Claire temporarily reverted to Mum and Erin laughed.

"He's my husband. I want to know what happened. Plus, I thought it would be fun." She turned her gaze to her daughter. "I enjoy being with you. And like you said, Deer Lodge is intriguing." Erin pointed the car out of town toward less populated areas and then fields, and down a rural farm road.

Claire gasped, and Erin slammed on the brakes.

"What? What is it?"

But her daughter didn't answer.

"What is it, Claire? Honey?"

But Claire could only stare open-mouthed out the window, then point to an old run-down farm with a dilapidated barn, fields, and horses running along the fence line. Tucked just behind two trees was a white bungalow with blue shutters.

"It's our house." Erin breathed in with a sharp intake, as if gasping in pain, then let it out with a shudder. All his life, Chase had needed to come home and now they'd found it. Neither spoke for what must have been minutes, until Claire opened her car door and strode to the replica of their house on Manito Boulevard.

"This hasn't worked so well for you in the past!" Erin called out to her and then turned the car off and followed.

The house was poorly maintained, but Erin took that to be a good sign. An elderly person would have a challenging time keeping up with a property this size. She sidestepped the flooring with the missing board, which Claire pointed out. There was a porch swing and bench in the exact location of theirs at home. Could it really be a coincidence? Erin closed her eyes and then slowly opened them up to see a sky blue ceiling, just like theirs.

"Did our house always look like this? When you bought it?"

"There were three houses. All bungalows. One was blue, one was green, and one was white. Dad wanted this one," Erin said and then corrected herself. "I mean the white one in Spokane. He said it didn't need painting."

Claire knocked. A young woman holding a baby came to the door, a little girl clung to her leg.

"Hello. I think my dad used to live in this house?"

"I'm sorry, we're just renting." The lady shrugged, unwilling to open the screen door.

"Your landlord. Is he older or younger?"

"Well, it depends what you call old or young," the mother laughed. "I'd say the couple is about forty."

Erin craned her neck to see an antique needlepoint hanging over a dilapidated mantel, recognizing the Craftsman home but unable to read the writing. "Do you know anything about the history of the house?"

"We haven't been here long. My husband works in Butte."

Claire pursed her lips, then smiled. "Well, thank you."

"How old is your daughter?" Erin smiled at the toe-head with pigtails.

"Emily, can you tell the lady how old you are?"

Emily hid her face, then turned and teased with a sly grin. With pinkie and thumb pressed together, she raised her three remaining fingers.

"Free."

Chase couldn't have been much older when he left Deer Lodge. Did he once cling to his mother's leg? Why did she let him go? More importantly, *how* could she let him go?

They said their goodbyes, but Claire headed toward the barn instead of the car. "I just want to look at it a sec."

Claire slid the barn door open, and it squealed in resistance. Slits between the gray planks let in shards of light. The barn was clearly just for storing equipment and hay. The haymow was stacked with bales. A pulley extended from one corner of the roof to the other side. Erin could imagine someone had once sailed across the barn on a swing. Suddenly, a barn swallow darted at her head and Claire ducked, screaming.

"Let's go. This place gives me the creeps."

"Well, at least we know he lived here," Erin said, as they pulled out of the driveway.

"You know, this would be a really wonderful place if it weren't . . ."

"A ghost town?" Erin interrupted.

"Yeah. Kind of dead."

"There's potential for rebirth. Revitalization."

"It could be something. It's halfway between Glacier and Yellowstone. It's on the gold rush trail. It has a weird prison and loads of history."

"And the Grant–Kohrs Ranch. That's worth the price of admission. The Rialto, too."

Erin and Claire had developed a strange affinity for the place.

"Don't forget Hotel Deer Lodge."

"No, I might want to forget that."

Mildred Duncan lived in an apartment on Main Street above Cora's Café.

Claire and Erin had practiced every conversation starter to figure out a way the information might just slip out naturally, but Erin feared there was no way to get past the fact they wanted the name of someone who gave up their little boy.

From Mildred's apartment where she could almost see the prison, Erin prayed for a good opening. Mildred was GinnaBee's age but there was a sinewy toughness about her, nothing feeble in her mind or body and she had a full head of thick gray hair that she wore in a ponytail.

"My dad lived in Deer Lodge when he was a little boy. About 1930 or 1931. Did you live here then?" Claire sat across from Mildred.

"I've lived here on and off since I was twelve."

"Then you might remember him. His name is Chase."

"I've never met *anyone* named Chase."

"That was his name after he was adopted by the Ellises. Did you know a William and Geneviève Ellis?"

She didn't have to answer. Her sudden intake. The frown of concern. Her stoicism while she sized her up and down.

"And why would you want to know?"

"They're my grandparents. I'm adopted," Claire blurted out. "Chase is my dad." Mildred looked at her quizzically, adjusted her glasses and studied Claire. "But we think he might have been adopted, too."

"And what's it to you?" Mildred had a point. Chase should have been the one asking. In so many ways it wasn't their business and if Chase didn't want to know, why did they?

"My dad can't talk about it."

"Can he talk at all?" Mildred's question came too quickly. Her voice cracked in eagerness.

"Of course he can talk!"

Mildred exhaled slowly. Was that relief? Why that reaction?

"Why would you ask that?" Erin asked. "Did you know his parents? Or . . . are you his mother?"

"Oh, no!" Mildred laughed and then coughed as only a smoker could. "Cora's my only daughter. And that was an accident and a blessing."

"But you knew his mother. Or his father."

"I believe this is where I plead the fifth. Or say, 'No comment.'"

"Why would you hide that information? Don't you think his parents might want to know he's a lawyer? That he has a wife and three kids?"

"Congratulations." Mildred's face did not match the word.

"What are you afraid of?" Claire didn't back down. Erin was impressed.

"Nothing, ma'am. What are *you* afraid of?" At Mildred's tone, Erin moved behind Claire.

"That I'll never find out what happened to my dad. That he'll continue to blame himself for something he doesn't even remember. That people just discard children for no reason."

"They don't do it *for no reason*." Mildred leaned forward, glaring at Claire.

"And that there are things in our past that if we faced, we'd probably be stronger. That secrets and lies don't pull us together, they pull us apart. That somewhere out there, there might be a mother who wants to see her son. That there might be a father who cares. That whatever pulled them apart is fifty years in the past but it's still keeping them in prison. Just like this whole town." Claire took a huge breath.

Mildred whistled through her teeth. "You sure you're not the attorney?"

The jury was deadlocked on who'd win this argument.

"You ever met *your* mom?" Mildred asked.

"Yes. Sort of." Claire fumbled. Her voice wavered. Erin could tell she was losing her courage, her initial wave receding back with the tide.

"And it went well?"

"No."

"I'm not surprised."

"But this is different." Claire's voice was that of a child.

"How?" Mildred didn't lower her eyebrows, as if awaiting Claire's response. Then, finally, Mildred shook her head. "Look, his dad isn't alive and I'm not in contact with his mother."

"Just her name. We'll do the rest. Just her name?" Claire sounded like she was begging. Erin let her speak, proud that she was standing up for herself.

"She was a friend. I wouldn't want to hurt her by digging up the past." Mildred took a sip of coffee. Erin willed her to say the name. *Say the name. Give us the name.* "I'd call her myself and ask if it'd be okay, except I haven't heard from her in a long time."

"We'll go slowly. My dad will just call first and if she doesn't want to meet us, we'll stop right there."

"Did you stop right there when you looked for your own mother?"

Claire didn't answer. Erin held her breath. *Please just say the name. Say the name. Say the name.*

"We were friends. We never told on each other. I can't start now." Her eyes flitted between the two. "But I will say this. If you find her— she's one of the strongest, most loving people I know. Treat her well."

"But no name?" Erin couldn't hold it in any longer.

"No name." Mildred pursed her lips as if planning her next words. "I can say this." She looked to Claire. "Your dad. He didn't do anything wrong, and his mother would want him to know that."

Chapter Seventy-One
Erin

Deer Lodge, Montana
July 29, 1981

As soon as the William K. Kohrs Library opened, Erin and Claire were in, following an elderly woman pushing a cart down the aisle as if it were her own personal walker. Periodically, she stopped and shelved a book. Slow but sure and certainly accurate.

"Do you remember somebody giving up a child? It was 1931. The boy would have been about three?" Erin's heartbeat raced. This was the point in the conversation where people gave them weird looks. Chase could have been born out of wedlock. Placed in an orphanage. And with Chase's reluctance for answers, there was something that didn't want to come out. "His name was Chase?"

"Chase?" the woman almost laughed. "That's a strange name. Never heard of anyone named Chase."

"It's short for Charles," Claire murmured with a sigh. "And after a lake in Idaho."

"1931? That was a tough time. Lots of farms went under. Tough to feed your family. Some people left the area. That was the Depression."

"Do you have newspapers from then?" Erin steered back to their original goal.

"Ah yes, *The Silver Star*." The librarian motioned for them to follow her to the basement. "I'm gonna let you two go on ahead." She pointed downstairs, mumbling something about the stairs and not wanting to leave the library unstaffed. "Go through the large area and into the room in the corner. There you'll find collections of Silver Stars in large blue books."

Erin pulled thick catalogues from 1928 and 1929. "We're getting rather good at this stuff. Three decades earlier this time." She handed over 1930 and 1931 to Claire and they began reading out loud who was visiting who, the local dances, what was playing at the Orpheum or the Rialto. No birth announcements. Without a first or last name, it was hard to know what to look for. They swapped books and, after a thorough look, decided the library was another dead end.

As they turned to leave, Erin spotted a card catalogue, except it wasn't for books. Its drawers were labeled: Births, Deaths, and Marriages. Each drawer held a spread of years. After all their investigation, would it come down to one drawer?

It couldn't be that easy.

Each drawer held a spread of years. After all their investigation, would it come down to one drawer?

"March 7, 1928? That's what we're looking for."

"*If* he was born in Deer Lodge and *if* the *Silver Star* recorded it, and *if* a little historian with a pen made a tiny note card and stuck it in here for someone like us to find." Claire sounded skeptical.

Sliding the 1920–1930 drawer, Erin began thumbing through the cards, looking for a birth date that could be Chase's.

"Consider any date in March. You never know if Grandpa and GinnaBee had the right date." Claire tapped her hand nervously.

The 1928 births were out of order. November, January, April, June. Deer Lodge wasn't a big town. There couldn't have been that many births. She'd go through the catalogue as many times as necessary. She'd try every year in that catalogue.

But she wouldn't need to.

There was only one card for March 7, 1928.

Baby boy born to Jack and Siobhan Mason.
Caleb Andrew Mason

He existed. There were no other March births in Deer Lodge. Chase William, son of William and Geneviève Ellis, was once Caleb Andrew Mason. Now, where was his other mother?

Chapter Seventy-Two
Anna

Arlington, Washington
July 25, 1981

Anna lay on the floor crying, her body curled in a fetal position. How could she turn her daughter away? When Emma discovered her on the floor, Anna picked herself up and laid down on the couch. Her head pounded as she rehearsed how she would tell Ben what had happened.

Before he came home from work, she started cooking onions and browning the beef for tacos, the kids' favorite. She sprinkled red pepper into the mixture and tasted it. Though she could smell the strong aroma, it tasted flat.

"Hey, Mrs. Benanna," Ben said, sweeping her into his arms, then frowning at her tears. "Onions bothering you again?"

"Daddy! Play ball with me!" Aaron pummeled Ben, nearly knocking all three of them over.

"Mommy cry today." Emma stood at the door, seemingly unwilling to step out of the doorframe. "Mommy floor. I help Mommy." Even with her speech impediments, they understood her all too well.

Ben looked to Anna, puzzled.

"Aaron. Emma. Can you go check on Mei Mei? Daddy and I need to talk." Aaron reluctantly left but Emma stood her ground.

"It's okay now, Emma." Ben reassuringly kissed the top of Emma's head. "Daddy will take care of Mommy."

When RAFT had called, she was sickened by the thought that it could explode into something more, but she was assured the files were closed. They *said* the files were closed. But when Claire showed up . . .

Now she had no choice.

Anna had spent the day trying to figure out how to tell Ben the twenty-one-year-old secret.

She had to begin with uncovering a lie. A hidden truth. This time she told it all. Chronologically. Ending with today. Somebody had come to the house. Someone he knew nothing about.

"I hope you can forgive me. I never lied. I just never told you the whole truth. I did lose that baby. But . . . she's still alive." She knew her original story had been such a distortion. She had betrayed him by not trusting him enough to share the truth.

Ben closed his eyes and lowered his face into his hands.

"Say something. Anything. Are you embarrassed? Do you think I'm a terrible person?"

Ben shook his head. "None of the above. I'm just really hurt that you couldn't tell me."

"I know." Her voice sounded like she was pleading. "I know."

"I really thought we were a team. That we could work things out together."

Anna started crying. They *were* a team. But she'd betrayed him. Was twelve years of marriage with one huge secret too much to overcome?

"Didn't you trust me?"

What could she say? That when she first revealed everything, she had stopped short because her feelings were still so raw? That even now she felt sick over the guilt and embarrassment of giving away her daughter, who'd be twenty-one. How did she let her go?

"I've been living with this . . . this . . . and I tried to stuff it down, but it always came back up."

"Why couldn't you trust me?"

For her it was about privacy and pain. For him it was all about trust. She had wounded him in a way she couldn't have imagined.

"Maybe it's because it was so real and painful to me. If it was real to you, too, then two people would have to live with the knowledge. Two people, always thinking about it and living with the horror. Instead of just me."

"I need a little time to think. I'm going to take Aaron to the park."

"You're coming back . . ."

"Anna, of course I'm coming back." His voice was unusually terse. "The very thought that you could think otherwise . . . It's what's wrong with this whole thing." He turned his back and was gone.

Chapter Seventy-Three
Erin

Seattle, Washington
August 1, 1981

Erin and Claire traced Siobhan from Deer Lodge to Bothell to Seattle. Siobhan's last name hadn't changed; after all the years had she never remarried? Once they had Siobhan's address and phone number, Chase was finally willing to try.

Chase made the phone call, saying he was coming to Seattle and wanted to meet her. Chase's silence as he listened, confirmed they'd found the right person. The conversation was short. Then again, what could he say to someone he hadn't seen in fifty years? Did he even remember her? Siobhan had agreed to meet; that was all that mattered.

Chase said little on their five-hour drive crossing wheat fields, the Columbia, the Cascades, arriving in Seattle. Erin didn't know if he was mad at her or just apprehensive. The news filled the silence. *President Ronald Reagan; John Hinckley; a rare pneumonia contracted by homosexual men; six-year-old kidnapping victim Adam Walsh.* Which made Erin determined to check up on Elizabeth and Evan when she got to Seattle.

As they neared the University of Washington, Erin directed them up a hill and then along a winding driveway to a home overlooking Lake Washington. The Northwest contemporary couldn't be more different from Siobhan's home in Deer Lodge. Siobhan Mason had done well for herself.

Siobhan had to be about eighty. Erin had no idea what to expect.

Would Siobhan look anything like Chase?

When the door opened, Claire's sudden intake was so loud, Erin looked first to Claire, then Siobhan. Her first thought was that this woman might have just slid off a horse. She wore jeans and a soft yellow sweater, but it was the red hair fading into blonde that made her look far younger than Erin expected. Is that what Claire saw? What did Chase think?

"Welcome. I'm so glad you're here. I'm Siobhan."

Erin hadn't anticipated the accent. It added a buttery cream to her appearance. Chase's mouth fell open as if he, too, was affected by her tone and dialect. The Irish lilt was a complete surprise, so elegantly beautiful.

Siobhan's eyes softened when she saw Claire bite her lip as if holding something back.

"Sorry, I guess my dad didn't mention I was coming. And my mom, too." Claire pointed out Erin, then reached out her hand. "I'm Claire. His daughter." Siobhan held it in both of hers as she studied Claire's face. Was Siobhan going to cry?

"I'm adopted." Claire pulled her hand from Siobhan's. "Sorry."

Siobhan tilted her head curiously, frowned, then nodded.

The living room, straight out of a magazine, a European simplicity with a splash of color. Cheerful accents and unique décor. Everything had a place, it was clean and nicely furnished. A few spectacular photographs of what Erin recognized to be villages off the coast of Italy where she and Chase had hiked on their twentieth anniversary, and a few photos of what she thought might be Ireland. Photos of children decorated the piano and the hearth. Wingback chairs faced a fireplace filled with unlit candles. Erin could smell something sweet and fruity coming from the kitchen.

"Have a seat." Siobhan motioned to one of two small couches facing each other. "I've made a peach cobbler." She fluffed a pillow and set it back down. "You always liked peaches." Siobhan's voice was soft and gentle.

How to begin. Fifty years hung in the balance. This wasn't Erin's show. Claire tapped her foot nervously.

Siobhan folded her hands on her knees, her ankles tucked daintily together. "Thank you for coming." The clock on the mantel ticked loudly, filling the space of silence.

"I'm not sure where to start." Chase locked eyes with Siobhan.

"I've always wanted to see you. To know you." Siobhan's face was calm, unafraid.

Erin gazed out the full-length picture window. Boats cutting a line in the lake, the mountains in the background. How did Siobhan end up here after Deer Lodge?

"How about pictures?" Claire suggested. "Do you have any pictures?"

Siobhan lay her hand on a shoebox, conveniently placed on the coffee table. Her hands trembled as she lifted the lid, revealing squares of black and white. How odd that after all these years the pictures wouldn't be chronicled, remembered, cherished. But boxed.

"This was taken in 1931." Siobhan took out the top photograph, capturing a family of six. Chase moved behind the couch and peered over Siobhan's shoulder as Siobhan pointed out the people, her groomed nails, touching each face. "This is you." She pointed to what looked like a dark-haired boy squinting into the camera.

"Oh, Dad," Claire said suddenly. The boy could have been Evan. He held the hand of an older girl.

"This is Samuel, and this is Paul." Siobhan traced the faces of two older boys. "And of course, this is me." And then she hesitated. "And this . . . this is your daddy." Her face tensed noticeably. Chase frowned and pointed to the girl.

"I remember her." He gently pulled the picture from Siobhan's hand.

"That's something, Dad," Claire encouraged, turning back to him and smiling.

"Sarah. Her name is Sarah." And then he repeated it one more time but with a different accent. "Saraid."

"You two were very close. Sarah and you did everything together." Chase continued to stare at the picture.

"Did she sing to me?"

"All the time."

"That was 1931?" Claire asked. She sounded more like a journalist than a nurse.

Siobhan turned to Claire and took her time answering, studying Claire with the passing seconds. But at the same time, Erin realized that Claire was doing the same.

"Yes, 1931." She pulled out a handful of other pictures from the shoebox. "This is all I have." She placed the photos like playing cards in a specific, well-orchestrated order along the coffee table.

"This is Caleb as a baby."

"Caleb." Claire repeated as Erin was reminded of her husband's original name. Chase's face was pale.

"His name was Caleb. Caleb Andrew Mason." Siobhan handed the picture to Claire. "And this is Caleb with me." Siobhan set the photo on the table. If Chase had any memory of that moment on his mother's lap, he didn't show it. "This is Sarah and Caleb." A brother and sister holding hands in front of a house. Caleb held a toy rabbit in his arms. Sarah was the loveliest little girl Erin had ever seen.

Then Erin saw it. Sarah was missing a part of her arm. Erin couldn't take her eyes off the disfigured wing of the angelic child and her look of love for the little boy. Chase. Siobhan placed another picture of the little girl, slightly older, minus her brother but holding a doll by its hand, its body drooping sadly downward. Sarah's stare was as hollow as the look in the doll's eyes.

"Sarah and Claire." Siobhan pointed to her daughter and the Raggedy Ann doll and the significance of its name.

"What?" Claire turned first to Siobhan then to her dad whose look of shock told them it was a surprise to him as well. *Claire. The doll's name. Was that how her dad chose her name?*

Then very slowly, Siobhan played the final card, a photo of Chase's father, a man she called Jack, leaning against a stack of hay, holding a piece of straw between his teeth, Caleb sitting at the top of the stack, trying to imitate with his own piece of straw. Siobhan did not explain this photo, but she seemed to study Chase as he picked it up. Siobhan closed the box indicating show and tell was over. The oven alarm went off and Siobhan rose.

"You don't have a photo album or something?" Claire called out.

"I do." Siobhan set the hot cobbler on a pad, and then removed her kitchen mitts.

"Can we see it?" Claire pursued, as Siobhan stood in the kitchen.

"It's different." Siobhan sounded apologetic as she reluctantly retrieved a black photo album from the shelf beneath the end table. Claire paged through it, looking for her father.

"Is this my dad?"

"No, that's his older brother. Paul."

"How about this one?" Claire pointed out a skinny fair-haired boy.

"That's Samuel."

"I didn't think he looked like my dad."

"You won't find him in this book." Siobhan turned to Chase. "It was too hard after he was gone to keep remembering." She used third person as if she were not talking about the man in the room. The boy she had given away.

Chase frowned and picked up the picture of him and his dad. The man looked like both Evan and Chase. Erin returned to the family picture. Everybody stood close together, except the dad. He was looking off into the distance toward something that made him sad. Like going off to war. Chase walked away with the photo.

"I didn't even know if I should show it to you. I worried it might make you sad." Siobhan's voice dropped low.

"Something happened," Chase said, rubbing the edge of the photo between his fingertips. He sat back down on the couch across from Siobhan and Claire.

"Yes." Siobhan smoothed the fringed pillow on her lap. "He died." She stopped as if waiting for a response. "He died when you were three." Siobhan's voice almost seemed a question and the way she studied Chase, Erin had to wonder if she was trying to confirm her answer. Somehow, Erin could feel they were taking a path that could be painful. Why? Was it too late to turn back?

"Do you remember anything?" Siobhan asked, looking at Chase with what Erin would call a strange mix of fear and caution.

Chase stared at the photo, near expressionless. Silent.

"He was adopted that year. Why would you give him up?" Claire answered for him.

"Let me heat the water." Siobhan left for the kitchen. Erin watched as Siobhan gazed upward, took a deep breath, closed her eyes, and exhaled. She moved the tea kettle to a different burner and returned.

"Those were terrible times." Siobhan sat back down. "And Jack—your dad—was sick."

"There's more than that." Claire tapped her finger on the coffee table. "There's a reason why my dad can't remember what happened. Why he's not in your scrapbook."

"I loved you, Caleb," Siobhan said. "More than you can ever know."

"But you sent me away."

"You didn't send him away just because Jack was sick," Claire said.

"Something happened." Chase closed his eyes. "Was it my fault?"

"No! Of course not!" Siobhan's voice was abrupt. Claire and her father stared wide-eyed at one another. So, there was something, Erin frowned. Something Chase could think was his fault. Something Chase had blamed himself for, for over fifty years.

"I tried to hide it." Her voice softened to a whisper. "I spent a lifetime trying to shield everyone from it."

"I think it's time for the truth, Siobhan." Chase set the photo down.

"Do you regret the life you've had with the Ellises?" Siobhan asked.

"They were good parents. I was loved. I was *wanted*."

"You were always *wanted*," Siobhan countered. "You were wanted by me, too, Caleb. But you and I, we knew something. Something that caused only suffering for everyone. And if I tell you? If I remind you, will you hate me?"

"Tell me what happened." Claire didn't wait to consider.

And then Siobhan began reliving that day from the moment she opened the sliding barn doors and faced a horrible choice. Claire couldn't hide her shock when her dad's other mother described what she had done. But the worst was yet to come.

"I thought I could do this. I thought I could keep everyone from the truth and live the lie." Siobhan's voice wavered. "But when I turned to leave, I saw you. Hiding behind the ladder."

Claire gasped involuntarily. Erin took her hand and reached over to put her other hand on Chase's knee.

"I don't know how much you saw of what your dad did, but you probably saw enough. And you saw me. And what I did. And it had to be confusing."

Chase stood and walked away, unable to stifle a sudden cry of anguish. The cry a small boy behind a ladder should have uttered so many years before but had instead built up inside. Chase sat back down and put his head in his hands.

"I saw it. I think I saw it. I think I saw it *all.*" His face cringed as if he were in pain and he spoke in gasps. "I saw him with a rope. I thought it was a game. I thought it was a *game!*" He shook his head violently. "He yelled, 'Stay away!' But I didn't. I came back, and he was there. I saw it. I should have done something."

"There was nothing you could have done."

"Really? You know that?"

"You were *three.*"

Chase pressed his hands together and bowed as if in prayer. Was he crying? He rubbed his forefingers up and down his forehead then suddenly Siobhan enclosed her smaller hands in his, and he quieted under her touch. Mother and son, frozen together, as if in prayer. The tea kettle began to whistle softly and then scream. Nobody moved. At last, the water spurting onto the burner sizzled and popped and Siobhan rose to move the kettle.

"If I really wasn't wrong, then why did you send me away? What kind of mother does that?" His hands were open in a question.

"A mother who loves her son more than her own self." Siobhan returned, sitting across from him.

"You gave him away because he knew the truth and he could tell!" Claire accused.

"No! I *wanted* him to talk again." She looked directly at Claire, then turned to Chase. "But he wouldn't. Couldn't. I didn't think you'd ever heal if you stayed with us."

"I was only three! We were a *family.*"

"But you never spoke after that. I tried to get you to talk. Your sister tried to. Nobody could bring you back. I took you to the doctor and he said sometimes when children have a serious shock these kinds of things happen. Our doctor didn't know how to treat you. There was a specialist somewhere, but I was losing the farm, I had to go to work at the prison, I didn't know how I'd feed you all let alone try to find a specialist. It was the Depression, Chase." Siobhan stopped and took a breath. "And there was another baby on the way."

"You knew you had a replacement and so you just gave up on him?"

"Claire!" Erin corrected.

"No, I didn't give up on him, I gave him up," she corrected. "There was a couple in town who didn't have any children. She was a nurse and so kind to Caleb. Her husband had a respectable job. God forgive me, Caleb, but I asked them to take you. To help you. I wanted to rescue you and that's the only way I knew how."

"But you didn't 'rescue' everybody else. Just me."

"I thought you . . . I thought you would be better without me. I didn't know if you could ever love me again." Erin watched as tears ran down Siobhan's cheeks like rain on the window. "You could barely look at me."

"So, what about everybody else? My brothers and sister? The baby? Where are they?"

Siobhan pointed out the two boys.

"Samuel and Paul enlisted. One came back. One did not. Paul now lives in Italy."

"And the baby?" Claire asked.

"I lost that pregnancy."

"And Sarah?" Chase picked up the photo of the two of them. His voice cracked.

Siobhan sighed. "Sarah passed away before she turned twenty." Siobhan turned away as if it was too much sadness.

What was Chase feeling? Would he grieve for people he hardly remembered? Or grieve because he never really knew them? Erin was surprised to find Claire crying and that her own face felt hot and flushed. Claire reached for her dad who took her in his arms. Siobhan sat across from them, alone.

"I don't know where to go from here," Chase said at last, releasing Claire's arms from around him. "I don't even know what I want." Siobhan nodded, her face mirroring his grief.

"When you do, I'm here."

"Can I go wash my face?" Claire asked and Siobhan pointed down the hallway. Claire nodded to Erin and they both stood, silently recognizing Siobhan and Chase needed time.

"Second door on the left."

Typical Claire turned at the first door and Erin followed, embracing her daughter as the enormity hit her.

"I'm sorry, Mom. I shouldn't have done any of this. I feel so bad for Dad."

"I know. Me too."

"I dragged Dad here to learn he's lost his father, brother, sister, and that his mom's a liar. After all, that's what not telling the truth means, right? Lying?"

Claire wouldn't let go, her tears adding to her confession. "Do you know what? I have a father and a mother and two siblings who will never give up on me. I have family."

Over Claire's shoulder Erin looked out over the lake hundreds of feet below where sailboats drifted by, and a water-skier cut a spray. Her gaze shifted left to discover the books. One entire wall of books with a ladder that slid along it. Not just a study, a *library*. Eight shelves, floor to ceiling, wall-to-wall of books. A quick multiplication indicated that the one wall held fifteen-hundred books. Somebody was either a collector or a reader or both.

"This is magnificent!" Erin said.

No color coding, and clearly no organization by category or genre, though some were in chronological order as if Siobhan bought them as soon as they were published.

"Lots are underlined," Claire pointed out after pulling some of her favorites from the shelves.

Erin picked up *Jane Eyre*, near the end of the bookshelf and read aloud an underlined portion.

"I have for the first time found what I can truly love—I have found you. You are my sympathy—my better self—my good angel—I am bound to you with a strong attachment. I think you good, gifted, lovely: a fervent, a solemn passion is conceived in my heart; it leans to you, draws you to my centre and spring of life, wrap my existence about you—and, kindling in pure, powerful flame, fuses you and me in one."

Though there was no pattern, Erin sensed there was meaning to the order and a story behind the library. Each book had similar underlining, and two different sets of handwriting, as if a dialogue, and questions sprinkled throughout the pages. One script was flowing and elegant and the other was more like printing. Firm. Direct. Most books were signed by AMS.

"I wonder who AMS is?"

I've never seen such a comprehensive variety of genres in any home library." Erin observed.

Leaves of Grass, How the Other Half Lives, The Great Gatsby, The Sound and the Fury, How to Win Friends and Influence People, Invisible Man, Charlotte's Web, Merchant of Venice, Pilgrim's Progress, Fahrenheit 451, To Kill a Mockingbird, Catch-22, Silent Spring, The Autobiography of Malcolm X, Bury My Heart at Wounded Knee, Where the Wild Things Are, Paradise Lost, Crime and Punishment, A Tale of Two Cities.

Erin slid the ladder over to the left and reached for one of the first books, one she herself had never read. *My Ántonia.* Not even dusty, though on the top shelf. From atop the ladder, she read, *For Siobhan, my friend across miles and words.* AMS. She stepped down from the ladder and sat on the bottom step, continuing to read the underlined portions. Some beautiful, some like secret messages. How had she missed ever reading this novel?

"In the course of twenty crowded years, one parts with many illusions. I did not wish to lose the early ones. Some memories are realities and are better than anything that can ever happen again."

"This is reality, whether you like it or not—all those frivolities of summer, the light and shadow, the living mask of green that trembled over everything, they were lies, and this is what was underneath. This is the truth."

Truth? What was the truth? And why was it so important to Siobhan?

And why so many books? Siobhan's library took up over sixty years. It would take another sixty for Erin to read all the tomes. *A Tree Grows in Brooklyn,* 1943 marked the middle of 1919 to 1981, the exact center of the library. The story of Francie's Irish family struggling in the city was one of Erin's favorites.

"Let me be something every minute of every hour of my life . . . And when I sleep, let me dream all the time so that not one little piece of

living is ever lost."

The longer she stayed in this library, the more curious Erin became about the book collector, the secret keeper. This was her husband's mother, and Claire's grandmother. Claire, Elizabeth, and Evan might never call her grandma, but for better or for worse, she was Chase's mother and had changed his life. And this was something both Claire and her father shared.

"Have you ever read this?" Erin handed Claire *O Pioneers!*. Claire shook her head. Erin then stopped and listened to the silence. "Maybe we should go back?"

"What a beautiful bookshelf." Claire pointed out as they turned to leave. It was so different. Clearly handmade. Oak. More beautiful than the wall-to-wall built-ins. Erin ran her finger along its smooth shelves.

Suddenly Claire dropped her book. "Mom," she said with a shudder, pointing to the portrait above the bookshelf.

It was so familiar. So out of place. A stranger. Where had Erin seen it before?

Claire lifted the portrait off the wall and almost ran back to the living room, followed by Erin.

Claire was nearly breathless. "Why do you have this picture?" Erin stood behind, taking in Siobhan's reaction. Something was terribly wrong. Familiar and strange, an odd juxtaposition.

"Why do you ask?" Siobhan rose suddenly from her chair.

"Because I know her. Sort of. I met her."

"How? *How* do you know her?" Siobhan's face wrinkled.

"No. I want to know how *you* know her. Who is she to *you*?"

"You *met* her?" Siobhan gasped. "When? Why?" She wore the same look of fear, or was it protectiveness, as when Siobhan had told Chase what happened to his father. "What happened when you met her?"

"Answer *my* questions first."

"Why would you want to meet her?" Siobhan ignored Claire's pronouncement.

"What if I said that's my business?"

Just tell the truth. Tell her whatever is bothering you. Erin longed for one woman to bend.

"She's my mother." Claire confessed.

Surprisingly, Siobhan had little reaction. "And you met her?"

"Yes. And you're not surprised she has a daughter." Claire's comment was a statement not a question.

"No." Siobhan let that revelation hang in the balance. "What happened when you saw her?"

"Nothing." Claire bit her lip when it started to quiver. "Absolutely nothing," she repeated in a slow monotone.

"I see." Siobhan sank back to the couch, the color leaving her face.

"You obviously know her, and you're not surprised she has a daughter. Why?"

"I knew her family. Her mother and I . . . we were very close."

"So . . ." Claire began cautiously, "What was Aria like? You must know her pretty well if you have her picture hanging in your library."

"She was . . ." Siobhan began. "She was . . . well, she still is so smart and courageous and . . . beautiful." Siobhan seemed to relax, as if talking in the past about this woman they had in common was easier than talking about her own family.

"And she's a singer?" Claire sat on the couch across from Siobhan. Erin had never seen Claire's eyes sparkle so.

"She *was.* I don't think she performs much anymore, but she teaches music." Siobhan sounded hesitant, confused.

"Why did she stop? Was it me?"

"No. I don't think so."

"Do you know my father, too?"

"No. I do not." Siobhan's voice became sharp. Claire frowned. It seemed like there was something more. "That's the truth." Siobhan brushed an imaginary fleck off her pants.

"Do you remember anything about my birth? Did she consider keeping me?"

"From what I understand, she always planned on giving you up for adoption."

"So she never wanted me." Another statement, not a question.

"Never *wanted* you?" Siobhan scoffed. "She wanted you so much she gave you up."

"More than once." Claire's voice was a mixture of anger and anguish.

"What?" Siobhan shook her head. "Whatever she did was for you."

That response sounded familiar.

"What else?" Erin asked quietly. She had stood by long enough. She had learned now that third revelations followed first and second ones.

"What do you mean?"

"There's something else, Siobhan. You're leaving something out." Erin's voice was steely but calm. Chase turned to her curiously. Siobhan kneaded her leg nervously as if cobbling her thoughts.

"You're right, there's more." She took a deep breath as if weighing the consequences of her words and turned away from Erin toward Chase.

Erin's next words matched the firm, slow gait of Siobhan's.

"How do you know her?" she asked. "How do you know her?" she repeated.

Siobhan's next four words changed everything. "Aria is Sarah's daughter."

Chapter Seventy-Four
Siobhan

There are in this world blessed souls,
whose sorrows all spring up into joys for others;
whose earthly hopes, laid in the grave with many tears,
are the seed from which spring
healing flowers and balm for the desolate and the distressed.
—Harriet Beecher Stowe, *Uncle Tom's Cabin*

Ballard, Washington
December 1941

The war with Germany now seemed far away. She had her own battle on the home front. Sarah was gone but Siobhan's granddaughter was a fighter.

Each time Siobhan pressed her hand against the glass incubator, she measured the baby's growth. The baby could have fit in her hand, were they to have let her touch her. But she could sing to the infant preemie.

Sleep, sleep, grah mo chree,
Here on your mamma's knee
Angels are guarding
And they watch o'er thee

She wanted to hold her, but from everything Siobhan had studied, Aria was alive because of the warmth and oxygen the incubator provided. Baby incubators had been the stuff of exposition sideshows, funded by the admission tickets of onlookers. But she was heartened to know that they had made progress in saving the lives of premature babies. Still, the doctor had shocked her when he said she had a ten percent chance for survival.

"We have an oxygen pressure system to keep her lungs inflated. She'll breathe against the resistance."

"Everything I've read says the premature baby success rate improves with round-the-clock care. I'm not leaving." Siobhan carried two dog-eared University of Washington library books in her briefcase. "I'm also very concerned about RLF. Have you read the recent article in the American Journal of Ophthalmology? Many premature births result in blindness."

"You're correct. We'll be monitoring her closely."

"If she needs blood, she and I are the same." Siobhan flipped to a bookmarked page. "And she needs human milk. It's essential."

The doctor almost smiled. "That might be a challenge."

"Not really." Siobhan smiled. "I've found a wet nurse."

Aria Grace Kildea Hanson beat the odds her doctors had given, and three months later Siobhan took her home, where she fed her first from a tiny spoon, then a bottle. All the while, Siobhan sang the songs her mother sang to her.

Siobhan could remember the first time she heard Aria sing. It was the little Irish tune she had taught all of her children. The one Sarah sang to Aria, her unborn child, and would have sung to her if she had survived. Hearing it startled Siobhan because Aria sounded so like Sarah. When Siobhan gasped, Aria looked up, concerned.

"I like to sing, Mama. Sing with me."

And Siobhan would, but ever so softly, so she could hear Aria's voice above her own.

Aria sang with Lincoln High School's choral program and with the best voice teacher in the Seattle area. It didn't surprise Siobhan when Aria chose to study vocal performance in the heart of NYC, but she was shocked when Aria returned wounded and broken, without a song to sing. Siobhan grieved that another voice was silenced.

Then they learned Aria was pregnant. Aria made it clear from the start that she was not keeping the baby. Siobhan couldn't comprehend letting another child go. She had done that once before and still carried the weight of empty arms. The loss of too many children. Sarah, who gave up her life to give life. Samuel, the boy of her heart but not of her blood. Caleb. Oh, Caleb. And now Aria's baby. She had to do something.

Chapter Seventy-Five
Anna

Arlington, Washington
July 25, 1981

Anna watched Emma and Mei Mei play with her childhood doll. Emma pulled the string and Mei Mei giggled as Chatty Cathy® repeated her lines. Anna's head throbbed and her stomach roiled. She burned the taco shells and sliced her finger when chopping the lettuce. Did Ben mean what he said?

When at last they returned, Ben flipped on PBS where a trolley chugged to the Mr. Rogers Neighborhood of Make-Believe and sat with Emma and Aaron for a minute before he stepped over a Malibu Barbie, the pile of Hot Wheels, and Aaron's Starship Enterprise. Anna sighed. That was for another day.

Ben made two cups of chamomile tea and they settled on the living room couch.

"This is really big, Anna. I'm hurt that you couldn't trust me with the truth."

"I'm so sorry, Ben. I really am."

"What you've kept to yourself changed us."

It changed *us*? Her choice changed them both?

"You look surprised, but it's true. There are areas of your life that you shut down. I always thought it was because of what happened. But I don't think that's all of it. You have a child out there and pretending you don't is not healthy."

"What's healthy for me might not be for her. The truth would kill her."

"So might hiding it."

He had a point. What was her rejection doing to Claire and how had her partial truth hurt Ben and herself? Why had she been so afraid to tell him?

But what if she got to know her daughter and realized she'd made a terrible decision and then had to live with regret? And now that she'd met this younger version of herself standing on her front porch, she already felt the absence of the intervening years weigh heavily on her heart.

"You've hidden your past, switched schools, moved to a new area, changed your name, and refused a child. You've denied who you really are."

She felt lightheaded. It was all true. She had two lives. She loved Ben and her family. But what had she done with her past?

"That needs to change. Your real name is *Aria*. It's a beautiful name. You lived eighteen years with that name. You do not have to hide from the person you were born to be." Ben took her hand. "And you don't need to fear somebody's going to find you. I found you and that's all that's important."

Could he be right?

"We need to start at the beginning, honey." He put his arm around her and drew her close. "I cannot imagine how hard it was to give up a child."

Anna let it all go. She could hardly talk through her sobs. She told him what she'd never told her mother. Never told her father. That no one except the two nurses in her room ever knew she'd held her baby. That she had sung to her infant daughter.

She told him everything she could remember about that day. A nurse had brought in her baby. Did she want to see her? *Her?* She had requested not even to know the gender. But her? She had a *daughter?*

Did she want to see her? Of course she wanted to see her! She wanted to *hold* her. She wanted to nurse her. She wanted to keep her. The assisting nurse had obviously not read the orders because letting mother hold baby had not been in the plan. For Aria to hold the girl meant opening her arms. If she could keep her arms crossed, closed, then her baby would never be taken from her. She would never have to reject her.

The baby was so tiny, soft, pink, all wrapped in a white blanket with pink and blue stripes. Could any baby girl be more beautiful? This was her daughter! Aria touched her baby's pink nose and caressed her cheek. Her daughter was so quiet. Those beautiful lips moving as if she wanted something. Aria stuck her pinkie in the baby's mouth and her sweet lips suckled. Aria had been given bromocriptine shots to dry up her milk supply. She had, in so many ways, nothing to offer her baby. Except this moment.

She bent down and sang softly into her daughter's ear, nuzzling her face against her baby's cheek. Was there anything so delicate?

Rest tired eyes a while

Sweet is thy baby's smile

That was how the song went, wasn't it? Wasn't that just how her mother had sung it to her so many times growing up? The tune almost a lament, a melody so varied, verse by verse, it seemed like a letter written on her heart.

Angels are guarding

And they watch o'er thee

Suddenly, the door had flung open, and the head nurse returned.

"I'm so sorry!" The other nurse reviewed the clipboard. "We'll need to take the baby to the nursery."

"She's mine." Aria clutched her to her breast, feeling the tears well.

"I'm only following what's on the chart, honey," the nurse said with so much compassion in her voice, such kindness that Aria knew she'd cry. Her hand on Aria's head mirrored Aria's on her baby's. Was this nurse a mother, too? "What is it you really want, Aria?"

Aria had no answer, because she didn't know. She wanted two things that couldn't both happen. And so, she let the woman pry the baby loose. And then her arms felt cold and empty, and she turned to the wall, holding a pillow against her, a sad replacement for the pink bundle she had given away.

The one she thought she'd never see again.

"But I did see her again. She looks just like me. I want to know her, but I don't want her to know me."

Ben didn't speak for what seemed minutes, and then drew a long breath.

"Aria, we're taking in children so they feel loved. But does your own daughter feel accepted? Does she feel loved?"

Of all the things he could say. He could have been angry. He could have shut down. But Ben saw to the heart. Hers. Claire's. He called her *Aria*. Anna was no more.

"That book. It's beautiful. You need to understand that your daughter is well. *Aria Claire*. She's healthy and she needs you."

He was right, but it was too late. She'd rejected Claire three times. There would be no more chances.

Chapter Seventy-Six
Erin

Seattle, Washington
August 1, 1981

As far as Erin was concerned, Siobhan Mason had a lot more explaining to do. Somebody needed to connect the dots. Sarah had died in childbirth and left a daughter? One more hidden truth. Was this the last secret or were there more?

Luckily, Siobhan continued without prompting. "I found you by your last name. *Ellis.* It helped that your father was so politically active. Then I studied yearbooks at the newspaper office."
Erin and Claire exchanged knowing glances.

"I watched for your graduation. I even *attended* it."
Chase's eyes widened and Erin's heart went out to her husband.

"You were out of my arms, but never out of my heart." Siobhan's fingers touched her chest as if holding the secret. "When Aria was pregnant, I wasn't going to give her baby away, too. If I lost that baby, I would lose everything. I had to let the adoption happen, for Aria's sake, but that didn't mean I couldn't keep track of my great-grandchild. You two could have a child and I could—"

"But how?" Chase interrupted, shaking his head. "How could you know that?" Then his face paled. "Wait. Genevieve knew about Aria and Claire?" Erin noted despair in her husband's voice. Had he been deceived by Genevieve all these years?

"No. No." Siobhan lifted her chin. "I don't think she ever learned anything about who Claire is." Erin sighed in relief.

"So, it was *you*? You arranged for Chase to adopt his great-niece?" Erin's hands were open in a question. "How?"

"I knew you didn't have children." She took a deep breath. "I had a possibility. That's when I contacted Geneviève and told her of an attorney and adoption agency. I gave her the opportunity to pass along the information if she thought you two would be interested. Then I prayed. A lot."

Still silence. How long would it take to process all this information?

Siobhan's arms were crossed, holding her elbows in the palms of her hands, as if rocking a baby.

"I wanted to draw this child out of the water. Like Moses."

Moses. The cycle sacrifice and loss redeemed with a child. One repeated decision drawing a child to safety. But Erin didn't know what to think. Was it some sort of social engineering?

"Were you ever going to tell me?" Chase turned to his mother, his voice curiously soft.

Claire, her face white with shock, stacked the photos and returned them to the box.

"Not today. I would have first asked Aria's permission, but I didn't have time. Even right now, someone is with her, telling her." She sighed and shook her head. "It's a lot."

"You never *told* her?" Chase's look was incredulous.

Claire shook her head sadly. "She never knew where I was placed? Even though we're family?"

"It was a closed adoption. That's what Aria wanted." Siobhan took a deep breath. "Of course, now that it's all opened, we have to figure out what to do."

The three studied one another awkwardly. It seemed no one knew what to say.

"I have the dessert." Siobhan returned to the kitchen. "I don't know if you still want some."

Erin suddenly felt strangely tired and hungry and the creamy ice cream with the sweet peaches and crunchy topping tasted like what a mother, or a grandmother, or even a great-grandmother should make. Chase didn't touch his and then finally took one bite and sat back, stirring his cobbler. Erin wanted to hold her husband and understand him in a way she couldn't before.

"I'm not sure Sarah ever forgave me." Siobhan also twirled her dessert. "She couldn't comprehend what happened and felt so lonely." Siobhan's guilt was palpable. "So she always dreamed of having kids. Of having a big family again."

"Aria came two months early. Lars wasn't even there. By the time Lars got off the ship, Sarah was gone, and Aria was in an incubator. It was terrible. He didn't think he could ever take care of a baby girl especially when everything reminded him of her. He claimed he'd come back. Send money, check on her. He didn't. Even though I kept his last name, I knew she was mine. She was a Mason, and I had a second chance with Sarah if I raised her daughter.

"Aria called me 'Mom' and she became my daughter, Aria Grace." She spoke the name slowly, as if treasuring its flow. "I used to think Aria was a silly impractical name, but Sarah wanted a girl's name to be a song. An *Aria.*"

Without that unusual name, Claire might still be looking for her mother. And Erin was right to name her own daughter Aria. Something to share. A song intertwined their lives.

"I always wanted to know if she saw me. Held me. I mean, would that have made a difference?" Claire persisted. She would find the truth.

"Maybe you think because she gave you up, she didn't love you. That's not true. I know one day she came home and said she'd been to a doctor who could take care of things. She was crying. Said she couldn't do it. Said you were going to have a life and it was going to be good one." Siobhan stopped as if weighing her next words. "And it about killed her to do so."

"How so?"

"Your delivery was long and painful. She was in the hospital for forty-eight hours and lost a lot of blood.

"I was so worried it was going to be just like what happened to Sarah. That I'd lose her, too. And I think that would have broken me."

Erin's heart raced and she didn't know if she could look at Claire. But she needed her to know that she had two mothers who loved her very much.

Siobhan left the room and returned with a different scrapbook. She flipped it open to reveal newspaper clippings and photos of a young woman with red hair twisted at the nape of her neck. So elegant, so poised, wearing stunning gowns and costumes. Siobhan flipped back to the front to when Aria was a little, gangly red head and Erin drew in a shuddered breath. They could have been looking at Claire's baby pictures.

This was what Claire had been looking for. The match. Someone just like her.

"I have this record," Siobhan continued, bringing out a disk with a beautiful redhead in a green velvet dress displayed on the label. "They recorded her recital. I made a tape. You could listen. If you want."

Siobhan turned to Chase. "And when I hear her voice, sometimes I hear Sarah."

Why did it seem Siobhan needed for them to hear the concert? "Aria's voice is quite a song."

"Until me. Did I stop it?" Claire's voice quivered.

Siobhan ran her hand over the scrapbook. "What if I told you I'll never know what happened and you might not either?"

Let it go. Let it go. That's what Erin wanted to tell her daughter. It was time to let it go.

"She has a family now." Claire's voice had an unforgiving edge.

"She does. You should meet them."

Claire turned away. *You have siblings at home, too,* Erin wanted to remind her.

"You have a lot in common," Siobhan rested her hand on Claire's hand. "They're all adopted."

Chase put his hand on Claire's shoulder, and she turned to her father as he enveloped her in his arms. Erin memorized the moment.

"I think it's time to go." Chase released her and nodded to Erin.

"I don't know if I did the right thing." Siobhan brushed the hair from her forehead.

"I think you tried," Chase said graciously. "Maybe there are times when living with a painful truth is better than living a painful lie."

"Do you hate me?"

"No, I could never hate you." His words fell off. "Do you hate yourself? I wouldn't wish that on anyone."

"I've learned to forgive." Siobhan's voice was soft.

"If you could do it differently, would you?"

"I don't know." Siobhan frowned. "I used to look at a reflection of myself to see how the other choice turned out." Siobhan extended her hand as if trying to reach the woman who kept Caleb. "But the reflection can't tell me anything." She rotated her gaze to her son. "Maybe that means you were better for the choice I made." Her fingers slowly curled together, and she dropped her hand. "But I was not." Siobhan closed her eyes. "I'm so sorry, Chase." Her voice snagged.

"I am, too," he said. "I am, too."

"I found I couldn't keep reliving my decision and also move forward." Her voice was so gentle. "I hope you can now. Go forward, that is."

Chase opened the door for Claire and motioned for her to leave and then he turned back and took his mother in his arms. It was stiff and uncomfortable, but he tried, and Erin sighed with what she thought must be relief.

Chapter Seventy-Seven
Erin

Seattle, Washington
August 1, 1981

O nce back in the car, they seemed to be waiting for someone to say something. Anything.

"You have her address." Chase said at last. But he didn't turn the key.

Claire nodded.

"I have to see her." Chase sounded resolved.

"Dad, not now."

"You said I should come here, and I did. You were right." He tapped the steering wheel on "said," "did," and "right," emphasizing his point and building a case.

"It's too soon, Dad. She said no. Three times."

"She's my sister's daughter. I think she'll want to see me."

"But not *me*."

"I didn't mean it that way."

"I don't need to see her." Claire's voice was surprisingly void of emotion. "It's weird. In the middle of all this—even before I found out you're actually my uncle." She stopped and shook her head. "Oh, that is so weird. Great-Uncle Chase . . ."

"I'm your *dad*. Nothing has changed."

"That's just the point. I have a family that loves me. Why should I go see her now?"

"Because she might need you. She's your mother."

"She's the woman who gave me up. Mom is the one who raised me." Claire turned and nodded to Erin. "*She's* my *real* mother."

Although reassuring, it wasn't the resolution Erin longed for Claire. Or Aria.

"There's something in Siobhan that reminds me of you, Claire," Chase said. "And Sarah's daughter? I have to meet her."

The car was getting too warm and when Erin rolled down the window, Chase and Claire copied, allowing the breeze to rush through.

"I can't help but think that one action set everything in motion." Chase's grip softened on the steering wheel.

"Which one? There were a lot of them."

"Jack. My father."

"Or Siobhan. Your mother."

"I'm not sure I can blame her."

"So, you can forgive her? You think it was for the best?"

"I could ask you the same question, Claire."

Erin wondered where this conversation would take them. East or west?

"I can remember a warm hay bale and holding our hands up to bright light." Chase leaned back and shaded his face from the sun. "I can remember falling asleep in the shadow of that hay bale."

"Little Boy Blue," Claire murmured.

"Yes." Her father laughed softly. "Yes, that's what Sarah called me," Then he shook his head and frowned. "At least I think so. I'm not sure what's true or if I want to know." Chase raised his palms and shrugged. "Who will I be if I remember? Jack Mason's shadow, or William and Geneviève's silent orphan?" He rested his hands on his lap. "I wasn't looking for truth. But now I'll have to face it." Erin was surprised at the number of words. This was all new.

"I'm sorry, Dad."

Erin felt the shared guilt. She had conspired with her daughter, never comprehending the repercussions for her husband. Maybe GinnaBee was right and that it was better not to know the full truth. And yet, had this opened a wound that could heal?

"It's been quite a day." Chase exhaled then started the engine, though their destination had not been determined.

"Hey Dad, this is when you could say, 'I forgive you. It's okay, I'll get through it and grow and we're all going to be stronger.'"

Chase didn't smile and that made it worse, for a beat, until he spoke, rubbing his hands over the steering wheel. "I don't think we ever know the full truth. Just faint memories and dim recollections and the feeling that we were loved. I have that. Maybe I wasn't sure about it before. But I am now.

"I can't really judge Siobhan's choices because I don't know what I would have done. If I couldn't provide for you or give you what you needed to survive—to thrive, to heal, I'm not sure I'd be unselfish enough to let someone else try."

Erin understood Chase might be talking about Aria as well. Her eyes blurred. This man, her husband. She would have to alter and change and the two would grow. They had years; marriage was good that way.

"I'd like to think she loved me so much she *couldn't* give me up. But maybe I need to realize she loved me so much she *had* to give me up. That she wasn't selfish—but sacrificial." How gently he spoke. She loved this man. His hand touched Claire's cheek. "But maybe not giving up a child might have been wrong."

"Oh, Mom. You're crying!"

"What're you thinking, honey?" Chase rotated to hear.

"I always wanted to meet her. I think your mom might be different than you think." Erin longed to encourage Claire, but knew she had to let the two figure it out. This was a journey she hoped would bring them closer, as they realized all they shared.

"I haven't been the father you needed, Aria Claire."

Claire closed her eyes and lowered her head. Erin could hardly believe Chase was recognizing a deficiency, perhaps now the fortress he had built around himself would fall. He pulled Claire close as she sobbed into his shoulder. It was a good kind of cry. Happy/sad, they called it.

"You know, honey, I don't know about my mother." Chase took a deep breath. "Some of those choices might have been wrong. But some had good results. You in our family. That was the best. You did come out of the water, Claire."

Erin sat back, exhausted and tired. There was room only for thanks.

Chase nodded toward the box of tapes. "You want to listen on the way there?"

"I think you want to hear your *sister's* voice, Dad. Sarah's. But she's gone."

"Yes, but a part of Sarah lives on."

Claire popped the tape into the slot.

A woman's voice. Italian. Opera. Erin shivered at the sound. Claire's fingers were motionless in front of the cassette, as if she were reaching out to touch the singer. "*Voi che sapete,*" the soprano sang. "*The Marriage of Figaro,*" Claire whispered.

The voice was free, full of the love of life. How could Erin describe it? A ballerina pirouetting across the stage, a water-skier spraying a rooster tail, or an ice-skater landing a jump. She made it sound so easy. And when she spoke, Erin couldn't believe the voice wasn't Claire's. She couldn't read Chase's reaction. Was it confusion? Longing? Was he hearing a different voice from long ago?

"I added the next number. It's an Irish lullaby dedicated to my mam, who always sang it to me. It's called the 'Ballyeamon Cradle Song.'" Aria began the lullaby without accompaniment. Erin closed her eyes, trying to imagine Aria on stage, connecting the picture on the library wall. A harp joined in, a simple accompaniment highlighting the voice of an angel. The ornamentation, grace notes. The sweet, modal song that sounded like a personal message.

Rest tired eyes a while
Sweet is thy baby's smile,
Angels are guarding
And they watch o'er thee

What was Claire thinking? How it might feel if Aria were singing to her? Mother to child?

Sleep, sleep, grah mo chree
Here on your mamma's knee,
Angels are guarding
And they watch o'er thee

"Sarah was like an angel guarding me." Chase sounded oddly different. "She sang me that song."

"Oh, Dad!" Claire turned suddenly. "You remember?"

Chase nodded, smiling faintly. "And I imagine Aria sang it to *you*."

Could music be more than notes and words? Could there be a faint recollection, a distant memory, a feeling of being loved? Could a lullaby heal their daughter's wounded soul?

"But what if it was the last time she ever sang?"

"That would not be your fault, sweetheart." Chase placed his hand over Claire's.

A lullaby. A story in song. How many mothers had sung a lullaby to their babies?

Chase started the engine. "I don't know where I'm going." He released the parking brake and looked at Claire. "But you do."

Chapter Seventy-Eight
Siobhan

Now I understood that the same road was to bring us together again.
Whatever we had missed,
we possessed together the precious, the incommunicable past.
—Willa Cather, *My Ántonia*

Seattle, Washington
August 1, 1981

"Hello? Anybody home?" Her husband threw open the door, and quickly scanned the room, disappointment registering. "They're already gone?"

Siobhan nodded, fighting back the tears as he enfolded her in his arms. Every hello and every goodbye, he held her close. Not just a quick three-second hug. He had once said as much: "I'll never let you go," and he meant it.

"Are you all right?"

"I am." She touched his cheek softly.

He waited as always for her to write her thoughts aloud.

"I had no idea what would happen. It wasn't perfect. But what could I expect?"

"Closure?"

"Yes," she sighed. "And also, something else. Maybe an open window. What about Anna?"

"*Aria* was a little surprised by my sudden visit." His voice was a gentle correction.

"Aria." Siobhan paused, nodding her head. "Yes. She was born to be Aria."

He fumbled in the pocket of his linen jacket. "Oh, and I'm supposed to give you this." Siobhan could tell the scribbled drawing of a sheep "To Gramma ShaSha" was from Emma Joy. Always sheep. Emma loved sheep. "Ben's good with her." He stopped and rubbed his jaw. "But this whole thing brings up bad memories. Whatever they are."

"I'm sorry you had to be the one to tell her about Caleb. Does she hate me?"

"No one could hate you." He caressed her cheek.

"But I gave up Caleb . . . Chase."

"As Aria gave up Claire, no?"

The circumstances were vastly different. But they did have something in common. Then there was her mother and Brigid.

"Actually, I think Anna seemed intrigued that she had another uncle. And even more surprised that Chase raised her daughter! And all because of you."

"All because of me," she repeated in blame. "She didn't hate me for it? If I had just let the baby be placed anywhere . . ."

"What then? Aria wouldn't have to deal with this?"

Siobhan shook her head and bit her lip. She didn't want to cry again.

"But I don't think that's all bad." Her husband guided her to the couch. "It was upsetting meeting Claire. But there was something else. Something hopeful."

"Really? Do you think . . ."

"In her own time," he said softly. "I think Anna, our Aria will want to see her again."

"Sooner than she's ready!" Siobhan's hope turned to desperation. "I feel so badly. Claire saw a picture of Aria. She asked how I knew her. I couldn't hide it anymore. I had to tell them both the truth."

"Then what happened?"

"They were hurt, angry."

"Those kinds of emotions come with love." He drew her close, holding her so tightly, she thought he'd never let go. She loved him more than he would ever know, the man connected not by blood but by words.

"I can go through anything as long as you're with me, Antonio."

Chapter Seventy-Nine
Siobhan

Bothell, Washington
Salerno, Italy
1943

Later, Antonio would tell her that he didn't need to see the hospital records confirming Paul's birth date and identity. Paul was more Giovanni than Siobhan. To find Paul, wounded in battle, meant he had reclaimed something lost. His loneliness was lightened by the presence of her son, his nephew, and if he could ease Paul's grief upon hearing of Samuel and Sarah's death, he would consider it an honor.

After Paul and Antonio's journey on the Queen Mary, the two traveled by train to Seattle. Siobhan stood next to the closest gate for the first glimpse of Paul. And yet she was anxious about Antonio.

Perhaps she'd let Antonio pick her out of the crowd. But she was no longer the seventeen-year-old he had hugged goodbye in the Boston train station.

She wore her best suit, ironically called a Victory suit. Such a practical garment, but she wore it well. The nipped in waist, the padded shoulders, the peplum. The gray green nearly matching her eyes. Fingering its covered buttons, she noted how the white Peter Pan collar of the blouse peeked through at the neck. She checked the A-line flare and the hem that skirted her calves.

She styled her hair half up and half down, her auburn curls resting on her shoulders, smooth finger waves framing her forehead. Did she look so terribly different from two decades before? Her felt Stetson topped off her outfit. She hoped she didn't disappoint. Would Antonio recognize the woman she had become? Would she still identify him? The boy Antonio, younger than her sons, was gone. Would they have anything in common beyond twenty-four years of messages scribbled in books?

One by one, the passengers stepped off the train, some searching for loved ones, others businesslike, lonely in their pursuit to get to wherever they were going. She held back, behind a ring of families.

Suddenly, Antonio filled the door frame, his dark hair slightly peppered with gray, his face stubbled from the long train ride. He had lost the boyish softness and his features were chiseled. Remarkable. His eyes scanned faces until he locked on hers and he smiled. The same slow grin. The man Antonio was here. A presence that both overwhelmed and exhilarated her.

She exhaled and then gasped as her son emerged, smiling, waving to her as if to say, "I'm all right." The two men moved toward her in slow motion until Antonio hung back and set down their bags. Paul took her in his arms and twirled her. She closed her eyes to his embrace and when she opened them, she motioned at the redheaded toddler standing below. Antonio was kneeling down to Aria's level to talk to Siobhan's granddaughter face to face.

"Free," Aria said, using her left hand to capture her thumb and pinkie so her three fingers stood proudly. *How like her mother.* Antonio held out a peppermint, which Aria lifted from his open palm. She smiled and rubbed his face gently. "Ouchy," she said at the bristles. Surprisingly, Antonio scooped Aria up in his arms and after the peppermint was safely secured in her mouth, she rested her head on his shoulder in complete trust, her long red hair in curls down the back of her green wool coat.

Siobhan marveled at the strangeness of seeing the "brothers" together, like a young Giovanni next to a mature Antonio. "Hello, Siobhan," Antonio said simply, Aria's arms securely encircling his neck. Hearing his voice after so many years made her thrill in a way she didn't think possible. Then they both laughed, as if that were the only thing they knew to do, oblivious to whatever anyone else thought. The words between lines over years and books; their thoughts underlining what was in the hearts formed a connection she didn't know was still possible.

"Hello, Aria, I'm your Uncle Paul!" Paul lifted Aria's chin and she smiled back. Then he pressed them all together in an embrace that, acknowledging months of sadness and loss, contained their now smaller family.

"One of us has to get back soon," Antonio said, stepping away. Siobhan was speechless. Her gaping mouth then met with laughter from both men. "It's good news, Siobhan," Antonio continued. "A wedding." Siobhan felt everything that was hope fall into a crack in her soul.

"Don't worry, Siobhan, she's a wonderful girl. A nurse. And she's Italian." Antonio's eyes twinkled with pride. Italian, of course. Siobhan nodded. She tried to be happy for him.

Siobhan nodded. She tried to be happy for him.

"Mam, you'll like her." Paul winked mischievously. "Sofia reminds me of you."

That was a blow Paul would never understand. Siobhan's legs felt weak. She looked suddenly to Antonio. *How? Why?* Antonio returned a happy grin.

"We're getting married next month." Paul added.

"You? . . . *You're* getting married?" Siobhan didn't know whether to laugh or cry. Why did she feel such a reprieve? Antonio turned to Paul with raised eyebrows and a smile. They both shrugged at Siobhan's response.

Siobhan hugged Paul in relief. He whispered in her ear, "Don't let this one go. He's a catch."

Her heartbeat quickened and, she didn't know why, but she was crying and laughing at the same time. Antonio dabbed her tears with his handkerchief, then cupped her chin with his hand. His touch brought the rush of words to her heart, and she felt she knew him as though they'd never been apart. Then little Aria reached out her hands and touched her Mam's face in imitation.

Paul and Sofia's Italian wedding was followed by Siobhan's marriage to Dr. Antonio Savelli, professor at University of Washington, where

Siobhan Mason later completed her PhD from the Department of Speech and Hearing Sciences. She had kept her last name, Mason, just in case one day somebody wanted to find her.

Keeping her name . . . it had worked, hadn't it?

Now thirty-eight years later, in their Seattle home overlooking Lake Washington, Antonio was as handsome as when he stepped off the train in Seattle and fell in love with a little girl born not of his blood but of his heart.

Antonio was even more striking than over fifty years ago, when he'd handed Siobhan a manila package and sent her on her way, on a train to a different life and a different man. Perhaps Antonio truly was the love of her life. Was that possible? That Antonio Marius and Moira Siobhan shared the bitter and the sweet?

"Shhhhh-avahhn." He spoke so gently, so musically, touching his lip, then hers, as if sharing a secret. "Saaaaah-velli." After all these years, he still recited her first name the way he used to whisper it in the Boston library but now possessively adding his surname. They were two old people who better understood not only the words on the page but the quiet space between the lines.

"*You are my sympathy—my better self—my good angel*," he quoted Brontë, his voice rough, as if something was breaking. "You're the beginning, middle, and the end of my story, Siobhan Savelli." These were his own words, rich with emotion.

Siobhan held his hand to her face and blessed it with a kiss.

Epilogue

I was entirely happy.
Perhaps we feel like that when we die and become a part of
something entire,
whether it is sun and air, or goodness and knowledge.
At any rate, that is happiness; to be dissolved into something
complete and great.
When it comes to one, it comes as naturally as sleep.
—Willa Cather, *My Ántonia*

Arlington, Washington
December 19, 1981

Aria Grace Kildea Hanson McMahon stood backstage, unaware that the auditorium seats were filled with friends, family, and so many students from years past. She knew only that Ben was in the second row with their three children and she would sing for him. And she had to admit—for herself.

Ben claimed the emerald green velvet dress he had bought her perfectly complimented her auburn hair, which her mother had styled into a French twist that morning. Her father slipped a corsage of tiny red roses and baby's breath on her wrist. Up until the last second, she would hold the card her children had drawn for her. *We Love Mommy. SING GOOD!* Teachers from her school had prepared hot cider and gingerbread cookies for the reception. Claire had insisted on using her GinnaBee's recipe. After sampling their cinnamony deliciousness while waiting in the green room, Aria understood why. The falling snow was the perfect accompaniment to the Christmas holidays and the kickoff to a family reunion like none other.

In so many ways, Aria's life had come full circle. She'd been given back her voice, her name, and her daughter. Now she would sing the abandoned recital from long ago and reunite her family.

In the audience, Siobhan squeezed Antonio's hand. Their girl was singing again. Paul, his wife and their four adult children had flown in the day before. Paul leaned into his brother Chase and said something which made them both smile at the same time. Paul had never forgotten his little brother Caleb and they had fifty years of catching up. Separated by miles and years, they'd found more similarities than differences and it made Siobhan's heart swell. Claire held baby Mei Mei, helped by GinnaBee's funny distractions. How much the child understood was not fully clear, but she relished the added attention. Elizabeth entertained Emma with sheep puppets made from socks and cotton balls. They were a family, connected by love and sacrifice.

Evan's greatest fear, that he would lose his sister, did not come true. Aaron Joshua was certainly not a rival but a friend. AJ's collection of Star Wars figures exceeded his, and AJ had a trampoline in his backyard, and neither one of them was looking forward to sitting still for over an hour listening to songs that were not in "American."

Suddenly Aria stepped into the warmth of the bright lights, which blinded her to the rows of family below and her retired voice teacher, Montserrat, whom Ben had invited as a surprise. Claire drew a deep breath and pulled Mei Mei near. She felt Erin's arm around her and saw the tears running down her mother's face. It would have made Claire sad, except she knew her mother was actually happy for Aria and for Claire. She leaned against her mother, sharing her anticipation.

Aria closed her eyes, and a quiet calm came over her as she began to sing a cappella.

Sleep, sleep, grah mo chree
Here on your mamma's knee

A simple Kildea lullaby sung by Moira, carried to America by Siobhan and handed down from one mother to another.

Angels are guarding
And they watch o'er thee

A lullaby Aria had sung to four children, who now smiled proudly up at her. A lullaby as pure as her heart and her mother's and her grandmother's and the heart of any mother who ever loved a child.

About the Author

Ann Marie Stewart's first novel, *Stars in the Grass* won The Christy Award® for best debut novel.

When she's not writing a story, she may be acting it out, or telling it through song, as a coach for musical theatre.

Waterskiing is her favorite sport, but in the offseason Ann lifts weights in her voice studio and walks eight miles a day on the trail near their home. Ann loves hanging out with her husband and two adult daughters watching UVA Basketball, and shepherding a whole flock of fuzzy sheep on Skyemoor Farm, in Virginia–where unscripted drama provides plenty of entertaining material for her next story.

Acknowledgements

I love a good adoption story both true and fictional. After my agent prompted me to work on my next novel, I knew that was my topic. But I had no idea it would cover seventy years, five states, three countries, with dozens of literary references and fascinating characters crisscrossing familiar territory decades apart.

That territory is dear to my heart.

I have vacationed with family at Priest Lake, Idaho for over forty years, hearing about the earlier settlers and the history of the region. I've always loved Boston and enjoyed a return to explore the streets of "Italy." Alerted to the Boston Public Library in Back Bay, I was fascinated with its museum-like architecture and art. I walked the bridge to Charlestown as Siobhan did a hundred years before. A return to my hometown of Seattle both on paper and in person made this location an easy site to share.

A former roommate kept telling me about Deer Lodge, Montana, this quirky town she now called home. Because this old-time jewel was on the railway from Boston to Seattle, both Siobhan and I stopped there. Now that I've been to Deer Lodge three times, I have a great appreciation for all it could be. Where else can you tour a former prison, see the expansive Montana sky, visit a working ranch, and take in a rodeo or two on your way to or from Yellowstone National Park or Glacier?

I confess, I didn't get to Ireland. Yet. However, my good friend Siobhan Kildea McMahon did. She picked my village of Kilrush,

Ireland, fielded questions with her Irish Da, and gave me my heroine's name.

Siobhan's story morphed in surprising directions. Who knew that the Pandemic of 1918 would become more real because of Covid-19? The more I wrote, the more I was shocked by the background of each character. I had no idea! Some revelations were sad, others shocking, and others ever so satisfying. Still, the initial question remained: Is it better to know the truth? I wonder how each character would answer.

I wish I could step onto the page and meet each of them and I hope that you do, too. Maybe, just maybe, we can one day see them on the big screen in a restored W.A. Clark Theatre in the Montana State Prison. Now THAT would be exciting. Of course, I'd want all those who had helped along the way to join me in jail for the event.

I'm thankful for:

1. Inspiration. Thank you Sherrill Ellis Kraakmo for enticing me to Deer Lodge, Montana; Kitty Eisele for all things Boston and Irish; and Siobhan Kildea McMahon for being my Irish eyes.

2. Smart friends who know about adoption, trains, literature, or all things medical from preeclampsia to Alzheimer's. Louise Monda Eskew, Jen Ducharme, Cheri Dillon Verham, Sherry Saunders Haynes, Deborah Raney, Jimmy Lambert, Ava Wilson Santos, Carrie Leslie, Elizabeth Pickett, David Agnor, Chris Stafford, Virginia Theerman, Karlah Louis, Julia McClenny, David and Sarah Sanders, Arne Spekat, Bobbi Kliepera, Jill Dye, Kim Zeidman, and Lori Galloway.

3.Research experts: Melanie Sanchez, Curator Deer Lodge Prison Museum; Lincoln Konkle & Mary English with Thornton Wilder Society; Stephen Puleo, author of *The Boston Italians*; and Gabrielle Gruber, University of Washington Department of Speech and Hearing Sciences.

4. Honest readers: Alane Redon, Heidi Veldman, Joan McClenny, Barb Boughton, Rebecca Reed, Pam Bass Rowell, Lori Galloway, Judy Greene, Shaunna Bohan, Laura Goheen, Christine O'Connell, Kim Zeidman, and Ruth Roetcisoender.

5. A book club to test drive the manuscript. Thank you BIBLIO BABES Kimberly Zeidman, Barb Jackson, Kristy Pittas, Kelly Young, Kelli Linville, Janet Spencer, Ann Doss, Annette LeVan, and Christine Miner.

6. A great agent. Thank you, Chip MacGregor of MacGregor & Luedeke for not only prompting the novel and being my friend, but for connecting me with Hidden Shelf Publishing House.

7. Technical help for website and promotion: Sarah Cahaly, Edward Viera, Timothy Deegan, Amy Sauerlender, and Aliyah Dastour.

8. Editors. Thank you Rachel Wickstrom and Holly Lorincz.

9. A book launch and street team to BLAST it out of the water! Amy Sauerlender, Lori Galloway, Hilary Alexander, Patti Ayers, Stacey McKenzie, Carrie Leslie, Kimberly Zeidman, Melissa Henderson, Celesta Miller, Dena Murray, Beckie Burnham, Ann Petrin, Laura Young, Kimberly McDaniel, Kitty Eisele, Betsey Bishop, Julia Tomiak, Shawn Marie Carnall, Ruth Wiechmann, Sherry Larson, Tammy Hansen, Elizabeth Roden, Michelle Grudi, Sheila Donoghue, Rachelle Knight, Chris Storm, Jackie O'Hara, Sandie Williams, Aliyah Dastour, and Theresa Green.

10. YOU! Thank you for reading my second novel!

Siobhan's Library

The following list includes books that are quoted, referenced, or mentioned in Out of the Water. *Citation accurate to the best of our knowledge, may have been serialized or written under a pseudonym.

Alcott, Louisa May. *Little Women*. Two volumes. London, Roberts Brothers, 1868, 1869
Austen, Jane. *Pride and Prejudice: A Novel*. London, T. Edgerton, Military Library, 1813
Baum, Frank L. *The Wonderful Wizard of Oz*. Chicago; New York, G.M. Hill, 1900
Bradbury, Ray. *Fahrenheit 451*. New York, Simon and Schuster, 1967
*Bronte, Charlotte (Currer Bell). *Jane Eyre*. London, Smith, Elder and Co., 1847
*Bronte, Emily (Ellis Bell). *Wuthering Heights*. London, Thomas Cautley, 1847
Brown, Dee. *Bury My Heart at Wounded Knee*. New York, Holt, Rinehart & Winston, 1970
Bunyan, John. *Pilgrim's Progress*. New York, G.H. McKibbin. 1899
Burnett, Frances Hodgson. *Secret Garden,* London, Heinemann, 1911
Burnett, Frances Hodgson. *A Little Princess,* New York, Charles Scribne's Sons, 1905
Carnegie, Dale. *How to Win Friends and Influence People*. New York, Simon and Schuster, 1936
Carroll, Lewis. *Alice's Adventures in Wonderland*. New York, Macmillan, 1865
Carson, Rachel. *Silent Spring*. Boston, Houghton Mifflin, 1962
Cather, Willa. *My Dear Antonia*. Boston, Houghton Mifflin, 1918
Cather, Willa. *O Pioneers*. Boston, New York, Houghton Mifflin, 1913
*Cather, Willa. *Prairie Spring*. Prologue to *O Pioneers,* Boston, New York, Houghton Mifflin, 1913
Cather, Willa. *Song of the Lark*. Boston, New York, Houghton Mifflin, 1915
*Chapman, George. *The Odysseys of Homer, Vol. 1*. First English translation, London, J.R. Smith, 1857

Dickens, Charles. *Christmas Carol*. London, Chapman & Hall, 1843

Dickens, Charles. *A Tale of Two Cities*. London, Chapman & Hall, 1859

Ellison, Ralph. *Invisible Man*. New York, Random House, 1952

Faulkner, William. *The Sound and the Fury*, New York, Jonathon Cape and Harrison Smith, 1929

Field, Rachel. Hitty, *Her First Hundred Years*, New York, Macmillan, 1929

Fitzgerald, F. Scott. *The Great Gatsby*, New York, Scribner's Sons, 1925

Ford, Maddox. *The Good Soldier*. London, John Lane, The Bodley Head, 1915

Grey, Zane. *Riders of the Purple Sage*. New York, London, Harper & Brothers, 1912

Haley, Alex, X Malcolm. *The Autobiography of Malcolm X*. New York, Grove Press, 1966

Hammett, Dashiell. *Red Harvest*. New York, Alfred A. Knopf, 1929

Hardy, Thomas. *Tess of d'Ubervilles*. New York, Modern Library, 1919

Hawthorne, Nathaniel. *The Scarlet Letter*, Boston, Ticknor, Reed & Fields, 1850

Heller, Joseph. *Catch 22*. New York, Simon and Schuster, 1961

Hemingway, Ernest. *Farewell to Arms*. New York, Scribner, 1929

Hugo, Victor, *The Hunchback of Notre Dame*. translation by Frederic Shobert, Paris, Gosselin, 1831

Hurston, Zora Neael. *Their Eyes Were Watching God*. New York, J.B. Lippencott, 1937

Lazarus, Emma. *"The New Colossus"*. Statue of Liberty. New York, 1883

Lee, Harper. *To Kill a Mockingbird*. Philadelphia, J.B. Lippincott, 1960

Melville, Herman. *Moby Dick*. London, Richard Bentley, (England) Harper & Brothers (US), 1851

Milton, John. *Paradise Lost*. London, Samuel Simons, 1667

*Munk, Arnold. *The Little Engine that Could*. as retold by Watty Piper, location unknown, 1930

O Henry. *The Gift of the Magi*. New York, The Four Million, 1906

Orwell, George. *Coming Up for Ai.*, London, Victor Gollancz, 1939

Dostoyevsky, Fydor. *Crime and Punishment*. The Russian Messenger (series), 1866

Rawlings, Marjorie Kinnan. *The Yearling*. Charles Scribner's Sons, New York, 1938

Remarque, Erich Maria. *All Quiet on the Western Front*. English translation. Boston, Little, Brown and Company, 1929

Riis, Jacob, et al. Photography by Riis, Jacob A. *How the Other Half Lives: Studies Among the Tenements of New York*. New York, Charles Scribner's Sons, 1890.

Sendak, Maurice. *Where the Wild Things Are*. New York, Harper & Row, 1963

*Shakespear, William. *Merchant of Venice*. England, James Roberts, 1598

*Shakespear, William. *Macbeth*. England,

*Shakespear, William. *All's Well that Ends Well*. England,

Sinclair, Upton. *The Jungle*. New York, Doubleday, Page & Co., 1906

Smith, Betty. *A Tree Grows in Brooklyn.* New York and London, Harper & Brothers, 1943

Spyri, Johanna. *Heidi.* First English edition, London, W. Swan Sonnenschein, 1882

Steinbeck, John. *Grapes of Wrath.* New York, Viking Press, 1939

*Stowe, Harriet Beecher. *Uncle Tom's Cabin.* Serialized in The Abolitionist Journal, 1851

Tolkien, J.R.R. *The Hobbit.* London, George Allen & Unwin Ltd. Of London, 1937

Tolstoy, Leo. *War and Peace.* New York, English translation, William S. Gottsberger, 1886

Wharton, Edith. *Ethan Frome.* New York, Dover Publications, 1938

White, E.B. *Charlotte's Web.* New York, Harper & Brothers, 1952

Whitman, Walt. *Leaves of Grass.* New York, James and Andrew Rome, 1855

Wilder, Thornton. *Our Town: A Play in Three Acts.* New York, Coward McCann, Inc., 1938

Woolf, Virginia. *To the Lighthouse.* London, Hogarth, 1927

Wyss, Johann David. *Swiss Family Robinson.* Johann Rudolph Wyss, 1812

CPSIA information can be obtained
at www.ICGtesting.com
Printed in the USA
BVHW040418061021
618236BV00007B/152